Second Chance
with the Rancher

A YOUNG SISTERS NOVEL

WHITLEY COX

Print ISBN: 978-1-989081-88-4

Cover art: EmCat Designs

Editing: Proofreading by the Page

Beta-reading: Proof Postive Author Services

For Katie Hommey, my homey, my friend.

Thanks for being cool as fuck and never skipping leg day when you teach.

Also, you're a fucking badass, just saying.

Love you!

Don't Forget

Be sure to sign up for my newsletter to stay up to date on new releases, deals and more.

Sign up here —> http://eepurl.com/ckh5yT

Become a Patreon Patron to get short stories, secondary character stories, favorite character update stories, exclusive cover reveals, exclusive excerpts from WIPs and more!

Support here —> https://patreon.com/authorwhitleycox

A few other books by Whitley Cox
The

Single Dads of Seattle
Grab book 1 here
https://books2read.com/HBTSD-SDS
*

The Quick Billionaires
Grab book 1 here
Quick & Dirty
https://books2read.com/QDirty-QBS
*

The Harty Boys
Grab book 1 here
Hard Hart
https://books2read.com/HH-HB
*

The Young Sisters
Grab book 1 here
Not Over You
https://books2read.com/not-over-you
*

Doctor Smug
https://books2read.com/DoctorSmug
*

Hot Dad
https://books2read.com/Hot-Dad
*

Snowed In & Set Up
https://books2read.com/SISU
*

Love to Hate You
https://books2read.com/Love2HateYou

Contents

Chapter One

"Stupid piece of shit Ford," Nate muttered, as he hunched over even more under the hood of his pickup to get closer to the problem. "Found on road dead. Fix or repair daily. Stupid fucking piece of shit." He let out another string of colorful words that would probably make a sailor turn scarlet in mortification when the crunch of gravel broke through his soliloquy of swear words. He didn't recognize the sound of the approaching vehicle's engine, and normally he could tell which truck or car was ambling down the long drive of the ranch just by the engine and the way the tires rumbled over the gravel.

No riding tours were on the books for today, and they hadn't officially opened the petting farm on weekdays yet. They'd do that soon, once all the kids got out of school for the summer. It was nearly the end of May and although the mornings and evenings were still cool, the days had already grown hot and sweat beaded on his brow like a string of salty pearls. They also hadn't had rain all month, so things were already bone-dry and dusty.

The car probably just belonged to one of the many families that paid to board their horse on the ranch. As another stream of income, Nate and his brother Asher made a sweet killing offering stables to those who wanted horses but had nowhere to keep them. They boarded them, looked after them and charged the owners a pretty penny to do so. The weekends were busier, of course, but there was usually an owner—or their horse-obsessed teenage daughter—milling around, brushing their horse or taking it for a ride.

He lifted his head to greet the new arrival only to bash it mighty hard on the inside of the hood.

"Jesus Christ, motherfucking piece of shit! Fuck!" He closed his eyes and rubbed his head. He'd have a goose egg for sure.

The vehicle came to a stop.

A door opened. Another door opened but only one closed. There were voices. A man and a woman. Then feet on the gravel followed by another door closing and tires spinning in the gravel as the car—he'd determined quickly that it was a car not a truck—turned around and headed back toward the main road.

Still rubbing his head from where he'd smashed it against the hood, he squinted into the afternoon sun at the slim figure walking gracefully toward him.

Shielding his eyes with his hand—even though he didn't have to, he knew that walk and those hips well—he sucked in a sharp breath and watched Mieka Young walk toward him, awkwardly pulling a suitcase behind her with one hand, while her other arm and wrist were in a cast that covered the length of her forearm from her elbow to her wrist.

Help her, you dumbass.

As if smacked in the back of the head by an imaginary Nana somewhere, he shook his head to free the cannoning thoughts that had left him paralyzed, and raced forward. "Let me help you."

Mieka smiled shyly. "Thank you."

His heart lurched in his chest. It'd been a while since he'd seen her. And the last time that he had it'd been under unusual and *difficult* circumstances.

"How are you?" she asked, her full lips pulling sideways into a small, awkward smile.

"Busy," he said, doing everything he could to slow down his heart rate. His knuckles ached from how tightly he was squeezing the handle of her suitcase. He needed to calm the fuck down.

"Never a moment's rest when you run a ranch I suppose," she said, throwing in a sexy, husky chuckle.

"Nope."

Casting her gold-flecked brown eyes around the big open driveway that separated the main barn from the farmhouse, she cradled her broken arm against her abdomen and allowed her shoulders to droop. "Is my sister around?"

"Triss and Ash are out in the back field. They've gone to give Dare some news. He's a daddy. Little Daria was born last night."

Her eyes perked up. "A new foal?"

Nate nodded and his pulse relaxed a bit. Anything to do with horses eased his troubles, and right now, he was troubled. "Wanna come see?"

Her smile was big and bright and only added to her incredible beauty.

He tucked her suitcase next to his truck and jerked his head toward the barn just as a series of barks erupted from the south side. A moment later, Nate's Blue Merle Aussie Shepherd came racing around the corner, his tongue lolling out the side of his smiling mouth. He recognized Mieka right away and zoomed up to her.

"Hello, Bruno," Mieka said, pausing to bend down and pet Bruno who was lapping up her affection like he hadn't been given any attention in a month. "I love his different colored eyes—brown and blue," she said. "They're so cool."

"It's why I picked him," Nate murmured, waiting until Mieka and Bruno got reacquainted and the dog stopped trying to smother her with love and kisses.

Eventually, Bruno settled down and the three of them got back to their task of going to check out the new foal.

Curiosity burned hot inside him as he tossed some side-eyed glances toward the caramel-brown-haired beauty. What was she doing here? Did Triss know she was coming? Was it as awkward for her as it was for him? How long was she staying?

3

He opened the side door for the barn and allowed her to walk through first. He tried hard not to inhale when she walked past him, but it was fucking impossible. Her coconut shampoo went straight up his nose and made a beeline for his balls. Fuck.

"Which mare did Dare have a foal with?" she asked, turning to look up at him with those unusual brown eyes he'd gotten lost in one night. He'd never seen eyes with so much gold in them before, and then he met the five Young sisters and saw five sets of the unique and beautiful eye color. But Mieka's were lighter brown than the others and seemed to sparkle more, too. Or at least that was his opinion. It might be because he was also hung up on the woman. Who knows?

He cleared his throat and answered her. "Greenleigh. Moved her to a bigger stall since there are two of them now. They're down at the end."

Mieka nodded and continued on down through the barn, petting the cheeks and long faces of each horse she passed. She was a lot like her older sister, Triss. Both women seemed to be naturals with animals. He'd noticed it first when she came last summer for Asher and Triss's wedding. All the creatures on the ranch were drawn to her. And that was one of the things that had drawn Nate to her. She had a wildness about her, but as much as she was wild, she was also soft and gentle. Which was something animals—particularly horses—needed.

She poked her head over two adjacent stalls. "These mamas look ready to pop, too."

"Callie and Hula-Hoop are due with Mercy's foals any day," he replied.

"Oh, how fun. A field full of foals for the summer."

She reached Greenleigh's stall and peered over the side where Greenleigh was busy nursing a healthy little filly they'd named Daria after her late father—Dare. Dare had been Asher's horse, but after a freak accident a couple of winters back, Dare had fallen into a gopher hole in the snow, broke his leg and they were forced to put the gentle giant down. Fortunately, they still had a few of Dare's samples left in the vet's freezer, so they were able to continue his legacy posthumously. That was where Triss and Asher were right now, telling Dare's ashes under the

4

old maple tree that he was a daddy.

"She's beautiful," Mieka cooed, opening up the stable door without asking and stepping inside. She'd been here before, and was very comfortable around the animals, so Nate had no issues with her opening the stable door and entering. Bruno nudged Nate's leg and Nate bent down and gave his trusty companion a thorough scratch behind the ears while eying the slim dancer as she cautiously made her way to the side of Greenleigh's head. "Hello, lovely mama. What a gorgeous little girl you have. Dare would be so proud, I'm sure." She scratched the long bridge of Greenleigh's nose until Daria stopped nursing and came over to sniff and check out Mieka, too. She nudged her a couple of times, pulling a laugh from Mieka, who eventually petted the foal, too. "Brazen little thing, hmm?"

"We're going to keep her and raise her to be a therapy horse for the clinic," Nate said, hating the awkward silence between them and feeling the need to keep talking like an idiot.

"That's a great idea. Triss said business is booming and the waitlist is getting longer by the day. It'll be great if you can offer therapeutic riding and camps for special needs kids and stuff." She wasn't looking at him, but rather giving all of her attention to the horses.

"That's the plan."

"Well, I'd love to help out any way I can with the upcoming other births." She finally turned to face him. "That is, if you *need* help."

"Can always use another set of hands during a birth. Can always use another set of hands on the ranch."

He glanced out one of the barn windows to see Triss and Asher making their way back hand-in-hand through the field. Several horses were grazing and he could hear their hired ranch hands feeding the chickens, mucking stalls and tending to the goats. A couple of other hands were out riding the fence looking for holes, and two homeschooled teenage girls whose parents paid for their horses to be boarded at the ranch, were in the outside coral practicing jumps. It was a weekday so things were quiet. It was the weekends and when summer was in full swing that things got hairy. Multiple dude ranch guided rides a day, the petting farm would open up soon, and all the kids with boarded horses would be around riding as much as they could while school wasn't in session.

It was their best money-making time, but it was also insane and they really could use all the help they could get.

She lifted her casted arm. "Not sure how much help I'll be, but I'll do what I can."

"What happened?" he asked, holding open the stall door so that she could step back out. Macklin, the attention-whore horse who would literally try to sit in your lap if you sat down in his stall made huffs and brays of frustration that he hadn't been given love yet, so Mieka made her way over to his stall, nuzzling him as soon as she got there.

"It was stupid, really. My own fault."

He waited for her to elaborate.

"I'm not a spring chicken anymore and can't do the moves I used to do in my teens and twenties." Her face fell and she kissed Macklin's cheek. "I did a flip and went to land on one hand—something I've done, or *did* thousands of times before—but this was a new routine and I was out of practice. My arm twisted, which messed with my balance, then I fell funny and snapped my radius."

"Fuck," he murmured.

"Yeah."

"How long are you out of commission?"

Her bottom lip wobbled for a moment, then she huffed out a sarcastic one-breath laugh. "Well, that depends on who you ask. My doctor says I'll be in a cast for about six weeks—it's already been almost two weeks. I might be able to get an air cast sooner if the healing is quick. I've got about six screws and two plates in it which will speed up the healing. But if you ask our choreographer and the manager of the production company I was with on the cruise ship, my career is over."

"What?" Anger lashed through him. "You broke your arm, not your ankle or hip."

"Thirty-four is old for a cruise ship dancer. They're surprised I've lasted this long without breaking something. My contract was up and they took this *break* as an opportunity not to renew with me."

A red heat wormed its way through Nate's body. "You've got to be kidding me?"

Tears welled up in Mieka's eyes and her throat bobbed on a harsh swallow. "That's what I said. But nope. So, I'm jobless, homeless—since I lived out of a suitcase on the ships for years, and—" she lifted up her casted arm, "literally broken." She sucked in a rattled breath and it looked as if she was about to break down into sobs, but Triss's voice interrupted them and caused Mieka to sober, wipe her eyes and throw on a big smile.

"Mieka?" Triss said.

"Hey, sis," Mieka said, grinning.

"I ... this is a surprise." The sisters embraced, but Triss cast a curious glance at Nate over Mieka's shoulder. "Is everything okay?" They broke their embrace and Triss's gaze fell to Mieka's casted right arm. "Oh my God, what happened?"

"Spring chickens are made of rubber, old stewing hens like me are apparently made of porcelain and break easily." Her tone was full of anger and sarcasm and Nate one hundred percent understood why.

"Huh?" Triss glanced at her husband, then at Nate, her brown eyes— slightly darker than Mieka's but with the same gold-flecks—narrowed in confusion.

"I did a move I'd done a million times when I wasn't a washed-up old hag and my brittle bones couldn't handle it, so they shattered like fine crystal on a tile floor," Mieka said. "Now, I'm jobless, homeless and according to my asshole choreographer *Martin*, I'm also washed-up."

"What the fuck?" Asher muttered. "He said that?"

"Martin has no filter," Mieka replied. "We've never *really* gotten along since he took over for Stefan last year. I was dance captain and Martin just came in with a chip on his shoulder and a hate-on for me. Apparently, he treated all the dance captains he's ever worked with like they were dirt." She shrugged. "I never let him bother me, until he called me *washed-up*, that is."

"We have a baby sister with no filter, but even Rayma wouldn't be so mean as to call you—or anyone *washed up*. A broken arm does not mean you're incapable. It will heal and you can go back to dancing on the ships, right?" Triss rubbed her sister's back affectionately.

Mieka sniffed and shook her head. "They wouldn't renew my contract. I'm old."

"Oh my God, you're not *old*. You're thirty-four. That's *not* old." Triss rolled her eyes. "They're idiots. You'll get hired on by another cruise line or production company or whatever, no problem. I know it."

Uncertainty shimmered in Mieka's eyes, along with fresh unshed tears. As much as she hoped her sister was right, Nate could see that Mieka was convinced her dancing days on the luxury cruise ships were over.

Nate knew nothing of that world or industry, so he wasn't planning to weigh in, but the look of pure defeat and sadness in Mieka's eyes had his protective instincts kicking in. He was a fixer. He fixed things. Broken vehicles, injured animals, rickety fences. He fixed.

But a sad woman—who he had carnal knowledge of—was a completely different thing and he wasn't sure he even knew where to begin when it came to mending her broken heart and tattered spirit. He sure as hell wanted to try, though.

"So, I'm here to drink until I forget how to dance, cuddle foals and bake bread, or pies or whatever. Put me to work. I don't know how much use I'll be mucking stalls and stuff with only one arm, but I'm happy and willing to pitch in wherever I can. And we can get shitfaced every night and talk trash about our parents and Royal Olympian Cruise Line."

Triss's mouth twisted in a funny way and she cast a cursory glance at Asher who shoved his hands deep into the pockets of his jeans, then rocked back on his heels. "I um ... I won't be getting shitfaced with you, unfortunately," Triss said.

Mieka studied her sister in confusion for half a second, then her eyes went wide. It took Nate a couple more seconds to clue in, but then he did, too, his eyes shot to his brother who was all cocky grins.

"A baby?" Nate asked, all excited.

Asher smiled wider. Nate knew that his brother and Triss had been trying to conceive for the last six months, so the fact that it'd finally happened, had joy replacing all the anger that he'd felt in his heart a moment ago over the injustice of Mieka's circumstances. His brother also looked happy enough to explode, and that was saying a lot since Asher was typically always mildly irritated in some way.

"We're going to have a little cowboy or cowgirl," Triss said softly, resting her hand on her flat belly.

"Rancher," Asher corrected.

Triss smiled and rolled her eyes. "Right, rancher."

Mieka swallowed, blinked and forced the fakest smile Nate had ever seen on anybody ever. "That's amazing. I'm so happy for you." Then she threw herself at her sister and hugged her tight.

When they broke their embrace this time, Mieka was teary-eyed, so she wiped her fingers beneath her eyes and smiled. "This calls for a celebration. You might not be able to drink, but I sure can." She turned to Nate and Asher. "Boys, don't make me drink alone."

"I've got some stuff to do in the barn still," Asher said.

Mieka turned to Nate. "Nate?"

It was only four o'clock in the afternoon, he still had shit to do, too, and his truck was making that weird clunking sound and he hadn't been able to figure out where the problem was. But the look of pure desperation in Mieka's eyes tugged at his heart until he thought it might be ripped clean from his chest, so he nodded. "Sure."

She beamed, but it was all fake. "Excellent." Then she linked arms with her sister and the two of them headed off toward the house through the barn.

Asher turned to Nate. "A little early to start drinking."

"She's in pain," he said plainly.

"From her arm? Can't she just take some ibuprofen? I'm sure the doctor prescribed her some fun painkillers like T3s or oxy."

"Not her arm," he said, shaking his head as he watched the two women continue to walk away. "It's her heart." And he was determined to find a way to fix it, even if it broke his own in the process.

Chapter Two

She could do this.

That wasn't nearly as excruciating as she'd anticipated it being. Nate wasn't being weird... well, he wasn't being *that* weird.

And given the past they shared, there was plenty of weirdness to be had between both of them.

And he was up for getting shitfaced, so...

You really think that's a good idea? Remember what happened the last time the two of you got shitfaced? And what happened after that?

Triss held open the door to the farmhouse and Mieka wheeled her suitcase inside. It was just like she remembered it the last time she was here, only with a few more homey and feminine touches. A vase of flowers on the table, a throw blanket over the couch, a few decorative pillows and a picture of Mieka and her sisters sitting on the mantle next to a picture of Nate and Asher with their arms around each other, dressed in their wedding attire at Triss and Asher's wedding.

"You know where the guestroom is," Triss said, heading into the kitchen. She took down two drinking glasses from the cupboard and filled them with water from the tap. "How long are you planning to stay?"

"If I said that was undecided, would you glare at me and tell me to leave? I know that guests are usually like fish. Three days and they start to smell. But ..." Mieka asked cheekily, accepting the water from her sister and taking a sip.

Triss smiled sweetly. "You can stay as long as you need. I'm assuming you'll need to find a doctor in Denver, though?"

Mieka nodded. "I'm hoping you have a recommendation?"

"I'll make a call. I have a client who owes me a favor since I bumped her son up on my waitlist and took him as a client even though I didn't have space. She's a physician."

"Look at you making contacts and wheeling and dealing," Mieka teased her sister. "This country life has done a world of good for you. Married with a baby on the way and a thriving business. And you seem more confident and at peace than ever."

Triss grinned. "It's the fresh air ..." Her smile turned sassy. "And the hot cowboy sex."

"I bet it's more of the latter and less of the former."

Triss sipped her water. "Ranchers have stamina, not gonna lie. Might do you some good to find one of the ranch hands and get him to scratch your itches on a hay bale or something"

Oh, Mieka knew first hand that ranchers had stamina. Nate was like the Energizer Bunny.

But she wasn't interested in any of the ranch hands, not that they were terrible to look at. Nate and Asher had very nice-looking employees. But that could get messy, and unfortunately, there was only one rancher she was interested in having on a hay bale and scratch her itches.

"So, any idea what the next step is?" Triss took a seat at the kitchen table, so Mieka abandoned her suitcase in the hallway and joined her. "Where do you want to live? I suppose the possibilities are endless."

It might seem that way to those on the outside, but in reality, the possibilities were slim. She was a dancer. That was it. She'd done nothing but dance as a hobby, career, and every hour in between for over twenty years. Ever since her mother bought her her first pair of ballet flats at six, Mieka knew that dancing was her life. And she never looked back. It was a way to combat her ADHD. It kept her mind and body busy. If she was too fidgety or couldn't concentrate, she knew that she could get up and practice dancing. Move her body to keep her mind from wandering. Eventually, she did have to be medicated because it was the only way she could get through school without failing since she still struggled to sit still and study, read or write, but the dancing helped a lot.

She was hired by a dance company in New York right out of high school and danced and trained with them for three years, touring all over the country and over to Europe, then a fellow dancer recommended her for the cruise ships and the rest was history.

She'd traveled all over the world, made loads of friends and memories, but her body was suffering. She wasn't twenty-two anymore. Her hips and knees hurt. The life of a cruise ship dancer was exhausting. They trained on land for four to eight weeks before boarding a ship for a two-week sailing. During that sailing they had anywhere between five and nine shows a week, as well as a welcome performance. Then there was practice and training on top of that, guest dance lessons, "meet the cast" nights, and murder mystery nights where they dressed up and engaged with the guests. She also ran the spot-light for the ice show.

When she was younger, she'd do all of this and *then* party all night with the crew on the ship or off. Only to wake up and do it all over again the next day. But her wild party days followed by two-hours of sleep then six cups of coffee were behind her. She liked her sleep. She liked not being bone-tired in the morning. Even though she wasn't necessarily an introvert, at the end of day, she was often peopled-out and in need of some time to herself to decompress.

She knew her sisters thought her life was glamorous and wild, and for a time it had been. But now, everything hurt. Her body, her arm and her heart.

Because even though she knew it was for the best that she stopped dancing on the ships, stopped the insane schedule, she didn't know anything else. All she knew was dance. All she *had* was dance. The only friends she had were other dancers on the ships, and just like her, they had no actual address. They lived in the rehearsal dorms in Fort Lauderdale, or on the ship. Then when their contract was up, they went home to visit a family member for a few weeks, then the entire process started over again. She was lost without her fellow dancers, lost without the need to get up every morning and perform.

"Trapped in a vortex of thoughts?" Triss mused softly, breaking Mieka out of her own head. Apparently, she'd been sitting there not saying anything staring at a knot in the wooden table.

But Triss and Mieka were close and Triss knew that Mieka would often get caught up in her own thoughts and go quiet.

Mieka smiled shyly. "Sorry."

"What's going on, Mieks?" Triss reached out and grabbed Mieka's hand that wasn't in a cast.

It was that little bit of contact, that touch, that connection that was like a pin prick on a water balloon and suddenly the tears just started falling.

She didn't even say anything. She just cried.

Sobbed at the table until her big sister pulled her into her arms and they sat there, knees touching, arms wrapped tightly around each other as Mieka's whole body shook.

Triss said nothing. She rubbed her sister's back and made shushing sounds. But she never said it was going to be alright, or that they'd figure it out. Because she knew that Mieka didn't want those platitudes right now.

She wanted to wallow. She wanted to grieve her past life, mourn what used to be, and then once she was out of her funk, then they could figure out the next step.

Eventually, the tears stopped falling, her breathing calmed and her body quit trembling. She pulled away from Triss, wiped her eyes and took a sip of her water.

"Feel better?" Triss asked.

"A little."

A throat cleared behind them and Mieka froze. She didn't have to see him to know that Nate was there.

How long had he been there and why didn't Triss tell her?

"Did you get the truck fixed?" Triss asked her brother-in-law.

Mieka wiped beneath her eyes again, she probably had horrible raccoon circles from her mascara, but whatever. She spun around in her seat and faced Nate. He looked how she felt. Helpless and uncomfortable.

"No," Nate said with a sigh. "I'm gonna take it to Larry down the road tomorrow and have him look at it. It's beyond my capabilities."

"And that's just killing you, isn't it?" Triss said with a knowing smile.

Nate grunted. "You know I don't like it when I can't fix things."

"I am aware of that trait of yours," she replied with sass. "Seems to be something the Harris brothers have in common. Drives Asher nuts when he can't *fix* my period cramps."

"Well, you won't have to worry about those for a while," Asher said, coming into the house. "'Cause you're knocked up with my baby."

Triss rubbed her flat stomach. "With your little cowboy or cowgirl."

"Rancher," Nate and Asher said at the same time.

Mieka snorted and Triss winked at her husband.

"I thought you had work to do in the barn?" Triss asked, directing her question to Asher.

"I do," he replied, "but I gotta change into different pants. Callie's in labor and it looks like it's going to be a quick one. She started showing signs when we were out there. Tested her calcium secretions earlier today and they said she was close. Figured it would happen sometime today." He pecked Triss on the side of the head, then headed upstairs.

Mieka turned to Nate. "I suppose binge drinking will have to wait until the foal is out?"

He gave her a resigned smile. "Then it can be celebratory drinking. Did you want to come watch?"

She perked up and nodded. "I'd love to. Should I change? Is there a splash zone?"

He chuckled and his eyes drifted down her body appreciatively. "Might be a good idea."

She was not dressed for a farm or a ranch, and certainly not for the birth of a foal. Though, she'd learned last time she was here that this place was not conducive to heels, so she wore flats, but that didn't mean she couldn't still be stylish. She had on black and white gingham capris that reached her mid-calf, a tight-fitting black tank top and a billowy white vest cardigan thing that hung past her flat ass. She knew she had no butt. That was what getting up at four in the morning and running ten miles on the treadmill did to her body. No tits and no ass.

Maybe she'd grow both now that she wasn't dancing anymore.

Maybe she could just eat chocolate and bread and grow boobs and a butt. That could be her new purpose in life.

Asher came bounding down the stairs wearing faded jeans and a flannel shirt rolled up at the sleeves. It was exactly what he'd been wearing before, just slightly more worn and tattered. Nevertheless, It was a good look on her brother-in-law. "I'm gonna go move Callie out to a vacant pasture so she can foal outside where it's more comfortable," he said, kissing Triss on the cheek again.

"Good luck," Triss called after him.

"I'm already dressed for getting covered in placenta, so I'll see you out there?" Nate directed his question to Mieka.

She nodded and stood up. "I'll go see if I can find something I don't mind burning afterward."

His chuckle lasted until the door closed behind him.

"You coming?" Mieka asked her sister as she grabbed the handle of her suitcase.

Triss shook her head. "I would love to, but I'm honestly exhausted. I can barely keep my eyes open, so I think I'm going to go lay down upstairs for a bit."

"I remember Pasha saying the first trimester is brutal and all you want to do is sleep." Mieka remembered that part of her own first trimester, too. Though it only lasted for a couple of weeks. But the exhaustion was hard to forget.

Triss stood up and nodded. "I remember Pasha saying that, too. And she's not wrong." Her expression softened and she hit Mieka with a probing look. "I don't want to say it because I know that's not what you want to hear, but..."

"I know," Mieka said, knowing exactly what her sister was planning to say. "I'm just having a pity party right now. So let me wear my pointy hat, hit the piñata, and play pin-the-tail on the depressed donkey, okay? I'm sure I'll snap out of it eventually. Watching new life come into the world in a field under a blue bird sky might do the trick."

Triss's expression said she wasn't so certain Mieka would just *snap* out of it that fast, but she nodded anyway. "Okay."

Mieka knew watching a foal being born wasn't going to get her out of her funk, either, but it was still worth a shot.

They hugged again, then Triss disappeared upstairs, while Mieka rolled her suitcase down the hallway to the guest room. "Now to find something I don't mind getting horse vagina gunk on ..."

"Dystocia," Nate said, facing Asher as they all stood in the field with two of the ranch hands. "Foal's not in the proper position. She's struggling." He was wearing long rubber gloves that ran over his thick biceps and all the way up to his armpits. Before putting them on, he'd ditched his flannel shirt and was now in just a white ribbed tank top.

"Fuck," Asher grumbled. He approached Callie who was making all kinds of worrisome noises. Her nostrils were flaring on her silky black head and her eyes were wide with fear. He patted her cheek. "It's all right, baby girl. We'll get you sorted. We'll get your baby out. Don't worry." He kissed Callie's cheek then turned to Nate. "You want to or me?"

"Don't mind doing it," Nate said. "Already got the gloves on."

Mieka knew both Asher and Nate had been in the armed forces, but it still made her pause and caught her attention when Nate's dog tags swung out from under his tank top and bounced against his chest as he bent down and opened up a gray rubber tote and pulled out various pieces of equipment. The tags glinted in the late afternoon sun, but he quickly tucked them into his shirt again, then stalked back toward Callie.

"Hold her steady while I get in position."

Asher did as he was told and stayed at Callie's head. The other two ranch hands stepped up and helped keep Callie from moving too much. All of them were rubbing her, scratching her ears and speaking softly to try to keep her calm.

Mieka felt like a helpless idiot.

"What can I do?" she asked, hating that she couldn't be put to work like the rest of them. Her sister probably wouldn't have to ask, she'd just jump right in and know how to help.

Your sister also lives on the ranch, is married to a rancher and has witnessed many foals being born.

Right.

She couldn't compare. At least she wasn't shying away and not offering to help.

"When I ask for something, give it to me, okay?" Nate said, jerking his chin toward the tote.

She nodded. "Okay."

"I've called Jacob," Asher said, "but he's at another birth and can't get here for at least an hour."

Jacob was probably the vet.

"She doesn't have an hour," Nate said. He turned to Mieka. "Can you put more KY Jelly on my glove, please?" he asked.

She bent down and grabbed the big tub of lubricant.

"Smear it on for me, Minx."

She barely startled at his nickname for her. He'd started calling her that when they were planning the joint bachelorette and bachelor party for Asher and Triss. When the flirting had started. She'd liked it.

She smeared the jelly onto his gloved hand and watched as he carefully inserted it into Callie again. The horse's tail was taped up to her back using green painter's tape, and she'd watched them use soap and water to clean her vulva and teats.

Nate went in all the way up past his elbow.

She watched his face more than his arm. He grunted and twisted slightly, then closed his eyes to probably better picture what he was feeling around for. "I know the foal is in a fucked up position, I just don't know how bad," he said, continuing to feel around with his eyes closed. "I can only feel one leg."

"Fuck," Asher muttered, his blue eyes going wide.

"Backward. Posterior presentation with one leg," Nate confirmed, still armpit-deep in Callie.

The ranch hands exchanged worried expressions.

"What does that mean?" Mieka asked.

"It means we need to get that foal out fucking fast before it drowns in amniotic fluid," he said.

"Oh my God."

"Straps are in the tote," Asher said.

Nate nodded and stayed with Callie while Asher went to the tote and grabbed the straps.

Asher put on gloves, as well, then approached Mieka. "Can you go up to her head where I was? It's going to take two of us to get this foal out."

Mieka nodded and went to the front of the horse where Asher was to keep her still and calm, while Asher donned gloves, as well, and the two brothers went to work.

Mieka couldn't really see what they were doing, now that she was at the front of the horse, but she heard their muttered curses and whispered discussion, not that she could understand it all.

So she did what she could. She pressed her forehead to Callie's long nose and spoke softly. "You got this, sweet mama. You're going to be alright. Just stay with me. Breathe."

Callie's nostrils flared, she trembled and tried to step away.

"Keep her in place," Asher barked.

The ranch hands steadied Callie, and Mieka moved around to the side of Callie's face so that she could look into the big animal's eye. "Stay with me, sweetheart. Look at me. Focus on me."

She wasn't sure the horse understood her, but she hoped that her calm voice was at least doing something.

"Ready?" Asher said.

"Next contraction, we pull," Nate replied.

Callie's body went tense, her muscles tightening, her nostrils flared wildly and both Asher and Nate started to grunt behind the horse. Mieka pushed up onto her tiptoes to try to see what they were doing, but one of the ranch hand's heads was in her way.

"Need more hands," Asher called. "Hank, Ronny, come here."

Hank and Ronny disappeared, leaving Mieka alone to keep Callie calm and from moving too much.

"Stay with me, sweetheart. It'll be over before you know it. Then you'll have your baby to love and cuddle."

"On three," Nate said. "One ... two ... three."

"Catch him, catch him," Asher shouted.

"Got him," Nate said.

Callie stepped away a couple of feet and that's when Mieka saw Nate cradling the foal in his arms, suctioning mucus out of its nostrils with a bulb.

"Come on," Nate said, rubbing the foal's chest. Then he slapped its ribcage.

Still nothing. "Hand me a piece of straw," he said to Asher.

Asher did just that and Nate tickled the inside of the foal's nostrils, but still nothing.

"Come on, little guy." He set the small horse down on his right side, extended his neck, then covered one nostril tightly with his hand, held the foal's mouth closed and breathed into the other nostril causing the foal's chest wall to rise.

Mieka tasted blood and that's when she realized she was biting her bottom lip. Smoothing her tongue over the puncture, she held her breath as Nate continued to fill up the little horse's lungs, then let the air flow back out.

He pressed two fingers to the side of the foal's ribcage, behind his elbow.

"There's a heartbeat," he said.

Mieka exhaled in relief.

"But he's still not breathing." He resumed the mouth-to-nose resuscitation, and then, as if just waking up from a restful sleep, the foal's eyes blinked open, his feet kicked and he started to struggle to get up. He fell, attempted again, fell again, then on his third try, he succeeded and trotted over to his mother where he immediately started looking for milk.

"Thank fuck," Asher breathed, on his knees, as well, and tilting his head skyward.

Nate ditched his gloves, then wiped his hand over his mouth. "Thank fuck, indeed."

The two ranch hands exhaled in relief and Mieka wiped the tears of joy and relief from her eyes.

Nate and Asher stood up and wandered over to Callie and her newborn.

"He looks good," Asher said, running his hands gently over the damp fur of the foal. "Healthy little colt from what I can tell so far."

"Need Callie to pass the placenta otherwise we'll have to give her a shot of Pitocin," Nate murmured, walking up to Callie, pressing his forehead to the side of her head and whispering something. He scratched her ears, stroked the length of her nose and squeezed his dark blue eyes shut.

Mieka watched him, mesmerized.

He continued to whisper and it was almost as if Callie understood.

She huffed a couple of times through her nostrils, stomped her foot, then out came the placenta.

"Got it," Asher said, using a shovel to scoop up the bloody mess and place it into a wheelbarrow. "Looks fine to me. All one piece, no tears."

Nate was still talking softly to Callie and stroking her shiny black neck. Her colt was black, as well, and after a few more healthy sips of milk, he broke away and did a little hop to the side on wobbly legs before wandering over to the ranch hands and sniffing them.

"Little guy was lucky," the taller, older ranch hand said. If Mieka remembered correctly, he was Ronny, and the big, muscly red-haired guy with the rusty beard and neck tattoo was Hank. Ronny scratched behind the colt's ears. "Need to find you a suitable name."

"What about Lucky?" Hank offered.

"Had a colt two summers ago named Lucky," Asher replied.

"Chance?" Mieka suggested.

Nate nodded and broke away from Callie, leaving her to graze while her son trotted back over and started to nurse again. "Chance is perfect."

Mieka beamed and a pleasant warmth filled her chest.

Their eyes locked. His dark, stormy blue to her brown. She smiled. He smiled.

"I can stay out here and keep an eye on them, boss," Hank offered. "Then bring them back into the barn for supper."

Asher and Nate nodded and thanked Hank just as another ranch hand came running into the pasture where they were, with panic all over his face.

"Fuck," Asher muttered, knowing the news wasn't good.

"Hula-Hoop's in labor," he said, slightly out of breath. "It's progressing fast. She's already showing the allantoic membrane."

"What the fuck is with these fast-progressing mares?" Asher grumbled, gathering everything they'd used and tossing it into the tote before picking it up and running back toward the barn with the other ranch hand. Ronny was already running back, too.

Nate went back to Callie, said something to her, then with a quick head jerk toward the barn, while his eyes were like two blue burning coals on Mieka, he indicated they should catch up.

"Sorry, we won't be getting sloppy drunk to wallow in your sadness just yet, Minx," he said as they jogged toward the barn, side-by-side.

Mieka shrugged it off. She hadn't thought about her shitty life since she heard a mare was in labor. If anything, this was a better distraction than drinking. "Is Callie going to be okay?"

He nodded. "We got Chance out, got him breathing. There was no tearing for her, I checked. It was just a freak circumstance. One out of every ten foals is in a weird position and the mare requires our help getting the baby out. We're just lucky that we got him out quickly and he started breathing." He craned his head around to glance back at the new mother and son. Mieka did the same.

"They look perfect," she mused. "You'd never know the chaos that just was, looking at them now."

They faced forward again and kept moving.

"Hopefully, this birth is smooth. You up for another one?" he asked.

"This is the most fun and excitement I've had in ages. I'm totally game."

They slowed their roll as they reached the barn and he glanced over and smiled at her. "We're going to make a rancher out of you yet, Minx. Just you wait."

Where did those butterflies in her belly come from, and why did the idea of Nate *making a rancher out of her*, warm her all over?

With another sexy grin, he reached over and grabbed a Stetson off the wall and plunked it on her head. "I knew it. You were made to wear one of these, Minx. Hot as fuck." Then before she could reply, not that she could untangle her tongue to say anything, he left her melting like a puddle of goo and joined Asher and the others with Hula-Hoop.

Chapter Three

Nate was fucking beat.

Hula-Hoop's birth had been far less eventful than Callie's and required no intervention. Thank fuck.

They led her out to another fenced-off portion of the pasture and she birthed a healthy little filly with zero complications.

He let Mieka name this foal, too, and she chose the name *Skipper* since the filly kept doing a cute little skip rather than a walk or a trot when she first got up and started moving. She was a feisty thing and would make a fine therapy horse in the future.

After making sure all the horses were fed, had water, and that Callie, Chance, Hula-Hoop, Skipper, Greenleigh and Daria were all doing well in their stables, he joined Asher and the two of them headed toward the house.

He knew his brother was bone-tired, too.

Asher wasn't much of a talker even when he wasn't exhausted, and even though Nate was fine with or without conversation, he was too bagged to even form a complete thought, let alone a complete sentence, so they crossed the yard in silence.

Mieka had returned to the house to go help Triss with dinner after

Hula-Hoop delivered Skipper, and as much as she hadn't been in the way and he'd enjoyed having her around, he was grateful for the reprieve of her company.

She did funny things to his head.

He hadn't thought about her in ages—well, that was a lie, he *tried* not to think about her and had been attempting and failing to do so for ages—and yet, now that she was here, back in his life, on his land, and in his house, all he wanted to do was relive history and their one night together over and over and over again.

He'd been with other women since.

Asher liked to say Nate fell in love with a new woman every Friday night, and although he couldn't say that he actually *fell in love*, he did enjoy the company of women and often it was a different one from the previous week.

But Mieka ...

Minx.

He'd come up with that nickname last year when they were planning Triss and Asher's joint bachelorette and bachelor party. Mieka had come to Colorado a week before the wedding to help with planning and organizing. Then the two of them, along with Nate and Asher's niece Hannah who was Triss's best friend, the three of them planned a wild day and night in Denver for all of their friends, complete with a stretch Escalade and zip lining.

Asher heaved open the front door, and they stepped inside.

The delicious smell of barbecue wafted up Nate's nostrils and he nearly collapsed into the wall from how hungry he realized he was.

"Dinner is in ten minutes, boys," Triss called from the kitchen. "Enough time to scrub the birth goo off your arms and put on some clothes that don't smell like horse."

"Everything I own smells like horse," Asher retorted.

"Horse afterbirth, then," Triss said with a chuckle.

Nate wanted to see where Mieka was, but he thought better of it and just headed upstairs. Things were already awkward enough between them, he didn't need to add fuel to the uncomfortable fire by finding her and having nothing to say.

He and Asher took turns showering since the pipes in the farmhouse were old and there wasn't enough water pressure for them to shower at the same time in separate bathrooms. They were also a little too old to be having a bath together anymore.

Exactly nine and a half minutes after they entered the house, Nate and Asher were dressed and heading downstairs, drawn by the intoxicating aroma of fire kissed meat.

Triss was a great cook, and although Nate and Asher were no slouches in the kitchen, it was nice having his sister-in-law around to add her finesse to their meals. She knew when to give a dish a squeeze of lime or a splash of fish sauce to take it from good to great. Often, before Triss arrived on the scene, Nate and Asher ate dinner at nine or ten o'clock at night after a chaotic day of work, and that dinner quite often consisted of pan-fried sausages, packet mashed potatoes and some steamed broccoli. Food was food. They needed full bellies to function and that was all that mattered. And pan-fried sausages, packet mashed potatoes and steamed broccoli were food fit for royalty in comparison to some of the ration packets and meals they'd eaten when on missions.

But Triss knew flavor, so having her around had not only made Nate's brother less of a miserable bugger, but it also helped make their meals taste better.

Nate entered the kitchen behind Asher, who immediately sought out his wife, squeezed her butt and kissed the side of her head. "Smells amazing, babe," he murmured against her hair.

"Figured you boys would be hungry after a day of bringing new life into the world," Triss said, kissing Asher on his stubbled jaw. "Got steaks on the barbecue, Mieka's bringing them in, baked potatoes, Caesar salad, roasted veggies, and a blackberry pie for dessert."

Nate's belly rumbled again. That all sounded incredible.

The door to the backyard where the barbecue and hot tub were located opened and Mieka walked in carrying a tray with steaming steaks and barbecue tongs. "It's been ages since I barbecued anything, so I hope I did it all right. All my meals are just *there* for me on the ship either in the crew dining area or the guest buffet. I can't remember the last time I cooked for myself, let alone barbecued."

"I'd eat shoe leather slathered in barbecue sauce at this point I'm so hungry," Nate said, coming over to check out the steaks. "They look good to me. Nice grill lines."

"They need to rest a bit," she said, not meeting his eyes.

He reached into the fridge and pulled out two beers, twisting off the caps before handing one to his brother. "Drink?" he said to Mieka.

"I have something on the go already," she replied, pointing to a stemless wine glass with a clear liquid in it and ice cubes.

"I won't be getting high or drunk anytime soon," Triss started, "So I'm giving my stash to Mieka."

Nate's eyes went wide and he turned to Mieka who was taking a sip of her drink. "Have you ever done pot before?"

She nodded. "Not for a while, but I have. Never had it in liquid form, though. These lemonades are amazing. They go down *so* smooth. Gotta be careful since it's like drinking juice."

"I love them," Triss said, drying her hands on a towel. "They don't make my throat scratchy like the joints. Half a bottle of the peach lemonade on ice mixed with some sparkling water and I am a fantastic version of myself in an hour." Her husband snorted. She smiled even wider. "A *full* bottle over ice with sparkling water and I am the absolute *best* version of myself. Plus, sex and orgasms when I'm high is out of this fucking world. I can edge forever."

Asher snorted again. "Is it the weed, or the person you're fucking?" He came up behind her and pinched her butt again.

"The weed," she teased, which earned her a nip to her bare shoulder from her husband.

"We'll see about that," Asher replied. "You'll be sober for nine months plus however long you decide to nurse. I'll change your mind."

"Challenge accepted, Cowboy."

"Rancher."

Normally, Nate didn't give two shits about his brother and his wife flirting and being all lovey dovey together, but with Mieka in the room, too, and their history acting as the giant third wheel between them, made every second of this situation damn near unbearable.

He avoided eye contact with Mieka and took a sip of his beer, studying the ceiling like it was the damn Sistine Chapel.

Eventually, they all sat down at the table and despite his generally respectable table manners, Nate was too hungry to practice them and dove into his steak before he put anything else on his plate. His mouth filled with saliva as he brought the first bite up and snagged it with his teeth.

"Jesus fuck," he groaned, chewing, closing his eyes, and nearly coming in his sweatpants in front of everyone at the table. "That's so damn good." He chewed and chewed, keeping his eyes closed and just enjoying the peppery flavor of the rub and the perfect sear.

When he opened his eyes, he found Mieka watching him. Asher and Triss chuckled, but paid him little mind as they filled up their own plates, but Mieka seemed frozen in her seat.

"Did you put that rub on?" he asked her.

She nodded. "I befriended one of the chefs on the ship and he was big into barbecuing. He made his own secret rub and when I left, he sent me away with a big bag of it as a parting gift."

"It's amazing."

"Raul was a fantastic cook."

Was Raul more than just a fantastic cook, but also a fantastic lover? How friendly did they get?

"He was like a father to me," she went on. "He said I reminded him a lot of his daughter Katerina who's roughly my age." She glanced at Triss. "Though, he was nothing like dad. Way cooler."

A father figure. *Phew.* Nate swallowed down the masticated chunk of meat in his mouth and exhaled in relief. Not that he had any claim to Mieka, and he'd certainly been with other women since their one night together, but that didn't stop the idea of her being with another man from making the blood in his veins begin to simmer.

He sawed into his steak and put another bite into his mouth. "Well, my thanks to Raul, this is delicious. And you cooked it perfectly."

Her cheeks turned a sweet shade of pink before she put her head down and speared a broccoli floret with her fork. "Thank you."

Every bite of dinner was amazing, not that Nate expected anything less. But he could tell that despite her lack of time spent in a kitchen recently, Mieka knew her way around a spatula and frying pan—or in this case a barbecue and some tongs. Everyone chatted as they ate, though it seemed like Triss and Asher occupied the majority of the air time, with Mieka eating happily in silence just listening, and Nate too caught up in his food to do more than just add a sentence here or there to the conversation.

He and Asher cleared the table and put the dishes in the dishwasher, while Triss pulled a fresh pie from the oven where it was warming and Mieka grabbed a tub of vanilla ice cream out of the freezer.

"Where'd we get the blackberries?" Asher asked, taking down four plates from the cupboard. "They're not in season yet. Too early for them."

"I found a bag of them in the bottom of the chest freezer," Mieka replied. "Asked Triss if I could bake a pie."

"*You* baked it?" Nate asked, instantly regretting how surprised he sounded.

But she didn't seem offended and just laughed and nodded. "I did. Raul was also a master pie baker and taught me all of his secrets. Though, he refused to tell me what goes into his steak rub and just told me to message him when I'm out and he'll mail me more. Said that recipe he's taking to the grave. Won't even give it to his kids."

"Raul sounds like quite the character," Nate said, grabbing another beer for both him and Asher from the fridge.

Mieka was still chuckling and nodded again. "He is."

She and Triss worked like a well-oiled machine as they served up the pie and ice cream. Nate had to hand it to Mieka, besides the visual reminder of her cast, she didn't let it hold her back from much. It also helped that she was right-handed and broke her left arm, so at least she wasn't struggling as much as she could have been.

He dove into the pie with the same level of gusto he had the steak. Even though his stomach was no longer trying to digest him from the inside out, he was always hungry. He would never turn down food, least of all fresh, home-made pie.

"Raul's recipe?" he asked, wiping a bit of ice cream from his scruffy chin.

"The man knows how to make a pie," she said, putting a forkful of pastry into her mouth. "Though, to be fair, he taught me how to make a blackberry and rosemary galette, but I just used the same principles and made it into a pie. The trick is to overstuff the pie and make sure your dough is cold. But I really like the savory component of the pie with the rosemary."

Triss nodded. "Gives it a real earthy and almost fall-like feel. It's delicious, Mieks."

Asher reached for another slice, then scooped himself more ice cream. "Well, you can tell I like it."

Mieka's cheeks turned that sweet shade of pink again. "Thanks, guys."

"You could always open up a pie stand," Triss offered. "Pregnant and non-pregnant me will definitely be some of your best customers. Though, I expect the sister discount."

Mieka dropped her gaze to her plate and pushed her fork into a plump blackberry. "Thanks, but I think if I turned my hobby into a job, I wouldn't enjoy it as much. And I'm not even sure baking is a hobby since this is the first time I've baked in nearly two years."

"Yeah, but it's like riding a bike. It's not something you forget." Triss reached for the ice cream and scooped a big white ball onto her plate before adding another slice of pie.

Nate went back for seconds, too, as did Mieka and between the four of them they finished the pie.

Asher leaned back in his chair and rested his hand on his belly, giving it a rub. "Wife?"

"Hmm?" Triss said sleepily, leaning back in her own chair and smiling serenely.

"I'm bagged. I'm going to head to bed. You staying up to chat with your sister for a bit?"

Triss shook her head. "Unfortunately, I don't think I can. I can't keep my eyes open. I'm making a brain and a spinal column and stuff and it's kicking my ass."

Nate snorted. He'd never thought of it that way. She really was making all of those things. Eyeballs and organs, bones and ligaments. No wonder she was tired.

"It's all right," Mieka said, standing up and taking everyone's plates. She swayed where she stood a little and set the plates back down on the table. "Oh wow, I'm stoned."

"Too stoned?" Triss asked, her voice full of concern. "Did I give you too much?"

Mieka opened her soft brown eyes and focused on her sister, though it seemed to take her a second to actually focus. "No, I don't think so. I just didn't realize how high I was until I stood up." She giggled. "I'm really freaking high." She gathered the plates again and took them to the dishwasher.

Nate stood up, too, and returned the ice cream to the freezer.

Asher helped Triss stand, even though she wasn't far along enough in her pregnancy to need the help, but Nate's brother was incredibly attentive to his wife.

"Before we pass out can you massage my feet, Cowboy?" Triss asked, linking her fingers through Asher's and tugging him toward the staircase.

"Rancher," Asher corrected. "And I'll see if I can stay awake."

"Goodnight, Mieks. I'm glad you're here. 'Night, Nate."

"'Night, sis," Mieka called after Triss as she stood at the sink scrubbing the pie plate. "Thanks for letting me crash unannounced. I promise I won't be like a fish."

The creak of their steps on the stairs echoed through the house, followed by the closing of their bedroom door, their footsteps and muffled conversation. Asher and Triss's bedroom was directly over the kitchen and living room, while Nate's room was also upstairs but on the other side over the two guest rooms on the bottom floor. So above *Mieka's* room.

The moment his brother's bedroom door closed Nate became acutely aware of the only other person in the kitchen and the fact that she was quietly staring into the soapy water, high as a fucking kite.

"You okay?" he asked, approaching her slowly.

"This is really enjoyable," she said. "The scrubbing. The warm water. Watching the soap bubbles pop." She poked the nail of her pinky finger into a big bubble then giggled. "*Pop!*"

He snorted a laugh. "You're really stoned."

"Just call me a cupcake because I. Am. Baked." She turned and grinned at him. "Do you do the weed, too?"

His lip twitched at the funny way she worded it. Did he *do* the weed? But he kept himself from smiling in a way that wouldn't offend her and simply bobbed his head. "I do. Asher and I both got medical marijuana cards after we retired from active duty. It helps with the PTSD and invasive thoughts. Helps me sleep. Sometimes I struggle to fall asleep, you know ... memories and shit. We do it most nights. Usually head out to the hot tub with a couple of joints and lowballs of scotch to help knock us out. Though, I'm going to guess he's just going to take some THC oil or gummies tonight, rather than leave his wife to go smoke and soak."

"Ah, so you do the joints?"

This time he was unable to keep himself from laughing. The way she kept saying *the* before words was funny and he had to believe it was because she was high. "Yes, I *do the* joints."

All she did was nod. "So, I guess you saw some pretty bad stuff then, hmm?"

He nodded. "Yep."

"Good thing it's legal now, huh? At least in Colorado."

"We grew it for a while and just smoked our own, but our demand outgrew our crop and when things with the ranch picked up and got too hectic, we just decided to start buying it again. I don't need to get stoned. I just have a joint or a few puffs of the vape pen some nights and it's enough to help me sleep. That's all. Some vets do it all day long to function. That's not me. I won't drive after I've done it. If I've been triggered or had a harder day I might need more. It keeps me human, honestly."

"*Human*," she murmured.

Their conversation was interrupted by the squeak and creak of the bed upstairs, then by the pounding of the headboard against the wall and some deep, guttural grunts from Asher.

Jesus, fuck.

"I thought they were too tired?" she said with a groan and an eye roll as her face turned pink.

"Try living with them. Those two are like goddamn rabbits. Honeymoon stage every day."

"Oh God!" Triss cried.

"Oh come on!" Mieka shouted, slapping the dish cloth onto the counter with vigor and stalking through the kitchen. A second later, Nate heard the front door open then slam closed.

Chapter Four

He found her out in the barn nuzzling Macklin who was eating up her affection like the attention-whore that he was.

"This is usually where I come, too, when I'm tired of hearing them," he said, startling her only slightly when he approached. "Here or the hot tub with a joint and two ounces of scotch. But they're often out there fucking, too."

"You need your own place, dude," she said, kissing Macklin's velvety nose.

"Asher and Triss are already planning to build. They've mapped out the section of the property they're going to develop and have blueprints. I think they're breaking ground in a couple of weeks."

"Thank fuck, huh?" she said with a snort. "Until then, you might need to move to the hayloft. I've heard pregnant chicks can be freaky horny."

That made him laugh. "If she demands more of my brother than she already does, the man's dick is going to fall off."

"He still has a tongue, so I don't think she'll care." She kissed Macklin once more, then moved down the line to the next horse, which happened to be Nate's horse, Umber.

"Fair enough," Nate said with a grin. He'd never gotten to use his tongue on Mieka the way he wanted to. They'd made out like sloppy drunk morons, then she hiked up her bridesmaid dress and he pulled down his dress trousers and took her up against the wall of the barn outside.

If he was being honest, he was a little ashamed at how unromantic and kind of crass the whole thing ended up being. Sure, it was hot, and she got off—though it took her a while—but Mieka deserved so much more than a quick drunk fuck in the dark against rough wood that could put splinters in her ass cheeks.

He pulled his vape pen out of the pocket of his gray sweats, turned it on and took a couple of puffs, making sure to blow them away from the horses' stalls. Not that vape smoke was anywhere near as bad as real cigarette or joint smoke, but he wasn't going to be a dick either way.

"That's the smoking pen?" she asked, scratching behind Umber's soft brown ears.

"Why do you keep saying it like that?"

"Like what?"

"*The* smoking. *The* joints. You keep adding *the* to the beginning. It's weird."

She shrugged. "I'm stoned. I also give zero fucks. I have no fucks left to give. I broke my arm, essentially got fired because I'm old and washed up. And did I tell you that I was sort of seeing a bartender on the ship and when he found out they didn't renew my contract and *why*, he dumped me, too? My well of fucks to give hath runneth empty."

Nate's eyes went wide. "You never said anything about a boyfriend." His forearms began to tingle and he had to clench his fists to keep from wanting to put them through the face of the dumb fuck who thought dumping Mieka was okay.

"He thought I was younger. Thought I was twenty-six."

"Did you tell him you were twenty-six?"

She shook her head, reached for his vape pen and took a long pull off it. She held it in her lungs for a while, then when she went to expel the smoke, she started to cough. "That's strong," she said through coughing fits, her eyes beginning to water.

"Careful."

"I never told him I was twenty-six. Our ages never came up. We didn't do a ton of *talking* about ourselves if you know what I mean?" She rolled her eyes. "I'm not broken-hearted about him. He was just a good time and I knew it wasn't going to go anywhere. And I guess I should be flattered that he thought I was younger. But there is such ageism in this country—in this world—and it fucking sucks."

Nate nodded and took back the vape pen. Tonight was one of those nights he would need more than just a couple of puffs. Hearing about Mieka's bartender friend with benefits or whatever he was made him see red even though he knew it shouldn't.

"So are you like some sort of horse whisperer or something?" she asked, changing the subject and moving on to the next horse, Jim Jam, who was a horse they boarded for a local family. She was a beautiful Palomino with a sweet disposition and the patience of a saint. She gave Jim Jam some attention which the horse ate up as fast as she could.

"Horses are easy once you understand that all they want is love, kindness and patience. They're skittish around big noises and abrupt movements, and they learn people and their true intentions quickly. I get that because I'm like that, too. So as long as I recognize what they need and give that to them, then we never have any issues."

"I only ask because you were whispering a bunch of stuff to Callie and I thought maybe you two had your own language or something." She moved over to the next horse, Pom-Pom, a brown mare they'd owned for several years.

"I just told her how amazing she did and that I loved her and wouldn't let anything bad happen to her. It's more the tone than anything. The attention and the kindness that they respond to. I could have been reciting a recipe for pickled eggs and as long as the tone was right and she felt my calm it wouldn't have mattered."

Mieka made a garbled noise in her throat that was probably some kind of a laugh. "Pickled eggs?"

"Fucking delicious. Especially in an egg salad sandwich." Shit, now he was hungry again.

"I might have to try it."

He took another puff on his pen, blew out the smoke, then before he could stop himself, the words were coming out. "About that night."

Her head jerked up and those gold-flecked brown eyes bore right through him until they hit bone.

Fuck. He was an idiot.

"What about it?" she asked slowly, her gaze sharp but guarded.

He swallowed. "Are you uh... are you okay after that?"

She scoffed and her top lip curled up in derision. "We had one night, Nate. Don't read too much into it. I'm not broken-hearted if that's what you're worried about. We had one fun, drunk, sloppy night. We were stupid and didn't use protection. That resulted in an unwanted pregnancy. Which we—*I* dealt with—I'm fine. No regrets."

"How drunk were you that night?" he asked carefully. He'd been super drunk, but now that he thought about it, what if she'd been too drunk to properly consent? Had he taken advantage of her? He didn't think he had, but things from that night were still a little fuzzy.

"Blottoed. Why?" She took the pen back from him, took another puff, not as big of one this time, held in the smoke for a moment, then blew it out into the middle of the barn before moving to the next horse, Princess Sparkle Glitter Fairy Blossom. She was another horse they boarded for a family and their daughter had renamed the horse when they got the mare. Their daughter had been six. She was now eleven and simply called the horse Princess, thank fuck.

Worry spun through him. "Did I ... did I take advantage? I thought it was consensual."

She rolled her pretty brown eyes. "It was. You didn't take advantage. Just because I was forget-my-own-phone-number drunk, does not mean I was not one million percent on board with you sticking your dick in me. We flirted and shot fucky-eyes at each other for *days* before we finally acted on it. It was inevitable. Do I wish I hadn't been so drunk? Sure. It took me forever to get off. I had whiskey-clit something fierce."

"Oh, I remember. I thought my balls were going to fall off from how long I had to hold off."

"I told you to come."

"A woman always comes first. You're not a gentleman if you come before your partner. Leaving her to ride a softening dick is the lowest of the low."

She snorted. "Do gentlemen also stick their fingers in the ass of women they fuck for the first time?"

"If the woman agrees to it—which you *did, right?*—and it gets her off faster—which it did."

"Touché." She smirked, then her expression sobered. "I did agree to it, and you didn't take advantage of me, Nate. I swear it. But it was just one night. And if you're wondering if I regret the abortion, I don't. You're a great guy, but a baby was not in the cards for us. I was still dancing—I wasn't a shriveled up old crone like I am now—and you have your life here. As hot as you are, and as hot as that night was, it was an unwanted clump of cells that I was in no way prepared to gestate and raise. It wouldn't have made sense."

No, it wouldn't have, but that didn't stop him from wondering what would have been if things had been different.

He'd never begrudged her decision, and in reality, it was the right choice. It was *her* choice. He was over forty and with a good job, plenty of land and love to give, so a small part of him hurt that the clump of cells they made together hadn't grown into more, no matter how much he didn't want it to.

He also took note of the fact that she was using the past tense. A baby *was not* in the cards for them. It *wouldn't* have made sense.

Was she thinking differently now? Or was she speaking her weird stoned speech again?

Did she come here for more than just commiseration with her sister and to sort out the next chapter of her life? She had four other sisters, what made her choose to visit Triss as opposed to Oona in Montreal or Rayma and Pasha in Victoria? Why Triss?

A tremor of excitement shot through him at the idea that she didn't just come here to visit Triss, but she also came here for him. That even though she kept telling herself that it'd been *just one night*, deep down she knew they had a connection. She knew that it might have been just one night at the time, but it was more than that now. Or at least, it had the possibility of being more than that.

Bruno barked and came trotting through the barn. The dog slept where ever he pleased. He had beds in the house, in the barn, and sometimes during the summer when it got particularly warm, he just crashed on the wrap-around porch outside. He knew not to go onto the road and to stay on the property, and he could hear Asher or Nate whistle for him from over a mile away.

The arrival of Bruno seemed to break the tension that had grown tighter than a harp's cord between them. He bent down and scratched the dog's ears as Mieka moved on to the next horse, Tiberius, which was the horse Asher bought for himself after Dare passed away.

He was probably destroying any chance they had of rekindling anything, but the curiosity and concern for her well-being burned too hot inside of him to ignore. "And you're okay after ... after the procedure?"

"You mean after the abortion?"

He nodded.

"Say the word, Nate. It's not a bad word."

He rolled his eyes. "You're okay after the abortion?"

"I am, thank you." Her eyes held his. "And I'm not sure if I said it at the time, but, thank you for coming and being with me when it happened. You didn't have to."

Like fuck he didn't have to. He was responsible for putting her in that predicament in the first place, of course he'd be there. He was just glad that she called him and didn't go it alone and keep him in the dark.

Her sister, Pasha had worked at a hospital in Seattle for a time, so she got in touch with a former colleague there and arranged for Mieka to fly from Florida to Washington and have the abortion performed legally by a trusted physician friend. Pasha had intended to go and be there for her sister, but ended up having to stay home with her sick children last minute. That's when Mieka called Nate.

Did it hurt that she only called him when her other support system fell through and she would have otherwise kept him in the dark? Of course, it fucking did. But he never said any of that to her. He just flew to Seattle and held her hand.

She opted for the pill version of an abortion, which in Nate's opinion had been the wrong choice. Mieka was in a lot of pain. The cramps had her in tears and she sat on the toilet for hours bawling. And in the end, she needed a D&C anyway because an ultrasound showed remaining cells that didn't expel from the pill and if left in her body could cause infection. So she ended up going through both procedures.

He stayed with her through everything. Brought her whatever she needed, food, warming pads, hot water bottles, pain meds. And then when it was all over, she got on a plane and left, disappearing in the morning from their hotel room without so much as a goodbye note.

"Why'd you leave like that?" he asked, emotion choking his throat to the point where his words came out strained.

"I thought you were mad at me for going through with it," she said after a long pause of quiet. Her bottom lip wobbled slightly and her nostrils flared. "I wasn't going to tell you. But then ... then when Pasha canceled, I knew I couldn't do it alone and I didn't want anyone else to know."

"Why didn't you tell me until you needed me?"

"Because I thought you'd try to convince me to keep it. That you would paint a picture of a beautiful family life out here in the country where we could raise the one-night-stand baby on a farm in the fresh air and with his, her or their cousins."

"And that sounds like a terrible way to raise a child?"

"That sounded like hell to me, at the time. I wasn't ready to give up my life, to give up my career ... to give up my body to someone else. And we ... what are we?" She pointed her finger back and forth between them. "We had sex once, Nate. Your brother married my sister. But that doesn't mean we should be forced to be something we might not necessarily be destined for, right?"

That hurt like a fucking riding crop to his bare ass.

A life with him, here, sounded like hell.

Her gaze softened as his hardened. "I'm not trying to offend you. And a life like that doesn't sound like hell, *now*. It's not the life for me, but it also doesn't sound like hell, either, and I apologize if me saying that offended you."

"It's fine," he ground out.

Her lips pursed for a moment. "I can see that it did."

Sucking in a big breath through his nose, then pushing it out as he raked his fingers through his hair, he stood up from where he'd been rubbing Bruno's belly and approached her. Her brown eyes went wide and a tremor of fear had her blinking rapidly. He could see the pulse in her neck pick up and she swallowed.

"Let me show you what a life on this ranch can be like, Minx. You've got time. Nowhere to be. An arm and a heart to mend. Let me show you." He wrapped a strand of her caramel-brown hair around his finger and tugged until their faces were less than six inches apart. "It's hard work, but it's not hell."

She pulled in a big breath through her nose and when she pushed it out through her mouth, they were standing close enough that it hit his lips in a warm puff. "Are you upset I had the abortion?"

He shook his head slowly. "I'm upset you assumed I would try to talk you out of it, and didn't trust me enough with the truth until you were desperate. That tells me you don't know me well enough and I think now's the perfect opportunity to change that."

Her eyes widened.

"I'm not a bad guy, Minx."

"I know that."

"Do you?"

She nodded but just barely since he still had hold of her hair. "I do."

His lips twisted and he gauged her warily. It would be so easy to just tug on that strand of hair a little more and crush his mouth to hers. He could tell by the way she licked her lips and her gaze softened and warmed that it was what she wanted. But if he wanted a chance with Mieka, not only to show her what a great life could be had on this ranch, but also with him, he needed to play the long game. He wasn't going to fuck up this opportunity by jumping into the physical with her. Even a kiss could make things blurry.

The next time they kissed he wanted it to be romantic. He wanted her to want it for the right reasons. Not because she was high, lonely and depressed. But because she wanted him.

The next time he took her to bed it was going to be in an actual bed and he was going to make sure they remembered every second of it.

He saw what his brother had with Triss and Nate wanted that, too.

He wanted a partner. A person, and a family to love, and the more he stared into the gold flecks of Mieka's eyes, the more he realized he wanted it all with her.

Now, he just had to figure out a way to show her that it was what she wanted, too.

Releasing her hair, he took a step back, enjoying the confusion in her eyes as she wondered why he hadn't kissed her. "They're probably done fucking and asleep by now. Remember that you have to turn the shower nozzle all the way to hot, let it get hot, then adjust the temperature in the guest bathroom?"

She nodded. "O-okay."

He smiled, put the vape pen in his mouth and headed deeper into the barn.

"Come on, Bruno. Goodnight, Mieka." Bruno gave a little yip of excitement and scampered after Nate. It was all he could do not to turn back and look at her. He knew she was still standing there.

"G-goodnight," she stammered.

He grinned as he turned the corner outside and sat on a bench that allowed him a perfect view of all his land. It wasn't until he heard the side door at the other end of the barn close that he knew she was gone and he was finally alone.

"Give me a month, Minx," he said more to himself and the stars above than anyone else. "Give me a month and I'll show you what kind of a life we could have here." He took a long pull on the vape pen, then watched as the smoke disappeared quickly into the night air when he breathed out.

Now he just had to figure out what to do in that month to convince her.

Good thing he liked a challenge.

Chapter Five

Mieka collapsed into bed after a long hot shower. She'd bought one of those cast cover things that you can wear so having a shower wasn't impossible, or at the very least challenging and involving plastic wrap and duct tape. It was a lifesaver since she loved her showers. The hotter the better. The longer the better. Hot showers were endless on the cruise ships, but in the farmhouse where they had old pipes and a standard size hot water tank, the water ran cold long before she was ready to get out.

Damn Nate.

Damn him and his beautiful blue eyes that reminded her of the Atlantic Ocean at sunrise. Or his cocky smirk and the way it made that one dimple in his cheek dig in extra deep.

She thought for sure he was going to kiss her. Plaster her up against the wall of the barn and ravish her mouth—and her body. But he'd done nothing other than tug on her hair, make her panties soaked from the rakish look in his eyes, and ask her to let him show her how good a life on the ranch could be.

So many parts of her told her to say *no*. That this was not the life for her.

It was too quiet. Too removed from the rest of civilization. Too ... country.

But she didn't say a word. She didn't nod. She didn't shake her head. All she did was stare into his eyes like a love-sick fool as her tongue got more and more tangled in her mouth.

How did he expect to *show* her what life on the ranch could be like? She'd seen what life was like when she was here last year for the wedding. It was hectic, it was hot, it was dirty, and it smelled like hay and horse twenty-four-seven. She woke up to the smell and went to bed to it, too. Not that it was a terrible scent, but it was just ... everywhere.

She loved the horses, in fact she loved all the animals, but that didn't mean she wanted to set up a cot in Macklin's stall and send out change of address notices to all her friends.

You have nowhere to be and nothing better to do. Let him try. What's the harm?

The harm was that she had no idea what she wanted to do with the rest of her life, no idea where she wanted to set down roots—if she even had any roots to set down—and she was worried that her vagina and heart would get all wooed and seduced by the sexy rancher with dog tags and she'd make a huge mistake deciding to stay. This was not the life for her. It might be for her sister, but it wasn't for Mieka.

She knew Nate's bedroom was above hers. Triss and Asher's room was over the kitchen and living room. She hadn't heard him come in, but he probably did while she was showering. The squealing pipes drown out the sound of everything else, including her own thoughts.

Turning over onto her side under the covers she pinched her eyes closed and hugged her pillow, willing sleep to come. The weed was wearing off, and she made sure to take some regular-strength painkillers before bed since last night when she forgot, she woke up with a throbbing ache in her arm.

The sound of the front door opening and closing gently, had her eyes popping open. Shuffling, followed by the creak of feet on the stairs.

Nate.

She followed him with her ears as he made his way upstairs, down the hallway and into his room.

She'd never been in his room since there was no need for it. She'd been in Asher and Triss's room only because that was where Triss got ready for their wedding, but Nate's bedroom door had been closed and she respected his privacy.

Was he a minimalist with just a bed and a nightstand? A few pairs of jeans and flannels in his closet and one pillow? Or did the man like a few secret luxuries like a flat screen television, a wooden dresser and a nice bedside table? Did his bed have throw pillows?

She snorted at the thought of Nate's bed having decorative throw pillows. She'd never met a man who had throw pillows. Those seemed to come with a woman when she moved in, but no man that she'd ever met actively went looking for decorative pillows or had them in his bachelor pad. Not for their bed or their couch. They used their hoodie rolled up if they needed something for their head.

Her arm started to ache the way she was laying so she rolled over onto her back again and stared into the dark at the ceiling. The groan of bed springs as Nate climbed onto his bed echoed through the floorboards and Mieka held her breath.

Did he sleep naked?

She hadn't actually seen him naked even though they'd had sex. She hadn't even seen his cock. It'd been so fast, so dark and they'd both been so drunk that they just lifted her dress, pulled her thong to the side and went at it.

It wasn't her first one-night-stand, and she knew that it wasn't Nate's, either, but it was the first one-night-stand that she'd ever had with a guy and then been forced to see him again.

Exhaling a deep breath, she pinched her eyes shut again, determined to finally get some sleep. Maybe she needed to go and find more of Triss's lemonade?

She'd give it another twenty minutes and if she was still awake, then she'd go find something to help knock her out.

The house was quiet, save for the quaint creaks and groans that came with something that was nearly a hundred years old. She wasn't even thirty-five and already she creaked and groaned, what did that say about her?

She was just feeling the pulling effect of sleep when her phone buzzed on her nightstand.

Get some sleep, Minx. I have a full day planned for us tomorrow.

Well, now she was wide awake. How did he know she was still up? Did he have a camera in her room somewhere like he did in the stables? She knew they had cameras in the stables because Triss had told her about the time she and Asher got busy for the first time—which was in the barn—and Nate saw them on his phone. It was how they kept a close eye on the horses, particularly the pregnant ones.

She texted him back immediately. *I was asleep, thank you. And maybe I don't want a full day of plans.*

Liar. You weren't asleep. And yes, you do want a full day of plans. You can't wait to see what I'm going to do to show you how great a life in the country and on a ranch can be.

She pulled her phone away from her face, activated the camera option, flicked on her table lamp and took a picture of herself giving the camera the middle finger with a sassy glare on her face, then she sent it to Nate along with the message. *Get to sleep yourself, Cowboy. I don't have horses to milk in the morning.*

He replied immediately with a laughing emoji and the message: *Neither do I. We don't milk horses here, you weirdo. Just another thing I guess I'll have to teach you. Put your hair in a braid, too. Goodnight.*

She glared at his message for a full minute. Did he just tell her how to do her hair? The nerve!

Well, she'd show him, she'd put it in a braid all right, but she'd do it her own way. He probably wanted her to do a simple French or Dutch braid down the back, but she'd learned some pretty fancy updos working as a dancer for so many years. She'd braid her hair, but it wouldn't be what he was expecting at all.

Ooh, you rebel.

She rolled her eyes at her own thoughts, growled and flopped over to her belly, splaying her arm out like a starfish. Normally, she slept on her left, but with her broken arm that was impossible, which made getting comfortable for sleep a task and a half.

She growled again, sat up, fluffed her pillow and tried again.

Over twenty minutes passed and she still wasn't asleep, so careful not to wake the house with the noisy way the door stuck to the jamb when you tried to open and close it, she padded barefoot out into the dark kitchen. Only the light over the stove was on.

Triss kept her lemonades in the fridge and told Mieka to help herself, so she did just that, grabbing a brand-new bottle and drinking half of it straight. It tasted great and went down too easy.

A creak on the floor upstairs made her pause mid swallow and stare into the darkness.

She wasn't ready to see Nate again. Not after their moment in the barn, or his confusing text messages.

A door upstairs opened and she quickly stowed the rest of the lemonade back in the fridge and ran down the hall to her room, opening and shutting it way too fast and noisily. She cringed as she closed it, then jumped back into her bed and pulled the covers over her head.

Why was she doing this? It wasn't like Asher, Nate or Triss would open her door to check if she was actually asleep. She was a grown ass woman, she could get out of bed and go into the kitchen if she wanted to.

She was behaving like an idiot. An idiot child.

Pulling the covers off her head, she glanced up at the ceiling, gave it two middle fingers since beyond the ceiling was a sexy and infuriating man, then she closed her eyes and refused to open them until morning. Which she knew would come faster than she wanted it to, bringing with it a blue-eyed rancher with a dimple and dick she couldn't forget even if she tried.

And boy had she tried.

"Mornin', Sunshine," Nate said with a smile as he took a sip of his coffee at the breakfast table. "Trouble sleeping?"

"My arm was throbbing last night. I'm used to sleeping on my left and I can't so... yeah, sleep was hard." She sat down at the table across from him and thanked Asher for the mug of coffee he placed in front of her.

"Cream?" her brother-in-law asked.

She nodded. "Please."

He went to the fridge and brought back a carton of half and half.

"Where's Triss?" she asked.

"Triss likes to get in a run before breakfast and work most days," Asher said, plopping a bowl of savory oatmeal in front of Mieka. It smelled delicious. Two runny fried eggs, crumbled turkey bacon, salt, pepper and melted Monterey Jack cheese. Her belly grumbled.

"Oh, I forgot that she has to work," she sipped her coffee, feeling like a fool.

"I'll keep you busy, Minx," Nate said with a wink over his coffee mug.

Her face grew hot.

"How are you at decorating, Mieka?" Asher asked, plopping an identical bowl of oatmeal in front of Nate and then another one for himself at the table before taking a seat.

"Well, I've never really had a place *to* decorate myself, but I don't think my eye for what works and what doesn't is terrible, why?" She picked up a big piece of crumbled bacon and popped it into her mouth.

"We've built three log cabins along the river about a thirty, forty and fifty-minute ride, then a fourth one up on the hill roughly a ninety-minute ride from here. They're small and rustic, but we need to add furniture, dishes and décor. The plan is to rent them out as mini getaways. We'll ride guests out there on horseback, pack in all the food and guests can stay out there and go hiking, fishing, swim in the river or whatever. Little retreat-style things." Asher sipped his coffee. "It was Triss's idea. The cabins, and you decorating them."

"What do you think, Minx?" Nate chewed his breakfast.

"I think it's a great idea. Where do you want me to find the furniture? Am I ordering it or ..."

Nate nodded. "Yep. I'll direct you to the websites and you can just order what you think will work. We can take a ride out to one of the cabins today if you'd like to get a better idea. They're all identical."

Alone on a ride with Nate? Butterflies took flight in her belly, along with a few worried ladybugs, too.

"Minx?"

"Hmm?" She shook her head and blinked a few times, lifting her gaze to Nate's probing one.

"Do you want to take a ride to one of the cabins so you can make a list of what we'll need?"

"Uh yeah, sure. Sure."

He nodded.

"How will we get the furniture out there once it arrives?" she asked.

"Well, hopefully you get stuff that can be assembled after delivery, and we can take the boxes out via trailer and ATV," he replied. "IKEA is your friend in this case."

"After what happened with Dare, we decided ATVs and snowmobiles were a good idea." Asher's expression turned sad. "We should have had them at the very beginning, but we were trying to cut costs. And ended up paying the ultimate price."

She met her brother-in-law's eyes and mirrored his sad frown. She'd never met Asher's horse, but Triss filled her in on what happened and the story had absolutely ripped out Mieka's heart.

"Do you guys need to still go out and feed the horses and stuff?" she asked.

They both snorted and dug into their oatmeal. "Been up for two hours already, Minx," Nate said. "Everybody's been fed. Now it's our turn."

"Oh!"

He smiled. "You'll learn ranch life soon, don't worry."

"Will I be able to ride with a broken arm?"

"We'll put you on Macklin, he loves you so he'll be gentle and take it easy. It'll be like riding on a cloud." He sipped his coffee, but the twinkle in his eyes said he was smiling and found her concern amusing.

The front door opened and a sweaty and rosy-faced Triss came in. She ditched her running shoes and pulled her earbuds out as she wandered over to them in the kitchen and kissed Asher on the top of his head. "Good morning." She was still slightly out of breath.

"Running is okay for the baby?" Mieka asked.

"I asked my doctor and Google and both said it was fine," she said with a smile, her chest still heaving slightly.

Asher wrapped his arm around his wife's butt, but then made a face and pulled his hand away.

"I'm sweaty, what do you expect?" Triss asked, laughing.

Asher got up from the table and took his empty bowl with him. "You showering before breakfast or after?"

"I'm going to shower first." She took off upstairs and the squeal and groan of the pipes echoed through the house a moment later.

Nate finished his breakfast, too, and took the dishes to the dishwasher. He finished his coffee, then turned to Mieka. "Leave in half an hour?"

She nearly choked on the coffee in her mouth. "For the cabins?"

He lifted a broad shoulder in his sexy flannel shirt. "Lots to do today, need to tick that off the list sooner rather than later. We'll bring out a couple of pack horses, too, since they can use the exercise and I need to take out some supplies."

Mieka could only nod. Her mouth was full of delicious oatmeal and egg and her mind was racing. Nate was dead-set on showing her how great life on a ranch could be and it appeared he wasn't wasting any time making good on that promise.

"I uh ... I'll meet you in the barn in half an hour."

His nod was quick and curt but his smile made her insides do some serious Olympic gymnast worthy flips. "See you out there." Then he was gone with Asher in his wake.

Mieka finished her breakfast in quiet, but her brain wouldn't allow her any peace. After the way her panties flooded and her heart raced last night when Nate was right there, tugging her hair and giving her a look that promised a kiss. How was she supposed to think of anything else today on their ride?

The shower upstairs turned off, so she went to the sink, rinsed her dishes and put them in the dishwasher.

Triss had clients today, so Mieka needed to keep herself busy. She stupidly figured that since her sister ran her own practice, she could make her own hours and take some time off while Mieka was here. But she couldn't.

Triss was a speech and language pathologist, and after moving to Colorado to be with Asher, she opened up a private practice on the ranch. Asher and Nate built her a beautiful building where she met with clients of all ages and circumstances. She then hired a couple of occupational therapists, clinical counselors and behavior therapists, and the clinic operated with a holistic approach, using all of their resources and providing their clients with everything they needed in one safe space.

They were also planning to open up the ranch for therapeutic horseback riding, but as far as Mieka knew they hadn't hired a trainer yet, and only had one horse that was certified. But from what Nate said, Daria—Dare and Greenleigh's filly—would become one, as well as Mercy and Hula-Hoop's filly, Skipper.

In a pair of dark jegging capris and a billowy black top with cap sleeves, Mieka dug around in her bag for her Skechers slip-ons, then twisted her hair up into two elaborate braids, starting at her temples and moving toward the back of her head. She did them Dutch-style, folding the strands under each other as she went rather than over in the traditional French way, which made the braid sit on top of her hair. She pinned them and twisted them until they formed a delicate bun at the back. This was a style that a lot of the dancers had to wear for one of their performances and she'd perfected it. Executing the entire thing in under five minutes. However, with one arm in a heavy cast, it took closer to fifteen minutes for her to finish. But she did it, and that was all that mattered.

Grabbing a cardigan in case it got chilly, and slathering some SPF on her face, she was just leaving her bedroom when Triss came bouncing down the stairs. "How'd you sleep?" she asked.

"Shitty," Mieka replied, fastening some small pearl studs in her ears. "Arm was throbbing and I couldn't get comfortable. I ended up coming out here and grabbing more lemonade."

"And it helped?" Triss asked, making her way into the kitchen. "Before you judge, the doctor said I could have one cup of coffee a day. I'm not doing anything wrong. This is what keeps me from murdering people."

Mieka snorted and watched as her sister poured herself a cup of coffee then added a generous amount of half and half to it. "No judgment. And yes, the weed helped. I finally passed out around one, I think. You guys are freaking loud, by the way. Nate and I had to go out to the barn to get away from all of Asher's grunts and all of your, *Oh God's*. Seriously, get that house built and leave Nate in peace."

Triss clenched her teeth and frowned. "Shit, you heard us?"

"Uh, yeah. I think the coyotes in the fields heard you."

"Sorry. Nate's usually at the other side of the house and he puts in his earbuds to listen to podcasts before bed so he doesn't hear us. We totally forgot that you two were still probably downstairs when we started. Asher said he was tired, but he started giving me a foot massage, then his hands traveled up my legs and then between my legs and—"

"I got it!" Mieka put her fingers in her ears. "Don't need the details. You're saving a horse and riding a cowboy and I couldn't be happier. But I'm in a bit of a dry spell, trying to figure out what to do with my life and coming to terms with the fact that I'm a dried up, crusty loaf of bread in the dancing world, so hearing my sister get her rocks off with her hunky husband isn't high up there on my list of *fun things* to do at the moment."

Triss's mouth twitched like she was trying to hold back a smile. "Doesn't have to be a dry spell. I'm sure Hank would be more than happy to dampen your—"

Mieka cut her sister off with a stern headshake. "That metaphor is not going to work so I'm going to stop you now."

Triss laughed and took a careful sip of her coffee. "You know what I mean."

"I do, and no. I'm not going to go pick a ranch hand Bachelor-style and hand one of them a rose, then pull them up into the hayloft."

Triss merely shrugged. "Where are you off to? My first client isn't until nine-thirty so I thought we could hang out until then."

Mieka checked the time on her phone. It was only eight. She let out a deep sigh. "Nate wants me to join him on a ride to one of those log cabins you guys built along the river."

Triss perked up. "Oh right! I thought you'd be perfect for that. What do you think?"

Her sister wasn't wrong. The idea of getting to decorate and furnish a bunch of cabins sounded like a lot of fun. Mieka was itching to get on some of the websites Nate was going to direct her to, as well as the IKEA website and start planning each cabin. She already had ideas, but she needed to see the space first. "I appreciate you thinking of me. I think it's going to be fun."

Triss beamed. "I was going to do it, but I'm more than happy to pass the torch."

"Well, consider the torch passed. I'm excited."

"To spend someone else's money?"

"That, too."

They both laughed.

"Enjoy the ride. Nate's a great guide."

Nate being a guide was not her concern. It was what he was trying to do—show her how great country life could be—and the fact that she'd dreamed about kissing him last night.

Yes, she finally fell asleep, but then she had to dream, and all of those dreams involved Nate and his lips on various parts of her body. She woke up with soaked panties and flushed cheeks. Then seeing him all sexy and looking like a cover model for Farmer's Weekly magazine or something made all those dreams come rushing back and her body got insanely warm.

If you made the ranch your home, you'd get to feel those lips all over your body all the time. It wouldn't just be a dream.

She resisted the urge to smack herself in the forehead to clear that internal dialogue. It was her vagina talking—her stubborn cat—nothing more. Her vagina was lonely and talking like a desperate lunatic.

"I'm going to be late," she said, clearing her throat and heading to the foyer. "What time does your last client leave?"

"Five, so maybe we could run to the store and pick up something for dinner afterward? I was thinking tacos, but I need to buy lettuce, sour cream and jalapeños."

Mieka's hand landed on the front door handle. "Sounds perfect. I'll meet you back here at five. Have a great day."

Triss leaned in and the two hugged quickly, then Mieka was out the door, bringing her butterflies and ladybugs and a few horny hornets in her belly with her. It was going to be crowded in the saddle.

Chapter Six

For someone who admitted to having never been on a horse before in her life, despite how worldly she was, Mieka did surprisingly well.

It helped that Macklin was such a docile beast and just followed Umber in front of him as Nate led them through the field toward the trails.

It was an idyllic May day, with a bright blue sky, a warm sun and just enough of a breeze to keep the sweat from pouring down his face. The perfect day for a ride into the woods with the woman he was sweet on. Now, if only he could get her to stop gripping the pommel on the saddle like it was a life raft and she was sloshing about the sea in the middle of a hurricane.

He decided to load up their donkey, Sasquatch with a bunch of supplies, as well as Rubix, a newer horse they'd acquired about six months ago. He was a gentle brown stallion with white socks and seemed to have acclimated well to the group. He was a good addition and they hoped to breed him with Pom-Pom or Carolina next year.

"How you doing?" he asked, trotting back to ride beside Mieka whose knuckles were white she was gripping the pommel so tight.

"Fine," she squeaked.

He chuckled. "Grab the reins, you'll feel more in control."

She didn't move.

"Minx, grab the reins." He sidled up closer to her. Umber and Macklin merely snorted, but neither did anything to stop him from getting them so close, then he reached over and pried her fingers off the pommel before sliding the reins in between them. "Hold on with your thighs. But not too tight, otherwise he'll think you want to run."

Her brown eyes widened. "I don't want to run."

"You're not going to fall off. Macklin won't let that happen. Just relax. You're tense and he feels that. If you relax, he'll relax."

Macklin was so used to this kind of thing, that her stress wasn't really fazing him, but Nate needed to drive home the point of how astute and empathic horses could be. They picked up on your emotions, on your stress and your tension, and even though Macklin wasn't appearing to be affected by it, Umber was. Nate could feel Umber tense beneath him and he made a couple of huffs and puffs like he wanted to get away from Mieka because she was stressing him out.

"Easy, buddy," Nate murmured, leaning forward and stroking his horse's neck. "Just be patient." He turned back to Mieka. "Loosen your grip."

She did as she was told and loosened her grip. Her shoulders rolled back and she sat up straighter, breathing out slowly through her mouth.

"There you go," Nate said. "Macklin's not going to let you fall. Neither will I. This is supposed to be fun. Have some fun."

She shot a glare at him, but he just smiled wider until her stony expression faded and she reluctantly lifted her lips into a half-smirk of amusement. "So when do your first guests for the cabins arrive? Have you opened up the booking calendar yet?"

He led Umber away a few feet and the horse relaxed beneath him. "Two weeks."

Her eyes widened. "Two weeks? Cutting this a little close, don't you think?"

"We had some issues with getting the plumbing and generators set up. And

Triss was supposed to order the furniture and décor but she got pulled away last week for a work thing in Sacramento, and the furnishings just slipped mine and Asher's mind. We'll get it done though. With you helping us for sure. The stores we're going to order from are all in Denver, so we'll place the orders online, then go into Denver a couple of days later and pick up the orders. Faster than having them ship them to the ranch. We'll just take a truck and trailer with us. It'll be great."

She didn't seem convinced, but she focused her eyes forward again and relaxed her shoulders. "So how rustic are we talking? You mentioned plumbing, so the places have bathrooms and running water. What about Wi-Fi and electricity? What appliances are you providing?"

"Each cabin will have a fridge, albeit a small apartment-sized one, those are already out there since we took advantage of our friend with a helicopter and he dropped them off for us a couple of weeks ago. They're just not plugged in or anything. Smart ovens, and hot plates. We thought about gas stoves, but then we'd have to run gas lines out there, or constantly be worried about refilling the tanks. Plus, the risk of a fire or explosion just increases when you bring gas into the mix. There is running water, but the tanks will be heated via the generators, which our buddy with the chopper also delivered for us. Each cabin will have a queen-sized bed, a couch or futon, no television because that's not what this is about, some tables like coffee tables, kitchen tables, side tables or whatever, and books and maybe board games or something. I'll let you decide on that."

"How do the generators run?"

"Solar power. We have solar grids on the roofs and placed in ideal locations around each cabin."

"And who is going to be cleaning these places in between guests?"

"Triss said she would help, or Asher, or me, or we can send a ranch hand. We've talked about hiring a cleaner, too, if it gets too demanding."

He could see the cogs spinning in her head and he liked it.

"And your target demographic for guests is?"

"People with money and a sense of adventure. They want to get away from it all and unwind, get reacquainted with nature and go off the grid for a bit. We'll have a radio for them and us in the event something goes wrong, but for the most part, they'll be on their own. We'll take them in, then come and get them when their stay is over. Minimum three-night stay is required, otherwise it's not worth our time."

"And what are you charging a night for these cabins?"

"Three-forty a night in the peak season, two-ninety during the off season and we'll shut 'er down completely for winter since it'll be too risky to take people out there in the snow. Don't want them to get stranded."

"And how many reservations do you have so far?"

That was the question he was waiting for. He grinned. "We're completely booked until October thirty-first. Then we shut down from November first to March thirtieth for winter.

Her jaw dropped. "Completely booked in what way?"

"Starting May thirtieth, we have guests in all four cabins nearly every day until Halloween. We have one-day gaps between guests to go out and get the cleaning and set up done."

"That's amazing."

"Thanks. It's sure to bring in a lot more revenue and interest in the ranch. We're still doing the petting farm, too, which opens up fully even on weekdays at the end of May, then the ranch will be crazy-busy from sun up to sun down."

"You guys have certainly created a thriving business. Add in Triss's practice, the place is just a money-making machine."

"Costs a lot to run, too. Gotta pay the staff, feed the animals, something's always broken down—right now it's my truck apparently. I'll run it to Larry when we get back. We might make a lot of money—*now*—but we spend a lot, too. Sometimes it feels like it just bleeds out of us."

"Gotta spend it to make it." She cringed. "Sorry, that was so cliché. I know it takes a lot to keep a place like this running."

He chuckled. "It's okay." She was uncomfortable, he could tell. Was it because she was with him? Or what happened between them last night in the barn? Or his text messages? Probably all of the above. He wasn't doing a very good job at making her feel comfortable. If anything, he was probably succeeding more at making her feel extra *un*comfortable. He needed to fix that. "I like your hair," he said, lifting his chin to indicate her complex double braid and updo at the back of her head.

"I was *ordered* to wear my hair in a braid today. But I decided to do the braid *I* wanted, not what was expected of me." Her nose tipped up into the air and he had to keep himself from barking out a laugh that might startle the horses.

"All I meant was, you'll want your hair up so that it doesn't get caught on anything, or whip into your face when you ride. It wasn't an *order*. And I don't care what kind of braid you do. Though, this one is very pretty. Did they teach you how to do that at dance school?"

The sideways glare she shot him had him smiling. He liked teasing her. It made a pretty pink flood her cheeks and the way her nostrils flared and eyes widened just took her from beautiful to stunning.

But he needed to back off a bit if he wanted to win her over.

"Yes, they *taught* me how to braid my hair like this at *dance school*," she finally replied.

"Must have been challenging to do with only one real working arm. Well done."

He was still learning Mieka's tell, and although he didn't really like to compare people to horses, and knew that most people preferred *not* to be compared to horses, he felt that he could apply a lot of his horse whispering skills to the skittish dancer. She was trying hard not to react to his praise, in fact, she was trying to appear insulted, but it wasn't working. She responded to his "well done" the way any person who thrived on praise did. Her chest puffed up, her mouth lifted into a smile and her eyes twinkled.

"You're doing great. See how easy it is to ride when your shoulders aren't kissing your ears and you're not white-knuckling the pummel? It can actually be enjoyable."

"How much further?" she asked, not responding to his second compliment even though he could see her visceral reaction to it and the way it made her beam.

"Another twenty minutes or so. We'll just go to the closest one. They're identical pre-fabs, so once you get a feel for the size and design of one, you can just buy in bulk for the other three."

She nodded, then they rode in silence.

Nate itched to say or do something else that could help Mieka see how great life on a ranch could be, but at the moment, he was stymied. It would have to come naturally. He couldn't over-plan things.

He did, however, plan to have her help tag and name the new goat kids that had been born over the last two days. Three of their nannies had birthed six kids between them and all babies were healthy, but currently nameless. They often waited for one of the teenage girls with a boarded horse to name the goats—which was why they had goats named Eleven, Geronimo, Kombucha, Craddock, Dustin, Hilda, Marley, Alfonse, Billy the Kid, Hashtag, Jolene, Barbara, Nancy and Karen (who was such a Karen). But he figured Mieka might enjoy helping to pick out the names since she'd done such a great job with Chance and Skipper.

They also had to brush the miniature horses, Sam and Frodo, and the pony, Magic. He didn't want to lay on the work-load too thick to start, since mucking stalls and getting covered in chicken poop could turn her off ranch life. So he made sure to pick some fun chores to start.

Another twenty minutes of quiet riding in the morning sun, with the dew glistening on the leaves and tall blades of grass like little balls of glass, and the first cabin came into view on the river bend. They already had troughs and hitching posts outside of each cabin, so all he had to do was turn on the outside tap and fill the trough for the horses and donkey.

She helped him unload, which was mostly just wooden boards and planks to finish boarding up the bottom of the cabin to help with the insulation, as well as things like caulking for the window sills and extra grout for the tile in the bathroom. He didn't have a ton left to do, but enough that they'd be at the cabin for at least an hour.

"Did you bring a notepad?" he asked, unloading the last of the supplies from Rubix who was happily nibbling on some nearby grass.

She held up her phone. "I'll just dictate what I need into a note-taking app."

"Smart."

He opened the door into the cabin for her to walk in first.

"Oh wow!"

Oh wow good? Or oh wow bad?

"This is ... *cozy*."

He chuckled. "You mean *small*?"

"I mean, my cabin on the ship wasn't much bigger than this. At least after I became dance captain. They were significantly smaller when I was just a regular dancer and forced to share with other dancers and entertainment crew. No windows in those bunks, either." She shuddered. "A bit claustrophobic, honestly." She was rambling, which was something he noticed she did when she was excited. Not that it bothered him. He actually found it cute and endearing. It was like her brain was overflowing with ideas and thoughts and she couldn't get them out of her mouth fast enough. But he liked that she was excited about the cabins and talking a million-miles a minute. "And people are willing to pay over three hundred a night to stay in a shoebox?"

"It's the experience. Getting away from civilization, connecting with nature. Plus, we've hired a killer designer who is going to decorate and furnish this place so it's got everything our guests could possibly want."

Her brows pinched. "But I thought you hired m—" He was lifting one brow at her and smirking. "Oh! I'm the killer designer you hired."

"Smart and pretty." He winked. "We will pay you."

She wandered around the small cabin. It had three rooms total. A bedroom, or more accurately, a loft for a bedroom which sat over the living room, then there was the bathroom with a claw-foot tub and small stand-up shower on the lower level along with the living room and kitchen. There were windows in every room and the one in the living room was big and pointed directly at the river, the same with the window in the loft.

"Stunning view," she said, wandering over to the big picture window and standing in front of it.

"I couldn't agree more," he said, though he wasn't referring to the river.

"Did you bring a measuring tape?" she asked.

"Sure did." He handed her the one he had attached to his belt. "Let me know if you need any help. I'm going to start caulking the window sills."

"And I will start measuring the space for furniture." He went to the tool bag he'd brought and found the caulking gun and tube of caulking. They were quiet as they worked for nearly ten minutes. She made notes on her phone, but didn't dictate like she said she would.

The silence between them was driving him crazy.

"Tacos," he blurted out.

"Huh?" she was in the kitchen taking pictures with her phone.

"My favorite food is tacos. My favorite color is green. My favorite drink is an old fashioned, but after a long, hard day of work I prefer to kick back with an ice-cold beer."

Her right brow lifted. "Ooookaaaayyy."

"I told you I was going to help you get to know me, since apparently you don't know me at all, so this is me starting."

She slowly nodded. "Okay."

"Feel free to reciprocate."

"I'm good."

A growl rumbled in his chest. Why did she have to be like this?

"Hunt for Red October."

"Favorite movie?"

"Yes," he replied.

"Okay."

"Fall."

"Fall what?" Irritation glimmered in her eyes, but he was enjoying poking this bear. She needed to loosen the fuck up and try to have fun. It was almost as if as much as he was determined to show her how great ranch life could be, and help her get to know him, she was just as determined to *not* get to know him or see how great ranch life was. Stubborn minx.

"Fall is my favorite season."

"Oh."

"Horses, obviously."

"Favorite animal?"

He nodded again. "Yep. But dogs are a close second. Bruno wanted to come with us, but the bears are just coming out of hibernation and are hungry. I don't need him running off and either getting in trouble or eating a bunch of bear shit. I'm also not a big snake person. I wouldn't call it a phobia, but you won't see me volunteering to foster any snakes or put one around my neck at a carnival."

That seemed to pique her interest. "I've done that. In Thailand I put a massive albino Burmese python along my shoulders. It was really cool." Her smile was cheeky and did all kinds of things to his balls and lower belly.

Shuddering, he shook his head emphatically. "Nope. No thank you. No bueno."

She giggled. "So the big bad rancher slash SEAL has a weakness?"

He narrowed his eyes at her and stalked across the cabin until he was right up in her space. "Snakes aren't my weakness, Minx. They're a rational fear, since they can kill you. My *weakness* is sassy, stubborn women who make me work impossibly hard for their attention." He had her crowded against the small kitchen counter now and could tell that she wasn't as unaffected by his proximity as she wanted to be. Her chest heaved, her nostrils flared and her brown eyes widened. "Stubborn women who can't see all that they have to offer the world, and everything that's being offered to them."

She swallowed.

They held eye contact for nearly a minute, neither of them saying anything although he could read her thoughts pretty clearly based on how quick her pulse was beating in her slender neck. He took a risk and trailed his index finger down the side of her neck and over the delicate bone of her clavicle.

Her lips parted and her breathing picked up. He could feel the warm puffs of her breath on his arm.

"What's your favorite color, Minx?"

Her nose scrunched in a cute way and her brows knitted. "Huh?"

"Favorite color?"

"Uh ... purple."

He nodded and stepped away, showing her his back. "Good to know."

When she growled in frustration, he had to stifle his chuckle. He resumed caulking the window sill, while she muttered to herself behind him.

"Can I go up into the loft and measure?" she asked after a few moments of opening cupboards and drawers. "Do I need to order dishes and cookware, too?"

"Everything, Minx. Linens of every sort. Bedding, towels, clothes. The works."

She hummed in thought, and he turned around to face her.

"And yes, you can head on up to the loft. I'm done here anyway and need to caulk the window sill up there, so I'll join you."

She didn't say anything, but headed for the ladder to the loft and started to climb it. He was at the bottom of the ladder and about to start climbing, as well, enjoying the view of her ass as she used her long legs to propel her up, when she squeaked, swore and was suddenly falling.

Like a damsel in distress, falling from the tower, he caught her in his arms. "Whoa, there, Minx. Careful. You know I'm interested, you don't need to *throw* yourself at me."

She glared at him and sprang out of his arms, only to resume her climb once more.

"You're welcome," he said loudly.

She merely turned around while half-way up the ladder and shot another glare at him.

He was all grins and started to climb the ladder just as she reached the loft.

"This is bigger than I was expecting," she said. "I wonder if we could fit a king-sized bed up here?"

"We could," he said, making his way over to the big square window that offered the most amazing view of the river and mountains. "But it's getting the bed here that's the challenge. I suppose we could ask Cal to deliver it with his helicopter." He faced her. "You think a king is better than two twins or a queen?"

"Infinitely," she said without a second's hesitation. "Also, you can buy the memory foam mattresses which come in a vacuum-packed box, so they're small in the package, then when you open the box and air gets to it, it expands."

"Like one of those dinosaurs you put in water?"

She nodded. "Yeah, sort of."

Tapping his chin, he retrieved the tape measure from her and took some measurements of the room. "And what do you propose we do for a bed frame?"

"IKEA. You can get frames that have wooden slats rather than a boxed spring. That would cut down on not only expense, but the bulk of getting supplies here."

He measured the distance between the floor and the peaked roof, and the peaked roof to the railing that separated the loft from the rest of the house. "Yeah, we'd have to do that since there isn't enough clearance to get a boxed spring over this railing." He retracted the tape measure and handed it back to her with a wink. "Good thinking, Minx."

Her blush was sexy and she quickly hid her face from him. "What is your maximum occupancy?"

"Four. Why?"

"Well, I'm just wondering if we could increase revenue and availability by offering cots or rollaway beds, as well, and increasing the occupancy to a max of six. It's a small space, but you just charge extra for more than four people. I mean, in theory, you can advertise the place as perfect for two, but can sleep up to six, and just charge more for the additional four people. Since that's more linens to wash and stuff."

Stroking his chin, he mulled it over. "You might be onto something."

Again, she beamed and the smile and twinkle in her eyes had his cock twitching.

"No closet," she murmured.

"No, you'll need to get armoires or dressers or something."

She nodded and punched in some notes into her phone. "Curtains?"

"Up to you. My room at the house doesn't have them. I'm always up before the sun and go to bed when it's dark, so it's never an issue."

She responded with another nod and more notes into her phone. "I'm going to go down to the living room and take a few more measurements." She made her way back over to the ladder and climbed down.

He finished what he was doing, then joined her. Once he was done with the windows, he touched up the grout in the bathroom, then went outside to nail the boards to the underside of the house for better protection from the weather.

She remained in the house, but just as he was packing up the supplies, she met him near Sasquatch and scratched the gentle donkey's ears. "I'm done."

"Me, too."

"Are we heading to the next three or going back to the ranch?"

"My intention was to just visit this one. I brought out all the boards for all the cabins, but I was just going to leave them here and come out another day to finish up, but if you're game to keep riding, we can visit the other three and I can take care of all my projects today?"

She shrugged. "Nowhere else to be. Not until five when Triss is done, anyway."

He was finding her difficult to read at the moment. Quieter than he remembered. Normally, she was a fairly transparent glass house and he could see exactly how she was feeling and what she was thinking. Particularly when she blushed and the pulse in her neck picked up tempo. It was why he knew that she was so game for them to have sloppy sex the night of the wedding. Their flirting and suggestive banter had only been one of very many blatant clues that she was interested in him. Her facial expressions, fucky-eyes and rosy cheeks were the other major clues. But right now, she was more opaque than transparent.

She's got a lot on her mind. Her lack of a job, her lack of direction and uncertainty about the future. Cut her some slack.

Fair enough.

He finished loading up the supplies, then strapped the remaining lumber back onto Sasquatch before untying the horses from the hitching post and helping Mieka back into her saddle.

"Oh shit, sorry," he murmured, when his hand accidentally—and yes, it was truly an accident—slipped and his thumb pressed right between her legs. "I honestly didn't mean to."

"It's fine," she said quickly, putting her shoes into the stirrups.

He cleared his throat, and with warm cheeks, swung his body up into his saddle. "Are you having even a little bit of fun?" he asked, hopeful that she wasn't going to dismiss him with another "it's fine" or a shrug. He was trying to strike a balance here. Keep her engaged and help her get to know him, while also letting her stew in the pity party she had clearly thrown for herself before she even arrived at the ranch.

"I am," she said softly, as he guided Umber back to the trail and Macklin followed, along with the donkey and Rubix.

He craned his head around to look at her and smiled. "I'm glad. Can you picture a life here on the ranch yet?"

Thank fuck, that got her smiling. "Hold your horses there, cowboy, I haven't even been here twenty-four hours."

"Rancher," he said with a big grin that made her smile grow, too. They knew they were mimicking his brother and her sister with their cowboy-rancher joke. But he was here for it. If it brought a smile to her face like it did just now, then he was here for all of it.

He'd do anything he could to keep Mieka smiling like that, especially if life on the ranch—life with him—was what made her smile.

Chapter Seven

It was nearly four o'clock by the time they got back to the ranch. Nate hadn't packed anything more than a few granola bars and some apples, so Mieka was starving by the time they returned. Nate offered to go foraging or fishing in the river, but she said it wasn't necessary.

She was willing to deal with hunger more than she was her rampant libido, because she knew that watching him go all mountain-man and live off the land would have gotten her engine revving more than it already was. The man just had a way of making her panties get drenched and her belly turn into a warm pile of horny goo.

"Thank you for the gentle ride, Macklin," she said, as she finished brushing the horse that had kept her safe all day, and gave him some carrots from the bucket. He nibbled them happily from her palm before nuzzling her chest with his nose. She giggled and stroked his forehead. "Getting a little brazen there, Macklin. Need to buy me dinner, first."

"Is that what it takes?" Nate asked with a cheeky smile, approaching her with the hose and entering Macklin's stall to fill up his water trough. "Dinner and then I get to nuzzle your bosom?" He winked at her as he filled up the trough.

She rolled her eyes, but couldn't keep the smirk from lifting on her mouth.

"Not a lot to nuzzle, I'm afraid. And I only let those hung like Macklin nuzzle me."

He snorted and his smile grew to a dangerous size. Her clit pulsed and her belly tingled. "I think you can attest that although I'm not Macklin size, I'm no slouch, either."

She shrugged. "It was dark and I was drunk. I honestly don't remember. But I do remember it took me a really long time to come so ..." She flashed him a cheeky smile.

Heat blazed in his eyes. He'd been trying to get her to open up all day, but she'd worked just as hard to keep up her guard. She knew what he was doing. He was not only trying to woo her, offer him a second chance at *whatever* they'd been for a hot, sweaty minute, but he also wanted her to see what life on the ranch could be like.

She had to hand it to him, he was doing a good job. She'd had fun today.

The idea of getting to furnish and decorate the cabins was a dream she didn't know she had, come true. They were blank canvases ripe for her vision. She planned to do a different theme for each cabin. Nate said she could just order four of everything—four sets of dressers, four beds, four sets of bedding and linens—but she wanted to make each cabin unique.

Even though her belly rumbled like approaching thunder, she was glad that they'd gone to all four cabins so she could take pictures of the surrounding area and get a feel for what kind of a vibe she wanted each cabin to adopt. The three on the river would be more nature forward with lots of greens and browns, natural fibers and things that complemented the river and forest. But the last cabin—her favorite—was on a small hill with the entire valley and mountains in full view. The river was a five-minute walk down the hill and only visible from the window in the loft. She wanted to go more rustic and country with that one. Flannels and plaids, country-chic style furniture and décor.

Her heart was close to bursting and the cogs in her head were on overdrive by the time they returned to the ranch. She barely registered her hunger until another rumble, loud enough to make Macklin startle, reminded her that she should eat.

"My last client canceled because he caught a cold at the pool on the weekend, want to head to the store now?" Triss joined them at Macklin's stall where the tension between Mieka and Nate was thick enough to choke on.

Mieka's sister cast her a curious look before bouncing her gaze to Nate. She lifted one brow and cocked her head to the side. "What's going on with you two? I feel like I interrupted something."

"Nothing!" Mieka blurted out at the same time Nate shrugged and casually said the same thing.

That only made Triss more suspicious. Thankfully, though, Macklin realized there was a new person there to give him attention, so he made a snuffling noise and nudged Triss with his nose until she started to scratch his neck. "Yes, yes, you big baby." She kissed his cheek. "You're a bit pathetic, you know that, Mack? So needy."

"He doesn't care," Nate said, exiting the horse's stall. "He has no shame as long as he gets attention."

"I know men like that," Mieka said, which caused Nate's head to whip around and his eyes to burst into two blue flames in his skull.

Her lips twitched.

"Ready to go?" Triss asked.

Mieka nodded. "Sure. I'm starving, so I'm going to be the worst grocery shopping companion."

"We'll stop by the bakery and grab Danishes then, if there are any left," Triss replied.

"What's on the menu tonight, ladies?" Nate asked, moving to Umber's stall to fill his trough, as well.

Mieka wanted to keep it a secret then surprise him, since he'd divulged on their ride that his favorite food was tacos and they were in fact planning to make tacos for dinner. But Triss was oblivious to all that was passing between Mieka and Nate and just said, "Tacos."

Nate's eyes once again turned fiery.

"Pick me up a Danish," he called after them as Triss linked her arm through Mieka's and they made their way toward the side door at the south end of the barn.

"We'll see," Mieka called back, unable to resist teasing him.

She heard him growl behind her and that sent the butterflies with saddle-sores into a new frenzy in her belly.

It wasn't exactly the easiest thing in the world, climbing up into Asher's big truck with one arm in a cast, but she finally managed, with Triss giggling at her struggle.

"You okay?" her sister asked, still laughing while Mieka buckled up her belt and nodded. Triss turned on the truck and it rumbled to life. A moment later they were ambling down the driveway toward the main road. "How was your ride today?"

"It was great. I've got loads of ideas for the cabins."

"I knew you'd like this job," Triss said, turning left onto the country road that would take them toward the general store roughly two miles away. "Nate wasn't too annoying?" She said this with mirth, since Mieka knew that Triss and her brother-in-law had a great relationship. Triss had never had a negative thing to say about Nate, so she was just calling him annoying to be funny.

But Mieka was quiet.

"Shit, did he actually do something?" Triss asked, her brown eyes—a similar shade to Mieka's, but maybe a little darker—going wide with worry.

Mieka shook her head and sighed, staring out the window. "No. He's just ... he's trying to convince me that ranch life might be something I could like."

Her sister's brows pinched. "Why?"

Mieka went quiet again.

"Mieks?" Triss demanded, forcing Mieka to face her sister again. "What's going on with you and Nate? Has something already happened? I know you two were flirty at the wedding but—" Her eyes nearly exploded out of her face. "Did you two sleep together at the wedding?"

Mieka's mouth twisted.

"When?" Triss exclaimed.

Mieka's shoulders fell and she laced her fingers together in her lap, fixing her gaze on the lock for the glove compartment. "The night of the wedding. The reception. It was late, we were both stupidly hammered and we snuck out of the reception and had drunk, sloppy sex up against the barn. Then I took off back to work the next morning but apparently, he thought it was going to be more than just a quick fuck."

"And was upset you left without saying goodbye?"

"Among other things, yes." It wasn't that Mieka didn't trust her sister and feel comfortable telling Triss about her abortion, she just was more concerned with how that kind of information could affect Triss's relationship with Nate. They lived on the same ranch, were in each other's lives daily, so Mieka didn't want to give her sister any fodder to harbor resentment toward Nate. Mieka and Nate could go years if not a lifetime without ever seeing each other again, or at the very most, remaining civil and amicable when in the same space. So she needed to prioritize Triss and Nate's relationship above everything else.

Pasha knew about the abortion, obviously, since she had been the one to set it up for Mieka in Seattle with her former colleague. But Mieka hadn't told her other sisters. Would they be mad? They were all progressive women, and as far as she knew her sisters were pro-choice, just like her. But it was easy to say that you were pro-choice when those getting abortions weren't close to you. People changed their tune when the issue suddenly got closer to home. She also knew that Triss and Asher had been trying to conceive for months to no success—until now. She didn't know how Triss would take knowing that Mieka was Fertile Myrtle while she and Asher struggled to conceive.

Triss pulled over to the side of the road and put the truck in park. They weren't near anything but fields. A field of brown cows on one side of the road and a field of wheat on the other. "What aren't you telling me, Mieka?" Triss said, adopting her best big sister and mom-to-be voice.

Mieka swallowed.

"Mieka Contessa Young—"

"I got pregnant and had an abortion. Nate knows. He came with me when I had the procedure. Pasha set it up with a former colleague in Seattle."

Now she really was worried that her sister's eyes were going to burst free of her skull.

Triss sat there in stunned silence for several heartbeats. Mieka wasn't sure what to do. Her bottom lip wobbled.

She wasn't upset about having the abortion. She knew it was the right choice. She hadn't been ready to have a baby. She was still dancing, had no roots to put down and she and Nate hardly knew each other. It made sense.

But tears marred her vision as she stared at her big sister. "Are you mad at me?" She tipped her head to Triss's flat belly. "I know it took you guys a while to conceive. Are you upset that I ... that I terminated my pregnancy when it was so hard for you to *get* pregnant?"

Triss snapped out of her trance, unbuckled her seatbelt and lunged across the truck, wrapping her arms tight around Mieka. "What? Oh God. No, not at all. I'm so sorry you went through that. You know you could have called me, too. I would have come to support you. Me being pregnant and struggling to conceive has nothing to do with your accidental pregnancy. Nothing. I could never be mad or resent you for that. You have to know that."

"I know," Mieka said through sniffles. "Pasha was going to come with me, but Raze got sick so she had to cancel. I called Nate and he flew out to be with me. It was okay."

"Is he mad you had the abortion?" There was ire threatened in Triss's tone, but she withheld it until Mieka responded.

"No. At least he says he's not. He held my hand, brought me food and tea. He was ... wonderful."

They broke their embrace, and Triss wiped the tears from beneath her eyes. "Honey, I'm so sorry you had to make that choice. I mean, I'm glad that we still *have* that choice ... for now." She cast her eyes sideways and frowned. "Fucking patriarchy. But I'm glad that you did what was right for you and that you weren't alone."

Mieka nodded. "Me, too."

"So what's Nate trying to do now? Win you back?" A smile tugged at the corner of her mouth. "'Cause, I'm not going to lie. I think you guys are actually pretty perfect for each other and I would *love* to have you move here and for us to get closer."

"Way to pile on the pressure," Mieka teased.

Triss shrugged. "I want what I want, and I want my sister close."

Well, that warmed Mieka's heart more than she was prepared for. "I want to be close to you, too. But I just ..."

"You're sorting shit out. I get it. I wasn't in *exactly* the same boat as you when I ended up on the farmhouse doorstep a couple of years ago, but my life *was* at a crossroads. Lorne had just dumped me and I was wondering what to do with my life. Yes, my career was fulfilling and I loved it. I still do, but we can't get so wrapped up in our careers that it is all we use to shape our identity, you know?"

Mieka nodded. "I know."

Triss reached for her hand and gave it a squeeze. "We'll figure it out. But in the meantime, don't get mad at me for jumping on the bandwagon with Nate and trying to convince you how awesome life is on the ranch. I'm also totally team Nate and think if we married brothers, it would be AMAZING!"

Rolling her eyes, Mieka shook her head, but the smile on her lips was something she couldn't control. "He did a bang-up job convincing me today, I will admit it."

"Now he just needs to *bang* you in other ways."

"Uh, no. The man is virile, we don't need to make that mistake twice."

"Wear a condom."

Mieka sighed. "Yeah, I suppose ..."

Triss snorted and scooted back over to her seat, refastening her belt and putting the truck back into drive. "You didn't use protection, did you?"

"You saw me at the wedding. I was hilariously, fall-down drunk." She held up one finger. "But our coitus was one-hundred percent consensual before you ask."

"I wasn't going to. Nate is a lot of things, but he'd never take advantage of a woman."

"He double-checked that with me, too."

"Because he's a great guy."

"Yeah," Mieka sighed.

"You and Rayma did get pretty plastered after mom and dad went to bed."

"Rayma was fucking nuts. Dancing on the table, talking about going to see if she could ride a goat. Poor Jordan was having a hell of a time keeping her from breaking her neck. I wasn't *that* bad."

"No, you just went and rode a cowboy instead."

"Rancher," Mieka corrected, which caused them both to erupt into giggles.

They were still giggling when Triss pulled into the parking lot of the small shopping complex. There wasn't much, but there was a little bit of everything. A small tack shop, a small hardware store, a post office, a pharmacy, a bakery and a grocery store.

"Thank you," Mieka said as they climbed out of Asher's truck and Triss looped her arm through Mieka's while they walked toward the door to the bakery. "I hated keeping it from you, but I just ... I didn't want to jeopardize your relationship with Nate in any way and I thought if you knew he knocked me up you might get mad at him."

Triss smiled serenely and held open the door for Mieka to step in, she was instantly hit with the decadent aroma of yeast and sugar. Her belly made an angry rumble. "Never be afraid to tell me anything, Mieks. I know you. I love you. I know Nate. I love Nate. But I'm also an adult and can see the big picture.

I wouldn't have gotten mad at him. Though, I appreciate the thought behind your omission."

They approached the glass case that was still teeming with pastries. Mieka wanted one of everything.

"Is it wrong that I just want to fill my face while I'm here so I can finally grow tits and an ass?" she asked as her mouth flooded with saliva.

Mieka chuckled and approached the counter. "We'll take four of everything, please, Daniel."

Mieka's eyes nearly popped out of her head. "Four?"

"Well, I'm growing a person, and my husband and his brother would kill us if they found out we went to Daniel's and didn't bring them back anything. Plus, I can never decide, so it's easier to just *not* decide."

Mieka wrapped her arms around her belly as it grumbled and roared. She and Triss stood back and watched Daniel fill a big white cardboard box with all the different pastries.

Triss leaned over so that only Mieka could hear her. "I can not only see the big picture, little sister, but I can also see into the future, and I see us, and our husbands watching our children play in the field, loving life on the ranch. The fresh air, the wide-open spaces and the freedom." She bumped Mieka's shoulder. "Or maybe I'm deliriously hungry from the pregnancy and seeing things. Who knows?" She stepped forward and took the box from Daniel then paid him.

Meanwhile, Mieka suddenly had a very clear view of the image Triss had just painted. A blue bird sky, waist-high grass, children laughing and a husband staring at her adoringly. The only thing that was blurry was her husband and children's faces.

She did, however, know that all of their eyes were blue.

Blue like the Atlantic Ocean at sunrise.

And there was only one man she knew with eyes like that. Eyes that made her body tingle and her heart clench. And he was waiting back at the ranch for her, determined to convince her that this was the life for her.

Too bad she wasn't so sure it was.

Chapter Eight

It was nine-thirty at night, their bellies were full of tacos and pastries and Triss was yawning more than she was breathing.

"I can't keep my eyes open, guys. I'm sorry," she said, standing up from where she'd been cuddled up on the couch with Asher. "I have to head to bed. The baby is making me sleepy."

She leaned over where Mieka sat on the couch with her laptop, and pressed a kiss to the top of Mieka's head. "Goodnight, little sister."

Mieka tipped her eyes to Triss's. "Goodnight." She pressed her hand to her sister's belly. "Goodnight, baby cowboy or cowgirl."

"Rancher," Asher and Nate both grumbled.

Triss grinned, then headed to the stairs.

"I'm going to go check on the foals once more, then I'll meet you up there," Asher said, getting to his feet.

"I can go," Nate offered, though he looked mighty comfortable in the recliner with his big feet up and a beer in his hand.

Asher shook his head in dismissal. "I promised Tiberius I'd give him a few more carrots before bed." He disappeared behind the wall to the entryway, the door opened and shut a moment later.

"And then there were two," Nate murmured, tipping his beer bottle to his lips. "Whatcha looking at, Minx?"

"Furniture," she said, glancing at all the tabs she had opened. "Furniture and linens. Décor, dishware. All of it."

He was out of his chair and squeezing into the loveseat beside her before she knew it was happening. "Shove a bum, chum," he said, giving her a gentle hip check.

Despite her lack of an ass and slender dancer's frame, there really wasn't enough room for both of them on the loveseat. The man had breadth to him, and when you added in his big presence and his ego, she felt like a third or maybe fourth wheel crammed up against the arm of the two-cushion couch.

"Let's take a look," he said, reaching for her laptop. "Ooh, I like these." He was on the tab for beds she'd chosen for the riverfront cabins. All dark reclaimed wood that showed the natural grain and unique knots. "And matching night-stands. These are great." He was clicking through all the tabs. "These are a lot of tabs. How does your brain function with so many open?"

She snorted. "If only you knew how many tabs were open in my brain at one time."

He grinned. "Yeah?"

All she did was nod.

"This is a cool coffee table. It's that live-edge stuff that has become so popular. But the wrought iron legs make it look rustic yet modern. Another awesome choice. And there are matching end tables."

"Not exactly IKEA, I know, but I really think that you need to elevate—"

He held up his hand and shook his head. "We trust you, Minx. As long as they can get here by our first reservations and we can get them out to the cabins, do what you think is best."

Hope poured through her and she leaned over until their shoulders touched, the heat of him branding her like an iron. But it wasn't an unpleasant heat. It was welcoming and calming. She pressed the touchpad and went to a different tab. "They also make dining tables and chairs. Look at these."

"Oh, we definitely have to get those. Look at that cool acrylic river running through the two slabs of wood. That is really neat." He hit "add to cart." "What else, Minx?"

Grinning, and elated that he approved of her choices so far, she flipped to the tab with the linens, then proceeded to explain to him her vision for each cabin.

She was talking a mile a minute, but her thoughts were moving a mile a second. She thought for sure Nate was going to ask her to slow down or that his eyes would glaze over as she brought up drapery and throw pillows, but he didn't. He nodded and smiled, actively listened, asked relevant questions, and just seemed to absorb and enjoy her excitement.

The door opened and closed and for some reason, Mieka leaped off the couch, away from Nate's warmth and her computer.

Asher came around the corner and lifted a brow suspiciously at them.

"How're the moms and babes?" Nate asked his brother, completely unbothered by Asher's presence and Mieka's sudden departure from the loveseat.

"Callie is a bit engorged, not sure if Chance is nursing enough. I helped her, but we might need to call Jacob, have him come by in the morning to check on her."

"Mastitis?" Nate asked.

Asher shook his head. "Not sure. That doesn't usually happen until weaning if it's going to. He might just not be drinking enough. I'll give Jacob a call now and see if he can pop by in the morning."

Nate nodded as Asher ascended the stairs, pulling his cell phone out of his back pocket as he disappeared.

"You should get some sleep, Minx," Nate said, setting her laptop on the coffee table and standing up to stretch. "You'll be sore tomorrow after sitting in that saddle for so long."

"We'll see," she said cheekily. "I *was* a dancer not too long ago. With a rigorous practice and show schedule. Not to mention I got up and ran on the treadmill in the gym everyday. I'm sure a little *sitting* won't make me stiff."

His mouth curled into a smirk. "We'll see about that." He headed to the entryway while she grabbed her laptop, then followed him. "Where are you going?"

"I'm going to go check on Chance and Callie."

Fear shot through her. "But Asher didn't seem too concerned. He was just out there."

He shrugged. "And he's probably right. But I'm going to go double-check. No harm."

She opened her mouth, about to ask him if he wanted company, but thought better of it and pinched her lips shut, choosing to just follow him to the foyer and watch him slide into his work boots. Why did even that action make the butterflies in her belly go berserk?

Because he's big, sexy and the way the flannel shirt stretches across his broad shoulders as he leans down and tugs on his boots is hot.

Standing back up, he shot her another panty-shredding grin. "See you in the morning, Minx." The wink he gave her had those butterflies swooning, and the horny hornets in her belly flying around like they were drunk. Then he was out the door.

Mieka stood there and stared at the closed door for an inordinately long time. Too long, but she was simply stuck in place, her brain, heart, and vagina at war. Leaving her feet full of concrete and unable to function.

Her brain told her that she should go to bed. Her heart told her to go check on the horses, too. And her vagina told her to climb up on the cowboy and ride him off into the sunset.

Her vagina didn't know that Nate wasn't a cowboy, but rather a rancher and that the sun had already set. Her vagina was an idiot.

People joked about men having a one-track mind and thinking with their "little head." Well, women had the same problem. Her "big head" was struggling to keep up in the argument, while her vagina, or her "little head?" .... "little tunnel?" ... "love tunnel?" GAG! No! *Not* "love tunnel" ... she'd have to workshop it. Either way, her brain was losing while her vagina's argument was gaining momentum.

Clenching her fingers at her sides until her nails dug trenches into her palm, she let the pain snap her out of her horny stupor and she shook her head. "Argh!" she growled, spinning on her heel and stalking off down the hall to her bedroom.

Why did Nate have to be so freaking charming? Why did he have to be single, sexy, smart, handsome and a plethora of other appealing qualities that Mieka hadn't found in a partner in years? Why did the air have to smell so fresh here? Why did all the horses have to be so sweet?

This wasn't fair.

Life isn't fair, sweetheart.

With another growl, she undressed—albeit not with the vigor she started out with given her cast—then she put on the cast cover, wrapped a big fleecy towel around her body, and ducked across the hall to the bathroom.

She probably spent too long in the shower, given how the water was turning cool by the time she got out, but masturbating when you only had one good hand and the pipes squealed like a tortured pig wasn't the easiest or quickest of tasks.

But it was necessary.

She needed to clear her head and rid that sexual tension inside of her that was strung tighter than a bow string.

As much as she wanted to jump Nate's bones and have a good old-fashioned roll in the hay, she knew it was a bad idea. A terrible idea, no matter how much Nate and now Triss supported the notion.

She was back in her room and dressed in a black tank top and flannel pajama pants, keeping her ears peeled for the open and close of the front door.

But she heard nothing.

Did he already come back inside while she was in the shower?

Probably.

Curiosity niggled at the nape of her neck like an irritating mosquito, so she flung open her bedroom door and quietly padded down the hallway to check to see if Nate's boots were in the entryway.

They weren't.

This was a shoes-off house, given how much manure, dirt and other *stuff* was on the ground outside, so they kept the floors clean by keeping their shoes on a mat by the door. He wouldn't have worn them upstairs.

Before she could over-analyze the situation too much, she was throwing on the first coat she could find which she was pretty sure was Nate's given that it smelled like him, sliding into her slip-on Skechers and heading out into the cool, dark night.

The stars above were brilliant, bright, and winking at her like they knew what was going to happen. Nothing was going to happen. She was just concerned about the horses, that was all. She'd watched both Chance and Skipper be born, of course, she was invested in their well-being.

The gravel crunched under her shoes, but it sounded like rocks in a blender given the quiet of the evening. Nothing but frogs. It was still a little early for crickets, but the frogs were taking the opportunity to sing their night song extra loud since nobody was interrupting them. A hoot of an owl startled her and she jumped as she gripped the handle of the side door for the barn and yanked it open.

The barn was warm and most of the lights were off. Slowly, quietly, she made her way past the stalls. A few horses huffed and snuffled when they saw her, but only Macklin made a fuss for attention. He really was a sweet, pathetic attention-whore. But she was here for it, and went to him, giving him a couple of kisses and pets before continuing on down the barn toward Callie's stall.

"Everything okay, Minx? Are the honeymooners boning loudly again?" Nate's voice startled her. She hadn't come into view of him yet. How did he know it was her?

She asked that very question when she hung her head over the stall to find him sitting on the concrete with a blanket over his body, his head against the side, eyes closed.

"Triss is too tired to come out. Asher would cause more of a stir with the horses, particularly Tiberius. And Macklin is a big attention-whore. Plus, I can tell by the sound of your gait."

"The sound of my gait?"

"Every person has a unique walk and a unique sound to their walk. I know yours."

She often forgot that he was a former SEAL, trained in this kind of stuff. Of course, he knew it was her. He also probably knew she'd rubbed her clit until she came in the shower just by looking at her.

"What's up?" he asked, blinking those dark, dangerous blue eyes at her.

"I ... I was worried about Callie." She opened the stall and stepped inside, the scent of fresh hay hitting her nostrils. It was a nice smell.

He opened up his blanket and she didn't even hesitate to sink to the floor beside him and snuggle in close, allowing him to drape the blanket over both of them.

"How's she doing?"

"I think she has a clogged duct. It's not mastitis, but it's worrisome. Chance just favors the other teat which means the clogged one can't unclog."

"How do you fix that?"

"By milking the clogged one, but when I try, she gets frustrated and steps away from me. It might hurt. I don't want to upset her, but I am worried. Jacob will be here by eight tomorrow, then he can let us know what's really going on."

"You can't get Ronny or Hank or one of the other guys to come sit out here with her?"

He shook his head and yawned. "These are *our* horses. Our responsibility. I'd never forgive myself if I wasn't here and something happened to Callie, Chance or any of the horses. But you should go inside, Minx. There is no reason for you to be out here getting hemorrhoids on the cold concrete."

She giggled. "That's not how you get hemorrhoids. That's just something our parents' parents told them and they told us. It's from sitting too long and not getting proper circulation. Truck drivers get them."

He grunted, but didn't say anything.

"Besides, I'm invested in their well-being, too. I was there for Chance's birth, was a horse doula for Callie. I want to see them thrive, too."

He still didn't say anything.

Mieka's eyes drifted closed and her head slowly made its way to his shoulder. She was half-way into dreamland when a big, warm arm wrapped around her and pulled her tighter into his heat and protection. She snuggled in.

"I had a really nice day today, Nate," she said sleepily, not bothering to open her eyes. "And I'm sorry I didn't call you first when I found out I was pregnant. That was wrong."

"It's okay, Minx. I get it." His voice was dark and raspy and seemed further away than right next to her.

"Triss knows."

"She does?"

"Mhmm. She forced it out of me. I was worried it would affect your relationship which is why I didn't tell her. I didn't want her to be mad at you. She loves you."

"And I love her. She's the best thing that has ever happened to my brother."

"Mhmm."

"Is she mad at me?"

"No."

His grip around her tightened. "Sleep, Minx. Busy day ahead of us tomorrow."

She yawned, but never opened her eyes, rather, she snuggled deeper into his embrace and fell further into that purgatory between sleep and awake. "Nate?"

"Mmm?"

"I really hate the term 'love tunnel' for vagina."

He snorted. "Who calls it that?"

"I don't know. I'm workshopping something and that popped into my head. It made me cringe."

"Yeah, me, too." He paused. "What are you workshopping?"

"Well, guys think with their 'little head' right?"

"Mhmm."

"But women have the same problem. We also get overruled by our ... vaginas. But we can't call it our 'little head' because it's not a head. It's a—"

"Tunnel."

"But that's terrible. To be overruled by your *tunnel*. Barf."

His chuckle stirred the warm coals in her belly into flickers and flames. She still hadn't opened her eyes and was fighting the pull of sleep more and more as each second passed.

"Why are you workshopping this?"

"Because I am. My brain and heart and vagina are in a Mexican standoff."

"Oh yeah?"

"Mhmm. But I need a better term for my *vagina. Lady garden?*"

"Oh God." She could hear the cringe in his voice.

Pursing her lips, she thought for a moment. "What about my *cat is just being stubborn*."

Despite how close to sleep he sounded, Nate barked out a laugh that echoed through the quiet barn. "Go to sleep, Minx. You're delirious."

"Probably," she agreed, letting out a contented sigh. "Thank you."

"For what?"

"For being you." Then she turned her head just enough, kissed his shoulder and finally allowed sleep to claim her. And even though she was sitting on the cold, hard, unforgiving ground, she couldn't remember the last time she slept so soundly. Her dreams were pleasant, her body was warm and she felt protected and safe with Nate.

Mieka woke up alone in Callie and Chance's stall. Both the horses were still here, but Nate was gone.

Her butt was numb, but her body was warm under the flannel blanket.

She took her time getting up, stretching thoroughly. Chance was nursing, while Callie munched on hay. Other animals in the barn were making noises—munching, stretching, nursing and drinking—but Mieka kept her ears open for the tell-tale sound of Nate.

A quick good-morning scratch behind the ears for mama and baby, and she was exiting the stall, walking a little more bow-legged than she was prepared for. Her butt and inner thighs were tender after the ride yesterday and sitting on the ground all night.

She really wasn't as young as she used to be. A day like that ten years ago wouldn't have affected her at all, but now ... now her body was rebelling and telling her to ease up.

She grumbled and groaned as she slowly made her way down the barn past the stalls toward the side door. The need to pee came on fast and she picked up speed.

Macklin hung his big brown head over his stall door and made a demanding sound at the same time he locked eyes with her and held her gaze unwavering.

Rolling her eyes, she approached him. "I need to pee, Mack. Have you seen Nate?"

Macklin nuzzled her and nudged, asking for more scratches and attention, but eventually the need to pee was too great and Mieka gave the attention-whore one final kiss, then ran the rest of the way to the end of the barn. She was sprinting now as she headed across the yard to the house, flinging open the door and not even bothering to remove her shoes as she bolted down the hallway to the bathroom.

She nearly didn't make it, and practically started crying in relief as she relieved herself.

Once she was done and washed her hands, she exited the bathroom and removed her shoes, stowing them at the front door. Beside Nate's boots.

"Everything okay, Minx?" came his deep, manly rumble from the kitchen.

"I needed to pee," she said, entering the kitchen to find Nate, Asher, and a man she didn't recognize sitting at the kitchen table, all of them cradling steaming mugs.

"This is Jacob, our vet," Triss said, setting down a cup of coffee on the kitchen table and indicating that it was for Mieka.

"We didn't want to wake you," Nate said, sipping his coffee. "So Jacob came in for a quick bullshit and a coffee."

"Nice to meet you," the handsome vet with the gray eyes said, giving Mieka a slight head nod followed by an appreciative up and down with his eyes. "How did Callie and Chance look when you left?"

"Chance was nursing, but I couldn't tell which teat he was on."

Nate pushed away from the table and stood up. "Well, let's go take a look. I checked her this morning before I left and it wasn't warm to the touch, but when I gave it a squeeze, I could tell it was clogged. She flinched and tried to nip her flanks."

Jacob stood up, as did Asher. The three men drained their coffee cups, thanked Triss, then one-by-one they filed out of the kitchen. Nate was last and lingered, waiting for Triss to turn her back, then he dropped his mouth next to Mieka's ear. "We need to talk about last night, Minx."

Everything inside her clenched.

"Need to talk about that stubborn cat of yours." Then the man purred. He fucking purred. And not like some playful kitten or a barn cat basking in a ray of sun. It was a deep, throaty rumble, like a lion on the savannah who'd just caught the scent of a lioness in oestrous. Was she in heat? She was certainly warm, nay on freaking fire, when she was around this man. Maybe she was in heat. At the very least her cat was.

She swallowed, waiting ... for what? She had no clue. But she waited.

Then it came.

It was barely a brush of his lips against her temple, but it was enough to make every one of her hairs stand up and gooseflesh to break out across her arms. Then he was gone, leaving her a complete puddle. Confused, aroused and cursing her cat more than ever before.

Chapter Nine

He probably shouldn't have been such a dick bringing up last night and the fact that she was workshopping a term for the female equivalent of "little head" but it was impossible to resist. She made it so easy to push her buttons and get under her skin, not to mention the fact that calling her pussy a "stubborn cat" was just fucking hilarious.

But she'd said other things last night, too. Things he wasn't even sure she remembered. But he remembered. They kept him awake most of the night. That and the fact that having her that close to him, snuggled up in his arms was probably the most incredible feeling in the world, and he wanted to enjoy every second of it conscious.

He also struggled to sleep when one of the horses was ill, and even though he didn't think what was going on with Callie was cause for too much concern, he couldn't stop his worry. They'd lost six horses since they started the ranch over seven years ago.

They lost Dare, Asher's horse the winter they met Triss, then Callie's foal last summer. The colt had been in the breech position, and was stillborn by the time they were able to get him out. It'd been hard on all of them.

But Nate blamed himself, he was sure there was more he could have done for

Callie and the foal she lost, even though Jacob said it was a doomed situation from the very beginning. But it was why Nate had been so diligent this time around, staying with her and Chance the moment Asher said something was amiss.

The three of them entered the barn where ranch hands were busy mucking stalls and leading horses out to pasture for the day. Hank had Mercy by the bridle and was slowly, patiently leading him outside. The black mustang took one look at Asher and snorted in derision. Asher merely rolled his eyes.

The two had a very tumultuous beginning to their relationship, and although they were far better now and Mercy was able to mount mares without killing them, he and Asher still treaded lightly around each other. Both were skittish creatures and reacted poorly to loud and abrupt noises.

They reached Callie's stall and Asher opened up the door allowing Jacob to step inside. He checked out Chance first, determining him to be a perfect little colt, then he moved on to Callie.

"It's rare but it could be early onset mastitis. We normally don't see it with actively nursing mares, it's usually toward the drying out period when weaning, but it does happen. He's favoring the right teat which has caused the left to get engorged and," he attempted to milk the left teat, then clucked his tongue, "clogged." Jake ran his hands down Callie's legs, put his stethoscope into his ears and listened to her heartbeat, then he checked her teats again. She tried to move away from him when he attempted to milk her once more, then she turned her head and went to bite her flank.

"So antibiotics?" Asher asked, scratching his chin scruff which brought attention to the big white scar running down the length of his jaw and chin. He'd taken a piece of metal to the face during an explosion while in active duty. Luckily, all he had was the scar as the reminder. The scar and a big tattoo of angel wings on his back to commemorate all of his fallen brothers. Nate had a tattoo on his back, as well, but it was different.

Jacob nodded. "I've got some in the truck. Brought it in case. We'll also do a warm compress to help unclog the duct. But we need to encourage this little guy to not play favorites." He ran a hand over Chance's back while the colt nursed. A second later, Jacob gently reached down and encouraged Chance to unlatch, then he guided a frustrated colt around his mother to her other teat. He milked Callie, much to her annoyance and encouraged Chance to nurse from the clogged teat.

It took some finessing but eventually Chance latched. He suckled a bit, but didn't stay latched for long before pulling away and trying to get back to the other side to reach the non-clogged teat.

Jacob let him, then began to gently hand milk Callie. She wasn't too happy about it, but eventually, he got her expressing and she seemed to calm down.

"Still only coming out of one duct steadily," Jacob said, still expressing. "Ash, want to run to my truck and bring my big medical bag to me? I only have my small one here. Nate, can you get some warm compresses?"

Nate and his brother grunted, then took off to do as they were told.

When Nate returned to the stall with the warm compresses, Asher was already back and Nate was administering the antibiotics as well as applying a salve to Callie's swollen teat.

Nate handed the vet the warm compresses and Jacob applied them, holding them to Callie. "I'm not too concerned. She's not feverish, and there isn't any blood in the milk. We caught it early. It's really rare for mastitis to happen this early, when the foal is only a day or two old. I'm guessing the traumatic birth may have caused her some stress which can affect milk production. Or he just favors one side and isn't nursing the other side as much, which can cause engorgement. But you caught it early, so I'm confident we'll get this nipped in the bud in no time." Jacob nodded at Nate, who came around behind Callie, careful to keep a distance in case the mare kicked out, then he took up Jacob's spot, holding the warm compress against her.

"Thanks, man," Nate said, rubbing Callie's side affectionately.

"No worries." Jacob gathered up his supplies. "I'll give Ash the lowdown on the antibiotics. But I might as well check out the little fillies you just had, as well, while I'm here."

"I'll show you," Asher said. "Skipper and Daria. Both beauties."

"Good to see you," Nate called out, over Callie's body.

"You, too," Jacob replied.

Nate pulled the compress away, then tried milking Callie again to see if the other duct could express. Still no luck. He put the compress back on.

"Can I help?" came a voice like pure honey and velvet. She let herself into the stall, paid attention to a curious Chance, then circled around Callie to stand beside Nate where he was crouched. "Is she okay?"

He blew out a relieved and exhausted breath. It wasn't even nine o'clock in the morning and yet, he was ready for bed. "Engorged and a clogged duct, but Jacob thinks we caught it before it turned into full-blown mastitis. Thank fuck."

"So you have to stay out here all day and hold the compress against her?" Mieka asked.

He nodded. He didn't *have* to. They could get the ranch hands to rotate doing it, but he would stay. Callie was a good horse and she'd already lost one foal, he couldn't bear the thought of her undergoing anymore stress or pain. So he'd stay with her as much as he could. He would probably get a ranch hand to relieve him when he needed to piss, but otherwise, he'd hang out with Callie and Chance until Callie started to show signs of improvement.

She slid down to her knees and moved her good hand without the cast next to his where he held the compress against Callie. "I can do this for a while if you have other things to do." Their fingers touched and electricity raced from his hands right down to his balls.

"Just need to grab something quick to eat," he said, moving his hand away. As if on cue, his belly rumbled in protest and his back and knees cracked when he stood up. "You eat?"

She nodded and got more comfortable on the ground. "Triss made us fried egg sandwiches."

"Ooh, that sounds good."

"She's still in there, made one for you and Asher." Her gold-flecked brown eyes blinked at him, fanning those lashes that had to be extensions; they were just too long to be real. But they weren't too gaudy or thick to make them look unnatural. They were just long and only enhanced her beauty.

"I'll bring out a stool when I come back," he said, closing the stall behind him.

He ran to the house and scarfed his breakfast, then grabbed a couple of stools and high-tailed it back to the barn.

She was chatting with Callie and Chance when he arrived back at the stall.

"You're such a good mama, Callie," Mieka said softly. "Taking such good care of your baby boy. He's going to grow up to be strong and beautiful just like you."

Grinning, Nate opened the stall door and stepped inside, setting the two stools down in the stall, and handing Mieka a to-go mug of coffee. "Figured you might need a second cup since you slept sitting up on the cold ground last night."

Her moan of appreciation and their fingers once again touching when she reached for the mug sent another electric charge down to his nuts.

Reaching for the coffee, she removed her hand from the compress, so Nate took that as an opportunity to try to milk Callie again.

"Can you show me how to do it?" Mieka asked, setting her mug down beside her stool.

He nodded and took her hand in his, bringing it to Callie's engorged teat. "Put it between your thumb and forefinger like this." He placed her fingers where they needed to be, her thumb on the front, her finger behind. "Then pull down toward the tip, like so." He guided her fingers and after three pulls milk squirted out of both ducts.

"Is that?"

"Coming full stream out of both ducts," he exhaled. "Thank fuck."

96

He guided her a couple more times, more for himself because he liked touching her, then he left Mieka to try it herself. She did very well.

"Good girl, Mama Callie," she said, pressing a kiss to Callie's side.

Nate stood up, exited the stall, then returned a moment later with a glass mug. "Here, no sense wasting it."

Her eyes became dinner plates. "To drink?"

"Well, it's perfectly safe to drink mare's milk. Nomads used to do it. It's sweet and watery—"

"Wait, you've tried it?"

"Of course, I have. I'm a rancher. Tried goat's milk and chicken eggs, too."

She rolled her pretty eyes. "Not the same, smart ass."

"It is, though. Horses are herbivores and livestock just like cattle. I don't see the harm in it. They only have two teats as opposed to four like a cow, so we don't *actually* milk the horses for their milk, but I have tried it. We all have."

She made a face like she couldn't decide if she should be disgusted or not. Her brows were pinched, her mouth and her nose were scrunched and she just stared at the mug in his hand. But she continued to milk Callie. He placed the cup under the stream and started to collect the milk.

"We'll let Chance drink it," he said. "But you're welcome to try it first."

She shook her head. "I'm good, thanks."

"You'll stick to cow milk?"

"I mean, in truth, I prefer almond milk, but you guys don't have any so I make do with cow."

"Never seen nipples on an almond before."

She nudged him playfully. "For a man who barely slept last night, you're sure a smartass this morning."

"My ass is extra brilliant when I'm running on fumes."

Grinning at each other like idiots, they worked in companionable quiet until the mug was half-full. Chance had stopped nursing on the right side and wandered around Callie to stand over them, curious about what they were doing.

He nudged Nate several times with his head, running his velvety nose up and down Nate's back.

"He's worried you're going to take his milk," Mieka said with a chuckle as she continued to milk Callie.

"It's all for you, bud," Nate said, kissing Chance's cheek as the colt bent his head to get a better look at what they were doing. "Wanna sip?" he pulled the mug out from the stream and held it to Chance. The colt sniffed the mug and moved his head around a bit, but Nate persisted, put the rim of the mug to Chance's mouth and tipped it up enough that the milk hit his lips. Understanding flashed in the smart little guy's eyes and he sipped.

"Hey, that's cool," Mieka said. "I didn't know horses could drink from cups."

"Horses can do a lot of things." He let Chance finish the mug, then put it beneath Callie again so Mieka could resume the milking. "I think this is really helping her. We just have to keep the stream steady and relieve her engorgement."

"I'm happy to stay here and do this if you have other pressing matters," she said. "I feel useful."

He shook his head and bumped her shoulder. "You're definitely useful, Minx. You still have to order all the furniture and décor."

"Done," she said proudly. "Did it before I came out here. I can eat and spend money at the same time believe it or not. Particularly when it's someone else's money. Then I can eat, sing, tap dance *and* spend money. Actually, that's not true. I have severe ADHD and although medicated, I'm still really bad at multitasking. Executive dysfunction and all that." She waved her hand in a way to dismiss what she'd just said, or minimize it. "That's why I dance. To keep my body and brain moving."

Nodding, but a little overwhelmed at the sudden personal information overload, he forced a smile. "So when is it ready for pick up?" Did he know she had ADHD? He couldn't remember Triss ever mentioning it about Mieka. It explained some of Mieka's behaviors, though. How scatter-brained she seemed sometimes and fidgety.

"Day after tomorrow the order will be ready to go grab in Denver."

He was still nodding. "We'll take the horse trailer so that we can fit everything in. Do I need to book the helicopter?"

"Not a terrible idea. Do I get to ride in it?"

"You've never been in a helicopter?"

"I've done a lot of things, but riding in a helicopter is sadly not one of them."

"Well, then, lady, we will definitely have to fix that."

She beamed at him, then her lips twisted in a playful, but peculiar way, like she was thinking, but thinking suggestive things. "I don't remember much of that night ... unfortunately."

His brows lifted. "Of the night ... we ..."

Her head bobbed. "Did we even kiss?"

He was about to say, "Of course we did," but he had to stop himself and think for a second. He'd been shitfaced, too. Maybe they hadn't kissed.

"I don't remember," he finally said, deciding to be honest.

She huffed a laugh through her nose and shook her head. "Quite the pair, huh? We got so drunk that we can't even remember if we kissed or not when we had sloppy drunk, UNPROTECTED sex up against the barn. Not my finest moment, that's for sure."

"You worked your ass off all week helping out with wedding stuff, then you gave a killer speech. I say you deserved to cut loose. Particularly, after having to deal with your parents for four days." He made a *yikes* face with buggy eyes and a grimace. "How are those scared-of-their-own-shadows two?"

She exhaled through her nose. "Yeah, Royce and Yanna Young are *a lot*. They're fine. I haven't told them about my arm, or about my contract not being renewed. I have no idea how they'll react, and I'm honestly not in the mood to answer their millions of questions, or hear all the *shoulda, coulda, woulda* that would spill out of my mother's pie hole." Her top lip curled. "You *should* be more careful. Mieka. You *could* have paid more attention to where you were putting your hand. You *would have* been fine if you'd just watched what you were doing and practiced more." The voice she adopted to imitate her mother wasn't at all how Yanna sounded, but it was comical. Nasally and whiny and with lots of animated facial expressions.

"Triss told them about the baby, yet?"

She shook her head. "I asked her when she planned to tell them and she said maybe when the kid turns three."

He barked a laugh that made Chance take notice and he nudged Nate's shoulder with his nose.

He knew from what Triss and Asher had said, then from his own experience meeting Mieka and Triss's parents that all the Young sisters avoided their parents as much as they could, especially after what they did to Rayma when she was seventeen.

Mieka and Triss's youngest sister had gotten mixed up with the wrong crowd when she was a teenager, so not knowing what else to do with her, they shipped her off from Baltimore to Mieka's oldest sister Pasha who was living in Seattle at the time doing her pediatric residency. They didn't even tell Pasha. Rayma just landed on her doorstep one day.

Rayma continued to rebel and got tangled up in more trouble. It took Pasha and her now husband Heath driving down to Vegas to save Rayma after she was kidnapped.

A real shit-show.

So, who could blame the girls for remaining distant with their parents after that? When a kid got tough, they just gave up and pawned her off on someone else. Someone who didn't even know they were being made guardian. Someone who had their own busy life to deal with. Asher and Nate felt the same way about Royce and Yanna. They tolerated them, but they didn't like them. He also knew that Mr. and Mrs. Young had run a very tight ship when the girls were small. They avoided trouble of any kind like it was a twenty-foot angry viper. The girls were considered guilty of indiscretions before they even committed them. The kids could do no right, even when they did no wrong.

They were "trouble duckers" as Triss called them. Pacifists and super judgmental about everything.

And Nate had witnessed all of that firsthand.

The grief and guilt-trip that Triss's mother had laid on Triss about having booze, let alone an open bar at the wedding, was enough to bury an entire village. Triss lost a fair bit of weight right before the wedding because of the stress, which pissed off Asher. He'd been close a few times to telling off his bride's parents and kicking them off the property, but Triss stopped him.

Thank God they had the sense to retire to bed early after the reception, so the real party could start.

The transformation of the Young sisters once their parents were gone was like watching five depressed caterpillars emerge from cocoons into vivacious, life-of-the-party butterflies. Rayma and Mieka both danced on the tables, Triss did a keg stand in her wedding dress, and Pasha and Oona—who had both started pole dancing classes in their respective towns—gave the entire guestlist a small show, after Triss surprised them with stripper poles in the reception tent. It'd been a fun and wild night, and one Nate wished he could remember better.

"Looks like you got a little lost in thought there, cowboy," Mieka said, bumping his shoulder with hers.

"Just remembering the reception," he said with a smile. "Or at least trying to. Things do get a little hazy after that sixth shot of Fireball."

She shook her head, grinning. "Yeah, I lost count of how many shots I had. I think if I were to ever get married, I'd get stoned instead of drunk."

He nodded emphatically. "Hundred percent."

"Plus, the consummation sex would be better. At least, that's what Triss said. She said she was stoned at the wedding and had amazing sex."

Heat tingled between his legs.

"We got ripped off, didn't we?" she asked, taking the cup from him and holding it beneath the spray as she continued to milk Callie.

"In what way?" Now, he was crazy-curious where she was going here.

Her shoulder lifted. "I dunno ... just that we don't even really remember having sex. And yet, we know we did because it resulted in a pregnancy. Because I hadn't been with anyone else before or after to muddle the timeline. But all I remember is running out of the reception tent and across the field laughing."

"Then you tripped."

She giggled. "Then I tripped."

"And I helped you up."

"You helped me up, we held hands and continued to run. But I don't think we kissed."

"I don't think we did, either."

"Then we made it to the barn, but we didn't make it inside. You plastered me up against the wall—"

"You hiked up your bride's maid dress—"

"While you unbuttoned your pants."

"Then you pushed your underwear to the side—"

"And leaped up onto your hips."

"And ..." He lifted an eyebrow and smiled.

"And ..." She mirrored him, but her smile was less playful and more seductive. "I remember struggling to get off—which, I know is not a reflection of your prowess—I hope—"

"It's not," he said quickly. He needed to make that point *very* clear. "I have a very nice sized cock and I know what to do with it."

Her lip twitched like she was trying not to laugh, but all she ended up doing was nodding. "It has to do with my whiskey-numbed clit."

He snorted. "Whiskey-numbed clit."

She pressed on. "But like, I don't even remember what your dick looks like."

He choked on his spit like a moron, coughing for no reason until he could say, "Not sure I whipped it out and swung it around, so ..."

That made her smile. "I think I'd remember that." Her gaze drifted down to the front of his jeans and she chewed on her bottom lip.

Fuck him. What was she trying to do? Kill him? 'Cause she was going to succeed. He would die from loss of blood flow to his brain for sure.

"What's going on here, Minx?" His voice came out far raspier and desperate than he intended, but it seemed to have the right effect on her because her cheeks turned pink and she sucked in a sharp breath.

She shook her head and blinked quickly. "Nothing, sorry. Sleep deprivation."

"Mhmm." But he let it drop, despite how badly he wanted to keep going down this interesting rabbit hole.

She still thought about that night. So did he.

He worried that she'd have regrets, and although it appeared that she did, it wasn't the regret of having sex with him, it was the regret of not being able to remember having sex with him, and not getting to kiss him or see his cock. That made him grin like an idiot.

She shoved him. "Get your head out of the gutter, Harris." Rolling her eyes, she turned back to focus on milking Callie. "Your face is like a glass house. I can read every depraved thought parading through that pea-sized brain of yours."

"Pea-sized brain!" he exclaimed. "What's with the insults, Minx? I thought we were getting along and having a nice conversation about how badly you want to see my dick. I can text you a picture, not a problem. But my understanding is that women don't really *like* dick pics. At least the unsolicited ones. But if you're soliciting ..." His smile was stupidly big but he couldn't stop it. She just brought out the goof in him. She was so easy to tease, but could dish it right back, which was what he loved. He wasn't someone who pushed the buttons of a person who didn't want their buttons pushed. He liked the give and take. He liked a person—a woman—who could hold her own and dish it right back to him on a heaping plate.

And Mieka could do that.

Her gaze narrowed. "No dick pics, thank you." The tug of her mouth to the left said her brain and lips were not on the same page. Her stubborn cat was meowing loudly. Loud enough that he could practically hear it. And when her eyes drifted back down to the front of his jeans, he knew for sure that she didn't agree with what she'd just said.

"How's she doing?" Asher's voice interrupted her heated stare off with the crotch of his pants, and Mieka blinked and lifted her gaze to Nate's brother.

She cleared her throat but Nate could see the pink creeping into her cheeks and he had to smother his smile in the crook of his arm. "Both ducts are producing now. We held a warm compress, then started to gently milk her. Chance has sipped from the cup, too."

Asher grinned. "Look at you being all ... ranchy."

Mieka lifted a brow. "Ranchy?"

Asher's face scrunched, then he shrugged. "I didn't know what to say. Cowgirl is obviously the wrong word ... so yeah, ranchy."

Mieka snorted. "I like being able to help. Callie is such a sweet mama. She shouldn't suffer in the slightest."

The sincerity of her words hit Nate hard in the chest and he reached up and stroked Callie's side. "She definitely shouldn't. Not after last year."

"What happened last year?" Mieka asked.

"Callie delivered a stillborn," Asher said. "Foal was breech and we couldn't get him out in time. She was devastated. We all were."

Mieka's face fell and her eyes welled up with tears. "Oh my God." She rubbed Callie's side and kissed the spot she'd just rubbed. "Poor baby. I'm so sorry."

"A colt a couple counties over, was without a mare due to birth complications, and we tried pairing him with Callie to see if she'd adopt him and nurse him, but she was just too depressed. We really waffled whether to try again with her so soon, but after a few months she snapped out of her grief and seemed okay. I've never had a stillborn foal before, or seen a mare react in such a way. It was scary." Nate rubbed Callie's side again. "But now you have a beautiful little baby to love and care for, right, girl?"

As if she knew she was being spoken to, Callie swung her big head around and sniffed then nuzzled Nate's head. He chuckled and kissed her velvety nose.

"I'm gonna head to the feed store, get more chicken feed. You need anything?" Asher asked.

"Goat pellets for the petting farm," Nate said. "I think we're almost out."

Asher nodded, smiled warmly at Mieka then headed out.

"What happened to the colt that Callie couldn't bond with?" Mieka asked, wiping tears from her eyes with the sleeve of her sweater.

"Another ranch had a lactating mare and they took him. She bonded with him and he was fine. Callie just wasn't in the right headspace. She knew it wasn't her colt. She tried to nurse, tried to bond with him, but her heart was already too broken to welcome anyone else into it. She needed time for it to heal."

The tears were back in her eyes. "You never really think about animals grieving. But they do."

"Oh, they do. Particularly animals of higher intellect. Dogs, cats, horses. I mean elephants will visit the grave site of their family members decades later. And that mother orca who carried the body of her dead calf for like three weeks ... animals mourn for sure." He reached forward and stopped her from milking. "You can probably stop for a bit. We'll check on her again later. But we should give Chance a chance to nurse from this teat now that we've unclogged it."

Nodding, she sniffed and scooted back, still sitting on the stool. "Is that why you were so ... "

"Manic about Callie's delivery and when her duct was clogged? Yeah. Seeing her depressed was one of the hardest things I've ever witnessed. After, of course, actually seeing her dead colt and having to put down other horses because of injuries and stuff. But it was rough. On all of us. The pain in her eyes was gut-wrenching. She would look at me and it was as if she was asking me *why?* Why did her son die? What happened? Where was he now?"

Mieka covered her mouth with her hand. "Oh God."

"Ranch life isn't easy. It comes with its share of heartbreak for sure. But," he welcomed a curious Chance into his space and gave the little guy some thorough ear scratches, "it also comes with rewards. Like this handsome dude. And joy. So much joy. We've had three healthy foals in two days. That's definitely worth celebrating."

There was a knock at the side of the stall. "Nate, Barbara is in labor, just thought you'd want to know." It was one of the ranch hands who Mieka didn't recognize from last year. He was probably new.

"Who is Barbara?" she asked.

Nate grinned, stood up and offered her his hand. "One of the goats, and she's having triplets. Want to come watch more life begin on the farm? You can name the kids."

She took his hand and smiled so bright the entire barn lit up. "Absolutely I do."

Chapter Ten

"Kiwi, Mango and Papaya," Mieka said proudly, grinning at Nate and bouncing a little on her toes.

"Which one is the male?" he asked, clearly holding back his laughter.

"Mango, obviously."

He snorted. "Obviously."

"They're so cute. When can I snuggle them?" Her speech was getting faster the more excited she got. It was something she knew she did, but didn't have a lot of control over stopping. When her thoughts went crazy and she got excited about something, her brain and mouth worked as fast as they could to get all her ideas out into the world. She rambled and spoke like an auctioneer.

"Five days or so. We need them to bond with their mother first."

"What kind of goats are they?"

"We mostly have Nigerian Dwarves. They're a really gentle breed and tend to have a lot of multiple births."

She nodded. Her heart was so full.

When Nate invited her to come to the goat kidding, she wasn't sure what to expect. Was it going to be like the horse birth? Or did they just stand back and make sure there were no complications?

Nope, it was totally different. They got right in there. Because there were three kids, they had to break the sacs, then make sure the kids were breathing. Nate tied the umbilical cords off with dental floss then covered them with iodine.

"So, do you normally assist in the goat births, as well?" she asked, after they'd washed their hands thoroughly, gave Barbara some warm electrolyte rich water, and made sure all the kids were nursing.

Nate shook his head. "Not all of them. I try to be involved in most, but the ranch hands are all capable and know what to do, so does Asher. But I thought you'd enjoy watching more new life come into the world."

Smiling, she leaned over and bumped his shoulder. "You weren't wrong."

He stopped at another goat stall and opened the door before she could see why, but when she did see what was inside, she squealed. "Oh my God!"

"These two are about seven days old," he said, quickly closing the gate before the bleating little monkeys could escape. "They're also nameless."

"This is my jam! This is where I bring my skills," she said doing a little fist pump that had him laughing.

"You can sit down and they'll just climb all over you."

She did as he suggested and sure enough, two little weird-eyed kids started treating her like a mountainside. They tried nibbling her hair, her clothes and the laces on her slip-on shoes.

"What's their mother's name?" she asked.

"Eleven." Nate rolled his eyes.

"Why?"

"No fucking clue."

Snorting, she scratched the top of the little black goat's head. "This one is going to be Onyx."

"Onyx is a boy."

"It fits." The white one with black ink blots on its back put its front hooves on her thigh. "And this one will be Ruby."

"Ruby is a girl."

"It fits."

They beamed at each other and Mieka's heart clenched while her belly warmed.

"We have four more kids that need names," he said. "Need to keep moving."

After another three or so minutes, they went to the next stall where two more little kids climbed all over her. She named these twin sisters Belle and Winnie.

Finally, they visited Karen. Nate had to keep her cornered while Mieka gave attention to her twin sons. It wasn't that Karen was protective of her kids, it was that she was just an attention-whore and would shove her children out of the way to sit on your lap, then she'd aggressively head butt you for scratches and pets.

As was the way of the Karen, always out for attention.

She named Karen's little boys Ruger and Trigger since they were speedy little dudes and kept zipping around the stall like little bullets.

"How'd you know about a Ruger?" Nate asked after they washed their hands again and exited the goat stall. "I'm impressed."

"I might have googled it on my phone when you were detaining Karen. *Gun related names for animals* produced a plethora of options."

His raspy chuckle made her nipples pebble.

They exited the barn into a bright, blue-sky day. The sun was bright and hot and that's when she realized she'd been out in the barn since last night. The day had started, the sun had rose and she was still in her pajamas, hadn't brushed her teeth or hair in ages, and she was ridiculously happy.

"What's that smile for, Minx?" he asked, guiding her over to the left, away from the farmhouse. She didn't question him and just followed.

Shaking her head, she stepped through the first gate of the double gate that would take them into the chicken coop. "This has just been a really great day. I witnessed new life born into the world, got to cuddle and name goats ... it's just been a lot of fun."

"And it's not even noon."

Laughing, she nodded. "And it's not even noon."

He took her around to the back of the coop, both of them careful not to step on any of the what seemed like millions of cute orangy-brown chickens that clucked and bawked around them. "I'm sure Asher already did this this morning, but we can check for some second lays." "What kind of chickens are these? They're very noisy."

"Rhode Island Reds, and yeah, it's a noisy breed. But we don't mind. They let us know when they're happy and when they're not."

"Just a whole coop of Karens, huh?"

He snickered. "Yup. But most of these Karens are pretty docile."

He lifted the door to reveal rows and rows of nests. Most were empty, but some had eggs.

Her eyes went wide.

"Never collected your own eggs before?"

She shook her head. "Only from the grocery store."

"Oh, Minx, this is where it's at. Farm fresh, free-range, organic, Omega-3 enriched eggs are the only way to go. They'll ruin you for the store-bought ones."

"Was it one of these eggs that was in my sandwich this morning?"

"We don't buy eggs, so yup."

"It was delicious. The yolk was a rich, dark orange and so creamy." Her face fell. "Are there baby chickens in there?"

"They're eggs. What did you think was in an egg?" He was looking at her like she'd just sprouted another head.

"I ... I thought it was just yolks. That the baby chickens weren't formed yet. But ..." She cringed. "Is it like ... developed?"

Laughing, he rolled his eyes. "Minx, these aren't fertilized. They'll never be chickens. All that's in here right now is a dark orange creamy yolk. No feathers, no beaks. They were just laid today, anyway. Each girl lays between six and eight eggs a week."

Her gag-reflex relaxed, and she exhaled through thinly parted lips. "You must think I'm an idiot."

"Not at all. You're learning, that's all." He bumped her shoulder playfully. "Never a dull moment and always an opportunity to learn when you live on a ranch. You'd never be bored here."

Her lips twisted, and she reached out and grabbed a couple more eggs from the nesting boxes, holding them in her palm. "Just yolk, right?"

He nodded. "Right."

They collected the remaining eggs from the nests and put them into a wire basket. They had fourteen, which didn't seem like a lot given how many chickens were scurrying around their feet.

"Asher or Triss usually came out in the morning and collect the eggs for us to sell at the checkout for the petting farm. After taking what we need for ourselves, we have about ten or twelve dozen for sale each day. But they always sell out, and usually before lunchtime."

"Wow! These are busy ladies. And they all seem so healthy and happy."

His head bobbed. "Rhode Island Reds are a generally very healthy, very easy to care for breed. They're gentle and produce a lot of eggs. Between a hundred and fifty and two hundred and fifty eggs per chicken per year. Some produce more." He pointed at one big, plump lady with glossy rust-colored feathers. "Like Abigail. She's a super producer. She puts out at least three hundred eggs a year." He bent down and stroked the hen's back, causing her to make a purring like sound. "Don't you, girl? You're an egg laying machine."

Mieka grinned and crouched down too to pet Abigail. Her feathers were silky soft and the chicken seemed to enjoy the petting because she settled right down into a sitting position in the dirt and her eyelids appeared to grow heavy.

"And as the chickens get older, the eggs get bigger," Nate went on. "I'd like to get more hens to increase our egg production at some point, but that might be an endeavor for next year." A bleat at the corner of the pen drew their attention and Nate murmured, "Fuck," under his breath. "Fucking Fumble."

"Who?"

"The damn goat. Fumble. He's always trying to escape, and it looks like today he succeeded." They exited the pen quickly. Nate set down the basket of eggs on a bench and took off after the goat. But the goat was fast and seemed to laugh and enjoy the chase. He scampered two hooves at a time across the yard, bleating at Nate, then laughing when Nate would get close, lunge, then Fumble would jump out of the way at the last minute.

Before too long, three ranch hands—Ronny, Hank and one Mieka didn't recognize—joined in the chase.

Mieka wished she could help, but she knew better given her arm, and in all honesty, it was hilarious to watch four grown men chase a goat—who kept getting the better of them, too.

She held her hand over her mouth to keep from laughing, when Nate flung himself at Fumble, but landed hard on his belly in the dirt. Fumble stood five feet away and proceeded to poop where he stood, all the while making uncomfortably intense eye-contact with Nate. After that, she couldn't contain her laughter anymore.

Nate shot her a glare, but it was only for show. His lips were twitching to keep from turning into a grin.

Fumble climbed up onto a pile of stacked pallets behind the barn, stared down at the three men and bleated loudly. A chorus of more bleats echoed from the goat barn, then a few horses whinnied and Sasquatch made a loud *hee-haw* somewhere out in the field.

"What the fuck?" Nate growled.

"He's taunting us," Hank, the redheaded ranch hand said, a big dirt smear across his forehead. "Getting the others to encourage him."

"This goat is going to be the end of me." Nate let out an exasperated huff only for that to be cut off by Fumble bleating again, then he did something ultra-disgusting.

"What is he doing?" Mieka cried as they all watched the goat, on top of all the pallets urinate but make sure he sprayed it all over his legs, beard and face."

Nate buried his face in hand. "Oh my God."

"He's preserving his strong musky scent." Hank's chuckle was like honey coated gravel. "Fumble thinks his piss is like Drakkar Noir or something. It's also just a giant middle finger ... or middle *hoof* to us because Fumble is a dick."

"That's disgusting," Mieka said, watching the urine drip from the goat's long pointed beard.

"Did someone tell you goats were clean animals?" Ronny laughed.

"I suppose not." Was this a common occurrence on the ranch? Was Fumble constantly trying to escape? Even though she knew Nate was probably not enjoying himself at the moment, it was certainly fun to watch him chase the goat. She could get used to this kind of entertainment. However, she wasn't sure what she'd do if she was the only one around to wrangle the goat the next time he escaped.

So, as much as she was having fun watching Fumble outwit Nate and the other two guys, Mieka knew that it had to be frustrating, not to mention embarrassing. It was also pulling them all away from their daily chores. She made her way into the main barn, found a bucket of carrots, grabbed two, then went back out to the yard where they were at a stand-off with Fumble.

Walking up to where Fumble was still standing on top of the pallets like the king of the ranch, she waved the carrot in the air until the goat caught sight of it. His attention narrowed in on the food, and he leaped down without hesitation. It had to be at least ten feet that he cleared, but he stuck the landing like a gold-medal gymnast and trotted toward her.

"Here you go, Fumble," she said, holding out the long carrot for him. His beard was still dripping with urine, so she made sure to keep her distance. He opened his mouth and nibbled. She switched the carrot to her casted arm, then gingerly reached out and grabbed the goat by his collar and held on for dear life. "Guys," she said. "Little help."

Nate and Hank approached slowly and carefully, because Fumble had proved himself to be unpredictable and if he knew he'd been bested, he could drop the carrot and dick off again. She held on tight to his collar, but if the goat pulled hard enough, she'd have to let go. She didn't want to fall and jeopardize the recovery of her arm.

Nate inched forward, slid his fingers along her arm and hand, sending tingles of awareness careening through her. Then he looped his fingers around the collar and she let go.

They all let out a collective sigh of relief.

"Fucking goat," Nate murmured as he took the carrot from her, as well, and let Fumble finish eating it.

"My auntie has a great recipe for jerked goat," the dark-skinned ranch hand said, revealing a slight Caribbean accent. "I bet Fumble would taste delicious. Maybe a little tough because he's a tough old bastard, but we could tenderize him first with our fists."

Nate snorted. "Don't tempt me, Ray."

"Let's go, Houdini," Nate said, keeping a tight hold on Fumble's collar and leading him back to the goat barn. "I don't know how you keep getting out."

"Sheer determination, boss," Hank said with a chuckle.

Nate merely rolled his eyes.

Mieka wasn't sure if she should follow him or just stay there, so she chose to wait for him to return. She picked up the basket of eggs and stood there watching the chickens peck and scratch. It was oddly therapeutic to just zone out and watch animals happily live their lives free of responsibility and burden. All the chickens had to do was live their best lives and lay some eggs.

"If only I could have such a simple purpose," she murmured.

But she didn't have any purpose. Her purpose used to be dance. It used to be performing, but now ... now she couldn't even do that. Nobody wanted her. So what was her purpose? What did she have to offer anyone?

Would any dance company hire her? Or was she really too old and washed up?

Before she knew it, the tears were falling again and she was walking toward the farmhouse. She barely registered Nate calling her name behind her before she stepped inside the house, toed off her shoes, set the basket of eggs on the kitchen table, then went to her room.

He was just entering the house when she closed her bedroom door and collapsed onto her bed.

The knock on her door came a moment later. "Minx? You okay?"

She didn't say anything. She was bone-tired, sore and so deep in the mosh-pit of her pity party she couldn't even see the exit sign if she wanted to. She knew that there were bigger problems in the world than her lack of direction, but she couldn't stop herself from feeling this way. Dance was all she knew. She had no home, no job, and no idea what to do next. Then the guilt of feeling this way swamped her hard and fast. An avalanche of remorse burying her alive. How could she feel so sorry for herself when there were children starving in Africa and floods in Pakistan and global warming?

Her tears continued to fall.

There was another knock, then another.

"Minx? What happened?"

She still didn't say anything though. What could she say? *I'm sad because nobody wants me anymore. I have no purpose and I'm old, decrepit and washed up.*

She was thirty-four years old. Nobody would understand how she felt. They'd say she had her entire life ahead of her. She could go back to school and do a million things.

But they just didn't get it.

Nobody did.

Dance had been her life since she was six. She'd never had a job besides dancing. It was all she knew. It was the only thing on her resume. Even if she could start over and get a job elsewhere, who would hire her with a resume that was so niche-specific? And going back to school? She'd struggled to get through high school with her ADHD, no way in hell was she going to put herself through that again.

Eventually, she heard Nate's footsteps disappear down the hallway, then the front door opened and closed.

He deserved a response, at the very least. She knew that. He'd been nothing but kind to her since she arrived. He'd been nothing but kind to her since the moment she met him. But she also knew that now he had an ulterior motive. He wanted her to give him a second chance. He wanted to show her how good life on a ranch could be and that maybe, just maybe, she'd consider giving them, and the ranch, a chance.

But as much fun as she was having, she just couldn't see herself living here for good.

What good was a dancer on a ranch?

Sure, she could help with the goats, collect eggs, and hold a warm compress against a horse's teat, but those were also jobs that a ranch hand could do. Nate was only getting her to help so she didn't feel useless. She wasn't *really* needed there.

Not truly.

She wasn't needed anywhere.

Eventually, the tears subsided, and she fell asleep.

She didn't mean to, but after sleeping on the hard ground of Callie's stall last night, her body was sore and tired.

A gentle rap at her bedroom door pulled her from her dreamless slumber. Wiping the drool from the side of her mouth, she groggily went to open the door.

Triss looked worried. "You okay? Nate said you disappeared after helping them catch Fumble, then you didn't answer the door when he knocked."

"What time is it?"

"It's five."

Mieka's eyes went wide. "Oh my God. I slept the day away."

116

Triss shrugged. "So?"

"So, I shouldn't be doing that when people need help around here. When there's so much to do."

Triss's smile was small, but knowing. "They're okay. They manage just fine when you're not here." That feeling of uselessness and being inconsequential crept back into her heart and made everything turn cold.

Triss didn't seem to notice. "Help me with dinner?" she asked.

Determined not to spend too much time in her one-person pity-party, Mieka slapped on a half-decent happy face and nodded. "Can I shower first? I smell like goat."

Triss sniffed. "I can't tell. But then again, everything smells like horse and goat now, so ..." She shrugged. "Shower, then come help me."

Mieka nodded and closed the door when Triss walked away.

The shower helped brighten her spirits a little, but not much. By the time she emerged, with fresh clothes, and her caramel-brown hair in a long Dutch braid down her back, there were more voices in the house than before. The squealing pipes kept her from hearing anyone else come into the house, but the deep rumbles confirmed it was Asher and Nate.

Her belly clenched tight as she entered the kitchen and met Nate's eyes.

Concerned filled his gaze and she could tell he was itching to ask her if she was okay and what happened earlier. But he didn't. He just followed her as she moved across the room to the kitchen counter, picked up the knife and started chopping up a bell pepper for the Greek salad Triss was making.

"I'm planning dinner for seven o'clock, boys, so you have time to do whatever you need to do," Triss said, her hands coated in raw chicken as she slid marinated chunks onto wooden skewers.

Asher kissed the side of his wife's cheek, then headed for the door.

But Nate lingered, still watching her.

After a moment, he made his way over to Triss, bent his head to her ear and whispered.

"Oh, that's a great idea," she said enthusiastically. "I'll try to stay awake for it."

Nate grinned, nodded then headed back outside, casting one final curious, worried look at Mieka before he disappeared.

"What was that about?" Mieka asked, using her elbow to cover her mouth when she yawned.

"Nothing," Triss said with a big smile.

Mieka rolled her eyes. "What are you two scheming?"

"No scheming," she said innocently. "He just asked me something, and I responded. No secrets. No scheming."

"Me thinks the lady doth protest too much," Mieka said sarcastically.

"Chop the veggies, Mieks," Triss ordered, but not unkindly. "And let's come up with ways to get you out of your funk. Because clearly, you're in a funk. Feel free to tell me why, or don't, but either way, let's get you out of it."

Mieka groaned and rolled her eyes, but a stern look from Triss had her sobering her expression.

"Just promise me it's not line dancing. Or square dancing."

Triss merely shrugged, then resumed impaling the chicken cubes on the skewers.

Mieka groaned again. "I hate line dancing."

"Line dancing? Seriously?" Asher groaned as they stepped into the cliché country tavern with country music playing and the scent of cheap beer and straw heavy in the air.

"Come on," Triss encouraged, as the four of them made their way to a vacant table. "It's Friday night, and we need to do fun things like this while we can, because once we're parents, we might not get another date night until the kids are in college."

Nate was all smiles, so was Triss, but Mieka and Asher exchanged glances and she could tell her brother-in-law felt exactly the same way she did. And she would rather be anywhere but at a bar line dancing.

The server came over and Nate ordered a pitcher of beer and a ginger ale for Triss.

There were about twenty people all up on a small platform, dancing in sync to the song. The rhythmic *clomp clomp* of their boots was hypnotic and despite how badly she didn't want to be there, Mieka found herself drawn to their feet and the way they all moved in time with the beat.

The server returned with their pitcher and glasses and Nate went to work pouring everyone a beer. "I should have asked, but do you like beer, Minx?"

"It's fine," she said, taking a healthy sip. "Not my favorite, but I'll drink it." The foam tickled her upper lip and before she could lick it off, Nate was leaning forward and wiping her lip clean with his thumb.

She was paralyzed. Then her heart nearly stopped beating altogether when he brought the pad of his thumb to his mouth. A deep, clenching twist formed in her lower belly, wringing liquid heat between her legs as her eyes fixated on his lips and the way his tongue darted out to lick off the foam from his thumb.

"The fuck's going on with you two?" Asher asked, well, more like demanded. "What the hell was that?"

Nate shot his brother a bored look. Mieka's entire face was on fire.

"Leave it be, dear," Triss said, patting her husband's arm. "Nate's just messing around."

But Asher wasn't buying it, and Mieka already knew Nate's motives. This was all part of his elaborate plan to convince her that ranch life wasn't so bad. To give him and Colorado a second chance.

"Drink up, then come dance with me," Triss ordered, pointing at Mieka's glass which was still two-thirds full.

Mieka shook her head. "I'm not dancing."

"Like fuck you're not," Nate said.

She shot him a glare. "Yeah, like fuck I. AM. NOT."

Triss pouted, pushing out her bottom lip until it was enough of a purchase for a bumblebee to land on like a flower petal. "Please?"

Mieka's glare settled on her sister. Triss just smiled wider.

Mieka finished her glass, slammed it down on the table and ordered Nate to pour her another.

His face was wreathed in smiles as he did so. So was Triss's.

It took four glasses of beer for Mieka to finally allow her sister and Nate to pry her flat butt out of the chair and haul her up to the dance stage.

She'd never line-danced before, but it was easy enough to learn and follow. They all got into position, Triss and Nate on either side of Mieka in the front row. The music started, and with her hands on her hips, right over the belt loops of her jeans, she moved to the beat.

Triss was terrible. She couldn't stay on beat to save her life and kept bumping into Mieka. Eventually, she gave up and, with a laugh, went and snuggled with her grumpy-looking husband.

Nate was good, though.

Why was Nate so good at this?

He glanced at her as they danced side-by-side facing the audience, his smile wide and beautiful. She could not keep herself from smiling back.

Then he did a spin during their grapevine, followed by an elaborate stomp when they all stomped. He was still smiling.

Her grin grew wider and the next time they did a grapevine, she spun, as well, meeting his glittering blue eyes as he turned around, too. They both stomped. A couple more kicks, another grapevine with a turn, a scuff, and the song was over.

The dancers and the crowd clapped and Mieka, whose goofy grin hurt her face, was about to step back down and return to her seat when Nate grabbed her arm and another song started up on the speakers. Dancer and locals obviously knew what it was because they hooted and hollered and the dance floor got full fast.

"You can't *not* dance to *Copperhead Road*, Minx," Nate said, taking her arm and pulling her closer to him so more people could join their line. "It's sacrilege. Only Asher can get away with it because everyone knows he's a grump."

She snorted and watched as the music picked up tempo and the people around her and in front of her moved to the beat.

The lyrics started and the total mass of them began to move. It only took her watching the person in front of her for twenty seconds before she picked up the moves and danced to the beat. It was a great song to dance to, and she liked this style better than the one before. There was more kicking and stomping, and the energy on the dance floor was electric and contagious.

She got right into it, stomping with vigor, whooping when others whooped and dipping her hips and shoulders as enthusiastically as everyone else.

Her heart sunk the moment the song ended and everyone on stage dissipated back into the crowd. A warm, calloused hand found hers and linked their fingers, tugging her off stage and toward the table with Asher and Triss.

She was a little out of breath, but not too much. Asher handed her a freshly poured beer, and she sipped it with vigor.

"Looks like you hated every minute of that," Asher said cheekily. "People are talking about your deep scowl and the way you just trudged like a sloth through the moves."

Mieka snorted and shoved her brother-in-law playfully on the shoulder. "Shut up."

"I knew this would cheer you up," Triss said, sipping her ginger ale. She also had a plate of fries in front of her. Mieka stole one. "Dance is part of your soul."

"And her soul moves beautifully," Nate added. "They do this every Friday and Saturday night, Minx. There's even a class on Wednesday nights if you're looking to learn new moves."

Swirling and confusing emotions crashed through Mieka and she stood up from her seat abruptly. "I need to use the bathroom."

"Just past the bar, on the left," Asher said.

She nodded, then left, having to slalom her way through people and tables. Thankfully, there was only a short line, and she was in and out of her stall in a fairly reasonable amount of time. She hadn't actually needed to go, she just needed the space, but once she was there, she figured she may as well relieve herself. There were three sinks, so she didn't feel too bad standing in front of one, just staring at herself in the mirror for a few minutes. A couple of women gave her curious looks, but nobody said anything to her.

She barely recognized herself.

Sure, she looked the same. Caramel-brown hair, brown eyes with the gold flecks, high cheekbones, and slightly olive complexion thanks to her eastern European roots. She was the Mieka Young she saw in the mirror every morning and evening, but the vacancy in her eyes, the loss of confidence and identity that she felt all the way to her marrow oozed out of her, making her unrecognizable even to herself. Who was she if she wasn't a dancer? How was she supposed to introduce herself? What was interesting about her outside of the fact that she'd danced her entire life and on cruise ships? Add in the loss of validation, the loss of praise and that nightly applause that made her smile grow wider and her heart swell.

Who was she?

"You're a great dancer," came a soft voice behind her.

She blinked out of her trance, threw on a smile and turned around to face the woman who'd just spoke. "Oh, uh, thanks."

"Are you with Nate Harris?"

"My sister is married to his brother. I'm just visiting for a bit."

Her green eyes went wide with excitement. "Oh! You're Triss's sister? We love Triss. She's helping my nephew with his speech impediment. She's done wonders with him. And she's just so lovely. Honestly one of the kindest people I've ever met."

Mieka smiled. "That she is."

"What do you do?"

Mieka swallowed. What did she do? A lot of nothing at the moment.

The woman's head cocked to the side, waiting for Mieka to answer.

"I uh ... I *was* a dancer." She lifted up her broken arm. "Not dancing at the moment, though."

The woman's mouth dipped into a frown. "That looks like a nasty break."

"Yeah, it is. But I'm hoping to get an air cast soon. There are pins and plates in it, which should speed up the healing process."

"Well, I wish you a speedy recovery and that you're able to get back to dancing again soon. Tell Triss I said *hi* and that I just put the kale seeds she gave me into the ground yesterday, so we'll have to see who yields the biggest crop this year." She rested a kind hand on Mieka's unbroken arm, gave it a squeeze, then disappeared out into the bar.

Mieka turned back to face the mirror once more, touched up her lipstick, and with a defeated sigh, left the bathroom.

She was just passing the bar when a hand shot out and grabbed her upper arm. Instinct had her jerking it away, but the look of alarm on the man's face had him releasing her immediately. That's when she noticed that it was the handsome, neck-tattooed, redheaded ranch hand, Hank, from earlier that day. "Sorry, ma'am," he said quickly. "I didn't mean to startle you. I just wanted to get your attention, and it's really busy in here."

She eyed him warily, but nodded. "It's fine."

He was sitting at the bar, nursing a pint of dark beer. "I'm Hank, I work at the ranch for Nate and Asher."

She nodded. "Yes, I remember you helping catch Fumble today."

His head bobbed and he scratched at his rust-colored beard. "That's right. Um ... Nate said you're a dancer?"

"Was," she corrected, which hurt her to say out loud more than it had to break her arm.

123

His face fell. "You don't dance anymore?"

"Not at the moment, why?"

He licked his lips and cast a worried glance around the bar. "I um ... I need to learn how to dance."

"Like line dance?"

He shook his head. "No, I tried that, but I couldn't get the moves down and kept knocking into people." His cheeks turned ruddy under his beard. "More like, uh ...ballroom, or ... or something."

"Why?"

"My little sister is getting married next month and since our dad died when I was nine and she was four and we don't have any uncles or a stepdad or anything, she's asked me to walk her down the aisle. I'm fine doing that, but then the wedding planner asked if she is going to do a father-daughter dance, or in this case brother-sister dance. She laughed and said that her brother was born with two left feet and couldn't dance to save his life."

"That's awfully mean." Mieka's brows scrunched.

He shook his head quickly, his gray eyes going wide. "Oh no, Sherise didn't mean it like that. I think it was more to just let me off the hook. She's also not wrong. I can't dance and probably couldn't do it to save my life. I don't want to break my sister's toes on her wedding day." His lips twisted, and he looked at her pleadingly. "I'd love to surprise her on her wedding day and actually give her that dance without stepping on her feet or embarrassing her. Do you think you could help me?"

What had started out as a scare with Hank grabbing her arm, quickly turned into a cry for help and it melted Mieka's heart. This man wanted to learn how to dance for his little sister.

That depressing, sinking feeling she'd had in the bathroom slowly started to fade, and in its place a warmth grew. A sense of purpose. She nodded. "I can try. Sure."

Hank's face lit up. "I'll pay you, of course. And we can do it on your schedule, ma'am. Early mornings, late evenings, whatever works. I can probably do it on my lunch break, too, if you want."

She chuckled. "Do you live on the ranch, Hank?"

He shook his head. "No, ma'am, I live about a mile away, but I don't mind driving."

"Stop calling me ma'am, please. It makes me feel old. We're probably the same age."

"I'm thirty, ma—Miss Young."

"I'm thirty-four, so yeah, stop calling me ma'am and start calling me Mieka, please."

He nodded. "Okay ... *Mieka*."

She grinned. "Let me find a space we can use to practice, and I'll let you know a time and where to meet me. Give me a day or two to get it sorted, but I'll be in touch, okay?"

Hank's nod was so enthusiastic Mieka thought his head might snap off his neck completely. "Okay. That sounds great. Thank you. Thank you."

She smiled at him, wished him a good night, then made her way over to the table where Nate, Asher and Triss were all watching her curiously.

"What were you chatting with Hank about?" Nate asked, not bothering to hide the unease in his voice. She liked that the cocky rancher wasn't so cocky all of a sudden.

Pouring herself another glass of beer from a new full pitcher, she sat back in her seat and smiled. "I just got my first dance student."

Chapter Eleven

It was impossible to lie about the green-eyed jealousy monster that whispered negative things in his ear as he saw Mieka chatting with Hank at the bar Friday night. And that monster was back to whispering when Nate went to find her Sunday so they could head to Denver and she was guiding the good-looking redheaded ranch hand with the neck tattoo around the indoor corral to the sound of ballroom music.

He knew he had no claim on Mieka. She was free to dance with whomever she wanted. She was free to do whatever she wanted with whomever she wanted.

But tell that to the green-eyed monster that wanted her all to himself.

He hung back in the doorway of the corral to watch her dance with Hank for a moment. The big ranch hand, and former army ranger, was clumsy as he danced, stepped on her toes at least ten times that Nate could count. He also kept apologizing for his sweaty hands, but Mieka just smiled, told her it was okay and to keep trying.

She was grace incarnate, and Hank was, well, Hank was trying.

When Hank attempted to spin her, but then stepped on her foot again, she was facing Nate, their eyes caught and she smiled which made him smile.

"Sorry," Hank murmured.

"It's okay, just try again," she said patiently.

Nate wandered further into the corral, his hands in his pockets, watching Mieka patiently adjust Hank and start over again and again.

The music stopped, so did their dancing.

"All right, let's end here for the day," Mieka said to a long-faced Hank. "You did great for your first day."

"I really do have two left feet," Hank said glumly.

"We'll get you sorted," Mieka said, resting a reassuring hand on Hank's broad shoulder. "Just practice the box step I showed you. We'll meet here again in a few days, okay?"

Hank nodded, then snagged Nate's eyes. A red heat bloomed in the big ranch hand's cheeks and he dropped his head to almost a bow. "Nate."

Nate's mouth twitched. "Lookin' good, Hank. We'll be calling you Fred Astaire in no time."

That comment only made Hank grow even redder in the face and Nate couldn't stop himself from chuckling as the broad-shouldered man lumbered out of the corral.

Mieka swatted Nate's shoulder. "Be nice."

"I am nice," he said, pretending to be offended. "I'm always nice."

Her side-eye and lifted brow said she didn't agree.

"Ready to go?" he asked. He'd hitched up one of the horse trailers to his now fixed truck—Larry was a miracle worker—and they were heading to Denver to pick up all the furniture and décor that Mieka had ordered.

Stepping out into the bright May sun, Nate and Mieka had to maneuver around all the families with young children who had come for the petting farm.

In just a matter of days, the petting farm would be open seven days a week and every day would be chaos like this. But it was a good source of money, so as much as it was annoying tripping over strangers and kids, Nate didn't really mind it for the summer months where they made bank.

"Seems busier than yesterday," Mieka said as they made their way over to his truck which was parked down the laneway and off to the side a bit. They had a designated parking spot for patrons, but that was already full and people were parallel parking on either side of the laneway. He was worried he might not be able to squeeze his truck or trailer through.

"Yeah, I agree." They climbed into his truck and he started the engine. It purred like a well-fed cat and he said a silent thank you to Larry and his mechanical wizardry.

It took them forever to get down the laneway to the main road, since even though his truck and trailer fit between the rows of cars and trucks, it was tight. Then there were families walking aimlessly without a care in the world down the gravel driveway, having decided to park on the main road and walk.

Twice he had to stop the truck, put it in park and yell at people to get out of the field, that it wasn't part of the petting farm.

Mieka was giggling the second time he climbed back into the truck and put the vehicle into drive.

"What's so funny, Minx?"

"You," she said, still smiling. "You sound like an old man yelling at kids to get off your lawn. *Hey, you. This isn't part of the petting farm. Get out of the field.*" She'd dropped her voice to a deep timbre, attempting to imitate Nate. She had done quite poorly.

"Well, it *isn't* part of the petting farm. If someone falls and breaks their ankle or something in one of the divots, we could have a lawsuit on our hands."

"Which your insurance would cover since this is all part of the same land."

"Not the point. If they're off in an unsecured area, they could get hurt."

She lifted a shoulder. "Fair enough. You just sounded really funny yelling at the kids to get out of your field."

He grumbled, but didn't say anything as he turned onto the main road that would take them to Denver.

They didn't ride in silence to Denver, but the conversation was minimal. He could tell she had a lot on her mind, could practically see the cogs spinning in her brain, and he wanted to give her the chance to open up, but she just wasn't giving him any kind of opening.

Her moods were all over the place and he was struggling to figure out where her sudden drops into a dark head-space were coming from. Like when she'd helped them catch Fumble, then she just disappeared into the house and her room, didn't answer his knocks on the door and seemed to be buried under a mantle of despair when he saw her again in the kitchen.

The line dancing helped change her mood, but even that didn't last. By the time they got home from the tavern, she was quiet and lost in her own head again.

Saturday had been a chaotic day with the petting farm open and everyone wanting to see the new foals and kids. All the families who boarded their horses were also at the ranch, and they all needed help with something which pulled a ranch hand or Asher or Nate away from a routine chore. There just didn't seem to be enough hours in the day or hands available to get everything done. And Sunday was proving to be the same, only busier.

He and Mieka really shouldn't have left the ranch to go to Denver. Their hands were needed, but they also needed to pick up the furniture. Those cabins had to get furnished and ready for guests. This was going to be a big bump in their income, so they needed to do it right.

"So, tell me about life on the cruise ships," he said as they sped down the highway toward downtown Denver. "Up until recently, I'm assuming you enjoyed it if you kept doing it for so many years."

She pushed air out of her nose vigorously. "It was a lot of fun. Busy and hectic, exhausting and demanding, but I loved it." Her smile was small. "But I thrive in that kind of environment with my ADHD. Never a dull moment. Always a million things to do. No shortage of physical or mental stimulation. Though, to be fair, as I got older, I craved my alone time in my cabin more and more. As much as I liked the hustle and bustle of the day and being around people, I also really liked that downtime, too." Her fingers twisted in her lap. She had a ring on her middle finger that she kept spinning, taking off and putting back on. He wasn't even sure she was aware she was doing it.

"Before they made me dance captain, I made extra cash working in one of the cafés, but then when I became dance captain a few years ago, I had admin stuff to do in addition to dancing and rehearsals. Emails, scheduling, department meetings, reviewing past shows to see where we needed to tighten things up and what we needed to change. I really liked that part of the job. I also just liked being in charge. I became like a bit of a big sister to some of the younger, newer dancers. At least once a week one of them would knock on my cabin door crying about something. Whether it was a broken heart because the crew guy she was seeing told her he wasn't interested in commitment, or two dancer roommates got in an argument over something like a curling iron. They came to me and expected me to fix things. I liked problem solving and being the one with all the answers and ability to help. Oona said it was a lot like her job as an RA in college. And I guess it kind of was, not that I went to college, but when we compared notes, the roles seemed pretty similar."

"I can totally see you as the big-sister fix-it type," he said. "You've got a real nurturing way about you that I think probably really helped your fellow dancers."

The pink in her cheeks was sweet, as was the smile that accompanied the blush. "I like helping people."

"I can tell."

"Also, other people's problems distract me from my own problems." Her laugh was forced. "It's a form of procrastination."

Nate slid her an amused side-eye. "I think we all do a bit of that."

She heaved another big sigh. "I loved my time on the ships. I met amazing people, traveled all over the world and did what I love—dance. Not everyone can say their passion is also their profession." Her gaze slid sideways to his. "I mean, I know you can, and Triss, and Asher. But a lot of people just work to survive. Their passion isn't something that will put a roof over their head or food in their belly. We're really lucky."

"We are," he agreed, loving how down-to-earth and appreciative she was of the unique situation they shared. It was true, ranching was his passion and he knew he was fortunate that his passion was also a lucrative profession.

"But it's also all I know, and I can't dance forever. Just ask Martin."

"Martin sounds like a douche."

She snorted a laugh. "You have no idea."

They drove the rest of the way into the city mostly in silence. She seemed miles away even though she was right there, lost in thought and staring out the window as she fiddled with the ring on her finger.

"Hungry?" he asked as they took the off-ramp from the highway down into the center of the city. It was just creeping up on noon and his belly rumbled at the thought of a greasy fast-food burger with a side of extra-large fries and a strawberry milkshake.

Mieka nodded. "I could eat."

"I need grease, calories and ketchup, what about you?"

Her brown eyes went wide and she nodded with enthusiasm. "I like the way you think."

He pulled into the line for the drive-thru of a fast-food burger joint he always visited when he came to Denver.

"How can I help you today?" the teenager over the speaker asked, his voice cracking slightly.

"Hey, yeah, I'll get a double-stack with the works, extra large onion rings, extra large fries, a strawberry shake and ..." He turned to Mieka. "What would you like, Minx?"

Nodding, she said, "I'll get the same."

Nate's eyes went buggy. "Holy shit." Then he grinned. "I like a woman who can eat." He turned back to the intercom. "Just double that order, man. Two double-stacks with the works, two extra large onion rings, extra large fries and two strawberry shakes."

The guy over the intercom rattled off what they owed, then told them to proceed to the first window.

"Thank you." Nate pulled ahead to the first window, paid, then they waited until they had to move forward to the next window to get their food. "That's a shit-ton of grub, Minx. You going to be able to eat it all?"

"I'm on a mission," she said. "Dancing and my rigorous workout and training routine have rendered me without an ass or tits, so since I'm not dancing for that militant cruise line anymore, I may as well grow my boobs and booty."

Of course, his eyes were on her chest. She'd been just talking about her tits, so naturally, his gaze would gravitate there to see if what she said was true, that she had no chest to speak of.

"For the record, I think you've got a great ass and tits, if my opinion is worth anything to you. Also, there's more to your beauty than just those parts of your body. I'm a leg man myself, and you have *great* legs. Loved when they were wrapped around my hips like a fucking ivy vine."

Her cheeks bloomed with color again, and she swallowed.

"However, I also fully support you sticking your middle finger up at the cruise line for canning you and eating what you want to eat. Life's too short to eat rabbit food every day. I get eating healthy so you can live longer, and generally I do eat healthy, but when I come to Denver, I always come here. Best burgers in the fucking city." He pulled up to the next window and a teenager with braces and a bright yellow uniform greeted them with a giant paper bag and two enormous milkshakes in to-go cups.

"I may have overestimated my capabilities," Mieka said, taking in the gargantuan size of the milkshake alone. That thing probably held more calories than she consumed in an entire day on the ship. Perhaps an entire week.

Nate pulled out of the line and into a vacant parking stall where he rolled down the windows, put some country music on, then turned off the truck.

"There's a park a mile away with picnic tables if you'd rather," he said, opening up the paper bag. "This isn't very romantic, or easy."

"This is fine," she said, accepting her foil wrapped-burger.

Probably working out the physics of how she could eat the monstrous thing with two patties, Nate caught her watching him as he unwrapped his burger, opened his mouth wide like a snake unhinging its jaw to devour an antelope, and he took a big bite.

A piece of lettuce fell into his lap and he picked it up, but not before he watched her eyes follow that leaf, then lingered on the front of his jeans for way too long.

The grin on his face as he chewed was unavoidable.

"Eyes up here, Minx," he said with a chuckle, his mouth still slightly full.

She shook her head and blinked, then ignoring his continued laughter, she unwrapped her burger and dove in.

The moan that came after she took a bite of her burger had his cock struggling to get out of his jeans. She closed her eyes and her head lolled back against the seat. She looked about ready to come in her pants.

"That was a pretty epic bite, Minx. For both of us. Did you get off?"

"Damn close," she murmured. "Fuck, that's delicious."

She took another bite, while Nate—who was already over half-way through his own burger—opened up the onion rings, fries and ketchup packets, making a bit of a smorgasbord on the bench seat for them.

"That's a lot of food," she said between chews.

"We'll take it home if we can't finish it." His brows scrunched for a second. "Scratch that, we'll take it home if *you* can't finish *yours*. This order is standard for me and I can always finish it." He grabbed his milkshake from the cupholder and took a hard pull. His eyes bugged out slightly from how hard he had to suck to get anything out of the straw. "Damn, they always make these so thick. I'm going to burst a blood vessel in my eye just getting it through the straw." But the threat of a broken blood vessel didn't deter him and he sucked harder until a satisfied smile curled his lips around the straw. "That's the stuff," he said, putting the milkshake back in the cupholder a moment later. "Worth the effort."

They continued to eat in companionable silence, sharing stolen glances as they chewed. Each time she caught his eye, or he caught hers, they would both smile, then laugh.

Crumpling up his wrappers, Nate stashed them into the paper bag. Mieka still hadn't finished her burger and had only had two onion rings and three fries.

"You don't *have* to finish it, Minx," he said, his smile cheeky. "It isn't a competition. And I definitely don't want to see you sick."

She took a final bite of her burger, then admitted defeat and wrapped it up for later. "My attempt at rebellion was bigger than my belly."

He chuckled again. "You can always have more later. But try your shake, it'll make you make those noises again."

Rolling her eyes, she grabbed her shake. She struggled to suck up much since it was so thick, but once she did, the moans she made had his cock twitching again. "Why does all the most delicious stuff have to be so bad for you?" she asked.

"Jesus, Minx, I've never wished to be a straw more in my life."

That line was cheesy, but it had her smiling anyway and she just reached over and swatted him, though it wasn't easy since she had to hit him with her right hand and twist her entire body.

"When do you see the doctor about an air cast?" he asked as she stored her leftovers into their containers and put them in the paper bag.

"Next week on Friday. That's the earliest they could get me in."

He nodded. "Ready to go?"

Grabbing the milkshake, she took another hard pull and nodded. "Drive on, Cowboy,"

"Rancher."

"Anywhere else you need to go, Minx?" Nate asked as he climbed into the truck after closing the horse trailer that contained all the furniture, décor and kitchenware they would need for the four cabins.

She'd done well. Extremely well. He was impressed with not only her eye for decorating, but her frugality, as well. She bought a ton of stuff on sale, second-hand and on clearance. It was a bit of driving around, since she'd organized pick-up times and locations for certain second-hand items from their sellers, but the savings were certainly worth the gas money.

One look at her in the front seat of the truck, and he was laughing.

She was shoving onion rings into her mouth and her cheeks were puffy. And the deer-in-the headlights look on her face like she'd just been caught rifling through someone's trash for stale donuts was priceless.

"This isn't what it looks like," she said, her mouth full.

"You mean, you're not filling your face with onion rings?" His laughter was unavoidable. She looked ridiculous, but also adorable.

Chewing a few times, then swallowing what appeared to be a large lump of food that had her wincing, she took a deep breath. "Well, yeah, I guess it is what it looks like. But the smell when I got in here ... come on." Her head rolled around on her neck. "It's just too good."

"I'm not arguing with you. I'm just wondering why you're eating like a raccoon trying to hoard all the grub for yourself. I'm not going to make you share with me. I've had my order. This one is yours."

She lifted up the container of fries. "You want some?" She popped one into her mouth.

Smiling, he shook his head and buckled his belt. "They're all yours." He started up the engine. "Though, I am wondering when you're going to let me take you on a proper date."

She startled. Choked, then coughed a bunch. He had to throw the truck back into park and swat her on the back a few times.

"Gonna live?" he asked when she brushed him off and nodded that she was okay.

"I think so."

"Just the idea of going on a date with me makes you practically choke to death, huh?"

Her side-eye had him grinning.

"No," she said, exasperated. "It's not that. You just ... you just surprised me."

He pulled out of the parking lot of the furniture store and onto the road. "I don't see how it comes as *that* much of a surprise that you nearly died by French fry. You know I'm interested in you. I've said that I am. We might have only had one sloppy, drunk night together that neither of us can really remember, but that doesn't take away from the fact that we have chemistry. There *is* an attraction here, right?"

She was quiet for a moment. A long moment that made him nervous.

Maybe she *wasn't* attracted to him anymore? Was the chemistry all in his head and she was just treating him like a friend? Had he been friend-zoned?

Finally, she released a breath. "Of course, there is an attraction, Nate. And yes, we have chemistry. I just ... why go down a road when we both know it's a dead end?"

They came to a red light, so he turned to face her. "Dead end?"

"I'm not going to remain in Colorado, so why start something when it'll only end in heartbreak and awkwardness? We're family ... sort of. Though, not in a banjo playing, move-to-the-deep-south kind of way. But we don't want to make this awkward for Asher or Triss."

He nodded and pressed his lips together. She was still convinced there was no life for her here. That she couldn't find happiness on the ranch, or with him.

He needed to do a better job of convincing her otherwise.

"One date," he said. "Let me take you on one date and show you it doesn't have to be a dead end. It could be a roundabout."

She lifted a brow.

"Or a ... an intersection? A four-way stop? An on-ramp? And off-ramp? A yield? Oh, I got it," he snapped his fingers and grinned, "a *merge*." His brows bobbed salaciously.

"Stop," she said with a giggle. "No, wait, GO! The light is green." And as if on cue, the vehicle behind him honked.

He gunned it. But his feathers weren't ruffled at all and he settled into the drive. "One date, Minx."

"I thought we had to go set up the cabins?"

"We do. We'll go on a date after that."

"I don't know if this is a good idea. I know it will be great when it's happening, and that I'll enjoy myself. But what about *after*?"

"What do you mean, *what about after*? After the date? After the date, I'll make you breakfast in bed, then have you sit on my face so I can have my breakfast."

The flood of pink to her cheeks made his dick twitch.

She was fighting a smile which only made his smile grow.

"One date, Mieka. And we don't have to have sex. Just let me... let me *woo* you."

"Woo me?"

"Yeah. Let me woo you. Court you. Do things properly. Because we certainly didn't do it properly the first time. I mean, yeah peg A went into hole A, or I guess it was peg *D* went into hole *V*, but we don't even remember doing it, so ... I don't consider us doing it properly."

"Peg D? You're really not selling me on any of it by calling your junk a *peg*."

"Pegs can be big. It's not a *clothes peg*. Pegs for construction can be big. Like timber frame pegs and stuff."

Her mouth twisted. "Me thinks the gentleman doth protest too much."

"This peg got you off in the end."

"I think it was the finger," she teased.

"Ah, yes, the finger." He wiggled the finger he'd pushed into her ass. "It really is magical."

Her eyes rolled, but she was still smiling.

"One date, Minx. Let me take you out, show you that this is in no way a dead-end, or a road destined to end in heartbreak."

Chapter Twelve

Nate had given her a lot to think about on their drive, and no matter how much Mieka tried not to, her eyes kept drifting to his finger. Yeah, *that* finger as it gripped the steering wheel. Then, when she'd realize she was staring at his hands—particularly that finger—she'd move her gaze elsewhere, and of course, her eyes drifted down to the front of his jeans where a *big peg* apparently lived.

Damnit, she was in a dry spell. Like a major dry spell. Her stubborn cat was starting to pace and meow and demand attention. Not to mention those horny hornets in her belly that buzzed every time Nate smiled at her, or she imagined those big hands of his holding onto her hips as he plowed into her from behind over a hay bale.

Even though she'd been sleeping with that bartender back on the ship, it'd been over a month since they'd done anything, mostly because their shifts didn't align. And when they did do things, he'd been mediocre at best. The man had no tongue skills, and zero stamina. Most of the time, Mieka had to get herself off *after* he came.

Yeah, Nate was right. A gentleman should always let the woman come first so she's not riding a soft dick, limping her way to her own finish line.

Staring out the window, determined not to look at his finger or crotch anymore, she wasn't even aware of the fact that she was chewing her nails until Nate's voice broke her out of her trance. "I didn't know you had ADHD," he said. "When did you get diagnosed with that?"

She spun around to face him, but then dropped her eyes to her hands and the horrible chewed, red and tender fingertips. "When I was five."

"And dance helps?"

"It keeps my mind focused and my body busy. I'm also medicated, which helps, too." She shrugged. "It's just a part of my life and who I am." Her gaze slid to his. "But it's also responsible for my fidgetiness, mood swings, impulsiveness and how my self-esteem can quickly take a massive nose-dive in a literal second." Heaving a big sigh, she balled her sore hands into tight fists. Well, she did it with one hand and attempted to with the other. "I just do the best I can. Every day is a struggle. Just some days are more of a struggle than others."

"If I'm doing anything to exacerbate that struggle, please let me know." The sincerity in his blue eyes and his voice was touching.

"You're not," she said. "You're keeping me distracted from wallowing... for the most part. So, thank you."

They were already back at the ranch, so he turned off the road and rumbled the big truck and horse trailer down the laneway. A quick glance at the clock on the dash said it was just after five-thirty, so of course the petting farm would be closed to the public by now, which explained the empty yard and parking lot.

Nate exhaled. "I know it brings in money, and it was my idea, but fuck, it gets claustrophobic when we have the petting farm open. People, big and small, are everywhere." He pulled the truck up in front of the barn, put it in park, and turned off the engine before hopping out.

Mieka did the same and met him behind the trailer.

"Feel free to go do what you need to do, Minx. I've gotta get this stuff out of the trailer and into the corresponding crates." He grinned wide at her. "Good thing you were organized enough to color code everything ahead of time so I know which chair goes to which cabin." He opened the trailer door to reveal boxes piled up to the ceiling. The bed of the truck was full of bedding, kitchen stuff, décor and everything else. The furniture was in the trailer and even then, not everything fit, so they paid for express shipping and the rest would arrive by tomorrow.

And just like he said, she had given each cabin a corresponding color code and put a big sticker of that color on the appropriate furniture. She wasn't always this organized, but she was really passionate about this project, and appreciative of the trust Nate and Asher had put in her, so she was determined not to mess it up.

"I can help," she said, watching Asher and Triss come down the front steps of the house.

"You've already done so much," Nate replied. "It's all good. Besides, we don't want to hurt your arm."

Asher sidled up beside his brother and whistled when he looked inside the trailer. "Don't want to know what this cost us."

"Then don't ask," Nate chuckled, hauling out a huge box that was part of a bed frame.

The two men went to work removing everything from the trailer and truck, while Mieka grabbed her leftover lunch and followed Triss inside.

"How was your day?" Triss asked, gauging Mieka carefully.

"It was good. We got everything we needed."

Triss's eyes fell to the fast-food bag. "Ah, you stopped at Gus's. I take it you're not hungry, then?"

Mieka puffed out her cheeks and shook her head. "I still haven't even finished this. But it's so freaking good."

"I know. I've gone to Denver with Nate a few times and he always stops there. It's good, but it's definitely a treat. I'm like a snake after I eat there. That's my meal for the week."

"You're okay that I'm going to skip dinner?"

Triss lifted a shoulder. "You're an adult and free to do as you like. It's why I haven't put the meat on the barbecue yet."

"The day here was good?" Mieka asked, pulling out the rest of her burger, taking a seat at the table and diving in. "We feel bad. We left when it was so busy."

"Great day," Triss said, taking up an abandoned spot at the counter to continue preparing a salad. "It was busy, but everyone had a good time. Fumble escaped again, so that was fun. Asher is so close to barbecuing that goat, I swear it."

Mieka chuckled. "Apparently Ray's auntie has a great recipe for jerked goat."

They continued to chat until the door opened and the men came in. "Minx?" Nate called out.

"In here," Triss said.

Nate and Asher both came into the kitchen, their faces red from exertion and a slight sheen of sweat on their foreheads.

"Cal says he can pick up a crate tonight and drop it off at one of the cabins. I'm keen to get these things set up. You interested in riding out there with me tonight?"

"Tonight?" Mieka squeaked.

"We'll take the ATV so we can haul more stuff and not make the horses sleep outside tethered to the hitching post."

"We're going to spend the night out there?" Confusion and unease swirled through her. Not because she was afraid to be alone with Nate because she didn't trust him. She was afraid to be alone with Nate because she didn't trust herself. She wanted him, he wanted her, and he was hell-bent on wooing her. He wanted to take her on a "proper date" for God's sake.

Plus, there was that chemistry that they had. That undeniable, practically tangible chemistry that, if shaken too vigorously, would probably blow up the entire county. She knew that the more time she spent with him, particularly alone, the less she'd be able to deny, let alone avoid that chemistry. And then the explosion was inevitable.

"Yeah. There's a futon and a bed in the crate. I'll set those up first." His mouth turned up into a cheeky smile. "You have somewhere else to be, Minx?"

"Well, I *am* teaching Hank how to dance, so …"

"We'll be back in a few days. You still have loads of time to teach the big lug how to do the cha-cha." He squeezed her shoulder as she held the rest of her burger in mid-air and gaped at him. "I'm going to go pack. You should do the same. And we'll grab food, too."

He disappeared, and Mieka pivoted in her seat with dinner-platter eyes and her mouth still open to stare at her sister. "What the fuck?"

Triss shrugged. "Welcome to ranch life, where the cowboys spring this shit on you all the damn time."

"Ranchers," Asher murmured.

An hour later, Mieka was plastered tightly against Nate's back on the ATV, her arms around his waist as they raced through the field toward the woods and hills. They had a trailer behind them with all their stuff—clothes, bedding, food, water, toiletries etcetera, as well as Nate's tools and a few things that didn't fit in the crate. Since it was mid-May they didn't have to worry about dusk setting anytime soon, and the warmth from the late-day sun bored into her back, making her squeeze her arms around Nate extra tight for just a moment. Then she realized what she was doing and quickly loosened her grip.

But, of course, he felt it and reached for her hands with one of his big ones and encouraged her to tighten her hold again.

Damn him. She could feel each hard ridge and plane of his abs beneath her fingertips and when he tightened his stomach muscles, she nearly had an orgasm.

And he probably knew she nearly came because his chuckle in front of her was deep, raspy and totally knowing.

Damn him.

"*I could get used to this,*" said her stubborn cat. "*Life with the rancher is titillating. Purrrrr.*"

She told her cat to shut the fuck up and ignored her damp panties as best she could as she climbed off the back of the ATV and away from the hot, solid wall of Nate.

They'd made it to the first cabin in no time. The helicopter flew by overhead and circled back, while Nate gave instructions on a radio. Soon, the enormous crate came flying over the treetops and was slowly lowered into a clearing. Nate stepped forward, continuing to give Cal instructions. He reached up and guided the crate softly to the ground, unhooked it from it's tethers and with the finesse of a true expert, Cal lifted off again and disappeared.

"Thanks, Cal," Nate said into the radio.

"No problem. Just let me know when you want me to grab the next ones."

"Appreciate it, bro." Nate gave a wave to the sky, even though Cal was already gone from sight.

"That was smooth," Mieka said, handing Nate the crowbar from the trailer so he could pry open the crate.

"Cal is the best of the best. He used to fly helicopters with us on missions. He and Wark."

"And where is Wark now?" God, she hoped he wasn't going to say that Wark was dead. She crossed her fingers behind her back, immediately regretting her question and the can of worms it could have possibly opened.

"Married and living the life on the Oregon coast with his brilliant billionaire scientist wife. He retired and now makes furniture as a hobby. I'd have loved to get him to make all the stuff for the cabin, but there just wasn't time. Man is anal retentive about detail and a dresser takes him fucking months. Asher's already commissioned a few pieces for their new place when it gets built. Dining table, coffee table, that kind of shit." He opened the crate and unloaded, handing things to Mieka, who took it all up to the front porch of the cabin, then used the key Nate gave her to unlock it and begin hauling everything inside.

She released her pensive exhale and uncrossed her fingers, saying a small thank you to the universe that Wark was okay and living his best life.

The sun was lower in the sky by the time they got everything into the tiny cabin, making the already shoebox size space feel like a shoebox for a mouse.

"I'll start up in the loft," he said, making multiple trips up the ladder with boxes. "I'll put the bed frame together, then we can open up this magical memory foam mattress you were so excited about."

The way he said that she was excited about a mattress sent all kinds of thoughts—most of them dirty—careening through her mind. And he must have picked up on her thought shift because his eyelids dropped to half-mast and the smile that curled his mouth made her toes curl and her belly get warm.

But he didn't say anything, and she wasn't sure if that was better or worse.

Nate brought along a portable speaker and connected it to his phone through Bluetooth, so in a matter of seconds country music was playing throughout the cabin. She cringed. Country music was not her cup of tea.

That didn't stop her from humming and singing along about a man's dog running away and his truck getting keyed after he cheated on his girlfriend.

While Nate was busy putting the bed frame together, Mieka went about putting all the dishes in the sink to wash—she remembered to bring over-sized rubber gloves that reached her elbows—and setting up the kitchen chairs. The tables were handcrafted by a local woodworker with live-edge slabs and an acrylic river running through it, but the chairs were just standard IKEA chairs that needed to be assembled with an Allen key.

Triss was going to wash all the towels and linens and have Cal drop them off when he did his next deliveries. So for now, they had towels from the farmhouse and sleeping bags. Nate had thought of everything.

"Wanna come up and help me with something, Minx?" Nate asked from the loft.

She dried her hands on a dishtowel and climbed the ladder to find him sitting on the floor next to a nearly assembled bed frame.

Her belly clenched as images of "breaking in the bed" or "christening" it with Nate took over every other rational thought in her head.

"Brain out of the gutter, Minx," he said, tossing her another cheeky smile.

She rolled her eyes. "What did you need my help with?"

"Hold on to that piece there so I can slide Peg D into Hole V, please." His smile grew as he pointed to the long piece of wood he wanted her to grab.

"Fuck off," she said, turning to head back to the ladder.

"I'm serious, Minx. I need your help," he said with an obnoxiously sexy chuckle that made white-hot tendrils of lust uncoil through her. "Though, the peg isn't called *Peg D*. It's just a wooden dowel, but I need you to hold the end for me."

Sucking in a breath she prayed would be fortifying and relaxing, she turned back around, crouched down and grabbed the piece he indicated giving him a look that said she was neither amused nor aroused, but irritated. She was actually all three, but would die before she told him that.

He slid the dowels into the holes, then had her do the same on the other side so he could fit in those dowels, as well.

"Thank you," he said. "Now for the slats, then we can open up the mattress."

She stayed in the loft while he put down the pseudo boxed spring, then watched as he slid the blade of his X-Acto knife through the binding of the slats.

Every move the man made, every smile, every glance had her panties getting wetter by the second. She was just heartbeats away from throwing all rationale and caution out the door and into the river and just jumping the cowboy's bones and making up for the time they were together that she couldn't remember.

But that was a slippery slope.

Rayma would say that your vagina is a slippery slope.

"Meow!" said her cat.

"Fucking Rayma," she murmured.

"What was that?" he asked, fitting the wooden slats into the bedframe.

"Nothing," she said, shaking her head. "Just something my sister said to me. Or *would* say to me if she was here."

"Triss?"

"No, Rayma."

"Oh God, I can only imagine. That woman has no filter."

"Nope."

"All right, now that those are done, let's check out this magical dinosaur mattress you bought us." He used his X-Acto knife again and sliced through the tape like it was warm butter. Her insides clenched.

Something was obviously wrong with her if she was turned on by the man cutting through a piece of tape. She needed to have her head examined. Maybe she needed to go visit her sister Oona who was a psychologist. Oona could hook Mieka up to some electrodes and pump electricity into her brain, so she stopped thinking that everything Nate Harris did was sexy.

The mattress was vacuum sealed in a big plastic casing, so once Nate freed it from the box, he carefully slid the blade of the knife into the plastic and as if the mattress was made of baking soda and the air was vinegar, it oozed out of the plastic casing and unfurled before their eyes, growing to six or seven times its normal size until Nate let it collapse to the floor, a fully formed king-sized mattress.

"Well, spank my ass and call me Sal, that was pretty fucking cool," Nate said, picking the memory foam up and heaving it onto the slats. Then he collapsed onto the mattress, gave it a couple cursory bounces and nodded. "I could sleep on this. Well done, Minx." He patted the bed. "Come try it out."

Getting onto a bed with Nate Harris, a walking, talking, horse-riding, lady boner maker, was a bad, bad, bad idea. A terrible, no-good, very bad idea. And yet, she wandered over like an imbecile and slid onto the bed, reclining down beside him until they were both on their backs staring up at the ceiling.

"This is nice," he said.

Her heart pounded.

"Thanks for coming out here with me, Minx." The music still playing on his phone switched to something romantic and croony. She resisted the urge to roll her eyes at just how imperfectly timed the song was.

The universe was messing with her.

This was not where she was supposed to end up.

Sure, she was happy here *now*. But this was not the life for her. She needed fast-paced. Go-go-go. She needed nightlife and an audience. She needed to dance.

There were only so many ranch hands she could teach to dance, and then what? That wasn't a career. That wasn't a purpose. It was hard enough that all of her sisters did things that helped others. Pasha was a pediatrician, Triss was a speech path, Oona was a psychologist and Rayma was a social worker. Mieka danced. Not that there was anything wrong with her career choice, but unlike her sisters who could find work pretty much anywhere, Mieka couldn't imagine making a career of dancing here in farm country. And since she had no other skills, what was there for her to do out here?

And as much of a nice bit of respite the ranch was—despite the fact that she'd been put to work the moment she arrived—the charm of it would surely wear off and then she'd be left with resentment and longing for the life she knew she should have.

Because the mattress was memory foam, Nate shifting to his side didn't jostle her at all, unlike a spring mattress. He was facing her now, and she resisted rolling over to face him for all of five breaths. Then she broke down and rolled over.

"I take you under the moonlight. My heart is full. Our bodies intertwined. Our souls as one," the portable stereo taunted.

Her body grew warm and her fingers twitched and itched to reach out and touch him. To run her fingers over his thick brows, or feel the scratch of his scruff against her palm. She remembered the roughness of that scruff against her neck from when they were together against the barn. She'd liked it.

She wanted it elsewhere. Like her cheeks, her mouth and her inner thighs.

Swallowing, she finally met his gaze and it damn near sent her entire body aflame. Heat sizzled in the deep blue, and the longing that she saw behind those eyes gutted her.

He wanted something she just couldn't give him.

Reaching up, he tucked a wayward strand of hair behind her ear, but his finger lingered and trailed down her cheek, then her neck and finally her collarbone before he removed it. It left a trail of fire though, and the flames were hot and big enough that it'd take jumping in the river outside to douse them.

"Save the Last Dance," she said softly.

Confusion creased his face.

"My favorite movie."

"Ah." His eyes widened in understanding and he smiled.

"Moroccan chickpea stew over Israeli couscous is my favorite meal, and summer is my favorite season."

His smile made everything inside of her clench and get happy. "Thank you."

They laid there for another couple of minutes, neither of them saying anything, or breaking eye contact and yet somehow his fingers found hers on the mattress and they intertwined. It felt wonderful and so natural to lay next to Nate in bed.

The contentment and warmth that filled her wasn't overwhelming like she thought it would be. It was healing and blissful. Despite the fact that they'd never been in a bed together before, it didn't feel weird at all. It didn't even feel like something she'd need to get used to. It was an experience she enjoyed and wanted to make permanent.

Permanent?

Where did that thought come from?

She was about to ask what they were doing when her belly rumbled like approaching thunder.

Nate blinked and sat up, unlacing their fingers and immediately making her bereft of his touch. "I guess we should eat, huh?"

The spell or whatever it was between them was broken and the song on the portable speaker changed to something less sex-in-the-back-of-a-pickup-under-the-stars. She was both relieved and disappointed by all of it, and her fingers still tingled from where they'd been touching his.

"I still have some onion rings and fries left, but I'm happy to make something for you," she said, sitting up and swinging her legs over the side to stand up and head to the ladder.

"Sure, thanks." He'd already opened up another box, this time for one of the nightstands and was pulling out the pieces to assemble.

Nate packed rations like he was stocking a doomsday bunker. Cans of stew, beans, soups and precooked pasta in tomato sauce. He'd also grabbed a package of steaks, some hotdogs, a couple boxes of mac 'n' cheese, bread, oatmeal, eggs, bacon, and coffee.

It wasn't exactly what Mieka would have packed, or at least she would have also packed a vegetable or piece of fruit, but she'd figure something out.

He was singing along to the music up in the loft, and as she stirred an unappetizing stew on the hotplate, she started to hum along to the song, too.

"I like this view." His voice over the music, and after such a long span of no talking between them, made her jump.

She spun around and stared up at him. "Meaning? A woman in the kitchen making you dinner?"

"Not *a* woman," he corrected. "And it doesn't matter what you're making, or that you're making anything. I just like that it's you. You could be clipping your toenails or plucking nipple hair and I'd still like the view."

She scoffed. "I do not have nipple hair."

His eyes rolled. "Sure you don't."

"Would it have killed you to pack a vegetable? A cucumber? Just one. Or an apple?"

He shrugged. "There's corn and potatoes in the stew, right?"

"'Cause you didn't have your fill of potatoes today already with those extra large fries?"

"There is no such thing as too many potatoes." He held up one finished nightstand and she applauded like a hoity toity woman at the opera.

"Bravo," she praised. "Encore, encore."

He put the nightstand down, bent over, and lifted up a second one.

She clapped again and grinned. "This dog food you call stew will be ready in a minute." She turned off the hotplate and moved the stew pot to a hot pad on the butcher block countertop.

"On my way down." He put the nightstand down, then gave her a solid five seconds to ogle his butt in those jeans as he climbed down the ladder. "Gonna go drain Peg D, then I'll be out." He headed to the bathroom. "How's Hole V, by the way?" he called out.

"Closed for asbestos removal," she replied, freezing the second she said it out loud, then slapping her palm to her forehead. What the fuck did that mean?

Apparently, Nate was wondering the same thing because he was laughing his ass off in the bathroom. "What the fuck does that mean?" he called out through the closed door.

Her face was on fire. Did she just tell him that her vagina had an asbestos problem? Yes, yes, she did.

Mortification had her body hot and her chest tingly.

The song on the speaker up in the loft switched again, but it was far too suggestive and romantic for ... whatever this was, so she scrambled up the ladder to grab Nate's phone and speaker. She was just coming down the ladder again, precariously cradling the phone and speaker in her casted hand, while holding the rungs with her other hand when the phone slipped, then the speaker slipped.

Instinct and firsthand knowledge of the disaster of a dropped phone had her sacrificing herself and letting go with her good hand to try to grab them. But she lost her balance and fell backward.

"Whoa!" Nate caught her in his arms, and somehow—the man was probably also a ninja in addition to a rancher, SEAL and walking, talking lady boner maker—he also managed to save his phone. His speaker fell to the wood floor but seemed unharmed. "Second time you've fallen off this ladder, Minx. I'm starting to think it might be on purpose just so I can catch you and hold you in my arms."

Her eyes snagged his and mischief, but also lust glittered back at her in those deep, dark blue orbs.

Her breath snagged. Her heart hammered against her ribcage, and before she knew it, she was grabbing him by the front of his shirt and crushing her mouth to his.

Chapter Thirteen

Nate only paused for a second before his grip on her tightened and he started kissing her back. Shifting their position, he swung her around the front of his body and plastered her back to the ladder, deepening the kiss and holding her up with his hips.

She could feel him growing harder against her inner thigh and she ground down against him, desperate for some friction. He growled and bit her lip, breaking their kiss and scraping his teeth along her jaw and down her neck. The stubble along his jaw scratched her, but the burn was delicious and she wanted more. She wanted that burn elsewhere. Everywhere.

Gripping the side rails of the ladder, Mieka tipped her head back against the rungs as Nate bit and sucked on her neck. Her pussy spasmed with each swipe of his tongue and scrape of his teeth.

Parts of her body remembered being with him, even if her brain was still fuzzy on the whole thing.

She had no idea what this meant for the future, but at the moment, she wanted—nay *needed*—Nate Harris inside of her.

But the man seemed to have other ideas and sunk to his knees, unbuttoning and unzipping her jeans and taking them with him, along with her shoes. He didn't even bother removing or shredding her panties and just pushed them to the side enough to get his tongue between her legs.

She nearly kneed him in the head.

Her fingers tightened on the sides of the ladder as Nate lapped at her center, swirled his tongue around her clit, and scraped his scruff along her inner thighs.

Yesssss.

Dear God, the man knew what he was doing.

He looped the backs of her thighs over his shoulders and settled better onto his knees, like he was aiming to get comfortable because he was going to be there awhile. But Mieka was already close. She'd been so revved up for days, just from Nate's flirting, being around him and when he'd wiggled that finger at her, that her body was running full-speed ahead for an explosive orgasm.

He must have known that, too, based on the way she was churning her hips and pressing her pelvis against his face, because he pushed one finger, then two into her channel, curled them up, pressed gently on her G-spot and she exploded.

Fireworks and starbursts erupted behind her closed eyelids and her body shook with each wracking wave of pleasure. Pure bodily bliss radiated out from her core in warm, beautiful ribbons and as hard as she tried, she just couldn't collect them all, and she knew she never would. Her toes curled and her fingers cramped from holding onto the side of the ladder so tightly. She had to let go with her left hand because of the cast, but Nate kept her propped up and in place.

She knew Nate would never let her fall.

As the aftershocks wore off and her soul slowly floated back to earth, Nate pulled his fingers free of her, gave a final swipe of his tongue up between the center of her pussy then sat back on his heels. "I didn't expect that appetizer, but fuck, it was delicious. Your cat might be stubborn, but it's damn tasty."

She blinked her eyes open and tipped her head forward to look at him as a heat of embarrassment crept into her cheeks. The erection in his jeans pulled her eyes away from his face and no matter how hard she tried, she couldn't look away. It was like a car crash or an eclipse. She knew it was wrong. That she shouldn't be staring at it, but tell that to her eyeballs, her pussy and her body after that soul-altering orgasm.

"My eyes are up here, Minx," he said with a laugh.

Now her face was going to burst into flames. She just knew it. Slowly, she lifted her gaze to find his penetrating one, full of cocky male bravado.

"That took *way* less time than last time. You were already wet for me and everything." His face scrunched, and he tilted his head to the side. "Though, I think you were also wet last time, but you had whiskey clit, so ..."

Goosebumps broke out over her legs, and that's when she realized she was basically naked from the waist down. She still had her panties on, thank God, but they were pushed to the side, showing Nate everything.

He just had his face smashed against me. I don't think he cares. Tell him to come back, I miss him already. Oh great, now her actual pussy was weighing in on the matter.

Even still. She adjusted her panties to cover herself better, then let go of the ladder and bent over to pick up her pants, but Nate grabbed them before she could, stood up and lifted them over his head so she couldn't get them.

She glared at him, then plunked her hands on her hips. "Give me my jeans, please."

"But we're not done yet. I've only just gotten started, Minx. And in my opinion, you're still wearing far too many clothes for what I want to do to you."

Her belly did a flip and her pussy did a clench. *What does he want to do? He can do whatever he wants. Cock, tongue, fingers. I want all of it.*

"Shut the fuck up."

His eyes widened.

"Sorry," she said, shaking her head. "That wasn't to you."

"Then who the hell was it to?" he asked. "It's only us here. Unless you have Triss on Bluetooth, then well, I'd prefer a heads up before I go down on you that we have an audience. I'm not against it if that's your kink, but trust and transparency is key."

Her eyes rolled. "It wasn't to Triss. I have no Bluetooth. It was to ... never mind. The voices in my head."

More like the voice in your pants. And, you're not actually wearing any pants right now, so ...

"I ... I think this was a mistake," she said, reaching for her pants again. "I don't want to lead you on. I'm sorry I kissed you. I'm sorry I let it go this far." She stepped toward him, reaching for her jeans.

But he was so much taller than her and his wingspan had him holding her jeans a full six feet above her head. "Nuh-uh, Minx." His gaze was heated and the way it swept across her exposed skin only caused more gooseflesh to rise. "You're not leading me on. I know what I'm doing. I know what we're doing. You know I want you."

She shook her head. "No, you want a *life* here with me. And I've told you, I can't give you that."

"No, I told you that I want you. And I want to show you how great life here can be. Whether it's with me or not, well ..." He shrugged and let that last bit hang. "I'm a big boy, Minx. And you're a big girl. You also brought up the fact that you were disappointed you never got to see my dick the first time we had sex."

"I was hoping you would forget about that," she murmured.

"I wasn't drunk when you said it and it's kind of hard to forget a smoking hot woman saying she wished she'd seen your dick before you stuck it in her. That kind of thing gets branded on your brain and keeps you awake at night." He bobbed his eyebrows up and down salaciously. "If you know what I mean."

"I think Fumble the goat would know what you mean." She made a half-assed attempt at jumping for her jeans, but knew it was a futile endeavour. Plopping her hands on her hips, she glared at him. "What do you want from me, Nate?"

His gaze turned heated which in turn made her body warm up. "I think you know."

"So, I don't get my pants back unless I have sex with you? You know that screams *Me Too* and sexual predator, right? I should just punch you in the nads, steal the ATV and head home."

He rolled his eyes, only to pin them on her a second later, the hunger in his gaze a taunting gleam that said he knew she wanted him just as much as he wanted her.

Fuck, he was right. Of course he was.

Everyone in the cabin knew it. He did, her pussy did, and even Mieka knew it, as much as she was trying to deny it.

Her pussy was still pulsing, still tingling from his attention a moment ago. All of this was just foreplay. She was going to end up beneath Nate—or on top of him—and finally get to see his dick as well as remember having it inside of her.

His grin changed a bit, growing wider and less mischievous, to happier.

"What?" she asked, the curiosity over his mood shift getting the better of her.

"You called it *home*."

Growling, she lunged at him and for her jeans, but he balled them up and tossed them up onto the loft, then pinned her against the kitchen counter.

"Don't read into it too much, cowboy. It's home *for now*."

He was still smiling as his fingers made their way to the hem of her shirt and he lifted it over her head. She allowed it. His mouth fell to where her neck met her shoulder and he sucked hard enough to send a straight shot of pleasure from that spot down to her clit. She tilted her hips against his erection involuntarily.

"Seriously, Nate, I don't want to lead you on." Her head dropped back against the cupboard when he moved his mouth down her chest, pulled a nipple free from the cup of her bra and sucked it into his mouth.

A moan she had no control over bubbled up from the depths of her chest.

"Not leading me on, Minx. Know exactly what I'm getting myself into." Sinking to his knees, he continued to press hot, wet kisses across her abdomen. "And I'm hoping what I'm *getting into* is you." He removed her panties, spread her thighs and pushed two fingers back into her channel.

She bucked against his hand and her eyes fluttered closed when the heel of his palm rubbed against her clit. She'd gone and gotten laser hair removal years ago, since it just made things easier. She never had to worry about hair, bumps or anything anymore. Some of their dance outfits were very high cut, but she also went to the beach and sat poolside while on the ships, so to have to keep everything tidy with monthly waxing appointments or shaving just didn't make sense.

Nate stood back up and she tipped her head forward, their gazes snagging.

Not saying a word, she reached forward and started to unbutton his flannel shirt. Her eyes raked his hard torso, his defined pecs and those insanely muscular arms beneath his tank top. She knew he was cut, but the sheer visual reminder of his strength had her pussy clenching around his fingers.

He had to pull those fingers free of her to allow for the shirt to come off, then he reached behind him and pulled his white ribbed tank top off, as well. His dog tags rested perfectly between his pecs and she licked her lips.

He was still in those ass-hugging jeans that fit him perfectly. And he had those twin lines running from his hips down under his jeans. The arrows, or the trails leading to the treasure below.

She reached for his button and zipper, but before she could pull the zipper all the way down, he grabbed her by the waist and spun her around, pushing her belly gently against the counter.

His lips trailed over her shoulders, down her back and even across the tops of her butt cheeks. "Were you on the pill last time?" he asked gruffly.

"Yes," she breathed. "But I have an IUD now and I um... I have condoms in my bag." Her cheeks heated at the mention of the condoms.

She hadn't been planning on sleeping with Nate... well, not *planning* on it, but she knew there was a possibility and she wanted to be prepared this time since last time they'd taken a risk and lost. Her ADHD and scattered brain kept her from taking her pill consistently. She often forgot, so the fact that she got pregnant wasn't entirely a surprise, but it had been a wakeup call that she needed a more permanent and worry-free form of birth control, hence the IUD.

His lips disappeared from her skin for a moment and she heard him rummaging around in her bag. Ordinarily, she'd be miffed at the idea of someone rooting around in her stuff, but in this instance, she didn't care. She also trusted Nate.

He was back a moment later and nipped her shoulder, making her shudder. The sound of the wrapper opening, followed by the drop of his pants, echoed loudly in the cabin, particularly since there was no music anymore.

He trailed his warm, calloused hands down her ass cheeks, squeezing slightly. One hand worked its way around in front of her and his index finger pressed her clit like a button, causing her legs to widen.

"Good girl," he murmured, scraping his teeth across the tops of her shoulders.

She trembled and smiled from the praise. She was such a praise-whore. An attention-whore, really. Her, Macklin, and Karen should start a support group. Attention-whores Anonymous or something.

The clasp of her bra was unfastened. She let the straps slide over her arms and the bra landed on the counter in front of her.

She was a maelstrom of conflicting sensations. Lust, desperation, curiosity, excitement, but also worry. She knew Nate wanted more, but she hoped that she'd been clear and upfront over their lack of a future, that he wouldn't let himself get his hopes up.

Why couldn't they just have fun? Scratch itches and do what came naturally?

Just because this kind of life worked for Triss, didn't mean it would work for Mieka.

Nate's cock, fingers and tongue, however... those definitely worked for her. At least for the time being.

One of his hands on her hip had her bending forward more and pushing her ass backward, into his cock which knocked her center. She could feel the condom and exhaled in relief at that necessary barrier between them.

"Minx," he breathed, hanging over her and pressing a kiss to her neck. "You've got me under your spell."

"Stick it in me, cowboy," she said breathlessly. "Remind me of what I forgot about."

He pushed forward slightly, breaching her center with the wide head of his cock. She sucked in a breath and relaxed her body, welcoming him home, then squeezing around him when he was fully seated.

The stretch to accommodate his length and girth felt amazing. It was exactly what she'd been craving for far too long. Not just since she showed up at the ranch unannounced, or since their last time together at the wedding in September. It'd been a long time since a man had filled her up like this, had made her come as hard as Nate already did.

His finger wiggled back and forth over her clit, pulling a shiver straight up the length of her spine and causing her to tighten around the base of his cock. He grunted and wiggled his finger faster.

He hadn't even started to move yet and already she was close.

"Get out of your head and into your body, Minx. Be in the moment, right here, with me. It's just us."

Just us.

"Just the three of us," he rumbled.

She paused and craned her head around to look at him. "Three?"

His grin made her clench around him. "You, me and your stubborn cat."

She rolled her eyes, but he stole her mouth and brought her back to the moment.

"You want me to make your kitten purr?" he asked when he broke their kiss.

"Need to start moving to do that, cowboy," she said, well, more like choked as he pinched her clit in such a way, she saw stars.

"Yes, ma'am." Then he started to move.

Boy oh boy did he start to move.

In and out of her, Nate plunged, pulling out all the way to the tip, then easing back in, torturously slow, but in a way that had his shaft scraping every inch of her trembling pussy. No part of her was left untouched. No nerve-ending remained unstimulated.

Mieka squirmed with the need to come, and yet, she wasn't ready. She didn't want to yet, because she wasn't sure what would happen after it ended. Would that be it? Would it be awkward between them afterward? They still had three more cabins to set up. Or would they just fuck on every surface of every cabin, then return to the ranch like nothing happened? Then she'd leave to ... who knows where? And see Nate when she came to visit after the baby was born?

"Get out of your head, Minx," he growled, pulling out of her roughly, spinning her around with one hand on her shoulder and removing his finger from her clit. He crashed his mouth to hers, pushed his tongue inside and challenged hers to a duel. She tasted the remnants of her earlier release on his lips, but that just turned her on more.

His rough hand cupped her breast, and he pinched her nipple, making her gasp against his lips. But he swallowed her gasp and continued to kiss her. Continued to knead and caress her breast, tug on her nipple and make her ride his thigh like it was the mechanical bull at the tavern they went to.

Only when she was so hot and bothered and the hollow ache of her pussy became unbearable, did he finally release her mouth, hook her thighs over his hips and plow forward, seating himself inside her fully in one hard thrust.

They both grunted, and he plunked her butt on the counter, dug his fingers into her ass cheeks and bucked upward, hitting her in all the right places. Even his pelvic bone scraped her clit in the absolute perfect way. She wasn't going to last much longer.

"We need to get you out of your head, Minx. Focus on us. On the fact that I'm literally inside of you right now. Our bodies are connected and that every time I push forward, you squeeze that perfect little cunt around me, begging me to stay." A quick bite to her neck and he pulled his face away. "Look at me."

She blinked open her eyes and gave them a second to focus on his face so close to hers. Goddamn it, he was beautiful. Rugged and scarred, rough-around-the edges, and with an almost haunted look in his eyes at times, but all of that just added to his beauty. He wasn't perfect. But neither was she. She didn't want perfect. She wanted real. She wanted a man who had lived, and knew how to live. And she knew for a fact that Nate had lived a lot in his forty-something years. He'd seen stuff that would probably give her nightmares, taken out a lot of bad guys and lost brothers and friends along the way.

An old soul resided inside Nate. An old soul with scars, faults and secrets. But she liked that. She liked everything about him.

"How does that feel?" he asked, sliding backward, dragging his cock against the inside of her pussy so slowly she nearly came right then and there.

"Good," she breathed.

"Just good?" he moved forward again, just as slow, filling her up once more.

"So good."

"So good, hmm?"

She nodded.

"I'm inside you right now, Minx. My body is inside your body. Think about that."

Oh, she was thinking about it all right. It was all she could think about. Well, that and the fact that she wanted his body inside her to pick up speed and hammer her into the next orgasm like a rabbit on cocaine.

"Think about how perfectly we fit together. How right this feels." He slid deep inside her, gripping her ass cheeks tighter to pull them closer together, and a rattled breath escaped her parted lips. "Look at me, Minx."

She tipped her eyes to his.

"Do you feel this?"

She felt everything.

Every inch of him inside her, she felt. His fingers on her ass, she felt. His dusting of chest hair tickling her nipples, she felt. She felt it all. Along with the growing frustration that he knew he was keeping her on the edge. That she was close to exploding, and he was deliberately withholding her orgasm from her. Oh yeah, she felt that frustration in spades.

Her hands had been on his shoulders to steady herself, but he removed one of his own hands from her ass, grabbed her right hand from his shoulder and placed it over his heart. "Feel how fast my heart is beating, Minx."

He wasn't wrong, it was thundering like crazy in his chest.

"That's what you do to me."

She swallowed. "Nate ... please ..." Her head shook, and she tried to look away, but he caught her chin in his fingers and kept her looking forward, looking at him.

"You're not leading me on, Minx. But I'm also not going to stop trying to convince you that this is where you're meant to be. That we have something. If you decide to leave, then fine, but while you're here, you're going to be wooed, seduced and showered with orgasms. Got it?"

She closed her eyes, but he started to retreat from her body, so she quickly opened them, grabbed hold of his shoulders again and pulled him back into her, meeting his challenging gaze. He lifted one brow, waiting for her to answer. Finally, she did, with a nod of understanding. "Fine. Now, can you please start moving faster? I'm about to lose my mind."

His grin was filthy, but it just shoved her closer to climax. He brought his hands to her waist, held on tight, then started to buck, hard and fast, seating himself completely inside of her, then pulling free, only to surge back in a second later.

The rub and slap of his lower belly against her clit was perfect and in less than a minute, she was tipping her head toward the ceiling, shutting her eyes and coming.

"Oh God," she panted, squeezing her muscles around him. "Yes. Oh God, yes." Her ankles locked around his back and she tipped her pelvis forward, taking him just a half-inch deeper. But it was enough of an angle shift to launch

Nate into his own release.

He stilled, his entire body stiffened, and a feral, masculine groan rumbled up from the depths of his chest. Dropping his head to the crook of her neck, he just kept it there as his cock pulsed inside her. She was caught up in her own release, but still managed to press a kiss to the side of his head as her soul threatened to rip clean from her body with each euphoric wave.

They stayed like that for some time. Enjoying the aftershocks that rippled through her. Every time she'd shudder, he'd twitch his cock inside her and they'd both laugh. But eventually, he softened and they knew he needed to pull out while he was still hard enough to keep the condom in place.

Slowly, he stepped away, holding onto the base of the condom. The moment he was free of her body, an overwhelming sense of longing eclipsed her. She missed him.

She'd felt nothing like that before.

He disappeared to the bathroom, bringing with him a gently folded up wad of damp toilet paper. "It was all I could find," he said, wiping between her legs. "Sorry." He didn't have much of a mess to clean up, since they'd used a condom, but she no less appreciated the gesture.

Once he tossed the paper into the garbage, he helped her down off the counter. He'd already pulled up his jeans again and refastened them. Her eyes fell to the front of his pants.

"What's up, Minx?" he asked, picking up her shirt from the floor as she refastened her bra.

"I still haven't seen it."

"Seen? Oh! Ha! Oh, Minx. You'll see it, trust me. Just give it a bit of time to regain some of its strength, then I'll give you an up close and personal *private* viewing. How does that sound?"

Heat infused her cheeks, but he didn't give her time to feel embarrassed before he grabbed her around the waist, tugged her against his rock-solid body and took her mouth.

When he released her lips, she was breathless and ready for round two. Or was it round three?

"How's that sound?" he asked again, grinning at her like a smug jerk she couldn't wait to climb like a tree again.

Her gaze dropped to the front of his jeans, and she licked her lips. "That sounds good."

Chapter Fourteen

Nate could have easily kept Mieka busy until the next morning. Spreading her out on the new bed up in the loft, atop an unzipped sleeping bag while he made her scream loud and long enough to wake the coyotes and concern the prairie dogs. But they had things to do. He also wasn't a spring chicken anymore and needed a longer refractory period than he used to in his twenties and thirties. He was forty-one years old and although he could still get it up a few times a day, long marathon sessions or a baker's dozen of erections in a day were no longer possible.

Mieka didn't seem to mind that he didn't throw her over his shoulder, haul her up to the loft and keep her there until morning. She finished her leftovers from Gus's while he ate some potato, corned beef and corn stew that was still warm on the stove.

"So um ..." she murmured as they sat on the floor in the living room, quietly eating their dinner and drinking wine.

"So, um?" he probed, pulling a grin from her face.

"That was fun."

"Sure was. *And*, we'll remember it. *And*, we remembered protection." He held his hand up for a high five that never came. She just rolled her eyes. So he high fived himself, then went back to eating.

"I know you said that I'm not leading you on, but I just need to be sure that once we get back to the ranch, and I've officially been told that I've overstayed my welcome that things aren't going to be weird between us. Not only when I leave, but when I come back to visit. Triss is my sister, and she's pregnant, so I'm going to want to come back and visit her and the baby."

"Not weird at all," he said, pushing some stew into his cheek. "And nobody is going to tell you that you've overstayed your welcome. I told you, Minx, I'm working to change your mind on this place." Cocking his head to the side, he asked, "By the way, how am I doing so far?" Then he waggled his eyebrows and stuck out his tongue in a dirty way. "Am I convincing you yet? Or do I need to spend the next several hours coaxing your stubborn cat into submission?"

"It's not my cat that needs convincing," she said while making a noise of derision in the back of her throat. "That bitch has already packed up everything she owns and sent out change of address cards."

That made him laugh and he tossed his head back. "I like your cat. She and I get along beautifully. She particularly likes it when I pet her with my tongue."

"She's a traitorous bitch," Mieka retorted. Her dismissal didn't deter him at all, though. It only convinced him he needed to work harder. Plus, he'd already convinced her cat, now he just needed to convince her heart. "And if you don't change my mind and I leave, things aren't going to be weird?" she asked.

He shrugged. "Only if you make them."

Her look was poignant, but then she picked up one of her onion rings and took a bite. "So we're going to keep doing what we just did until ...?"

"Until you say *stop*. Or until you leave. Or until you say you're going to stay forever. I mean, your cat already wants to stay and make a home on my face, I'd say we're halfway there already." He gave her a cheeky smile that had her rolling her eyes again.

"My cat is a pathetic, desperate slut who hasn't gotten—"

"Cream?"

Her glare just made him smile even more.

"I was going to say *attention* in a while."

"Potato, pot-ah-to," he mused.

"I disagree, but I digress. You're dealing with an attention-starved cat here, don't read too much into it."

"I'm not reading too much into anything." Oh, but he was. He wanted all of her. Cat, heart, body and mind. But he also didn't want to scare her away. Cats might be skittish, but they were brave, bold beasts compared to the timid, tender--hearted animal that was Mieka.

"It's just that easy, then, is it?" She took a sip of her wine. He'd brought a few bottles of red wine and she'd bought a beautiful set of stemless glasses for each cabin. "You think because you've won over my cat, the rest of me will just follow suit?"

"Maybe. A guy can hope. Besides, why does it have to be hard? The only hard thing about any of it should be my dick. The rest should be easy, and it is, because it's meant to—"

"Don't say it."

"Be."

She glared at him with those gold-flecked brown eyes. "I told you not to say it."

He shrugged and took another spoonful of the stew. "And I don't always do as I'm told."

"How can you say that we're meant to be? That *it's* meant to be when you know so little about me? When I know so little about you? Just because we have chemistry and finally had sex that we'll both remember doesn't mean we're compatible in the way you're making it out that we are. I could have a horrible nose-picking habit that I've been keeping under wraps."

Washing down the stew with wine, he swallowed before saying, "Do you?"

"No."

"As long as you're not eating it, I'd say that's not a big enough deal-breaker for me. Try again."

"I'm messy, I'm disorganized, I'm almost always late for things. I hate olives. I sometimes talk—and dance—in my sleep. I'm usually up at four in the morning running. I have serious body issues or what could be classified or diagnosed as body dysmorphia because of the decades-long need for me to be slim and have a 'dancer's body'. I'm oddly addicted to reality television shows like *Selling Sunset* and *Love is Blind*. You'll never see me in anything pink—ever. And I'm honestly not even sure that I want children. I figured one day I'd have them because you know, that's what society expects of women, or whatever, but I don't *feel* maternal. Sure, babies are cute, but do I want my own?" She shrugged. "I don't know." Her brows lifted as she brought a bottle of water to her lips and took a sip. "What say you now?"

Wow, that was a lot to unpack, but it also made him happy that she was finally opening up to him. That she trusted him enough to let him get to know the real, the flawed, the quirky Mieka Young, and not just the polished and poised dancer that everyone else saw.

"Well, I'm not a neat freak—that's Asher. So messes don't usually bother me. You seem pretty organized to me with the color-coded furniture for the cabins, so it seems that you're able to be organized when things are important. I love olives, so just give me all of yours. If I have a few puffs before bed, I will sleep like the dead, so not an issue. I'm up at five every morning to feed the animals, so four is nothing. I don't know what to say about the body dysmorphia thing, but whatever I can do to ease your personal judgment of yourself, or help you, just let me know. I think you're stunning and would still be stunning if you gained fifty or a hundred pounds. I don't watch television, so we'll never fight over the remote. Pink is overrated. And kids are not a make-or-break deal for me. If I have them, great, I'll be a kick-ass dad and love them with everything that I am. But, if I don't have them, I don't see my life being any less full or fulfilled without children. I'll have nieces and nephews from Asher and Triss, so I can just be the cool uncle." It was his turn to lift his brow. "Are you trying to scare me away,

Minx? Because you'll have to try a hell of a lot harder than that."

A huffed breath puffed out of her nose and her shoulders rounded slightly. "I'm also really stubborn."

"I've gathered that. But I train and work with horses who can be incredibly stubborn. Also, have you met my brother? You're as flexible as Gumby compared to that rigid fuck."

Her lips twitched, threatening a smile, and she took a sip of her wine to hide that smile growing wider. Her eyes found his, they were sad, but also held a glimmer of defiant determination. "Tell me something about you that— "

"That would scare the average person away?" he asked, reading her mind and body language.

She nodded. She'd been looking for a way to scare him off, but since she hadn't succeeded, she was switching gears and wanted him to scare her away.

Well, she'd find out eventually, so he may as well tell her now and see if it really did scare her.

"I need to know what I'm getting myself into, right? Any PTSD? Demons? Triggers? We know that abrupt loud noises are a trigger for Asher. What's your trigger?"

He was quiet for a moment, finishing his stew and having more wine while enjoying the curiosity that burned silently in her expressive eyes. He put down the bowl and spoon on the floor, then finished his wine and started to unbutton his flannel.

"You can't distract me with sex, Nate," she started. "Besides we have more work to—"

"Just be patient," he said, letting the shirt slide off his arms, then he reached behind him and pulled off his white tank top. With a deep, calming breath to help control his raging pulse, he twisted his body around, still sitting forward, but staring behind him so she could see his back.

He expected her to gasp, and she did.

But he hadn't been expecting her to reach out and touch him and he was startled at the cool, softness of her fingertips along the raised ridges of his scar tissue. He relaxed a moment later and allowed her to study his scars and the full-back tattoo he commissioned to cover it. While Asher had narrowly escaped an explosion at a hospital, ducking under his transport truck in the nick of time and just taking a shard of metal to the face, Nate had experienced something slightly different.

"What happened?" Mieka asked, still trailing her fingertips over the elaborate profile image of a male lion and a phoenix rising from the ashes. Roses encircled the two creatures and all of it was in grayscale.

He often forgot he had the tattoo until he shifted funny and the tight patches of scar tissue that rippled along the span of his back pinched or itched in an uncomfortable way. The tattoo covered most of them, but the edges were still visible at his sides.

"Nate?" she probed, her voice soft.

Slowly, he turned back around, taking the fingers she'd been touching him with in his hands and kissing the tips. "Fire," he finally said. "I was on a mission in West Africa. A bunch of children—all girls—were kidnapped from their school in a village and were being held for ransom. But they came from impoverished families, so the gang who kidnapped them—a religious extremist group known for their incel ideologies—knew their families couldn't pay. Some of these girls were as young as five. They were being sold off as child brides."

"Oh my God."

"There were four of us on the team. We snuck into the camp to rescue the girls, but something happened—I honestly don't even remember what. I was hit in the head, blacked out, and the next thing I know, I'm being shaken awake by one of the girls I was rescuing. She didn't speak any English. We were trapped inside a ramshackle building and it was on fire."

She pulled her fingers free of his grasp, reached up, and cupped his jaw. He leaned into her touch and briefly closed his eyes, trying his best to remember that night. Things were still fuzzy. The blow to his head had been hard and he was severely concussed.

"The blow to my head was worse than I thought and I couldn't stand without vomiting. The most I could do was crawl, which worked out since the whole place was full of smoke. We tied wet rags over our mouths and noses and I managed to get them to an exit where another member of my team—Ryke—pulled the girls free. But a beam came crashing down on me, pinning me in place on my stomach. I blacked out again from the concussion, and when I woke up, I was face down in a hospital bed in agony as a nurse debrided my back of the third-degree burns." His big hand cupped hers where it still rested against his cheek. "I'm not triggered by things like Asher is, but I'd be lying if I said I don't have a bit of a fire phobia now. I'm also not entirely sure I need to add children from my own bloodline to the world when there are just so many children elsewhere that are living in poverty and could be given a second chance at a decent future."

He glanced up at her, his heart heavy and his throat tight. He hadn't told that story to anyone in a really long time and as much as he liked to think he was over it, he wasn't and he probably never would be completely. Talking about it just brought it back to the forefront of his mind. He'd have a hard time falling asleep tonight, for sure. Good thing he brought a bunch of weed.

Tears shimmered in her eyes and her full lips were in a sexy little pout. "You're a hero," she said, her voice strained.

He shook his head stiffly. "No, I'm not. I'm just a guy who did his job. I knew the risks going in." He hated that word. *Hero.*

He was no hero. He was just a man with the skills that not everyone else possessed, so he used those skills to help others. Not enough people who were capable, whether by strength and size, or financial means helped others. This was a world full of selfish people—mostly men. Men who just took from others, who used others and believed they were impervious to any ramifications of their actions. He didn't know a damn person who had served that wasn't jaded as fuck about the world and the people in it.

But Nate and his team had been there to remind those men—those people—that they were as mortal as the rest of the world. They'd taken out a lot of bad guys. Even though Nate hadn't been able to, given his concussion and burn recovery, the rest of his team had finished the hunt and taken out every person involved in the kidnapping of those girls since most of them had fled the camp the night of the raid—after setting the place on fire.

He went on two more missions after that, then Asher had his accident and the two of them decided it was time to retire.

It wasn't his place to tell the public, but all of the ranch hands they hired were also retired vets—Hank, Ronny, Ray, Wes, Braiden—they'd all served somewhere, were honorably discharged, then thrown out into the world expected to assimilate back into society seamlessly.

Neither Asher nor Nate had worked with any of their ranch hands before they came to the ranch, but it was no secret that the ranch offered labor positions to veterans. So the men made their way to Colorado, rolled up to the ranch with lost and haunted looks in their eyes, then found themselves a new purpose and a place full of people who understood what they were going through. A place to call home.

It was often difficult for vets to find work when they returned to civilian life, so he and his brother made sure they offered their fellow soldiers a soft place to land when they ended their career in service. Working with horses was therapeutic, and the hard labor kept the men's minds from wandering back to their time overseas.

Her question pulled him from the dark rabbit hole of his thoughts and back into the light that was Mieka. "So, I understand the phoenix, but the lion? The roses?"

He twisted around again to show her his back once more. "Each rose represents one of the girls that we rescued and brought back to their family." He could tell she was about to ask how many roses there were, so he just answered before she could ask or count. "There are eighteen roses."

"Eighteen," she breathed. "Wow. And the lion?"

He shrugged. "It happened in Africa. The lion is the apex predator, and yet, the male lion isn't nearly as strong as a pride of lionesses. It just felt like a good reminder that no matter how strong I think I might be, those eighteen girls are a million times stronger. Not only individually, but collectively. The male lion can be usurped by a stronger one at any point, and wanders the savannah alone most of the time. It's also a cat, and cats are notoriously hard to kill. My nickname on my team used to be *Blaze*. Asher's was *Ash*, since we were both the explosive and ballistics specialists, but since that fire, I'm not really *Blaze* anymore. A couple of the girls we rescued called me "Lion Man" because apparently, I jumped and pounced around falling beams to protect them. I don't remember doing it ... Concussion and all. I didn't think I could stand without puking, but they say I did." He shrugged and scratched the back of his neck, the warmth of embarrassment creeping into his face.

Her eyes were wider than saucers, which caused a few rogue tears to slip down her cheeks. Blinking spiked lashes, she shook her head. "Nate ... if that story and those scars are meant to scare me away ..."

"It's not. They're not. I don't want to scare you away, Minx. I want to keep you here. But I want you to know me. All of me, so one way or another, it helps you make your choice more constructively. I don't have demons or triggers, just a rational fear of fire and fuzzy memories of a mission almost gone terribly wrong."

"Hence the lack of a woodstove or fireplace?" she asked, her smile small as her gaze drifted around the log cabin.

He nodded. "Yup. We're not open in the winter, so no need for a fireplace or woodstove. And you bought a couple of electric space heaters for each cabin. That'll be enough. I also won't light the woodstove in the house. That's on Asher or Triss. And they understand why I won't touch it. I don't remember being burned, since I blacked out, but I remember the fire. I remember being scared. I remember the debriding, and I never want to go through that again."

"I can only imagine the fear you felt. To not know if you were going to make it out alive. And I've heard that burning alive is one of the worst ways to go."

He nodded. "It is. I'm grateful that I was passed out when that inflamed beam landed on my back. Otherwise, I probably would have taken my own life rather than experienced that kind of pain, believing that I wasn't going to make it out alive."

"And the fact that you didn't break your back ..."

He nodded solemnly. "Another thing I'm grateful for. All-in-all, I'm tremendously lucky. And I know that. I don't take my life for granted. I'm not ashamed of my burns, but without the tattoo, they are very visible, and seeing them is just a constant reminder. They also scare people, so it was easier to just cover them."

Her fingertips traced the roses that spread out along his shoulder blades, then slipped down over his ribs, tracing the line of the phoenix. "It's beautiful."

"Asher and I used the same tattoo artist. He does incredible work." He turned back around, reached forward, and slid his hand to her hip, his thumb pushing up the hem of her shirt and down the waistband of her jeans so he could gently touch the small tattoo of five intersecting hearts at her hip. "And you got this one with your sisters?"

She nodded. "We each have one. Each heart is slightly smaller than the one before it, and the only one colored in is the one that represents our spot in the birth order. So since I'm number three of five, smack dab in the middle, I'm this one." She pointed to the mint-green heart. "I also have a wave on the top of my foot. A bunch of the dancers on the ship all got the same one at one of our ports. And then I have this small, single-line tattoo of a ballet dancer on the inside of my arm." She lifted her arm to reveal the delicate, tasteful single-line silhouette of a beautiful dancer en pointe with her head and arm elegantly tipped back.

His thumb rubbed over the heart tattoo on her hip again. "Are you scared, Minx?"

Their eyes met, and she shook her head. "Of you? Not at all. Of... *this*, very."

He got that. She was scared of what they could be. That her world could be flipped on its axis once more and she might just like the life he was offering her. But the only thing she knew was dance. She had convinced herself that a certain way of life was the only way, and the fact that he was offering her something entirely different scared her.

Slowly, he eased forward, sliding his hand from her hip, up her shirt until he cupped her breast and her back was on the floor while he hovered over her. "So scared that you're going to ask me to stop?" He pulled down the cup of her bra and swept his calloused thumb over her hardening nipple. His mouth hovered over hers, tasting her wine-flavored breath, as he was sure she was tasting his. His cock pressed painfully against the zipper of his jeans, but he restrained himself, waiting for her response.

She didn't respond with words though, but rather her body and lunged upward, snagging his bottom lip between her teeth while wedging her hands between them and reaching for his zipper.

He took her response as a green light and surged forward, taking her mouth and tangling his tongue with hers. She started to suck on his tongue like it was a cock, and he groaned into her mouth at the thought of watching his fiery Minx take him in her mouth. If she sucked cock like she did his tongue, he wouldn't last long.

Once she had his fly open, she pushed her fingers below the waistband of his boxer briefs to find him hard for her. She circled his length with her thumb and forefinger and began to stoke.

Pure, fucking heaven.

Then he nearly came like a teenager in the backseat of a Volkswagen after prom (not him, but other teenagers, he was sure) when she swept her thumb over his crown and swirled the precum around the tip.

He continued to cup and knead her breast, loving how hard the nipple grew when he pinched and pulled it, and the way she bowed her back and groaned when he delivered just a slight snap of pain.

They made out and stayed at second base for a few minutes until she growled in frustration, pulled her hand free of his pants, pushed his chest until he was forced to sit up, then pushed him more so he laid down on the blanket they were on.

He watched as she got up on her knees, pulled the top of his jeans down and waited for him to lift his hips so he could pull them down more. Then, his Minx wrapped her delicate fingers back around his shaft, dropped her head and took him in her hot, sexy little mouth.

"Fucking hell," he groaned, threading his fingers into her hair, but realizing it was bound in a ponytail and quickly pulling it free of the elastic.

She bobbed up and down in his lap, taking him to the back of her throat, then pulling him nearly free, only to swipe her tongue over the crown and wiggle it into the sensitive hole at the top. Her hand continued to work him up and down, her saliva creating a lube that felt amazing as her fingers stroked him with ease.

He wanted to come down her throat so fucking bad, but he was also aching to be back inside her in other ways. If she let him come in her mouth, he would, then he'd tear off her pants and make her sit on his face, but he'd leave that up to her.

Some women stopped giving head before the guy came, while other women were more than happy to swallow. He wasn't sure where Mieka sat on that spectrum, but he'd be cool with whatever. The fact that she was willing to wrap her lips around his cock at all was incredible, and he wasn't going to be greedy.

After their time on the counter and he went to the bathroom to dispose of the condom, he'd also washed his cock and balls. It was just good manners. And he was extra glad that he did that, because what happened next nearly made him explode. She released his cock, dropped her head low, and took one of his hairless balls into her mouth, sucking gently and swirling her tongue around the sensitive globe. She switched to the other one at the same time, her free hand, the one with the cast, navigated between his legs, and two of her fingers pressed up hard on his perineum. Fucking hell, this woman knew what she was doing.

She sucked on and swirled her tongue around his balls a bit more, then released the left one with a wet pop before taking his cock back into her mouth. Still stroking him, she glanced up his torso. "I'm fine if you come."

Oh God, was the woman trying to make him fall in love with her? Because she was doing a bang-up job of it. He'd already been feeling things for her since she arrived—hell, since she came for the wedding—but after sucking his balls and telling him he could come in her mouth, she was making it almost impossible for him not to fall in love with her.

Tightening his grip on her hair and bucking his hips up into her face, he gently forced her to take him deeper. She didn't gag or balk and took him with ease. Her hand around his shaft picked up speed, and she pressed those two fingers harder into the space between his sac and asshole, then pulled him all the way out until her lips just encircled his crown. She sucked hard on the crown, pulling all the remaining blood he had in his body into the head until it throbbed, then she dropped her head one more time, shoving him to the back of her throat and he came.

It was a reflex to tighten his hold on her hair and thrust up into her face, but she didn't seem to care. He came hard down her throat, relishing every contraction as she swallowed him down, taking what he gave her, keeping his cockhead nestled and pulsing between her tonsils like they were giving his dick a little hug. He'd never experienced head like this before and he never wanted to experience anything different ever again.

When the warmth in his lower belly dissipated and his balls relaxed away from his body, she gave one final swipe of her tongue over his tip and pulled away slowly, releasing his cock from her mouth.

He heaved a heavy sigh, opened his eyes, and glanced at her.

She was grinning. It was like staring directly at the sun and he had to shield his eyes from how radiant she was. "Unbutton your pants, Minx, and climb onto my face."

Her smile grew even wider. She stood up, did as she was told, and carefully eased herself over his face, settling her sopping-wet pussy over his mouth.

"Here, kitty, kitty," he coaxed, which earned him a smack to the head that had him laughing.

"Not funny," she replied.

"It is a little bit," he retorted, cupping her ass cheeks to tip her forward a little more. "Just call me the cat whisperer." He dropped his voice low. "Oh, my pretty pink kitty. Such a stubborn little cat you are. Come to Dadd—"

"Dear God. Shut. Up!" Even though her words were harsh, her tone was anything but and she giggled at the end.

"Make me," he growled, flicking his tongue out when a drop of her sweetness fell on his upper lip.

"Oh, I'll make you all right." She sunk down lower. "Put your mouth to better use."

All humor went out the window and his balls twitched and cinched up against his body. "Just like that, baby," he murmured, swiping his tongue over his lip to gather up that droplet. "Sink down and smother me."

Again, she did as she was told and he immediately pushed his tongue into her channel to lap up her sweetness.

"Nate," she breathed, rocking against him.

"Just relax, babe. Let me show you how good life on the ranch—how good life with me—can be." Then he fucked her with his tongue and made her come twice.

Cuddled up on the floor after two of Mieka's orgasms and more wine, her head rested on his chest and he drew delicate swirls on her bare back. They still had a lot of work to do, and it wasn't even nine o'clock, but after how hard they'd worked that day, they deserved an extended coffee and sex break. "I'm sorry I didn't use a condom that night," he said, pressing a kiss to the top of her head. "And I'm so sorry you had to make that difficult decision alone, experience the nausea and fatigue of the first trimester, and go through that procedure–twice." It'd gutted him when the medical abortion didn't completely work and she had to have the D and C after all. But Mieka was a trooper through all of it. She let him help her, but he could tell it went against her nature. She wasn't used to asking for help. She was fiercely independent, crazy-strong willed and incredibly stubborn, which were all things he admired about her.

He was one-hundred percent all for women's body autonomy and freedom of choice. Mieka hadn't set out to get pregnant and have an abortion, but he understood why it was necessary that she did. She wasn't ready to be a mother and her future shouldn't be fucked up forever because of one mistake.

But he also knew that Mieka didn't come to her decision lightly. She'd said as much. She told him that she'd weighed her options for weeks before deciding that an abortion was right for her. It couldn't have been easy to go through that mental turmoil, and he hated that he'd put her through that.

After a long period of companionable silence where they just held each other, she turned her head and pressed a kiss over his heart. "It takes two people to get pregnant, Nate. We were both at fault. But thank you. It means a lot. I really do appreciate your support and that you never tried to convince me to keep it."

"Not my body, not my choice."

"I know, but ... I'd be lying if I said I hadn't considered your feelings and how this would affect you, too. Just because it's my body, doesn't mean what we accidentally made wasn't half you. Not that you ultimately had a say, but ... I was distraught over the whole thing for a while."

He hugged her tighter against him. "Besides Pasha, did you tell anyone?"

"Triss knows now. But no, just you and Pasha. I didn't want the girls on my dance team to find out because ..." She shrugged. "They're all nice, but they can be gossipy and judgmental. I was already the oldest on the team. A few of them are also from right-wing religious families and have made their stance on abortion *well* known. I just didn't need any more side-eyes coming my way because I got knocked up at a wedding by a sexy cowboy."

"Rancher."

"Right."

"Well, now we have condoms—"

"And I have an IUD, so we should be okay to continue with our—"

"Torrid affair." He flashed her a big smile at the same time he reached down and pinched her butt.

"Yes, our torrid affair. Without the risk of making another clump of cells." He lifted his hand in the air for a high-five. "To condoms and IUDs."

She rolled her eyes and shook her head. "I am *not* high-fiving you for that."

With a growl, he rolled over on top of her, pinning her beneath him. "Oh no? Well then how about a fuck masquerading as a high-five?" He had another erection, and it was poking into her thigh.

She lunged up and bit his lip. "Now that I can get on board with."

Chapter Fifteen

As much as Mieka enjoyed the multiple orgasms that Nate was providing her with, they did have work to do. So after they had sex again, she cracked the proverbial whip and told him to get back to work. She did the same, and they worked until just shy of midnight, setting up furniture, laying rugs and hanging pictures. Then they had a shower and collapsed exhausted into the big king-sized bed up in the loft. She passed out in a matter of seconds after her head hit the pillow. Nate vaped a bunch of pot right before he went to bed, because he said talking about the fire would keep him up.

The pot seemed to work, and he fell asleep beside her quickly, curling around her body and providing a solid warmth at her back for the rest of the night.

Since Nate was used to waking up at five in the morning, he was up with the birds, and back to putting together furniture, while Mieka slept in until just before six.

They finished the rest of the cabin, then Nate radioed Cal to meet them with the helicopter and they jumped on the ATV to head to the next cabin.

Rinse and repeat. They finished the second cabin just before ten o'clock at night, which left them with loads of time to break in the bed.

"Triss said that high sex is the best sex of her life," Mieka said, taking a bite of toast from their late dinner. She'd made them breakfast for dinner. Toast, bacon and eggs. Still no vegetables or fruit, but she just couldn't bring herself to open up one of those cans of stew and call that dinner.

"High sex is the best sex I've ever had, too," he said. "I mean, besides sex with you." His grin was super cheesy, but it melted her heart nevertheless. "So I can only imagine that high sex with you will make my balls explode right off my body."

"Well, that sounds terrifying." She sipped her wine. "And not at all pleasant."

"Triss packed a few lemonades for you if you'd rather that than smoke. We can take a wander down to the river, go for a swim."

"Isn't it freezing?"

"Probably. It's glacier fed, and it's only spring. But it reminds you that you're alive. Just remember the size my cock can get when it's warm and hard because I'm a bit of a turtler when I get cold."

She snorted so hard that the wine went up from her mouth into her nose and started to burn. "Oh my God!" She reached for a piece of paper towel. "Don't say stuff like that. At least not when I'm drinking." Her eyes were now watering, and she was pretty sure that liquid she felt running down her nostrils was wine. She dabbed the paper towel to her nose, and sure enough, it came back red with wine. "A turtler?"

"Yeah, you know, like shrinkage."

"I don't think our relationship is there yet."

He took a sip of his wine. "Sure it is. You sucked my balls and nearly suffocated me with your beaver, our relationship is there."

"My *beaver*?"

"Beaver, box, pussy. Whatever you want to call it." He snapped. "Oh right, it's your *stubborn cat!* I almost forgot."

She didn't know if she should laugh or cringe. She was a liberal, thin-filtered woman, but this was a new side to Nate that she wasn't sure she was on board with. Or at the very least, it was going to take a bit of getting used to. She couldn't deny how his crass and filthy side turned her on, though. She'd be lying if he asked her if her panties were bone-dry and she said yes.

"Finish up your toast and let's go for a walk. I brought headlamps so you don't eat it on the trail and break all those pretty teeth."

"I have a cast. I shouldn't be swimming."

"Just dip in your toes." He reached out and grabbed her big toe inside her socks and gave it a pinch. "Come on, it'll be fun."

The big, boyish smile on his ruggedly handsome face had her agreeing against her better judgment and before she knew it, she was holding Nate's hand, carefully making her way over rocks and roots, down the trail toward the gently babbling river below.

"It doesn't sound like a rushing river, so that's good," she said, tightening her grasp on his hand when the trail turned steeper.

"No, it's just a brook. But it's pretty full right now from the snowmelt."

Eventually, the path flattened out and they came to a small clearing with the river in front of them. The moon wasn't quite full, and its light filtered through the trees—most of which were just sporting small new leaves for the spring. The light of the moon reflected off the water, lending the entire area a romantic and beautiful glow that just filled Mieka's heart with all kinds of giddy joy.

"This is beautiful," she said, releasing his hand and stepping closer to the river. "It's like something out of a fairy tale."

The flicker of his electric lighter was no comparison for the blinding light of their headlamps as he lit the joint pinched between his lips. She turned off her headlamp, and he did the same. Suddenly it was just the lighter flame and the moon which only added to the ambiance and romance of it all.

"Except the hero in most fairy tales doesn't get super baked."

He snorted. "Only in the best fairy tales." He took a long pull of the joint and she watched as he exhaled the smoke out into the night air.

She could only really see it as it drifted past the moonlight that dappled through the trees.

"I brought your lemonade if you don't want this," he said, taking another pull off the joint, then keeping it between his lips as he reached into his back pocket and brought out the bottle of cannabis lemonade.

She smiled and accepted the bottle. "I think I'll go with this. When I smoke it burns my throat and makes me cough." She unscrewed the cap and took a tentative sip, then a bigger one. He'd grabbed a peach-flavored one for her and it absolutely hit the spot. She was a little achy after two days of being on her feet non-stop and helping Nate assemble furniture. Not to mention all the sex. That left her achy in the best kind of way. Actually, all her aches and pains were well-earned and made her buoyant with satisfaction. She was accomplishing a lot and having the best sex of her life.

"What's got you smiling like that?" he asked, coming toward her and wrapping his arms around her waist. "Thinking about my tongue and where I had it earlier?"

She put the cap back on her lemonade before looping her arms around his waist, too. "Among other things."

She waited for the kiss she knew was coming.

It came, and it took her breath away. He tasted like weed and bacon, but she didn't mind. The kiss deepened, but not to where they took their clothes off.

Once they broke their lip lock, he peeled away, finished the joint that he'd been keeping precariously tucked behind her back, then undressed.

"You were serious about going for a swim?" she asked, opening up her lemonade again and taking a sip.

"Dead serious," he said, dropping his jeans to the earth, followed by his boxers. His cock wasn't quite the granite-hard column of love she'd experienced earlier, but it wasn't a shriveled, over-cooked breakfast sausage, either. He was sitting at what she'd had ex-boyfriends affectionately refer to as *a half-chub*.

He pulled off his shoes and socks, then he was gloriously naked as he casually sauntered his fine ass over to the sandy beach that was below the grassy bank.

"It's the perfect swimming hole spot," he said. "Best one of the four cabins.

Each place has something unique about it. This one has the swimming hole, the first one has a few apple trees, the next one from here has a small waterfall, and of course, the one on the hill has the view and the sunset."

"I love that," she said, unable to pull her eyes from his butt. They were Krazy glued to his tight, round, full derriere. She was jealous of such a nice ass. Meanwhile, hers was flat as a pancake.

He turned around, smiled a cocky smile at her, then spun back around and dove in, disappearing into the inky black water that gurgled and bubbled lazily over the smooth rocks.

Where was he?

Fear crept up her spine like a demon's claw scrambling for purchase on the edge of a cliff, and she raced down to the sandy beach, searching the water for a sign of him.

"Nate!" she called out, about to run into the river after him, her cast be damned. But just as she lifted her foot to run into the water, he popped up like a porpoise, his skin glistening in the muted moonlight.

"You okay, Minx?" he asked, his smile cheeky as he sauntered toward her, dripping, chiseled and causing her heart to hammer against her chest hard enough to break a rib.

She exhaled, then shoved his shoulder when he got close enough. "I thought you'd been swept away, or drowned, or were attacked by rabid beavers or something." Shamelessly, her eyes drifted down his rippling torso to the patch of trimmed hair between his legs, and what was not at all "shriveled" or "turtled" in her opinion. Her eyes widened, and she swallowed.

"Just cooling off," he said, reaching for her hand. "I'm a strong swimmer, no need to worry about me. But I like that you were, anyway." His head dipped, and he brushed his mouth over hers in a searing but brief kiss. "You feeling that lemonade, yet?"

She hadn't been a second ago when she was overcome with fear for his life, but now that she'd calmed down a little and that viper between his legs looked like it was preparing to strike, she was feeling the lemonade. And it was making her feel pretty good.

Scraping her top teeth over her bottom lip, she looked up at him with her best sexy doe eyes. "I think I am." Her hand made its way down his wet torso, through the damp patch of wiry hair and she took his cock in her hand, stroking him and feeling him grow and get warmer with each brush of her fingers.

Nate growled, dropped his mouth to her neck, and nipped it softly. "Not here, Minx."

"Why? Are there cameras or wolves?"

He snorted, took her hand and led her over to where he'd neatly stashed his clothes. "You're a lady and you deserve to be spread out on a bed and worshipped, not forced to scramble for an orgasm on the cold, wet rocks." She could see his teeth from his wily smile, glimmer in the moonlight. "At least, not this time. But I would like to bend you over a hay bale or have you straddle me on a tractor." Grabbing his clothes, he kept a firm grip on her hand, and together they walked back toward the path.

He didn't seem to care a lick that he was naked, or that his feet were bare, and the fact that he didn't, that he was so comfortable in his own skin and being nude turned her on. Even though she knew she was fit and had no reason to be insecure about her figure, she still was.

She always compared herself to the other younger, tighter, prettier dancers who would join the team. Some of them had natural curves, great butts you could rest a glass of wine on like a shelf, and the most enviable cleavage imaginable. So when they were forced to strip down to nothing in the changing rooms between sets, Mieka felt the unfavorable tingles of inferiority and insecurity with her long legs, flat butt and barely-there chest.

To line her and her sisters all up in a row, she was definitely the odd one out. The other four had curves, tits, and asses, while Mieka often felt like a twelve-year-old boy. Gangly and long-limbed, but otherwise unremarkable.

They had to go single-file for a bit as they made their way up the hill and riverbank toward the cabin. But Mieka wasn't complaining, the tight butt in front of her was a welcomed view. She ached to reach out and bite it, but wasn't sure how that'd be received. It could also cause Nate to trip. Then he'd fall, injure himself, possibly take her down with him and they'd end up a heap of blood and bruises in the dirt, dark and in the middle of the woods.

She clamped her teeth together and let him lead her quietly with his bite-mark free butt back to the cabin.

Like the gentleman she didn't know he was, he used the hose outside to spray off his feet, then opened up the cabin door and before she could even blink, Nate had her thrown over his shoulder and he was hauling her up the ladder to the loft.

She landed on the bed gently, her body not bouncing at all since it was a memory foam mattress. Nate was already completely naked, so he made quick work of getting her to the same clothes-free state as he was, then he hovered over her. "Fuck, you're beautiful, Minx."

She shouldn't be so shallow as to smile as widely as she did at that comment, but she did. Him thinking that she was beautiful meant a lot, because she definitely didn't feel beautiful when in a line with her sisters, or in a line with the other dancers. She felt plain and flat and boring. She tossed on a confidence that she didn't feel inside when she was forced to interact with people, hoping that one day that confidence might actually be real, but so far, it wasn't. She felt like a phony, like an actress pretending to live this care-free life of travel and adventure while being confident and happy in her own skin.

His lips traveled down her jaw and neck, across her décolletage, down her sternum, across her belly and to her hip bone. He swept his tongue across her tattoo, leaving it tingling when his mouth continued south. Even though her body was on fire and every touch of Nate's skin to hers sent electric zaps of pleasure careening through her, the tear that slid down the corner of her eye into her ear was involuntary.

Like the trained SEAL that he was, Nate stopped, lifted his head and furrowed his brows. "Minx, what's wrong?"

She shook her head almost violently, swallowed and plastered on one of those fake smiles she'd mastered when dancing on stage and her period cramps were nearly unbearable. "Nothing."

He wasn't buying it. Propping himself up on his elbow, he shifted up the bed, still hovering over her so the tip of his cock bounced against her belly. He gave her a hard look that had her squirming and her insides twisting. "Don't lie to me, Minx. Something's wrong. What is it?"

Her bottom lip trembled, and she looked away at the same time another tear slid down the other side of her face into her other ear.

With a firm finger on her chin, he turned her to face him. "Look at me. What's wrong?"

She closed her eyes, but his deep, rumbly growl had her opening them once more. "You called me beautiful."

Mieka didn't think she'd ever seen a man look more confused than Nate did at that moment. It was like she'd just asked him to describe what the number eleven smelled like. "You're going to have to help me out a bit here, Minx. Is that a trigger word for you or something? Should I have not called you beautiful? Because ..."

Her head started to shake. "No, it's not that."

"Because you're not *just* beautiful. It's not like I'm only attracted to your looks. You're also really smart, and funny, and a talented dancer, quick-witted, stubborn, sweet and kind. I ... I'm sorry if it felt like I was focusing on your looks."

"It's not that at all," she heaved a big sigh, wedged her right hand between them and swept more tears from her eyes. "I just don't *feel* beautiful. So hearing it just, it just makes me feel good. Good enough to make me cry, apparently." She laughed awkwardly. "I'm sorry. I didn't mean to ruin the mood. Continue."

Nate snorted, rolled over to his side, rested his head in his hand while his elbow was propped up on the bed and he fixed her with a look that said, "We're not *continuing* until you explain yourself, you crazy woman."

Rolling her eyes, she shook her head dismissively. "It's stupid, really."

"Obviously not, if it upset you. Talk to me, Minx."

"Look at my sisters and how gorgeous they are."

"All the Young women are beautiful. I won't deny that. Despite your parents being weirdos with sticks up their asses, they've got good genes. What are you getting at?"

"Compared to those four, I'm the ugly duckling trapped in the middle of four beautiful swans."

"You're a dancer for crying out loud. A literal swan in Swan Lake." His brows pinched. "Have you done Swan Lake?"

She nodded.

"See? How on earth can you think you're any less stunning than your sisters? Have they said something?"

"No. Never. I mean, we all tease each other, and one thing they tease me about is my flat butt, but they've never called me ugly. I do have a ridiculously flat ass. Like, how I am even able to sit down is beyond me."

Nate wedged his hand beneath her and gave her right butt cheek a squeeze. "Seems like enough to hold on to in my opinion."

"Because I'm doing a lot of eating on this little escape from reality, and I'm not running."

"Then stop running and do something else." His shrug said he didn't understand why she did something that clearly brought her such little joy. To be honest, she couldn't understand it, either. She hated running. And yet, she'd done it every morning for years, because it kept her fit. It was a great way to start the morning to get all those cannoning thoughts in some semblance of order, and she was good at it.

"I also never felt beautiful next to the other dancers. So many of the new girls came with these gorgeous bodies with curves. Butts you could rest a coffee cup on and breasts that filled out a bikini nicely. I often have to buy my bathing suit tops in the youth section. They don't have ones small enough for me. Do you know how humiliating that is?"

At first, he thought he had all the answers to her problems, but she could see the uncertainty in how to "fix her" slipping from his eyes. "I can see how that would make you feel bad about yourself," he said after a moment. "I'm sorry you had to experience that."

He dropped his mouth to her nipple and sucked on the peak until it turned hard and red before letting it go with a wet *pop*.

"But for what it's worth, I'm not a tit-guy. I'm a leg-guy and you have amazing legs. Long and lean, muscular and strong. I've already told you that."

He reached down, lifted her leg from the hip and slowly slid his hand along the bottom, from her hamstring to her ankle and back up again, chasing the goosebumps, then bringing on an entirely new batch of them when he pressed a kiss to the inside of her knee.

"We're all built differently, Minx. Our bodies are miraculous and wonderful. They allow us to do such great things. Run and jump, dance and swim. Bring new life, enjoy delicious food, feel pleasure, feel pain. They're works of art, every single one of them, and yours is no exception." Rising up to his knees, he cradled her ankle in his big hand and slid the other hand up the front of her leg from shin to quad. "In fact, I happen to think you're one of the most unique and priceless masterpieces ever created."

Pouting, she cupped her tiny breasts together. "You're telling me you wouldn't like these to be bigger so you could ... I dunno, push your dick between them?"

Nate snorted. "You've got big full lips, a beautiful pussy and an ass I'm dying to sink into, I think I'm okay without tit-fucking you."

Not quite convinced, even by his crass compliments that left her pussy drenched, she stared down the length of her body at her non-existent breasts. "I've always wanted to get fake ones. Nothing outrageous, but like a modest C-cup or something. Just enough to add some curves to my figure and fill out a T-shirt. But I couldn't risk the recovery time and taking time off from work. But now that I'm jobless ..."

"If that's what you need to help with your self-esteem, baby, then go for it, but I don't think you *need* to get them done. Breasts aren't what make you beautiful." He pressed his finger gently against her chest. "It's what's in here that makes you beautiful, and Minx, you've got a gorgeous heart." He moved his finger down her torso, over her hip and to her thigh. "You've also got incredible legs." Leaning forward, he gently nipped the top of her thigh.

How did she wind up so lucky as to find this man? She could count on one finger the number of guys she'd been with that hadn't asked her at some point if she'd ever considered getting implants. And that one guy was Nate. Every other man had in some way mentioned to her the size of her breasts.

"*Totally your choice, babe, of course, but like, have you ever thought about implants? It's just a question. I'm just curious. Why are you looking at me like that?*"

That was pretty much how it went down every single time.

Not with Nate, though. Nate genuinely didn't care whether she filled out a bra or had beestings for tits.

"Why are you so good to me?" she said through a tight throat. There were those tears again. She refused to let them fall, though. Not anymore. She was done crying over the fact that she didn't find herself to be beautiful and men wanted her to change her body—for them. If she was going to change her body, it would be for her and her alone. Besides, she was ruining the mood and she and Nate could be doing far better things with their growing high and their time.

"Good people deserve goodness," he said, surging forward so he was back above her, his cockhead once again knocking her belly. "And you're a good person." His lips brushed hers. "You high?"

She nodded. It didn't take much to get her feeling good in the head. She hadn't done cannabis in such a long time that half a bottle of the lemonade—so just a few sips—and she was cruising at an altitude of ten-thousand-feet on a magic carpet made of cotton candy. "You?"

"A little," he said, nuzzling her jaw. "Tell me where you want me. What's going to make you feel amazing? My cock? My tongue? My fingers? Tell me how to make your stubborn cat purr, Minx."

Again, she could count on one finger the number of men who had ever asked her that. And that one man was Nate. He cared about what *she* wanted and didn't just use her for his own pleasure, *hoping* she found some of her own in the process.

It really wasn't that hard to be a considerate lover, or good in bed, and yet, so many men she'd met and been with just didn't give a crap. Their orgasm was the only orgasm that mattered. She could have been a fleshlight for all they cared.

Quickly, though, she shoved those depressing thoughts out of her head because there was a man very dedicated to her pleasure, who found her beautiful and smart and interesting, waiting for her to tell him where to touch her.

"Decisions, decisions," she murmured, smiling when he dropped his head and scraped his teeth, then his stubble over one of her nipples, then the other.

"You can have it all, too. Start with one, move on to the other, and finish with your favorite."

"I can't decide. I love them all." The pot was taking its effect now and every touch of his skin to hers sent ribbons of pleasure dancing through her. All her nerve endings were awake, paying attention and hyper-sensitive. She loved it.

She'd heard some of the other dancers talking about how amazing sex when high on ecstasy was, but she'd never indulged in that. If it was anything like how she felt now though, she understood the appeal.

But she didn't touch drugs when she was abroad. The stories she'd heard about foreigners being carted off to jail for a hundred years or whatever for possession of a controlled substance was enough to make her question whether she should even carry Midol in her purse.

Trailing his fingers down her body, while continuing to torture her nipples in the best kind of way, he circled her clit with his index finger, pulling wetness from her center. Her hips leaped off the bed and he chuckled as he pulled her nipple into his mouth and sucked. Pushing two fingers into her channel, his thumb pressed her clit, and she was pretty sure she blacked out for half a second.

She squeezed her muscles around his fingers, bucking her hips up and moaning when he pressed up hard on her G-spot.

"Dear God, Nate," she crooned when he scraped his whiskery chin across her chest to her other breast, rubbed the stubble over her tight, hard nipple, then pulled it into his mouth.

"How many times can we make you come, Minx?"

"I don't know," she breathed, her hands coming up to grip the sides of the pillow. "I might black out after one. Good God, this is incredible."

Scissoring his fingers back and forth inside her, while his thumb wiggled over her clit and his mouth and chin played with her nipples, Mieka was close to combusting. And yet, she could also stave off the orgasm better than she'd ever been able to before. She was able to ride that delicious paper-thin edge of pure pleasure for much longer than she'd ever been able to in the past. Normally, when that tipping point came, she couldn't control herself from tumbling over. No matter how much she metaphorically windmilled her arms to stay up on the ledge, she would inevitably fall forward, off the cliff and into the full-on climax.

But not tonight. Not now. It had to be the weed. Or a combination of the weed and Nate. But either way, she'd never edged like this before and it was amazing.

She could enjoy the journey longer, experience more pleasure, let it build slower and stronger until she felt it in every cell of her body.

Nate lifted his head from her breast for a moment and brought it to her ear, biting the lobe before whispering, "I want to hear you come, Minx. I want you to squeeze my fingers in your tight little pussy. Then I'm going to put my mouth on you and make you come again before I finally slide inside you and we come together." Then he dropped his mouth back to her breast, scraped his scruff over the nipple and she finally, at long last, came.

And holy hell, did she ever come.

The orgasm was never ending. It started off strong and just kept going, building to a decadent crescendo that had her seeing stars, smelling colors, and hearing numbers. Or maybe those were angels and harps, she couldn't tell. The backside of the mountain was long and luxurious as her legs trembled and her body shook with the strong aftershocks. Pleasure seeped into every fiber of her body, every fingertip, every toe.

With a sigh of pure, unadulterated contentment, she relaxed into the bed and released her death grip on the pillow. Another rush of pleasure spun through her briefly when Nate removed his fingers from her and released her nipple from his mouth.

"God, you come so beautifully, Minx. The sighs and the moans, the calls to a higher power." His chuckle was dark and deep and made her pulsing pussy clench.

Wasting no time, he slid down her body and his mouth was on her, giving her not even a moment of reprieve to gather the scattered pieces of her soul before he was sucking on her clit and pulling another orgasm from her.

"High sex is the best sex," Mieka said after that second world-rocking orgasm and Nate climbed back up on the bed, flopping to his back beside her. "Or maybe it's just you." She paused for a moment to give it some thought. "No, it's the pot and you. Sex with you is the best I've ever had, but high sex with you is better than sober sex with you."

He snorted, reached for her and hauled her over him so she straddled him, sitting up. The steel column of his cock rested against his belly, a dewy bead of precum glistening on the tip. She licked her lips, picked up his shaft and swept her thumb over the top, then stuck it in her mouth, sucking off the salty tang of his cum.

His dark blue eyes flared for just a moment before dropping to half-mast. Heat and need burned behind those blue orbs as he raked them up and down her body. His hands followed, and he cupped her breasts, then slid his hands to her hips and lifted her up slightly.

But they both must have realized the same thing at the same time, and he plunked her back on his lap. "Condom, right? I nearly forgot."

"Me, too," she whispered, clambering off him and to her duffle bag. She found the little foil packet and climbed back onto the bed to straddle him once more. "Shall I do the honors?"

He grinned. "Let's see your mad skills, woman."

Snorting, she tore the packet open, pulled out the condom and carefully rolled it over his length, pinching the tip and making sure it was secure at the base. He double-checked her work, but nodded in approval. "Good job. That was hot."

With a big smile, she pushed up onto her knees, hovering over him as he tilted his cock up. She lifted up a little more until they were aligned, then sank down slowly, squeezing him inch by inch as she took him inside her.

"Fucking hell," he exhaled. "That feels so good."

All she could do was nod and bite her lip. She was still tingling all over from her last two orgasms, and with Nate inside her, she knew this next climax was probably going to kill her—at least for a second or two.

"Minx," he murmured, finding her hips with his hands and encouraging her to start moving. "So fucking beautiful. Honestly. I haven't been able to get you out of my head since last summer."

She'd be lying if she said she hadn't thought of him several times since last summer, either. Including when she was with other men. Even though their first time together had been sloppy, drunk and difficult to remember, it wasn't the sex that made her think fondly of Nate.

It was everything else.

The way they bantered and joked. How flirtatious he was, and that when she was around him, she genuinely felt beautiful inside and out. He really listened and seemed to care about what she had to say. And now that she was getting to know him even better, learn what made him tick and what scared the crap out of him (snakes and fire) it just made her think about him even more.

Bending over, she pressed her mouth to the side of his jaw, then his cheek and finally his mouth, tasting her own release on his lips. He wedged his tongue between their lips and tangled it with hers as she began to rock back and forth, allowing him to really fill her and for her to feel every inch of him.

The scrape of his lower belly against her clit was going to throw her hard and fast to the top of the cliff again, but she didn't care. She knew the weed could let her edge, so she just let her body do its thing, welcoming all the pleasure that Nate gave her.

Reaching behind her with one hand, he found her crease with his finger, then slid that finger down lower, gathering some of her arousal before trailing it back up to her puckered hole. Nate broke the kiss and asked for consent with lifted brows.

She nodded and carefully, he pushed one finger and then a second into her anus.

"Oh God!" she dropped her forehead to his shoulder and continued to move, feeling his cock inside her and now his fingers, as well. As much as she thought she could edge into infinity, that wasn't going to happen. Nate was pushing her harder and harder to that sweet leap into oblivion. His hips lifted and his fingers plunged. He drove into her deeper, and rubbed harder against her clit, making her body sing.

"Look at me, Minx," he ordered, releasing her hip with his other hand and bringing a knuckle under her chin, encouraging her to lift her head. She didn't sit up, but stayed hovering over him. It wasn't easy with her one casted arm, but she could manage for a little while longer. "You are so fucking gorgeous, Mieka. Never forget that. Inside and out you're the most beautiful woman I've ever met … but when you come, fucking hell." He rolled his head on the pillow before refocusing his gaze on her. "Exquisite. You're an absolute goddess."

Removing that knuckle from under her chin, he wedged it between their bodies until he found her clit.

"Are you going to come for me, Minx?"

She nodded.

"Are you going to come hard?"

She nodded again, whimpering slightly when he started to rub evocative little circles around her clit. Their eyes locked. She was so close. The way she was grinding against him was growing more erratic. Everything just felt so good.

"Come for me, Minx." He pinched her clit and her entire body detonated. She closed her eyes, but his order of "Open your eyes," had her flaring them open again and pinning them on him.

His gaze was heated and blue flames danced in his eyes as she came undone around him. Wave after beautiful wave crashed through her from her core outward until her fingertips tingled and her toes curled.

She vaguely recalled him pulling his fingers from her ass as he released her clit and found his own release. Their eyes stayed locked and as weird as it was, it was also really hot. The way his chest rose and fell frantically, his feral grunts and growls and that last big hip lift that nearly sent her crashing to the floor. It was all so ... wild. And she was here for it. She was here for all of it, and she wanted more. More tonight. More tomorrow. More next week and next month. She never wanted this feeling with Nate to end.

After he finished pulsing inside of her and she knew he was done and she was done, she carefully slid off him, feeling instant relief in her casted arm. He removed the condom, climbed off the bed, and took the ladder to get to the bathroom. He was gone for a long time, so at first, she thought he was having a shower, until she heard the bathroom door open and the tub running. "I ran you a bath, Minx. Come on down."

Her smile was idiot-big as she climbed down the ladder. No man had ever run her a bath before. She was giddy and hopped down the last rung straight into Nate's waiting arms. He carried her the rest of the way into the bathroom where LED candles (that she had ordered for décor) were set up on the windowsill next to the free-standing soaking tub. It was beautiful and perfect. He placed her gently in the tub, making sure to keep her cast out and resting it on a hand towel.

"You're not going to get in with me?" she asked, giving him a big dramatic pout.

"Won't fit me and you, Minx. As much as I'd love to. But you enjoy." Then he bent down, kissed her on the lips softly, and turned to go.

"Thank you, Nate," she called after him, settling into the warmth and bubbles.

"I'd do anything for you, Minx," he said before closing the door and leaving her with her warm bubbly bath, LED candles and a heart so confused it wasn't sure whether to beat or break.

Chapter Sixteen

By the time Mieka got out of the bath, the water was cool and her fingers resembled raisins. Nate helped her out so that she didn't slip and fall and get her cast wet, then he wrapped her up in a big towel, gave her a big glass of water and the two of them retired up to the loft where Mieka promptly fell asleep.

They finished up everything at the second cabin that morning, then raced ahead to the third cabin to meet Cal with the helicopter.

Rinse and repeat.

Assembling furniture, decorating, setting up house, a vegetable-free dinner, a stroll to the waterfall while consuming the drug of amazing orgasms, experiencing those amazing orgasms followed by a deep, dreamless sleep wrapped up in Nate's arms.

Then they made their way to the final cabin on the hill the next day where Cal met them with the last crate. He even found a spot to land his helicopter and came to join them.

"Cal, this is Mieka, Triss's sister," Nate said as they watched the big, broad-shouldered man with the dark red hair amble his way up the hill from where he'd landed it in the field.

Cal held out a tanned hand scattered with freckles and scars, and Mieka took it, grateful that he didn't give her a limp handshake because she was a woman. His hand was just as calloused as Nate's but she didn't mind. "Pleased to meet you, Mieka." Cal propped his hands on his hips after releasing Mieka's hand and gauged the cabin. "How'd setup on the other three go?"

"Pretty good. We're going to stop at the first one on our way back and stock it up with linens, but otherwise, everything is ready for guests, right, Minx?" Nate asked, bumping her shoulder playfully.

"I think so." She shielded her eyes from the sun and took in the vastness of her surroundings. Fields and hills, mountains and forests. It was breathtaking and made her problems feel so small and insignificant in comparison to how big and miraculous the world was.

"Need a hand unloading?" Cal asked, following Nate over to the crate where he used the crowbar in his hand to pry open the box.

"Can always use another set of hands," Nate replied as he got the crate open and started hauling out boxes of furniture.

The three of them worked quickly and smoothly. Cal stuck around to help assemble furniture and before Mieka knew it, they were done.

"Wow!" she said as the three of them sat on the hill staring out at the winding river below. Cal had packed a cooler with beer in it and ran to get it from his helicopter once they were finished. Now they were all enjoying a cold San Camanez lager after a hard but accomplished day's work. "That went way faster with three sets of hands." She turned to Nate. "Do we have time to head back to the house before dark?"

He shook his head. "Not the house, no, but we could probably make it to the first cabin before dark if you wanted to."

She shook her head and smiled. She wasn't ready to return to reality. She loved playing house with Nate where they could wander around naked, even outside, if they wanted to and not worry about being spotted by anyone. Not that she had, but he certainly did and she wasn't about to ask him to put his clothes on anytime soon.

The smile that met hers warmed her heart to a startling temperature. "Me either. We'll stay the night here, then head out in the morning."

"I'm not a fan of flying in the dark if I can help it," Cal said, standing up with a bit of a grunt. "I'm going to head home, but I'll pop 'round the ranch soon for a beer and a bullshit with you and Ash." He slapped Nate on the shoulder affectionately, smiled warmly at Mieka, then stalked down the hill toward his shiny black bird.

"He seems nice," Mieka said, taking a sip of her beer. It wasn't her beverage of choice, but after a busy day like today, it surprisingly hit the spot.

"Salt of the fucking earth, that guy," Nate said, not looking at her, but rather propping his forearms on his knees and staring out at the field below. The sun had already set, but hints of orange, yellow and pink still lingered in the sky along the ridges of the hills. "I would trust Cal—any of my brothers really—with my life. I'm glad he moved here. Not sure it's for him, but he seems happy."

"What makes you say you're not sure it's for him?" And more importantly, what made him think that this *was* the place for her?

He shrugged a big, muscly shoulder. "Guy never sits still in one place for long. He gets restless. Flies his chopper to a new town, sets up camp for a few months, maybe a year, then picks up and leaves again when he feels like it. I don't know if a city would be better for him or not, but I'm not sure he'll stick around here long enough to put down roots." He took a pull of his beer and shrugged again. "Then again, I've been wrong about shit before. Maybe he'll settle down. Find a nice woman and call this place home. It'd be nice to have more friends around."

She stared at his profile for a moment, studying the length of his nose, the definition of his cheekbones, his strong jaw and chin. She'd never noticed it before, but from the side she was looking at him on, his nose appeared a little crooked. She liked it. It added to his character.

"How'd you break your nose?" she asked after a moment of silence passed between them.

Nate snorted and took another sip of his beer. "Ash decked me. We were fifteen. I ran my mouth. Can't remember what it was about, honestly. But he got pissed off and decked me, broke my nose." His eyes bugged out. "Blood was everywhere. Our mother was furious. Kicked us both out of the house until dark for ruining her nice new rug."

Mieka smiled. "Did you two get into a lot of trouble growing up?"

That same shoulder lifted again. "No more than most boys, I imagine. Nothing illegal ..." He scratched his chin. "I don't think. Just stupid shit. I tried to ride two goats like water skis. Tore my taint and groin muscle. Nearly ripped my body in half." He dropped his knees and closed his legs. "I can still feel that one when I think about it too much. The stitches ... the recovery. That was probably the stupidest thing I've ever done. Nearly rendered myself a eunuch."

Mieka giggled even though she knew she probably shouldn't, but it was a funny story. She could just imagine a young Nate thinking he could ride goats like water skis, only to be horribly surprised that goats had minds of their own and didn't run next to each other.

"You think that's funny woman?" he asked with a growl that woke up the butterflies in her belly along with a hoard of horny hornets. He finished his beer, set it down on the grass and before she knew it, he was covering her.

Still giggling, she set her own beer down and looped her arms around his neck, blinking up at him. "I do, yeah. But I'm also really glad that you're not a eunuch."

He huffed a laugh and nuzzled his nose against her cheek. "Yeah, me, too."

Grinding himself against her, she lifted her hips up to feel his hardening length pressing into her thigh.

"I'm glad we're staying one more night out here," he said. "I like this time with you. Just the two of us."

She blinked and swallowed past a growing tightness in her throat. "Yeah, me, too." Wedging her right hand between them, she found his button and zipper, unfastened them, then pushed her hand beneath the waistband of his jeans and boxers.

"Minx," he purred, thrusting his hot length up into her hand. "We don't have to. Not out here anyway."

"You mean in the wide-open world under the puffy clouds?" she asked. "I think we really do have to. We can't come all the way out here to this paradise and only have sex in a bed."

"Well, there was the ladder, the counter, the floor ..."

"The ATV this morning," she reminded him, biting her lip at the memory of that hot, impromptu pit-stop they made on their way to the final cabin. The rumble of the ATV, combined with the friction of her crotch right against Nate's butt had warmed her up enough that while they were driving, she started to stroke him. He then stopped the ATV abruptly, hauled her around so she was straddling him on the vehicle and they had a wild quickie right in the middle of the woods.

"That was fun," he replied, scraping his scruff against her jaw.

She stroked him and bit his lip. "I have a condom in my pocket."

"Oh, you little minx, you think of everything. Did you plan this?"

Shaking her head, she smiled as he raked his teeth against her jaw. "Need to always be prepared when it comes to you." She stroked him a few more times, then they divested themselves of their pants. He laid his jeans and hers beneath her so she wasn't laying directly on the itchy grass, then he slid the condom on and was inside her.

They made love under the emerging stars and even though they'd only each had a beer and were essentially stone-cold sober, Mieka could say without a doubt that was the best sex of her life. Because it was with Nate, and when she was with Nate, she felt cherished, desired and beautiful. And that was a feeling that could never be mimicked by any kind of drug. Nate *was* her drug. And he was becoming pretty damn addictive.

As reluctant as he was to return to the ranch and reality, Nate knew he needed to get back and help his brother. They were gearing up for their busiest season to date with the cabins, the petting farm and more foals and horses than ever before. It was mid-day the next day when they returned to the ranch and as he expected, the parking lot was full and people were everywhere. The petting farm was officially open seven days a week until Labor Day. So they needed to make sure to keep Bruno in check so he didn't get run over by a speed demon soccer mom in a Dodge Caravan.

He parked the ATV in the shed beside the other ATV and the two snowmobiles, then helped Mieka climb off behind him before grabbing their bags from the trailer.

"Back to the real world," he said with a sigh and a heavy heart as she held open the door for him since his arms were loaded with their bags and the cooler. Last night their rations had been pretty low, so he convinced Mieka to finally try one of his canned stews. She choked it back, but told him to never serve her that again.

They made their way across the yard, nodding and acknowledging ranch hands as they went, and dodging families who were trying to find a parking space.

"Hey, buddy," Nate said, stopping next to a man who was smoking beside a small lean-to shed with a shake roof and shake siding. "You can't smoke here. The entire property is a smoke-free zone. Please put it out."

The man was probably in his late sixties with a grizzled appearance, thinning gray hair and a knobby nose. He squinted at Nate through his big thick glasses then dropped his cigarette butt to the ground and crushed it with his shoe. "Happy?" he asked, his tone dripping with sarcasm.

"Thanks, man," Nate said, ignoring the man's irritation. "Appreciate it. Enjoy your day." They continued on their way toward the house and Nate sidled up closer to Mieka. "Smokers piss me off. They think just because the tubes are made of paper and the tobacco is a plant that dropping their butts on the ground isn't fucking littering. It totally is. Plus, the goats eat the butts and then I've got nicotine addicted goats who need a Nicoderm patch."

Mieka snorted. "Have you actually had to do that?"

"No. But you know what I mean." They took the steps up to the farmhouse and once again she opened the door for him so he could lug all their stuff inside.

Asher and Triss were sitting at the kitchen table enjoying lunch, but both their eyes perked up.

"About time you two showed up. How're the cabins?" Triss asked, standing up from the table and taking her dishes to the sink. Asher was just finishing his sandwich, but lifted a chin at his brother in acknowledgment.

"Ready to make us a bunch of money," Mieka said, beaming as she took a seat at the table and thanked Triss for the coffee she brought over.

Nate did the same and nearly came in his jeans from how good the coffee tasted. They'd run out of coffee yesterday morning, so today they were running purely on fumes and adrenaline from leftover orgasms.

"I'm excited to see the finished products," Triss said. "You took pictures, right?"

"Loads," Mieka agreed. "So we can update the website and really draw people in. Rugged luxury is what I think we should advertise it as."

"I like that," Asher agreed, sipping his coffee. "Fits the brand and what we're striving for perfectly."

"You guys hungry?" Triss asked. "I made chicken parmesan last night and I made us both chicken parm sandwiches just now. Plenty left."

"I'd love one," Mieka and Nate both said at the same time, grinning like idiots who'd spent the last four days having copious amounts of wild sex. Because that's exactly what they did and he wouldn't regret a second of it, even if she did leave him broken hearted and took off to only God knew where when her arm was finally healed.

Triss made them both sandwiches and the four of them sat there and chatted about what went on at the ranch while Nate and Mieka were away, and how the set up of the cabins went. Nate was just licking the marinara sauce off his thumb when Hank came bursting through the front door. "FIRE!"

Nate and Asher both stood up so abruptly that their chairs toppled over. They ran after Hank out of the house and down the steps. Mieka and Triss were hot on their tail.

"Oh my God!" Triss exclaimed as they all came up on the same lean-to that they'd passed not too long ago and big orange flames licked up the sides of it and out the window.

Nate would bet his left nut that it was the same fucking smoker from before that lit up as soon as Nate was in the house, then he tossed his butt and it caught fire on the grass next to the shed. White-hot tendrils of fear—and anger—began to worm their way through his body as smoke billowed out of the gaps in the shake roof.

People were being ushered out to the muster point in the far field by Ronny and Ray, while other ranch hands were getting the animals out of the barn since the lean-to was right next to the barn and the wind was blowing in the perfect direction. If a spark leaped from the shed it'd land right on the barn.

Asher had run to get the big hose from the side of the barn and was dragging it over. Another ranch hand turned the knob and Asher started to spray, but it wasn't doing enough.

Ruff. Ruff.

Nate froze, then spun around. "Bruno!" he hollered. "Bruno!"

Ruff. Ruff.

Fuck, no. Please no.

The dog hadn't come to greet them when they arrived. He should have known something was up. How the fuck did he get in the shed and why was the door closed?

Ruff. Ruff. Ruff. Ruff.

Asher was still spraying the lean-to at the base of the flames while Nate swallowed his fear as best he could and ran toward the engulfed shack.

Ruff. Ruff. Ruff.

Bruno began to whimper and scratch at the interior walls. Nate's fear quadrupled inside his chest as his heart hammered against his ribcage, threatening to shatter all the bones. "It's okay, buddy!" he called through the door. He reached for the brass handle, but immediately pulled his hand away again when it was scalding to the touch. They used this shed as extra storage for various things like rakes, buckets and bags of goat and horse food they sold to those visiting the petting farm. The wind had probably blown the door shut, that happened pretty often if it was left open. And Bruno was always getting into places he shouldn't.

Asher continued spraying the lean-to, but the flames were still flying and Nate watched as sparks jumped from the roof into the sky and landed precariously close to the barn.

He tore off his flannel, wrapped it around his hand and reached for the door handle again, but before he could grab it, he was shoved out of the way.

"I got it, it's okay," Mieka said, opening the door with her gardening glove-covered hand. "Step back, Nate." Smoke flowed out of the open door like a dam in hell had just exploded. She had a rag tied over her face and construction goggles on. Where the hell did she find goggles? Then before Nate could tell her not to, she ran into the lean-to.

"Mieka, NO!"

But she was already inside. A second later, she came out, carrying a passed-out

Bruno in her arms. She took him far away from the shed and rested him on the ground on his right side. She pulled the rag away from her mouth and the goggles from her eyes, then placed her mouth over the dog's nose, blowing into it. "Come on, Bruno. Come on, buddy."

Hank had dragged a second hose from around the far side of the barn and now they had two water sources working to put out the fire. Finally, they were making some headway and the flames and smoke were beginning to dissipate.

But Nate wasn't really paying attention to that, he was focused on Bruno and Mieka.

The dog's body remained still. His chest wasn't moving.

Terror dug villainous talons into Nate's heart as he watched Mieka perform CPR on the dog, then cover his nose again with her mouth and breathed.

She did the whole thing again twice more, with dread and despair filling the cavities of Nate's chest with each passing second, then suddenly, Bruno's legs twitched, his eyes opened and he struggled to sit up so he was no longer on his side.

"Oh thank God," Mieka said, sitting back on her heels as Bruno got to his feet and went to lick her face. He was a crazy-smart dog—if not a bit of a delinquent when he was bored. He knew who'd saved him.

The dog's different-colored eyes swiveled to Nate briefly before focusing back on Mieka, his tail wagging.

He gave Nate no time of day because he knew Nate had chickened out. Nate had hesitated, but Mieka didn't hesitate at all. She went into the fire, ready to rescue.

What on earth possessed her to do that?

"Good boy," Mieka praised, reciprocating Bruno's affection and kissing his head. "What were you doing in that shed, Bruno?"

Triss ran over carrying a small oxygen tank and mask that she retrieved from the office. They needed it for insurance purposes because they ran a business. The same with a defibrillator, first-aid kit and a spine board. Nate, Asher, Triss and all the ranch hands were up-to-date on their human and animal first-aid, but all of that flew out the window for Nate when he saw the flames, apparently.

"Does he need this?" Triss asked, sliding down to her knees and holding out the oxygen mask.

Mieka held Bruno and placed the mask over his nose, but the dog shook his head trying to dislodge the mask. Eventually, she gave up. "I think he's okay?"

"I'll call Jacob and have him come take a look," Triss said, pulling out her phone and standing up again.

Bruno finally left Mieka alone and trotted over to Nate, licking his face, as well, and rubbing his body against Nate's legs. "Hey, buddy," Nate said, tears pricking his eyes. "You gave us quite a scare." He rubbed the dog's fur affectionately and swallowed past the lump in his throat.

Scratching behind the dog's ears, Nate glanced behind him to where Hank and Asher were still spraying the shed, even though no more flames or smoke seeped out.

"Thank fuck," Nate murmured, kissing a smoky-smelling Bruno on the head. "Thank fuck you're okay, buddy."

He made sure Bruno stayed with Mieka before he stood up and went to check on the charred remains of the lean-to as the black, burned wood dripped and steamed.

"What do you think happened?" Hank asked, releasing his finger from the trigger on the spray nozzle.

"I bet it was that fucker smoking," Nate murmured, enjoying the way rage replaced the fear inside his heart and the heat that encompassed it. He spun around and stalked back over to Mieka, placing his hands on either side of her face. "What the hell were you thinking?" His forehead pressed against hers. "You could have died."

"But I didn't," she said, her hands making their way to his hips. "And you shouldn't have had to run in there. That's a fear you shouldn't *have* to face. Not like that anyway."

He shook his head and pinched his eyes shut as his brain wrestled with all the colliding emotions threatening to bury him alive.

"How did you know what to do?"

"I remembered what you did when Chance was born and not breathing, I figured it was pretty much the same for a dog. And I saw the gardening gloves and goggles hanging up in the main barn a few days ago when I was visiting the horses. Not sure why you need goggles, but I'm glad they were there."

Fuck, this woman was something special. Something amazing.

"You could have died," he said again. "I could have lost you."

Her eyes flared, helping him realize what he'd just said. He released her head and spun around, breaking into a jog as he made his way around the barn to the muster point in the field.

It was easy enough to locate the fucker, since he'd lit right back up and was standing away from the majority of the crowd, sucking on another fucking cigarette. Nate didn't stop and he just ran right up to the guy and punched him with a hard right-hook clear in the jaw.

The man fell backward into the grass, but somehow managed to keep his smoke between his fingers. "What the—"

But Nate was already on top of him, sitting on the man's barrel of a stomach, straddling him. He was about to hit him again, but hands came up under his arms and hauled him off the bloody-faced man.

"Nate! For fuck's sake, Nate stop!" Asher yelled, his voice barely breaking through the ringing in Nate's ears.

Asher gripped him by the shoulders and shook him. "What the fuck is wrong with you?"

"It was this motherfucker. I caught him smoking, told him to put it out, that we're a non-smoking business. I know it was him. There is no other explanation. He tossed his fucking butts on the ground and nearly set the whole ranch on fire. Nearly killed my dog. Could have killed the woman I lo—"

Asher released him and spun to face the guy who was still on the ground.

Then that stupid son-of-a-bitch had the audacity to put his still lit cigarette back in his mouth and inhale. His face dripped with blood, and yet he still smoked. Right in front of everyone.

"Don't think I'm not going to sue the fucking pants off both of you," he said between coughing fits. "I fought hard for this country so we could have the freedom to smoke where we want and when we want. So you silver-spooned little pussies could have a life like this."

Asher reached into the collar of his shirt and pulled out his dog tags, shaking them toward the man. "We fought, too, you fuckwad. Every single man who works here did. So shut your fucking face and get the fuck off my property."

"Gonna sue the pants off this place," the man murmured, struggling to get up in between more coughing fits.

Mieka marched forward, plopped her hands on her hips and tipped her chin up. "Just try, buddy. The non-smoking signs are everywhere. As are cameras. And there are enough witnesses here, with their phones out that you won't have a leg to fucking stand on in court. You put every person here, including your family, and every animal in danger with your recklessness."

"What are you, their lawyer?" the man on the ground asked with a snarl.

"Not *their* lawyer, but I am *a* lawyer, and I'll happily represent them for free if necessary." She glanced back at Triss, Asher and Nate and smiled. "Family discount and all that."

What the hell was she going on about? She wasn't a lawyer.

And was it illegal to impersonate one like it was a police officer?

The thought of losing the ranch because this fucker decided to sue them sent Nate's head spinning, but the fact that for the second time in less than five minutes, Mieka was saving them, had the spots from Nate's vision disappearing.

Nobody helped the smoking guy up, but Asher did walk over, pulled the cigarette with a long stalk of ash from his yellow fingers and crushed it beneath his boot. Then he dug a small hole and buried it so none of the animals accidentally ate it.

Normally, it was Asher with the hot temper, but the fire combined with nearly losing Bruno, and Mieka running into the shack for him, it was all just too much and Nate had lost his cool.

It was nice to see Asher take the hot-head-helm again and grab the old guy by the collar and escort him—and his family, yeah, he was there with his grand-children and wife—to their vehicle. Then he followed them down the laneway in his truck to make sure they were good and gone, while Nate sat on the front steps of the house stewing in his own mental anguish.

Mieka was with Triss and the two of them were helping calm down guests and let them know they could return to the petting pens. They also started to lead the animals back into the pens and barns along with the ranch hands. The entire time Bruno was right on Mieka's heels. He was her furry shadow, never letting her out of his sight, let alone more than two feet away. If she stood still for too long, Bruno sat right on her feet. She took it all in stride, laughing at the goofy dog now made of super glue, and smiling at guests.

Her warm, inviting demeanor put everyone at ease and soon things were back to normal, as if nothing had caught fire and Nate hadn't nearly put his fist through a man's face.

Still sitting on the porch, Nate watched his brother lumber toward him, his hands in the pockets of his jeans, eyes scanning the property as cars full of families came and went. Asher sat down next to Nate. "That was something," he finally said, after a long tense minute of silence.

"Yeah," Nate exhaled. "It was."

Every year since they'd opened the ranch, they added something new to the property or business. Something else to make them money. Last summer it had been Triss's clinic, this summer it was the cabins. Next summer, who knows? But with those additional income streams came more stress, and more respon-sibility. They had to hire more people, get more insurance and as successful as the place was, the responsibility of it all could, at times, be crushing.

Asher had a soft place to land at the end of each day—Triss. Nate had nobody.

Nate had no one to bury himself in or a caring and patient shoulder to lay his head on and forget the stress and responsibility of this demanding job. At least not a permanent place. Mieka was here—for now. But as much fun as they were having and as much as he thought she was perfect for this life, he wasn't so sure he'd done enough to convince her of that.

"So you love her?" Asher said, breaking through Nate's plaguing thoughts as he stared blankly at a leaf on the gravel.

Nate's shoulders slumped and finally, he nodded. "I think so."

Asher blew out a breath. "That's a lot."

"It is."

"Does she know?"

"I think so, but I don't know if it'll be enough to keep her here."

They weren't looking at each other, but Nate could see out of the corner of his eye that Asher was shaking his head. "Bro, that's tough. I don't know Mieka *that* well, but I know the woman needs to be busy. At least that's what Triss says about her sister."

"She does, yeah."

"And the ranch is always busy."

"It is."

Asher blew out another slow breath, then rested his hand on Nate's shoulder. "And here I was worried that you'd break *her* heart."

Nate hung his head. "I know, right?"

"Speak of the busy, heartbreaking devil," Asher said with a chuckle as they watched Mieka bounce toward them with an enormous grin on her face, Bruno right behind her. "So, you're a lawyer that moonlights as a dancer, or a dancer that moonlights as a lawyer?"

Her smile was sweet and her cheeks filled with pink. "In addition to dancing on the ships, we took part in dinner theater. I participated in a lot of murder mystery nights and got pretty good at acting. I honestly didn't even really think about it before I was telling him I was your lawyer." Her eyes glittered and she bowed. "Normally, I play a Southern belle, or a French artist," she waffled between a drawl and a French accent. "Playing a lawyer was new, but I hope it did the trick."

Asher chuckled. "I think it did."

Mieka's lips twisted and her eyes went wide as she gave a goofy shrug. "Obviously, we'll hire a *real* lawyer if that asshole comes back with a lawsuit."

"He won't," Asher said, shaking his head. "His wife was berating him something fierce as I escorted them off the property. Even his grandchildren were mad at him. I think—I mean I *hope*—he's learned his lesson."

Mieka nodded, then pivoted her gaze to Nate. "How are you doing?"

He glanced up at her and met her eyes. Concern swirled through the brown flecked with gold. "I'll be fine."

Nate's brother snorted. "Dude, the barn nearly caught fire, and then you hauled off and punched a guy—*a customer*. In front of *other* customers. I'd say you're not as *fine* as you think you are."

Clearing his throat, Nate broke his gaze with Mieka and glanced at Asher. "I'll *be* fine. I just need to process. I'll get super baked tonight, have a couple of beers or an ounce or two of whiskey, a soak in the hot tub and I'll pass out and sleep too heavy to dream about this nightmare."

"Thattaboy." Asher slapped him on the shoulder. "Weed: it solves all the veterans' problems." His tone was chock-full of sarcasm as he stood up and shook his head again. "We can handle barn shit for the rest of the day, maybe just make yourself busy with other stuff until we get the charred remnants of the lean-to removed, huh?"

Glaring at his brother, Nate stood up. "I'll be fine. I'm not afraid of charcoal."

Mieka cleared her throat and stepped closer to him. Her presence was grounding and made the sadness and frustration that was swirling around inside of him like a cyclone, calm down—a little. "More goats were born last night. Can I name them? You know this is my jam. I was born to name animals."

Even though his heart was heavy enough to keep him sitting on the porch steps for eternity, he mustered up enough strength to plaster on a smile and approach her. "You were born for this, huh?"

She nodded and her grin grew even wider as she linked her fingers through his, giving his hand a squeeze that went all the way to the center of his chest and made the strings of his heart pull tight. "I was. We both know it. Can I name them? Twin girls."

He squeezed her fingers, too. "Let's go see these little kids then, hmm. Figure out what to call them."

"Oh I already know what I want to name them," she said, adding a little skip to her step. "I told you, I was born for this."

He smiled at her and squeezed her hand. "I agree. I really do think you were born for *this*."

Chapter Seventeen

"Dear God, I can't wait to scrub this arm until the skin is practically raw," Mieka said, holding out her left arm which was now in just an air cast and not the plaster cast. Even though Triss had offered to drive Mieka to Denver to get her cast changed, Nate said he would drive her. He had to pick up some stuff anyway, plus, he just wanted to spend more time with her.

It'd been six days since they'd gotten back from the cabins and the catastrophic excitement of the shed fire, and even though Mieka had moved up to his bed and they made love every night, he still missed her. They were both so busy during the day that he rarely had more than twenty minutes with her until dinner time. Ten minutes in the morning for breakfast and ten minutes for lunch. Then they saw each other at dinner and in the evening, but he missed that time with her in the middle of the day that he'd had at the cabins.

Which was why he *insisted* that he drive her to Denver.

"So are you going to keep the baby goats that were born this year or sell them?" she asked, sipping her milkshake from Gus's. They'd stopped again for burgers, fries, onion rings and milkshakes, since Nate couldn't go into Denver without stopping at Gus's. But Mieka had opted to get a smaller burger and smaller sizes of her fries and onion rings than last time.

"We'll keep a few, but we can't keep all of them. We sell the majority."

"Will you keep Chrishell and Amanza?" she asked, referring to the twin females that she'd named the day they got back from the cabins. Apparently, those were the names of two of the stars on *Selling Sunset,* a reality television show she was obsessed with. Nate had merely shaken his head and rolled his eyes when she told him the origin of her name choices.

"Yeah, we'll keep them. They're pretty docile, so they'll be a nice addition to the herd."

"Do you have any cats around?" she asked, peering out the window.

He nodded. "Yeah, we have six or seven barn cats that keep the rats and other rodents in check. They're feral though, not allowed in the house."

"What are their names?"

Wrinkling his nose, he gave her a strange look. "They don't have names."

The face she made had him bursting out laughing. It was as if he'd just told her that he'd committed murder. "They don't have *names?*"

"No. They're feral barn cats. Why do they need names?"

"Because!"

"That's not a reason. What do you call them then?"

"Barn Cat Number One, Barn Cat Number Two and so on and so forth."

"That's terrible. They need names. How would you like it if when you were born your mother just called you Child Number Two?"

"Would Asher be Child Number One or Asher?"

"Does it matter?"

"A little."

Growling, she rolled her eyes. "Those cats need names."

Nate laughed, reached over and squeezed her thigh. "You can name them if it will make you happy. But first you've got to find them."

Resting her hand on his that was still on her thigh, she grinned. "I'll find them."

"Bruno was pretty put out that you left without him," he said chuckling.

"You have a new number one fan, I think."

"He's a good dog, but it's too warm to leave him in the truck. I'm sure he's fine back at the house."

The first night after the fire, Bruno had put up quite a stink being excluded from the bedroom where Nate and Mieka were sleeping. He scratched and howled at the door until Mieka took pity on the manipulative little bugger and let him in—after they had sex—then Bruno curled up in the crook of her legs, his head on her thigh and snored like a bull elephant with a head cold. And since they let him into their room once, the dog figured that was the status quo now and wouldn't have it any other way. Nate was pretty sure Bruno was more infatuated with Mieka than he was. Not that he could blame the dog, she was pretty spectacular.

The sign for Harris Brothers Ranch came into view and he turned off the road and onto the laneway.

"You have dance lessons with Hank today?" he asked, checking out the horses that were grazing in the field. The three foals—Daria, Chance and Skipper—were out with their mothers along with Macklin and Umber who were in the far corner in the shade by themselves.

"Yeah, he's getting a lot better."

Since they returned from the cabins, Mieka and Hank had been practicing every day in the indoor corral.

He parked the truck in the gravel in front of the house and Mieka hopped out. "Thanks for driving me," she said, coming around the grill and lifting up on her toes to kiss him on the lips. "And thanks for lunch. I'm glad I went with a smaller order, otherwise I'd be waddling into dance lessons."

Nate wrapped his arms around her to hold her there for a moment, not ready to let her go. "Let's go on a date tonight," he said.

Her brows lifted. "Was that not what today was?"

"No. It was me giving you a ride to the doctor and buying you lunch. Let's go on a proper date. I told you before that I wanted to take you out and it hasn't happened. Let's make it happen."

Her smile made his insides turn to warm goo and his dick twitch in his jeans. "Okay. A date."

"I'll pick you up at seven."

"I'll be ready." Then she kissed him one more time, but even though she meant for it to be chaste, he clung to her and deepened it, wedging his tongue between her lips and savoring the lingering flavor of her strawberry milkshake.

Eventually, though, he had to let her go. She skipped a little as she made her way across the yard to the front porch of the house to go wash her arm before she met Hank, blowing him a kiss just before she disappeared into the house, taking a piece of his heart with her.

"You're doing so well, Hank," Mieka praised as Hank led her around the corral in time to the music on her phone. "I can't get over how you've improved in such a short time."

"It's the teacher," he said, spinning her out, then back in at just the right time. "You're also a doctor, apparently, because you managed to fix my two left feet." At his joke and compliment, the big ginger ranch hand turned red in the cheeks and averted his eyes as Mieka chuckled.

"I think it's the student. You've got to *want* to learn and improve. And you have such a great reason to want to learn how to dance. Your sister is going to be so surprised."

"I hope so," he said, continuing to move her perfectly around the corral.

The music stopped and to both of their surprise, clapping from several sets of hands followed immediately.

Poor Hank turned red in the cheeks again, but Mieka's praise kink kicked in and her heart fluttered. It'd been a while since she'd heard the intoxicating sound of applause and she resisted the urge to bow.

Turning around, they found a few adults and children standing there watching them from outside of the corral.

Mieka chuckled and patted Hank on the shoulder. "Well, that's a good sign, isn't it? They're not booing you."

Hank's lips twisted beneath his orangy-red mustache. "I think that clapping is for you."

"Not at all. There are two of us on this dance floor. It takes two to tango, remember?"

"We're not tangoing though," he said, confusion in his tone.

Mieka laughed and patted his shoulder again. "I think we're done for the day, Hank. I'll see you same time and place tomorrow."

Hank nodded and made himself scarce as Mieka approached their audience and grabbed her phone to turn off the music as the next song was about to start.

"Are you a dancer?" one of the women—probably in her early forties—asked.

"I am—or was—or used to be?" she said as sadness settled in her chest unexpectedly. "I am. I used to dance on the cruise ships and for a company in New York." She lifted up the air cast. "Not dancing right now, though."

"Are you also a teacher?" another woman asked, tilting her head to Hank who ducked out the exit at the same moment.

Mieka shook her head. "Oh no. No, no. Hank just asked me to teach him how to dance so he could surprise his sister at her wedding. That's all."

"You're Triss's sister, right?" the first woman asked.

"I am. One of them, anyway. There are five of us in total."

"And you're moving here?" a third woman asked as she played with her young daughter's blonde braid. "Or have you already moved here?"

Mieka shook her head. "I don't think so. And no, I haven't. I'm just here while my arm heals. Visiting my sister and naming some goats."

"That's a shame," the third woman said. "There's nothing in the area as far as dance studios go. We have to drive into Denver. I know of at least a dozen families with children who would love to find a dance studio and instructor closer." She glanced at her friends and they nodded. "And heck, I would love to take a dance class. I'm not the most graceful person, but I think an adult jazz or beginner ballet class would be fun. Don't you think, ladies?"

Her friends nodded again.

"Do you do all kinds of dance?" the first woman asked.

Mieka nodded. "I'm trained in everything. I even learned how to belly dance just for fun. It's a great workout for your core."

All three women's eyes went wide.

"That would be so cool," the second woman said. "My sister in Arizona does pole dancing."

Mieka nodded. "I've trained in that, too. A ship I was on a few years ago had a pole show. That's also a great workout. But you've got to learn to walk in heels."

"Well, you have three of your first customers standing right here," the third woman said. "Along with all of our children, if you do decide to stick around and open a studio." She laughed quickly. "No pressure, though. I'm sure this country life seems dull and boring compared to the exciting and adventurous world of cruise ships that you're heading back to soon." Her eyes sparkled. "I can't even imagine what that must be like."

All three women sighed and glimmers of longing and envy shone in their eyes.

"This is a pretty adventurous life, too," Mieka said. "I just got back from setting up four cabins for vacation rentals. The wide-open spaces, the mountains and valleys. Nothing compares to this beauty. And the training schedule and multiple shows a day on the ships is pretty grueling."

The women didn't seem convinced and gave a few more encouraging words to Mieka about the idea of setting up a studio, but eventually, their children pulled them away and Mieka was alone in the corral.

Bruno wasn't allowed in the corral, so even though he wasn't happy about it, he waited on the outside. His tail started to wag as soon as he saw Mieka exit the corral, stuffing her phone into the back pocket of her jeans, and he fell into step with her.

Her phone hadn't even been in her pocket a minute before it started to vibrate and warble. The caller ID said *Joanie*. A friend and fellow dancer on the ship. Originally from England, Joanie and Mieka had become fast friends after they were both hired by the same company in their third year of dancing on the ships. They worked together on the same cruise lines until Mieka's contract wasn't renewed. .

"Hey Joanie," Mieka said after the fourth ring. "How are you?"

"I just got sacked," Joanie said through muffled sobs.

"What?"

"Same thing that happened to you. My contract was up and they opted not to renew. Said I was *too bloody old*."

"You're thirty-two!" Mieka exclaimed, startling Bruno enough that he rose up onto his back paws and put his front ones on her thighs in concern. She petted his head and told him it was okay after he whimpered a few times.

"I know!" Joanie replied. "But that's ancient in the cruise ship dancing world, apparently. Fucking wankers."

"Fuck," Mieka shoved her fingers into her caramel-colored locks and shook her head. "I'm really sorry, Joan. What are you going to do?"

"Well, luckily, my brother is a real estate broker in Toronto and business is booming. He's going to help me study for my exam and get my real estate agent license then I'm going to start working with him. I've already applied for a work visa, but it shouldn't be too hard since I have family there. I told him you got sacked, too, and he said you could come on, as well, if you wanted to. Isn't your sister Oona still in Montreal?"

"She is, yeah."

"So it shouldn't be too tough for you to get approved to immigrate to Canada if she sponsored you or whatever." Joanie sniffled and the sound of a car horn honking filtered through the phone. "Sorry, I'm just heading to the tube."

"Where are you right now?"

"London. I went home as soon as they sacked me. Just to figure shit out, you know? Cry on my mum's shoulder and fill my face with Cornish pasties."

"Yeah, I know what you mean. I'm at my sister Triss's ranch in Colorado doing the same thing. You should have seen the burger I ate today, it was insane. When did you get let go?" Not that they were really "let go." Their job was contract-based so it made it easier for the cruise line dance companies to filter in new blood and younger dancers. Mieka had just always assumed that she'd be the one to not renew her contract when she was ready to settle down and start a family, not the other way around. Joanie had thought the same thing, apparently.

"Last week," Joanie said. "But then I had three more days left on the ship, which was absolute gobshite. How awkward. Dancing with all the girls whose contracts were renewed while they all knew that mine wasn't. Talk about hu-miliating."

Mieka cupped her forehead. "No kidding."

"You'd think all the tears would be done by now, but one of Genevieve's Instagram posts just came up on my phone and they're in Malta and it all just came flooding back which was why I called you. Because I knew you'd understand."

"Of course, I understand, Joanie, I'm glad you called and I'm so sorry."

"Thanks," Joanie choked. "Anyway, I'm flying to Toronto in a couple of days, so think about it. I think you'd be great selling real estate. We could become the dream team. Dance our way into million-dollar listings, you know? Become the next Netflix luxury real estate phenomenon. *Selling the Greater Toronto Area* or the *GTA* as my brother calls it. *Selling the GTA*. And done! I'll call Netflix and set it all up, you find us some stylists, because you know we need posh clothes and killer hair. I don't think I can do Botox or lip fillers, though. You know how I turn into an complete ninny when it comes to needles of any kind."

Mieka laughed. "Yes, I know. Two hours and half a bottle of tequila before you agreed to take that tetanus shot. I don't think I'll ever forget that."

"Lock jaw honestly didn't sound that bad, you know?"

Mieka was still chuckling. Joanie could always make her laugh. "I'll think about it. Thank your brother for the generous offer. I've been a little lost since they didn't renew my contract, so it's nice to know someone wants me."

"I miss you girl. We need to reunite."

"I agree. You take care, babe and we'll talk again soon. Love you."

"Bye, Love."

Mieka disconnected the call and stuffed her phone back into her pocket, her heart heavy for her friend, and for herself.

Another one bites the dust!

Who would be the next "geriatric" dancer to have the rug pulled out from under her? Who would Mieka be getting a phone call from next? It was only a matter of time, really. She'd been the oldest of their crew, but there were a few older-ish ones like Joanie. Jillian and Melissa were both over thirty, so they'd probably be next on the chopping block, feeling the cold steel of the axe on the backs of their necks before the end of the year.

Climbing the stairs into the house, Mieka opened the door, ditched her shoes and she and Bruno made their way into the kitchen where Triss was standing at the counter chopping vegetables.

"Can I help?" Mieka asked, needing to put the phone call with Joanie and the depression it threatened to envelop her into, out of her head.

"Nope," Triss said, smiling at Mieka over her shoulder. "You're not here for dinner. Go get prettied up for your *date*. Then come back here so we can have the safe-sex talk."

Mieka cringed. "I hope you're kidding."

Triss was already laughing. "I am. But seriously, go have a shower and put on something nice for your date."

"How do you know about my date?"

"I know everything that goes on around here."

"No, you don't. You didn't know Nate and I had sex on the night of your wedding."

"That was a one-off. But also, Nate told me about the date." Her smile was cheeky. "I'm excited for you."

"Do you know where we're going?" Mieka wandered over and grabbed a carrot stick from the bowl Triss was piling them into, and began munching on it.

"I do."

"Where?"

"It's a surprise."

"You know I'm not big on surprises."

"You'll like this one."

Munching her carrot, Mieka cocked her hip into the counter and studied her sister's profile for a moment. Triss was so naturally beautiful with thick dark caramel-colored wavy hair, high cheekbones, a straight nose and long lashes. She was honestly gorgeous. All of Mieka's sisters were.

"What's on your mind, Mieks?" Triss asked, not bothering to look at Mieka, but instead continued focusing on her vegetables. She moved onto celery.

"Do you think I'd make a good real estate agent?"

Triss put her knife down and turned to face Mieka. "Where did that come from?"

Shaking her head, Mieka reached for a julienned slice of yellow bell pepper and took a bite. "A friend of mine also didn't get her contract renewed. Her brother is going to take her on at his real estate firm in Toronto and he said he has a spot for me, too. Joanie and I could work together. Oona might be able to sponsor me, since she's in Montreal, so not too far away and has her citizenship now. Or I could ask Rayma or Pasha to do it."

"Is real estate something you're interested in?" Triss asked, making sure she kept her tone even and void of any kind of judgment. She was also keeping her face extremely neutral. So neutral that it was kind of bugging Mieka.

"I mean, I love all of those shows. *Selling Sunset. Selling The O.C. Selling Tampa, Million Dollar Listing.* Plus, all the ones on HGTV. The flipping shows. I like it all."

"Yeah, I like those, too, because it's fun to imagine and see the luxurious way some people live, but I would never want to become a Realtor and actually deal with those kind of clients and endure that stress. They have to be available to their clients twenty-four-seven. And it's such a cut-throat industry. No, thanks."

Mieka shrugged. "I might be really good at it."

"You are a people person and have a lot of energy." Triss's face finally displayed an emotion besides neutrality, and that emotion was sadness. "I'd miss you. I know we haven't spent *a ton* of time together since you arrived, but the time we have spent together has been great. It's made me realize how much I wish I had family closer." Her hand fell to her belly. "Especially now that my family is growing."

"Ask Mom and Dad to move here," Mieka offered, trying not to smile.

Triss snorted. "I'd rather have a lobotomy, thanks."

They both laughed. A couple of hours was all Mieka and her sisters could handle of their parents. Nobody had really forgiven them for what they'd done to Rayma, abandoning her with Pasha when she was only seventeen and essentially crying out for help. And no matter how much they tried to tell their parents that what they did was wrong, their parents didn't agree and refused to apologize.

Mieka looped her arm around Triss's shoulder and leaned the side of her head against her sister's head. "I know, and I've really enjoyed this time with you, too. But I can't stay here forever."

"Can't you?" Triss's question was full of sincerity and it tugged hard at the strings of Mieka's heart.

Mieka released her sister's shoulder and Triss turned to face her. Their eyes met and Triss regarded her with such sadness. Mieka hoped her own look conveyed her appreciation but also her resolute decision that her time on the ranch was temporary. "I need to find my own way. Find my calling."

"And you think that's real estate?"

"It could be."

Triss pulled Mieka into a tight hug which Mieka reciprocated and the two of them stood there in the kitchen for a long time just holding each other not saying anything.

"I just want you to be happy," Triss said after several long minutes passed between them. "No matter where that may be. I just want you to be happy."

Hot tears pricked Mieka's eyes and she squeezed her sister tighter.

"I mean, I *wish* that was here. Selfishly, I want my sister here. I want you to marry Nate and give me nieces and nephews that can grow up alongside my own children. But I understand if that's not the path you're meant to take. A pregnant, hormonal woman can dream though, right?"

"She can," Mieka chuckled through her tears.

They clung to each other a little longer, then parted, each of them wiping their tears and laughing at how easily they seemed to cry these days.

"You should go shower and get ready for your date," Triss said, turning back to her vegetables. "Dress nice, but practical."

"What does that mean?" Mieka exclaimed.

Triss shrugged. "I have no idea."

Chapter Eighteen

Nate laid down the flannel blanket on the grass at the far end of the field. He had hay bales directly behind them so they could lean back, and they also served as a base for the projector.

With the help of Asher, Nate had set up a white sheet that would serve as a screen, as well as strings of white lights. And since Triss was totally on board with Nate courting her sister, she helped him pack a picnic dinner, complete with all of Mieka's favorites—including the Moroccan chickpea stew she said she loved so much—as well as wine and a surprise for dessert.

"You did all of this?" Mieka asked, her eyes wide in awe as she took in his effort to impress and woo her.

"I had some help, but yes."

Smiling and blinking quickly, she took in all that he'd done. "It's incredible and so beautiful."

He grinned and kneeled down on the blanket, holding out a hand for her to join him.

Bruno, of course, wouldn't let Mieka leave the house without him, as much as they tried to get him to stay, so he hopped onto the blanket, too, sitting down and letting his pink tongue loll out the side of his mouth as he smiled.

Mieka joined them on the blanket, and Nate pulled her into an embrace, wrapping his arms around her waist and claiming her mouth. It didn't take long for Bruno to get jealous and rise up onto his back paws, while his front paws rested on Nate's shoulder.

Giggling, Mieka broke their lip lock and turned to Bruno, scratching him behind both ears. "Are you jealous, Bruno? Are you the only man I should be kissing?" She bent her head and pressed a kiss to the top of his furry head. "You need to learn how to share, buddy."

Nate reached up and turned on the projector, which in turn lit up the white sheet hanging fifteen feet in front of them.

"Are we watching a movie?" Mieka asked, settling down on the blanket and welcoming Bruno into her lap. Though, she didn't really have a choice in the matter, Bruno climbed into her lap, made himself comfortable and gave her zero room for argument. Nate was beginning to feel a little put out how quickly and thoroughly he'd become second fiddle to Bruno—and possibly even to Mieka.

"Perhaps," Nate said, starting the film, then opening up the big cooler he'd brought out with him. "Wine, m'lady?" he asked, pulling out a rosé he'd been chilling.

"Yes, please, good sir," she replied with a fake British accent as she beamed at him and accepted the plastic stemless wine glass from him after he poured them both a healthy portion. She lifted her wine in the air slightly. "To making the most out of the moment," she said, clinking her cup against his.

He forced a smile even though those words caused a sinking feeling to fill his gut. Yet another reminder that her time here was temporary. A moment. A blip. She was still planning to leave. Still didn't consider life on the ranch something she could love, or even grow to love.

He wanted to argue with her, to ask her what else he could do to convince her that this could be more than just a moment, but he also didn't want to ruin the mood, or come across as whiny and needy. He was still battling with the humiliation of hesitating when Bruno was locked in the shed and Mieka went in after him. If he started getting all weepy and whingy about her leaving, he'd drive her away even faster for sure.

"Oh my God, is this *Save the Last Dance*?" Mieka asked, the excitement in her voice pulling a real smile from Nate this time.

He glanced at her over his shoulder as he brought out the containers of food he'd packed into the cooler. "It's your favorite, isn't it?"

"It is," she said, all giddy. "I can't believe you remembered."

"You only told me like a week or so ago. I also have a great memory." He handed her some Moroccan khobz bread that was still warm from being wrapped in foil, along with a container of the chickpea stew. He'd googled a few recipes, but then Triss took pity on him and found the one most like Mieka's favorite. She also helped by making the bread. His sister-in-law was a lifesaver. Triss helped him prepare the stew, couscous and the bread while he and Mieka were in Denver, and then he stepped into the kitchen while Mieka was in dance lessons with Hank. The khobz was sort of like pita bread and naan bread had a baby, that was the best way he could describe it. But it smelled delicious, so hopefully Mieka liked it.

"Is this—" Her bottom lip dropped. "Is this Moroccan chickpea stew and couscous?" she asked, her eyes going buggy. "You really do have a great memory." Ignoring the spoon he offered her, she used the khobz bread to scoop up the stew—which was also still warm since it was in a stainless steel container—and she shoveled a big pile of it into her mouth. Her moans of delight had his dick twitching in his jeans. "Oh my God. Please tell me you didn't make this."

His brow scrunched. "Why don't you want me to have made it?"

"Because knowing you can make my favorite meal probably better than I can is going to make it even harder for me to eventually leave. Did you make the khobz, too?"

Now THAT made him smile. "All part of the plan, Minx. All part of the plan."

He laid out the rest of their meal. Fresh sliced figs, nutty crackers, hard cheeses and sliced vegetables. There was plenty of khobz bread, and yogurt if she wanted to put a dollop on top of the stew, but when he went to offer her a scoop, Mieka was already using a second slice of bread to wipe the last bits of sauce from her empty bowl.

"Jesus, woman," he said with a laugh. "I didn't know you were that hungry."

"I have no bottom to my stomach when it comes to this dish." She scraped her teeth over her bottom lip. "These are all my favorites. Did Triss help you?"

"She's shipping us pretty hard, not gonna lie," Nate said.

"Oh, I know she is." She reached for a cracker, fig slice and piece of cheese, popping them all into her mouth at once and humming in delight.

Bruno had wormed his way between them and was slowly inching forward toward the food. His nose touched a cube of cheese and his tongue swept out and he licked his chops.

"Not for you," Nate said, scratching behind Bruno's ears and gently nudging the dog backward away from the food. "You can have some cheese if there's any leftover."

"There probably won't be," Mieka mumbled through a mouth full of more cheese and crackers.

Nate chuckled. "Oh fine." He grabbed the cube that Bruno's nose had touched and gave it to the dog. "That's it for you, mister. We don't feed dogs from the table in this house."

"Well ..." Mieka said, reaching for another piece of khobz bread, "we're *technically* not at a table, or *in* a house. And Bruno is smart, I bet he knows all of these things and that's why he's trying to sneak some food." She glanced at Nate, held eye contact with him and bobbed her brows seductively, all the while slowly moving her hand toward the pile of cheese cubes. She grabbed a couple and still, while maintaining eye contact with Nate, fed the cheese to Bruno.

"I saw that," he said with a laugh.

"Saw what?" She was the face of pure innocence. The Virgin Mary had nothing on Mieka Young right now.

"I'm going to stay your favorite if I have to give you all the yummy cheese," she said, adopting a baby-talk voice and bending down to kiss Bruno's head.

"He'll be fat and have gout if you do."

She snorted a laugh, lifted her hand and gripped his chin between her thumb and finger, pulling him close. "Thank you for tonight. This is perfect." She pressed her lips to his and he was tempted to deepen the kiss, but Bruno—the infiltrator—sat up and started to whimper.

"You're still my number one guy," she said, pulling away from Nate and petting Bruno. "Nobody could ever take your place."

"Don't let Macklin hear you say that," Nate said, leaning back against the hay bales as the movie started on the DIY screen in front of them. "And also, should I be offended that the dog is ahead of me on that list? Am I at least *second*? Or am I behind a dog and a needy attention-whore horse?"

She crammed more khobz bread and stew into her mouth, shrugged, shook her head and pointed at her mouth to say that she couldn't answer because her mouth was full.

"How very convenient," he said slowly, smiling as he scooped up stew onto his own piece of bread. "I guess third place isn't *so* bad."

They nibbled on dinner while watching Julia Stiles learn to channel all of her pain into her dancing.

By the time the movie was over, the stars were out completely, the air was cooler and Mieka had had three helpings of stew and couscous. The figs, crackers and cheese were pretty much gone, as well, and they were into their second bottle of rosé. Nate was feeling good, and judging by the way Mieka's thumb was resting on the front of his jeans and sliding back and forth over his hardening cock, she was feeling pretty good, too.

"This has been the absolute best date of my entire life," she said, covering her mouth with a yawn as she leaned her head against his shoulder. Bruno was nestled between her legs which were spread out in front of her. He had flipped over to his back and all four of his paws were in the air as he snored.

"I'm glad I could deliver. Though, I find that a little hard to believe given how much you've traveled. Surely you've had some epic dates in epic places. Dinner on the beach in Australia at sunset? A gondola ride in Venice? Ice hotel and the northern lights in Norway?"

She shrugged and nodded. "I've done all of those things, and they were great, but honestly, this is still the best date. It beats all the others, no comparison. Because you listened to me and you gave me all the things I love. My favorite movie, my favorite food, and seriously, this set up, the night and being with you, I couldn't imagine being anywhere else right now."

Was now the time to tell her how he really felt? Tell her that he loved her and ask her to stay? She knew he was trying to convince her that she was made for ranch life, but he'd never come out and actually *asked* her to stay. A lot of it had been witty banter lobbed back and forth between them like a beach ball. But he was dead serious. He wanted her. He loved her and he wanted a life with her. Kids or no kids, he wanted Mieka.

They were facing each other now and he lifted his head to cup her cheek.

Her smile was small, almost sad as she leaned into his touch. "I've been offered a job," she said softly.

Like an arrow had just flown through the sky and landed directly in his heart, Nate sucked in a breath, then struggled to draw in a second one. "Huh?"

Her eyes closed and her lips twisted. "In Toronto."

"Toronto? Doing what? Dancing?" The arrow had pierced his lungs, too. He couldn't breathe.

She opened her eyes and shook her head. "No. Selling real estate."

"What?" He jerked back. He was expecting her to say with a dance company. That would have made sense. That he would understand and be on board with. But selling fucking real estate? What the fuck?

"My friend Joanie from the ships was just 'let go' the way I was. They didn't renew her contract, either. Her brother is a big real estate broker in Toronto and is going to bring her on as an agent at his firm. There's a lot of money to be made in this market right now. She told him about me and he said there's a spot for me, too. Joanie and I could get an apartment together, become a team."

"So that's what you want to do? Sell houses?"

Her brittle smile dropped. "I don't know. Maybe? I might be really good at it. You never know."

"Oh, I have no doubt you'd excel at it, Minx. But my question is, is it what you *want* to do? Will it make you happy? "

"Maybe?"

"Maybe?"

"I don't know." Her tone was getting more exasperated and he could see the shine of unshed tears glimmering more and more in her eyes under the strings of white lights. "But I need to figure something out."

Shaking his head, he started to pack up their picnic. "And selling houses in a city you know nothing about is it then, huh? What happened to making your passion your career?

"That ship might have sailed. Now I have to be like everyone else and find a job that pays the bills and turn my passion into a hobby."

"That's what you want, huh? You want to live in Toronto, sell houses and dance for fun on the weekends or evenings."

"I've been to Toronto before. And I'll have Joanie and her brother. I'll make friends. I always do."

"I don't doubt that," he said, his tone snider than he intended it to be. This date was taking a turn he hadn't intended it to at all. At this point of the date, he'd hoped to have her bent over a hay bale with her pretty floral dress up around her waist and his balls slapping against her ass. He took a deep breath. "So you've agreed to take the job?"

She shook her head. "No. I just wanted to talk to you. To communicate. I wanted to tell you about the offer. Get your opinion." She hung her head. "I don't want to hurt you."

He shook his head, dismissing her claim. She might not *want* to hurt him, but she was anyway. And he knew this wasn't the right path for her. She was desperate and scared and jumping at any opportunity that came to her, even if they both knew it was the wrong one. "What happens when work takes over your life and you can't dance at all anymore because clients want you to show them houses in the evenings and on weekends? Are you ready to give up what you love?"

They both knew his last question held way more meaning that just her giving up dance so she could cater to the demanding schedule of her hypothetical clients.

"I need a job, Nate. I need purpose. I'm floundering and I no longer feel like I have any kind of identity."

"When do you leave?"

Her shoulder lifted on one side and she returned her gaze to his face. "I have nothing booked. Maybe next week? Just to go talk to Joanie's brother and see if I might be a good fit."

Next week!

"I asked you to give me a month, and you can't even do that." Glancing skyward, he tried to collect his thoughts and rein in his temper. Bruno had stood up and his head was swiveling back and forth between them like he was at a tennis match. "Have I convinced you at all? Or have you just been humoring me?"

"I haven't been humoring you," she said quickly. "This has all been very real to me."

"Real but temporary." He regretted the scoff that came with his words, the moment it was out because the hurt in her eyes was debilitating.

"I just don't know if this is the life for me. I just ... I can't see myself here long-term, okay? I've always pictured myself making a home in a busy city, teaching dance in a studio, riding the subway, going out for cocktails with friends to a hot new lounge, running through a city park pushing a stroller. I thought I'd live in a brownstone or something or maybe a high-rise condo. I never even entertained the idea of living in the country. I need the hustle and bustle of a city. The go-go-go kind of life."

"We go-go-go here from before sunrise to long past sunset," he retorted. "And selling real estate in Toronto doesn't sound like the kind of life you just described to me either."

Her eyes closed and she sucked in a breath through her nose, held it there for a moment, then slowly released it. "I know. I just ... I'm feeling really lost right now and I think you're trying to force me to find something. You're trying to force a square peg into a round hole."

He finished his rosé and packed away the plastic wine glass. "Am I then?"

Her gaze turned impatient. "We both knew this was temporary, Nate. I've asked you several times if you knew that. I told you I didn't want to lead you on, and you said that I wasn't and that it was fine. That we could just spend time together, make each other feel good and enjoy each other's bodies, knowing that it would eventually end. You've been trying to convince me that I'm a cowgirl at heart—"

"Rancher."

She rolled her pretty brown eyes. "Fine, a rancher, but as much as I've enjoyed myself here, and with you, we both know this isn't the life for me."

"We both don't know that. I don't know that. I think you're kidding yourself. This is totally the life for you, you're just too stubborn to see it. You don't *want* to see it. You don't want this life. And why? What's wrong with this life? We work hard, we make good money, we contribute to our economy, help out our neighbors and have the respect of our county and everyone who comes here or deals with us. We ship our stud jizz all over the fucking world. The equestrian world knows and respects the Harris Brothers Ranch. We're not nobodies. We might be blue collar, but we're respected."

Her expression remained irritatingly neutral, but her eyes were sad.

Was Mieka a snob? Was she turning her nose up at this life because she thought she was better than it? He hadn't gotten that impression from her before, especially since she'd jumped into every activity and chore with gusto and got just as dirty as the rest of them. But maybe she really was a snob and thought this life was beneath her.

He continued packing up their dinner dishes, then reached up and shut off the projector.

"I just don't think we want the same things," she said slowly. "We're not connecting the way we should. We agreed to keep it casual and we couldn't do that. And now ... now people are hurt."

"Yeah," he snapped. "People are hurt." He showed her his back as he continued to clean up. He was close to fucking tears and the last thing he wanted to do was allow himself to be anymore vulnerable around a woman who clearly didn't want him or the amazing life he was offering her.

"So that's it?" she asked, her words coming out choked. "The date is over?"

He didn't know what to say. He didn't know anything anymore.

"Nate!"

"What?" he rounded on her. "What do you want from me?" Tears stung his eyes.

"An answer. Because I said I've been offered a job and am considering it, are you ending the date? Are you ending things between us right here and right now because you're not getting what you want? I was honest and upfront right from the beginning. You can't blame me, when you knew this was temporary right from the start."

Nate ground his molars, flicked his gaze up to hers and blurted out, "I fucking love you, Minx. I'm in love with you. I didn't plan on falling in love with you, but I did. I'm weak. You told me it was temporary and I agreed, because I thought I could make it permanent. I said I was going to try to show you how good ranch life could be—and I asked you to give me a month to do that. I knew it was a long shot, but I remained hopeful anyway. I fucked up and I fell in love with you. Does that not change anything for you?"

Her brown eyes were wide. "Nate ... I ..."

"I want you to stay. Build a life with me here. I thought I was doing a good job of convincing you that you were born for this life, that we were really connecting, but apparently, I failed at that, too. I failed at keeping it casual and I failed at showing you how good this life can be."

Everything in his body was strung so tight that it hurt to even blink. It hurt to breathe and the push and pull of his heart strings with every beat was enough to make him see spots and nearly pass out. Nothing had ever hurt this badly. He'd gladly get burned to nearly a crisp again, then go through what he was feeling right now.

"I think we should just end it now," he whispered, the words feeling like a thousand rose thorns ripping open his throat more and more with each uttered syllable.

"What?" she asked, her voice soft and shocked. "Why?"

He shook his head. "I just ... I'm done trying to convince you."

"So, because you're done trying to convince me to stay this all has to end?"

He closed his eyes and his shoulders rounded with the heavy weight of his pain. A hot tear sprinted down his cheek and he quickly swept it away. "I think it's for the best. A clean break. We can be friends. I hold no animosity or anger toward you, but I need to start getting over you."

"And you think that'll be easier to do while I'm still here?"

No. But he also wasn't prepared to torture himself for another week while she was here, knowing he'd failed to convince her to stay, and that she didn't and would never feel the same way about him that he did her.

He dug out a headlamp from the bag of stuff he'd brought with him. "Here. You can head back to the house. I'll clean up."

"Nate," she breathed.

"I'm sorry, Mieka, I just ... I failed and I'm sorry for that. I'm sure you'll make a wonderful real estate agent." And with that, he stood up and started to take down the sheet that had been their movie screen and the twinkling strings of lights.

He avoided looking at her at all costs, and he wasn't sure when she got up and left, but eventually she did. His chest throbbed as he watched the light from the headlamp bob through the field toward the main house. He knew she'd be safe. Bruno was with her, but he just couldn't spend another minute with her, wrapped up in a temporary cocoon of bliss, knowing that she wasn't even trying to give them a real chance. She was willing to take a risk on a job she'd never expressed any interest in, in a city she barely knew, but she wasn't willing to take a chance on him or a life together.

Eventually, the light from the headlamp disappeared and he was able to take a deeper breath. His chest still hurt and his brain still raged, but deep down, he knew he'd done the right thing.

Because wasn't it the age old saying, if you love something, set it free?

And Nate knew for a fact that he'd never loved anyone the way he loved Mieka, so he was doing what was right, and he was letting her go, even though it shattered his heart to do it.

Chapter Nineteen

Mieka's well of tears had run dry by the time she reached the farmhouse. Her nose was clogged, her face was drenched and everything hurt. Particularly, her heart.

Bruno grew more and more distraught the longer and harder she cried, stopping her several times on the walk through the field to whimper and put his paws on her thighs, asking what was wrong.

She'd also stopped, spun around and stalked back toward him several times with her fists bunched and a deep pinch to her brows. Had he really just dumped her?

But after a yard or two, she'd lose her fire and turn back around to face the house.

What would she say to him? Demand that they keep their temporary, casual thing going until she left, just so she could squeeze out a few more orgasms and kisses?

He'd said his piece. He'd fallen in love with her, tried to convince her to make their temporary arrangement permanent and call the ranch home. They wanted different things, and when she really thought about it, maybe ending it now rather than a week from now really was the best for all involved. They could take the week to cool off, return to being friends and hopefully part ways on truly amicable terms.

That didn't mean her heart wasn't broken currently and her eyes weren't blurry from all the tears.

She'd asked Nate multiple times if he could handle this temporary arrangement. She didn't want to lead him on, and he assured her that he was a big boy and could handle a fling. She knew he was still trying to convince her that ranch life was for her, but she also thought that he knew no matter how lovely life here seemed, eventually, she would leave.

She was a square peg and this life was a round hole. They just didn't fit.

Grateful that Nate was still in the field, she zipped up to his room and gathered her things, returning to the guest room on the main floor of the house. She showered, then fell into bed with Bruno curled up beside her as she hugged her pillow and surprisingly more tears fell, despite the fact that she was sure she'd depleted her stores on the walk back through the field.

She slept terribly, flitting in and out of consciousness, then laying awake staring at the ceiling when she heard Nate arrive and stomp upstairs. Then knowing he was laying in his bed alone upstairs just brought on a whole new batch of tears that soaked her pillow until sunrise.

Making sure Nate and Asher were out of the house and in the barn before she emerged from her room, Mieka dressed before she left her room, tossed her hair into two plaits that fell over each shoulder and made her way into the kitchen in search of much-needed coffee. She was exhausted after such a restless, tear-filled night. Bruno found his breakfast, ate it and took off outside to do his business, but she knew he wouldn't be gone long. Every time she woke up last night, so did the dog. He'd whimper, get up and lick her face, then settle somewhere on the bed closer to her than before. Eventually, he was curled up on her pillow with his chin resting across her neck. It wasn't overly comfortable, but she welcomed the companionship. She didn't want to be alone and Bruno seemed to know that.

"Good morning," Triss greeted her, sitting at the kitchen table sipping her coffee and finishing her toast.

Mieka's gaze met her sister's, Triss's eyes went wide as tears filled Mieka's and at the same time Triss stood up from the table, Mieka collapsed into her sister's arms.

"Fucking hell," Triss murmured against Mieka's shoulder as Mieka sobbed and shook against her sister's frame. "He did it, didn't he? He told you he loved you and went and fucked it all up."

"It's not his fault," Mieka choked.

"Of course, it is. Well, it's both of your faults, but you were upfront about this being temporary, and it's like he had horse shit in his ears and only heard what he wanted to hear. Thought he could change your mind." Triss stroked Mieka's back. "I mean, I *hoped* he'd succeed, but I know you. You're stubborn and stuck in your own head. I figured hell would have to freeze over before his efforts actually worked. And now you're crying, in the guestroom again, and Nate is wandering around with a giant black cloud over his head."

Mieka couldn't decide if knowing there was a black cloud over Nate's head made her feel better or worse. She didn't like the idea of him being sad or angry. That hurt her heart even more. But he'd also gone and done exactly what he promised he wouldn't, which was take this from a temporary fling of fun to something far more serious that he wanted to make permanent. That black cloud was his fault not hers.

"I think I'm going to take the job," she said between sniffles and sobs. "I think I could be good at real estate."

"Okay," Triss said carefully.

"I promised Hank I'd work with him until his sister's wedding, but that's this coming weekend, so after that, I'm going to go. I've overstayed my welcome and need to get on with my life."

Triss pushed her away slightly and held her by the shoulders. "You have *not* overstayed your welcome, okay? Just know that. You are more than welcome to stay here longer. We can ignore Nate together and I'll even let you spit in his food."

Mieka snorted and wiped away a tear that sprinted down the crease of her nose. "I don't want to spit in his food. Can I really be mad at him for falling in love with me? Isn't that the ultimate compliment?"

"We can be mad at him because you repeatedly made sure you weren't leading him on and let him know that this thing between you was temporary, then he went and changed the agreement. I mean, we can't exactly control who we fall in love with." Triss tipped her head in the direction of the barn. "I fell in love with a grumpy stoner rancher with PTSD for crying out loud."

"How do I even function around him now? It's going to be so awkward, which is exactly what I was worried about. I don't want it to be awkward or weird for you. He's your brother-in-law. He's your family. And we're going to share a niece or nephew. I want to come back and see the baby, see you. Now it's going to be weird. Especially if I start seeing someone else, or he does."

The idea of Nate being with someone else made her stomach spin and bile coat the back of her tongue. She wasn't sure she'd be able to handle that.

"Don't worry about my relationship with Nate," Triss said. "We'll be fine. And as far as the awkwardness goes, that's on him."

"Doesn't make it any less awkward."

"Just stay in bed until they leave in the morning after breakfast, then have Hank meet you in the corral at dinner time for dance lessons. Then you and I can go for a walk in the field or something until bedtime. Asher will understand."

"I hate this," Mieka said with a big pout.

"Me, too." Triss pulled her in for another hug and rubbed her back. "Me, too."

Nate was brushing Umber in his stall when Triss stomped into the barn and over to where he and the black cloud over his head were working. "You're a fucking idiot," she said, loud enough for everyone in the barn to hear. Loud enough for Mercy in the stall at the end to grunt and huff because of the abrupt noise. "Sorry, Mercy," Triss called out, before turning her attention back to Nate. "But I stand by my statement. You're a fucking idiot." She brought her volume down significantly the second time she said it.

"I know," Nate said, standing up to his full height from where he'd been brushing Umber's legs. "I spent the entire night berating myself, so you can save your breath."

Triss plunked her hands on her hips. "And what do you plan to do about it?"

Shrugging, Nate went to work brushing Umber's neck and mane. "What is there to do? I fucked up and fell in love with her, told her such but that doesn't seem to change things. She's still convinced this isn't the life for her, even if I might be the guy."

"Ever wonder if you came on a little too strong?" Triss asked, her nostrils flaring. "That she's still dealing with the complete and total faceplant of her career and life and that she's trying to figure out where she fits into the world? Then you went and *told* her that she belonged in this life, rather than letting her figure that out on her own, and attempted to manipulate her further by telling her you loved her in a last-ditch attempt to get her to stay. And when she didn't say it back, you went all passive-aggressive and apologized for falling in love with her. Then told her to leave. Ended the date in a big pout and told her to walk back to the house in the dark by herself. It was selfish and super manipulative, Nate. Not cool. I love you. But I'm pissed off at you right now."

He squeezed his eyes shut and pinched the bridge of his nose, counting to ten in his head before he spoke. "I thought I was being romantic. Isn't it supposed to be romantic to tell someone you love them?"

"Depends on the circumstance, and in this circumstance, it was manipulative. Then when your ego got hurt, you punished her for not saying it back and made her walk back in the dark. What the fuck, dude?"

"So what do I do? I can't leave the ranch and move to Toronto."

"She never invited you."

Ouch.

Heat flared in his cheeks at how candid and real his sister-in-law was being. She was dishing him a harsh dose of reality, but it was one he sorely needed. Here he thought that he was being romantic, putting his heart on his sleeve and showing his vulnerability to Mieka, but in reality, he'd been trying to manipulate her. To sway her to make a decision based on how he felt, not how she felt. Then, with his heart in shambles, he made her walk back in the dark alone thinking he was saving them both the awkwardness of walking back together.

He was an ass.

"I can see that what I'm saying is actually sinking in, and that's good. Your head isn't nearly as thick as your brother's, but either way you need to give her space and *not* make it awkward. You apologized for fucking up and falling in love with her, apologized for failing to convince her that this is the life for her, but you haven't apologized for how you treated her on your date. You haven't apologized for trying to manipulate her. And she deserves that. She did nothing wrong and we all know that."

Nate exhaled. "How do I do that? I'm worried it's going to be uncomfortable no matter what I do."

"Yeah, probably. But you can't be mad about it. This is a situation of your making, so deal with the awkwardness like a man. You can't show her any animosity, because we all know that the one who fucked up here, is you. You should be humble, regretful and apologetic, and *not* expect or assume that an apology is going to bring her back into your bed or you into her good graces.

But she deserves an apology."

His head bobbed and he leaned forward and pressed his lips to Umber's neck. "She does."

"Good." Triss's shoulders rounded and she heaved a weary sigh. "I'm also sad that it didn't work out between you two. I was really rooting for you. I wanted your plan to work as badly as you did, but she's stubborn and lost and—"

"Incredible," he said softly. "She's incredible."

"She is. And I think the two of you would have been incredible together, but we can't force things."

"No, we can't." He scratched his head and met his sister-in-law's brown eyes, eyes just slight darker than Mieka's, but with the same intelligence and kindness. The sisters looked a lot alike and were similar in a lot of ways, too, and yet, they were also so very different. Mieka had a wilder side to her than Triss. A more adventurous side that really spoke to and appealed to Nate. Asher was the responsible one, and Triss was a lot like that, too. Cautious and careful, cerebral and serious. Though Triss had more of a sense of humor than Asher, she was slowly drawing out Asher's more playful side which was nice.

But, Nate liked a woman with a sense of adventure and who wasn't afraid to take a few risks. Which was why he thought Mieka was perfect for him. And he still believed that.

"Just don't make her last few days here miserable, please. She's leaving Saturday since she promised Hank she'd finish helping him learn to dance, so it's only seven more days, then you can wallow how you please."

One week?

She was leaving in a week?

Was he having a heart attack? His hand came up to rest over his chest as an excruciating tightness filled the space between his lungs, and his breathing grew short and shallow. He tried to breathe through the pain, but it wasn't easy.

"She's inside booking a flight to Toronto right now," Triss said, coming up to kiss Umber on his long nose. "I'm really sorry it didn't work out, Nate. Truly."

Then she was gone from the stall, leaving Umber, Nate and Nate's broken heart as he fell to the floor of the stall on his knees and the tears started to fall.

If you didn't know Mieka was a dancer from talking to her, you'd know she was based on the way she expertly danced around Nate for the last seven days He hardly saw her, and when he did finally catch a glimpse of her, she was on her way out.

He never saw her in the morning, she stayed in the guestroom until he and Asher headed out to the barn to work for the day, then when they came in for dinner, she was quick to head out to the corral to give Hank his dance lessons. And if Nate was still up after dance lessons ended, Mieka and Triss went for a walk, or hung out in Triss's office.

He hated himself for what he'd done. To not only Mieka, but to himself, his brother and his sister-in-law. It was awkward for everyone and it was his fault.

He and Asher had taken the first batch of guests to the cabins on Monday, so Ray and Mieka rode out to the cabins on the ATVs Friday afternoon—after Nate had returned with the guests on horseback—and they cleaned and set up the cabins again for the next batch of guests who rode out on Saturday. Ray said that they needed to develop a better system, since it was a lot of work for two people to do four cabins in that short amount of time, and also pack out a vacuum and all the laundry.

Nate wished he could talk to Mieka about it all and get her opinion and ideas for improvement, but the woman gave him no room for a conversation, so he was left trying to figure out a way to simplify things himself.

He hated all of this. Every second of it.

And he was the only person to blame.

He'd gone and obliterated not only their romantic relationship, but their friendship, as well, and if he was being honest with himself, he missed not being able to just *talk* to Mieka about stuff and pick her beautiful brain more than anything. Sure, the sex was phenomenal and he missed that, too, but he missed her friendship, her sense of humor, her cheekiness and intelligence the most.

But he had to go and be stupid and selfish and try to get her to give him more, even though she'd been upfront from the beginning that that wasn't an option.

Not a night went by where he didn't lay in bed, staring up at the ceiling reliving that moment in the field on their date where he told her he loved her, and he wished he could just take it all back. Where he kept his mouth shut and just kissed her instead of confessing his true feelings. He'd ruined everything and now so many people were in pain because of it.

It was Saturday morning and even though he knew he couldn't, all he wanted to do was lay in bed with his self-loathing. She was leaving today.

But the horses and goats weren't forgiving or understanding when it came to matters of the heart. They wanted their breakfast regardless of Nate's five-day pity party.

It was almost like the animals knew that something was going on. Macklin was particularly put out this morning, huffing and snuffling more than usual. Nate tried to give the attention-whore horse more attention to settle him, but it didn't seem to work. Asher was leading the horses out to the fields with Ronny, while Ray, Wes, Braiden and Nate mucked stalls and got the place ready for when the petting farm opened at ten.

Hank's sister's wedding had been last night and apparently, he'd brought his sister to tears with his surprise dance skills. He sent them all pictures of him with his sister, a big smile under his bushy red mustache as his sister—beautiful in her white dress—beamed like a Disney princess as he twirled her around the floor. Nate didn't have to ask whether he sent the same images to Mieka, he knew Hank would have.

"Looks like Hank stole the show at his sister's wedding yesterday," Braiden said, returning with an empty wheelbarrow for Nate to shovel shit into.

"Not sure that was his intention, but I think he got the shock-factor he was going for," Nate replied. "Never seen the big ginger smile that wide before."

Braiden chuckled. "Yeah, me either. Mieka worked her magic on him, that's for sure. I was wondering about asking her if she'd teach me, since my sister is getting married next year and I'd love to be able to surprise her, too. But I guess I missed the boat." His face turned sad, emphasizing the cleft in his chin. "How are you doing with all of that?"

"How do you think?" Nate said, lifting an eyebrow.

"Shitty how it all went down. She'll be missed for sure."

"That she will be," Nate exhaled as he tossed a big pile of manure into the wheelbarrow.

He didn't know when her flight was, but Triss said Mieka would be leaving at noon. She'd already ordered her cab, even though all of them offered to drive her to the airport. Apparently, she didn't want to put them out anymore than she already had and wouldn't hear of taking them away from the busy petting farm.

The woman was honestly one of the most selfless people he'd ever met. No wonder she didn't want a future with him, not when all he ever did was take and think about himself and his own feelings.

The morning flew by and before any of them knew it, the first guests of the petting farm arrived. The parking lot filled up quickly and the raucous laughter of children and families could be heard all over the ranch.

It was hard to discern the different engines or crunching of gravel beneath tires from that of petting farm patrons or other vehicles, but he knew one of those cars would eventually be the cab to take Mieka to the airport. Nevertheless, he wasn't prepared for the bright yellow sedan to show itself at precisely noon, pulling up right in front of the house.

The driver got out and lifted his chin at Nate. "Cab for Mieka?"

"Right here," came her assertive, husky voice as she opened the door of the house and hauled her suitcase behind her. Bruno was hot on her heels, smiling and trotting beside her, completely unaware of what was about to happen.

Triss followed behind her sister, tears in her eyes.

Asher came running up from the barn and stood next to Nate, clapping him on the back, then squeezing his shoulder as a sign of support. They hadn't talked much about what had happened, Asher figured his wife took care of that. But Asher understood how Nate was feeling and was there for support, even if they didn't dissect it all which was something Nate appreciated. He extended his empathy to Nate, told him he was there if he wanted to talk, then let the whole thing drop. Nate appreciated that. He didn't need to rehash his fuck up over and over again. He felt shitty enough about it already and knowing Mieka was so close and yet so far away was punishment enough.

"Well, don't be a stranger," Triss said, drawing her sister in for a hug. "You're always welcome back. Though, I'm sure your new job as a big city real estate agent selling condos to billionaires is going to be *super* demanding. Don't forget about us little people when you get your own Netflix special, okay?"

Mieka laughed. "Forget about the little people? Never."

The two held onto each other for several heartbeats and although Nate couldn't hear what was being said, he knew they were whispering to each other.

Eventually, the sisters broke away from each other, then Mieka hugged Asher and thanked him for everything.

The moment was debilitating. Nate's palms grew sweaty, his pulse thundered and his gut spun until he thought he might puke. Was she going to hug him? How would they say goodbye? She hadn't even given him an opportunity to apologize. She'd avoided him like he had leprosy and the two hadn't been alone or spent more than thirty seconds in the same space since that night in the field. Mind you, he'd also been a bit of a coward and not sought her out, to create an opportunity to apologize.

Asher let go of Mieka and she stepped out of his embrace then lifted her head and fixed her gaze on Nate. Her smile conveyed her hurt, and the glimmer that was usually in her gold-flecked brown eyes was missing. All he saw in those eyes was pain, a pain he felt in his bones. A pain he'd caused.

"Don't work too hard, Cowboy," Mieka said, stepping forward and giving him an uncomfortable, stiff hug.

He pulled in a deep inhale, drawing the scent of her coconut shampoo all the way down to his toes as he ached to wrap his arms around her, press their bodies together and never let her go.

"Rancher," Asher murmured beside him.

Nate swallowed as she pulled away from him well before he was ready. She didn't meet his gaze even though that's all he wanted was to look her in the eyes and apologize.

"Well, I best be off. New life to start and all of that," Mieka said with a forced laugh as she let the cab driver take her suitcase and put it in the trunk. "Thanks for everything, guys. I really appreciate you letting me crash and helping me put the pieces of my life back together." She was still avoiding his eyes, but he could see the shimmer of unshed tears threatening to breach. Sniffing and smiling, she waved at Triss and Asher, avoided looking in Nate's direction, then spun around and climbed into the back seat of the taxi.

Bruno trotted after her and tried to climb into the cab. Mieka choked out a sob. "No, Bruno, I'm sorry. You can't come, sweetheart." She gently pushed him away, but he jumped right back up, putting his paws on her thighs.

"No dogs in the car," the cab driver said.

"I know," Mieka said. "I'm trying." She was crying now, trying to close the door, but Bruno was whimpering and scratching, jumping and barking. He didn't understand why she was leaving him. Watching him suffer, watching both of them suffer, was complete torture.

"Come on, Bruno," Asher said, stepping forward and grabbing Bruno by the collar. "We need to let her go. You'll see her again soon." He tried to tug Bruno out of the way so Mieka could close the door, but the dog dug in his heels and turned to snarl at Asher, shocking all of them.

Eventually, Asher managed, though, and Mieka closed the door. The taxi pulled out of the yard and rumbled down the laneway toward the main road as Bruno whimpered and barked in frustration and confusion.

"That was awful to watch," Triss murmured.

Asher was still holding Bruno, who was trying his hardest to break free and chase after the cab.

"You're an idiot," Asher said, turning to face his brother, after he tucked an angry and wriggling Bruno under his arm. "Even Bruno thinks so."

"I know," Nate said, his throat tight and full of rusty horse hoof nails as he watched the taxi turn off the property and onto the main road, then eventually out of sight. "I know."

Chapter Twenty

Her tears were big, fat blobs that made everything appear blurry as Mieka stared out the window of the cab, leaving the ranch and everything and everyone behind.

Bruno's whimpers still echoed in her mind. Saying goodbye to the dog and having to push him out of the cab was more painful than breaking her arm. Add in the look of agony in Nate's eyes, and the throbbing ache in her chest as she stiffly hugged him, and she'd gladly break every bone in her body than go through something like that again.

The further away from the ranch they drove, the more intense the pain grew. And the tears only fell faster and harder, until she was no longer suffering in silence, but sobbing and sniffling more than she had when the dance company said they weren't renewing her contract.

"Are you all right, ma'am?" the cab driver asked, his gravelly voice barely breaking through the din of her sadness.

Swallowing past a golf ball sized lump in her throat, Mieka nodded. "Mhmm. I'll be fine."

They continued to drive, and the tears continued to fall. They weren't that far from the ranch, but far enough that when a goat appeared in the ditch on the side of the road it made her gasp.

"Hold on!" Mieka said, lurching forward in her seat and gripping the back of the seat in front of her.

"Did you forget something?" the driver asked.

"Pull over, please. I know that goat. That's Fumble."

"Fumble? Only in the country would you *know* a goat." But he pulled over nevertheless, and Mieka flung open her door before the cab even came to a full stop. Wiping the tears from her eyes, she started walking, then picked up the pace to a run, keeping her eyes on Fumble the entire time.

"Hey, buddy, what are you doing out here by yourself?

Fumble bleated at her as if to tell her to fuck off.

Then, in true Fumble fashion, he pissed and made sure to get it all over his legs and beard again.

"Oh for crying out loud," she grumbled.

"*Mehhhhhh!*" Fumble brayed in response. He hopped sideways up and out of the ditch and into the middle of the road.

"Gonna be roadkill soon," the cab driver hollered out his window.

Mieka glared at him. "A little help would be nice. No need for the running commentary."

The cabby snorted, but opened his door and slowly ambled into the middle of the road so that Fumble couldn't take off down the road to Denver.

"Come on, Fumble," Mieka said again. "I'll give you some delicious carrots when we get back home. I promise. Anything you want. You want to eat my shoelaces? They're yours. You want a grilled cheese sandwich? I'll make you one with some of Asher's favorite expensive Gruyere."

"What kind of goat eats grilled cheese?" the cab driver asked.

"Goats will eat just about anything," Mieka said, slowly approaching Fumble. She was in a slight crouch. Anybody who drove up on this ridiculous scenario would think they were trying to disarm a bank robber or pry a toy poodle from the jaws of a mountain lion, not coax a delinquent goat to return to his barn.

"Come on, Fumble," the cab driver said. "The name suits him." He shook his head. "Fucking country folk."

At the insult, Fumble crapped himself in the middle of the road. A car zoomed by and honked, scaring the goat—and scaring more crap out of his rear end in the process—and causing him to jump back into the ditch. Mieka lunged for him, falling onto her belly in the gravel, but managing to hook the pinky finger of her left hand into Fumble's collar.

"Yes!" she breathed, wedging more fingers under the collar and tightening her grip. "Gotcha!"

The cab driver, who wasn't much for words it seemed, was already making his way back to his car.

She led Fumble over to the cab. "Can we go back to the ranch and return him, please?"

"You're not bringing that filthy, creepy-eyed thing into my car," the cab driver explained, eyeing Fumble with disgust. "I just watched him piss all over himself."

"Well, what am I supposed to do?"

"Don't know. Don't care. Not my problem. You hired me to drive you to the airport. Never said anything about a goat."

Mieka growled, but her grip on Fumble's collar tightened. "Okay, well, can you like follow me back to the ranch then?"

"It's your money." The cabby shrugged.

Rolling her eyes, Mieka pulled Fumble over to the shoulder of the road and they started to walk. But her back wasn't happy with the hunching over she was forced to do to keep hold of the goat, so she stopped, took off her belt and looped it through Fumble's collar to create a leash of sorts.

"That's better," she said, standing up to her full height, while still holding on to Fumble.

They'd driven farther away from the ranch than she thought, because it wasn't long before sweat started to bead on her forehead and trickle down her chest from the hot bright ball of fire in the sky beating down on them.

"Why do you keep trying to leave, Fumble?" she asked, not caring that she was having a one-sided conversation with a goat. The cab driver probably already thought she was crazy. She may as well feed that assumption even more. "The ranch is an amazing place to live. You have everything you could ever want or need. Food, shelter, family. Endless petting and attention from the children who come to visit, lots of things to climb. There are people there that care about you and love you. You could have been turned into Ray's auntie's jerked goat a long time ago, and you haven't been. So that's saying a lot."

The goat glanced up at her with his weird eyes. He blinked a few times but didn't say anything, then they continued to walk.

"The people at the ranch only want what's best for you, Fumble. What will make you happy and live your best life. The opportunities are endless. There's so much to do, I can't imagine you actually get bored. And the beauty of the land... I know you haven't been around the world, but the ranch truly is a gorgeous place. Triss, Asher and Nate... they love you. This is where you belong, Fumble. Where you're meant to be. Where you can live your best ... life." She stopped in her tracks hard enough to cause Fumble to choke a little on his collar and let out a *meh* of disapproval.

A tear slid down her cheek, but she smiled. The revelation was like a goat had kicked her in the back of the head, and a bubble of laughter forced its way out of her throat, abrupt and loud enough to make Fumble startle and try to step away from her.

"It's where *I* belong. Where *I'm* meant to be. Where I can live *my* best life."

Why did it take this long for her to see it? For her to realize that everything Nate was trying to show her was exactly what she needed?

She was an idiot. She'd wasted so much energy resisting the ranch and the idea that it was the right life for her, when all along, Nate and her sister knew better. They knew her better than she knew herself.

She didn't want a brownstone in the big city. She wanted the wide-open spaces of the great outdoors. She wanted the smell of hay and horse to be the first thing to hit her nostrils in the morning, not exhaust from an endless stream of taxis. She didn't need the hustle and bustle of a big city. She would never get bored on the ranch. This life was go-go-go enough for her, but more importantly, this life had Nate, and he was all she really needed.

Nate and Asher seemed open to the idea of adding more revenue streams to the business. They'd built Triss her clinic, maybe they'd build Mieka a dance studio. People in the area had already expressed interest and said there was a need for such a place. Why couldn't she give the people what they wanted? A place for her to do what she loved. Her passion.

A place to dance.

Before she knew what she was doing, Mieka was running down the side of the road in the direction of the ranch. In the direction of home. Fumble must have thought it was a game, because he kept up with her, giddily bouncing along beside her on the narrow shoulder of the road. She didn't even glance back to see if the cab driver was still behind her, because she didn't care. It wasn't what was behind her that mattered, it was what was in front of her.

Laughing and crying at the same time as she ran, Mieka yanked Fumble further over onto the shoulder when a big pickup truck started barrelling toward them. But she recognized that truck, even through the tears, and her smile grew wide enough to hurt her cheeks.

Nate pulled over, flung open his door, but didn't bother closing it, and ran up to Mieka and Fumble. "Why do you have my goat?"

"Because idiots love company," she said, slightly out of breath. "I found him in the ditch and was bringing him home. Were you coming to look for him?"

Nate shook his head. "No. I was coming to you. To apologize. I was going to chase you down at the airport and apologize for being such a manipulative asshole. For not finding you earlier this week and apologizing. I'm sorry that I let it go a week. I was just ..."

"Hurt. I know."

"I never should have told you that I loved you like that and expected it to change everything. I ruined what we had. I was selfish and I need you to know that I'm sorry and that I only want you to be happy. I just want you to live your best life and if that is in Toronto selling real estate then let me drive you to the airport myself to show you how much I support you. I don't want things to be awkward between us. We've been through too much together and I honestly just want you to be happy, Minx, no matter where that may be." He swallowed. "Or *who* that may be with."

Her smile fell a little, but her heart swelled. "Oh. I thought maybe you were coming to convince me to stay."

He shook his head. "That would be selfish of me. I would be trying to cage a bird that only wants to fly—or in this case sell luxury real estate—and I won't do that." He took Fumble from her hand and loaded the delinquent goat into the bed of his truck, securing a rope to the goat's collar so that he couldn't escape again.

A half-smile slid up the left side of Mieka's mouth. "Do it."

Nate faced her again. "Do what?"

"Convince me."

"Minx, I—"

"Just do it."

His brows furrowed and he cocked his head to the side, giving her a cute quizzical look.

"Ask me to stay. Ask me to give the ranch ... to give the *rancher* a second-chance. Then tell me that you love me and that you'll build me a dance studio on the property and make me the happiest woman in the world."

Now he understood and the smile that curled his mouth had her lower belly fluttering and warming like a kaleidoscope of butterflies dancing through the sky across the sun. Slowly, he approached her with purpose in his stride and fire in his eyes. He cupped her face and tilted her gaze to his. "Come back to the ranch, Mieka. It's where you belong. I'll build you the most beautiful dance studio in all of Colorado. And I absolutely will spend the rest of my life trying to make you the happiest woman in the world. As happy as you make me. I love you, Minx."

Smiling through all the happy tears she nodded and said, "Yes. Take me home, Cowboy. And I love you, too."

"Rancher," he murmured before sealing his mouth over hers, and kissing her like she held the only remaining oxygen molecules on earth.

Every stroke of his tongue, and brush of his lips just solidified her decision that this was where she was meant to be. With Nate, here on the ranch.

She'd been convinced that ranch life wasn't what she wanted, that it wasn't for her, but in reality, it was exactly what she needed. She'd never been happier or more at peace than she was when she was there. And it was as if the solutions to all her problems had presented themselves to her one-by-one, but she was too blind to see them.

She could open up a dance studio and teach. She already had willing students, and it'd be easy to find more. She loved decorating and managing the cabins, she could do that, too. Add in the fresh air, the sense of accomplishment and exhaustion she felt every night when her head hit the pillow, not to mention those orgasms, and she'd be an idiot to dismiss this kind of beautiful life. This kind of beautiful future.

This was hands down a much better life for her than selling luxury real estate in Toronto. No comparison needed. It'd just taken a delinquent goat and falling face-first in the gravel for her to finally see it.

Finally, they broke the kiss and Nate, still holding onto her face, beamed down at her. "What made you change your mind?"

"A rogue goat who doesn't seem to realize how good life on the ranch can be and that it's where he belongs. It's where we both belong."

They both glanced at Fumble who was staring at them like a creepy voyeur peering through bedroom curtains.

"Fuck, he's a weirdo," Nate said with a chuckle.

"But he's our weirdo."

"That he is," he said, letting go of her and jogging to the cab which was idling behind them. He leaned over to speak to the driver, then reached into his pocket, pulled out his credit card and a moment later he was wheeling her suitcase and lugging her purse and carry-on toward his truck while the cab did a U-turn and took off back toward Denver.

Opening up the rear door on his truck, he stowed her bags, then turned to face her. "Are we going home?"

"I think we are," she said, smiling up at him with so much love in her heart. "But, can I ask for a few favors?"

"Sexual?" His brows bobbed.

"Well, no, but we can discuss those after."

"Anything for you, Minx."

"Could we open up a dance studio on the ranch? Is there room?"

"I'll make room. So yes. That's a great idea."

Her grin grew even wider. "Could we also get pigs? And maybe some cows?"

"To eat?"

She shook her head. "No. To add to the petting farm. I love pigs, they're so smart and so cute. Plus, you know how I love to name animals. I've already got some great names picked out. Siobhan Swinestein, Beverly Bacon, Hugh Hamhock, just to name a few. And I think a Miniature Scottish Highland cow or two would be a wonderful addition to the petting farm. They're so cute and only weigh like seven hundred pounds."

"*Only* seven hundred pounds."

"Exactly, it'd be like adding a Yorkie to the mix, really. They wouldn't take up any space."

He snorted. "And I'm assuming you have cow names picked out, too?"

"Of course! Hillary Hefferson, Templeton Porterhouse and Jeremiah Wellington."

"Why do all your pigs and cows have last names?"

"Because they're *that* important. Can we get some?"

His laugh was warm and raspy as he swooped in, wrapped his arms around her waist and picked her up, spinning her around in a circle on the side of the road. "I'll get you a million pigs, and a hundred cows, Minx, and you can name them all. Anything for you. I just want you to be happy."

Looping her arms around his neck, she giggled. "A dance studio, pet pigs, Miniature Scottish Highland cows, and you. I don't see how I can't be happy."

Then they climbed into his truck and headed home. Back to the ranch, to start their life together, and what a beautiful, busy and fulfilling life it promised to be.

Epilogue

One year later...

"Condom?" Mieka asked slightly breathless as she and Nate ran toward the barn, laughing like stoned—but NOT drunk—fools out of the tent that held the guests for their wedding reception.

"Got like twelve of them in my pocket, Minx. I learn from my mistakes."

"Thank God."

They were holding hands and she had her long dress in the other hand as the grass tickled their ankles and the sound of music faded behind them.

"Fuck, I can't wait to be inside my wife," he growled, stopping them midway to the barn and hauling her against him for a lip-bruising kiss that made her panties get wetter than they already were. "Good call on the two of us drinking lemonades instead of champagne."

"No whiskey dick or whiskey clit for us," she said with a giggle as they took off running again.

The area surrounding the barn was dark and deserted. All the animals were in their stalls, and all the ranch hands and guests were dancing and partying up a storm under the tent, enjoying the open bar and the late-night pizza they had delivered twenty minutes ago.

Nate opened one of the side doors and pulled Mieka inside, plastering her body up against the inside wall and taking her mouth once more. She hummed and gasped as he bit her lip and ground his hard cock against her thigh.

"Inside me now, Cowboy. Please. Don't make me beg."

"Oooh, I like the idea of you begging for my cock," he mused, still holding onto her hand as he led her over to the stairs for the hayloft, grabbing a red and black flannel blanket off a bench as they went. "And it's *Rancher.*"

"So what does that make me now? A *ranchette?*"

"Never heard that term before, but sure. Though, right now, you're going to be a little sex pot with her legs spread wide and my cock inside her."

She grinned and giggled as he unfurled the blanket on a stack of hay bales, then went to work on his dress shirt and pants. Her husband was naked in mere seconds, his dog tags shiny against the hard muscular planes of his chest.

"Jeez, you waste no time, huh?"

"I'm contemplating an annulment right now, since you're still dressed. Strip, woman."

"This dress is a bitch to get into, so many buttons. How about we just push it up to my hips and you put your big love stick in my lady garden that way. I'll get naked later tonight when we go to bed."

"Your what?" he asked, referring to her *lady garden.* "I thought it was a stubborn cat? Or Hole V?"

She giggled again. "You know what I mean. Come here, big boy."

He grumbled, but obliged. Her dress had been a pain in the ass to put on. But it was so worth it. It was the dress of her dreams and she was going to wear it for as long as she could. Not even pre-wedding night sex could make her take it off before she absolutely had to. She was considering sleeping in it and wearing it tomorrow, too.

Ruffling the lacy fabric up to her waist, she tugged off her underwear and reached for him. "Come to Mama."

"I don't like this," he said, hovering over her and notching his Latex-covered cock at her center. "You're being weird right now."

"Yeah, but that's not going to stop you from fucking your wife on a hay bale. You're too much of a horndog to let this stuff kill your boner."

To prove her point, Nate thrust forward, impaling her with said boner. They both let out satisfied grunts as he seated himself to the hilt. "You sound like Rayma right now," he said, staring down at her. "No filter and deliberately pushing buttons."

"Yeah, but I'm not. I'm Mieka, your wife, so stop thinking about my baby sister and take me on this hay bale, Cowboy."

"Rancher," he grunted, dropping his mouth to her bare shoulder and starting to buck forward.

She lifted her hips and wrapped her legs around his waist, moaning when he sunk in just an inch or so deeper from the change in angle.

"We're married," he said, raking his teeth over her collarbone.

"We are."

"'Til death do us part."

"Death, or you know, a sexier cowboy rides into town and offers me something better. Like life on a ranch where the goats *don't* try to escape."

"Rancher," he growled, pulling out of her abruptly, yanking her up and turning her around. His hand on her back forced her to bend over and put her hands on the hay bale. He gripped her hips and sunk back in with one, deep thrust. "No sexier cowboy than me and you know it. You love it here, escaping goats and all."

"I do," she admitted. "This is totally the life for me. I love it here and I love you."

Hunching over her body, Nate released one of her hips, grabbed her chin roughly and turned her head for an awkward kiss.

Releasing her chin, he pushed the same hand down the front of her strapless dress and pulled her breasts free, tugging on a nipple hard enough to make her gasp.

Six months ago, she'd opted to undergo reconstructive surgery, getting modest C-cup implants. Nate said nearly every day leading up to her surgery that he didn't care what cup size she was, that she was beautiful to him no matter what. But she didn't do it for him, she did it for herself.

She'd gained a bit of an ass since moving to the ranch—finally. She ate well and changed her exercise routine to more squats, deadlifts and lunges than simply balls-to-the-wall running. But no matter how much she ate, her tits remained the beestings that they'd always been so she decided to take matters into her own hands—or in this case the hands of highly trained plastic surgeons—and go under the knife. It helped with her self-esteem, and she was able to fill out her wedding dress the way she'd always dreamed. She felt no shame in getting the surgery and held her head up high with newfound confidence every time she got dressed and saw that little bit of cleavage she'd envied her sisters over for so many years.

"Fuck, Minx, even with a rubber on, I'm not going to be able to last long. You feel so fucking good." He tugged on her nipple again, cupping her breast then moved over to the other breast to deliver it the same attention.

She wanted to reach down between her legs, find her clit and get herself there, but his vigorous pounding from behind required her to use both her arms for support.

"Dammit, Minx, you're so fucking hot," he pulled out of her again, spun her around, then flopped back to the hay bale himself, beckoning her to climb onto him. "I want to watch you come, baby. Watch you come undone as you squeeze my cock."

She climbed up onto the hay, straddling him with her knees on either side of his thighs. Her breasts were still out, resting on top of the tight corset top of her dress.

She notched him at her center, squeezed her muscles and slowly sunk down, taking him inch by luscious inch. They both moaned and Nate reached up to cup her breasts. "Minx," he breathed, rubbing his thumbs over her nipples.

Bobbing up and down on his lap, she leaned forward slightly so that her clit rubbed just right against his pubic bone, getting her there faster. The weed was doing the trick and amplifying all the sensations. Her body tingled with pleasure as every inch of his cock filled her up, rubbed and dragged against her inner walls, driving her closer and closer to sweet release.

"You want the finger, Minx?" he asked, his voice hoarse as he approached his own climax.

"Always want the finger," she said, smiling down at him as she continued to drop her hips. He wiggled the devious finger in front of her, pulling a raspy giggle from the depths of her throat, then he snaked it under her dress and around her backside, pulling some of her arousal from her pussy and up her crease. "Let me in, Minx," he said, his voice dripping with sex and longing.

He pressed once, then twice and she relaxed her muscles and allowed him to breach her hole.

"Gonna take you here later with my cock," he said, pushing his finger in further until it was all the way in. She sucked in a sharp breath, having stopped moving so he could do what he needed to do, but once he was in, she started to lift and drop her hips again. Her eyes threatened to roll into the back of her head and her pussy pulsed and spasmed as the need to come drew closer and closer with each rapid beat of her heart.

"Nate," she murmured, slamming her eyes shut and biting her lip. "So good. It feels so good."

"That's right, my wife. Come for me."

And because she was a dutiful wife who did what she was told—at least when it came to coming when she was already so freaking close—she leaned forward, took his mouth and leaped off the cliff.

Wave after wave of pure unadulterated joy crashed through her from her pussy and clit, her ass and her tits and out into every single cell of her body. Her fingers splayed across his hard chest, then slid down to the blanket he was on, bunching in the fabric with each spasm and clench of her muscles.

Nate's teeth found her shoulder and he paused beneath her, grunting and breathing heavily as he found his own release. The air from his nostrils hit her shoulder in warm, erratic puffs as he bucked up into her, stayed there for several quick heartbeats, and finally collapsed back to the hay bale as his cock throbbed inside her. They'd yet to go without a condom since they got back together over a year ago, knowing full well what being irresponsible could result in. But she had an IUD and the topic of children wasn't entirely off the table, so they planned to stop using condoms in a few months.

Because she was high on being married, drinking those delicious lemonades and being more in love and happier than she ever thought possible, Mieka's orgasm just kept going, then it rolled into a second one that saw her sitting back up on Nate's lap and riding him like a prize-winning race horse all the way to the finish line again.

Once that second climax shredded her to an unrecognizable version of herself, she collapsed against his chest, exhausted, winded and utterly content with the world.

Nate gently pulled his finger free of her ass and chuckled, the rumble of his laugh like a tractor starting up for the first time after the winter, beneath her ear. "I love you, Minx," he said, kissing the bite on her shoulder. "I think I might have left a mark that will let our guests—particularly your parents—know *just* how much I love you."

Smiling, Mieka lifted her head and rested her chin on his chest. "I don't care. I want all your bite marks and all your hickeys. We deserve to shout our love from the rooftops, particularly today. Fuck my parents and their prudish ways. Everyone with half a brain cell already knows that we snuck off to have sex. Though, I will admit, I *do* prefer when your hickeys and bite marks are on my inner thighs, but I'm not going to complain."

"I'll make those later," he said with a growl that she felt right down to her still throbbing clit.

The fingers from his non-butt hand trailed up her bare back. "You're happy?"

"Blissfully," she sighed, smiling and closing her eyes. Then it hit her. He was so concerned about her happiness, but she'd never checked in to see if he was happy, too. "Are you happy?" she asked, concern replacing the post-orgasm delirium she'd been feeling a moment ago. She blinked her eyes open and glanced up at him. It was dark in the hayloft, but her eyes had adjusted enough that she could see his face. The brilliant blue of his eyes was muted, but his overall beauty remained.

"So happy, Minx." He grinned. "Happier than I ever could have imagined."

The delirium began to return and she smiled again. "Me, too."

He twitched his slowly softening dick inside her and they both laughed.

"I suppose we should get back to our party?" she mumbled, pressing a kiss to his chest before resting her ear over his heart and closing her eyes. Her heart was so full it was close to bursting, and even though what waited for them back in the tent was all of their loved ones, she was loath to move from this spot of absolute bliss for anything.

"We should probably go make the rounds," he whispered, sounding half asleep. "Thank each person for coming and all of that."

Neither of them moved. Neither of them said anything.

Eventually, he slipped free of her and she rolled off him while he removed the condom and tied it off. Silently, Nate got dressed while Mieka tucked her breasts back into her dress and tidied her long fishtail braid as best she could. She probably had hay in it and a big tangled patch at the back of her head, but she didn't care.

They descended the stairs, Nate tossed the condom in the trash and washed his hands at the sink, then they laced their fingers together and walked back out into the warm night air.

Swinging hands as they traipsed through the grass, Mieka and Nate were all smiles.

"Minx?" Nate said, squeezing her hand and stopping halfway between the barn and the tent.

"Hmm?" She turned to face him and looped her arms around his neck while his hands found her hips.

"You'll tell me if you ever grow *un*happy, right? You won't just leave."

The worry and fear in his voice gutted her, but she tossed on a smile, lifted up onto her tiptoes and pressed her lips to his. "I'll tell you, I promise. But I don't see that happening. I love it here, truly. I know I was stubborn at first, convinced that I wanted a life that was go-go-go, hustle and bustle and full of skyscrapers, jet-setting and adventures, but deep down you knew what I *needed*. I needed you. I needed this and I am so at peace with my decision to stay."

His fingers tightened on her hips. "Your happiness is everything to me, Minx. Just being with you makes me happy, so I might forget from time to time to check in that *you're* happy. But smack me in the head if I forget to check in and things change with how you feel."

"I will. But I don't think I'll have to. I have everything I could possibly want here. A man who adores me and who I adore, family, animals, a thriving dance school—thank you for that, I can't believe how quickly we were able to break ground and get the whole studio up and running—and best of all, a sense of purpose. You gave me all of those things. You said you didn't want to cage a bird that simply wanted to fly, but I don't think you've caged me at all. You've simply given me the space and opportunity to spread my wings and fly while providing me with a nest to call home and return to each night."

Dropping his head, he claimed her mouth, deepening the kiss by wrapping his hand around the back of her head and dipping her low until the tip of her braid brushed the tall grass. "I love you, Minx, with everything that I am," he murmured, brushing his lips across her jaw.

"And I love you ... Rancher, more than I ever thought possible."

Then he scooped her up, and laughing like love-sick fools, he ran them back to the tent where they danced the night away with all their guests, celebrating love in all its forms, and appreciating second-chances, because if anything deserves a second-chance, it's love ... and a rancher.

Grab the Bonus Scene here —> https://whitleycox.com/bonus-material/
Preorder the next Book here —> https://books2read.com/done-with-you

If you've enjoyed this book, please consider leaving a review wherever you purchased it. It really does make a difference and helps an independent author like me.

Thank you again.

Xoxo

Whitley Cox

A YOUNG SISTERS NOVEL

DONE WITH *you*

WHITLEY COX

Check out the next Young Sidster Novel Coming October 2023

Preorder it here —> https://books2read.com/done-with-you

SNEAKPEEK

Done with You

Oona and Aiden

Coming October 14, 2023

Preorder here—> https://books2read.com/done-with-you

"You know, one of these days you're going to have to actually say something," Greg said with a slight chuckle to his voice as he rested a hand on Aiden's shoulder. "You can't come to an anger management class and not participate."

Aiden glared at the man and jerked his shoulder so Greg's hand slipped away. "Start seeing a therapist tomorrow. No need to talk here. Just gotta show my face so you can sign the papers."

Greg's brown eyes turned sad. "No, Aiden, it doesn't work that way. You need both. You need to participate in *both*. Therapy *and* anger management. The therapist is going to help you in a different way. Discuss your trauma and triggers more in depth, get to the root of it all and give you long-term coping tools. But anger management will help, too. It's comforting to be around others who experience similar intense emotions. To hear how they cope. To hear how they have slip-ups and how they handle day-to-day triggers, and come back from

274

difficult episodes and make amends with those they've hurt. We have tools here, too. But *both* this class and therapy are required for you to get back to work."

Aiden ground his teeth together and bunched his fists as he slowly turned around to face the gray-haired man old enough to be his father.

Greg's dark brown eyes shone like a glass of coke being held up to the light, with sincerity, then slowly drifted down Aiden's body until he focused on his fists. His mouth twisted beneath his thick gray mustache. "You want to punch me, don't you?"

"Did you drink then drive here?" Aiden asked through clenched molars.

Greg's brows pinched together in confusion. "No."

"Then I don't want to punch you."

"See, now we're getting somewhere. Why can't you discuss this in class?"

"Don't need everyone else knowing my business. I'm a cop and I've probably pulled over at least a few of these people. And I *know* I went to a domestic dispute regarding that tall motherfucker over there and his wife."

Greg pivoted for a moment to see Damien, who was closing in on six-foot-five standing next to the refreshment table with a paper coffee cup in his hand. He was smiling and talking with Terry, a long-time participant and a veteran.

Understanding flashed in Greg's eyes when he faced Aiden again. "That's fair. Perhaps this might not be the *right* class for you. Maybe you need to go to one out of town, or geared specifically for police officers. Where you don't run the risk being in a class with civilians you've witnessed at their worst."

Aiden snorted and rolled his eyes. "I just want to get the fuck back to work. So just let me come here, sit and listen and stay quiet. These people don't need to know why I'm here. We're all here for the same reasons anyway. We're angry and we can't control it."

Greg shook his head. "No, that's not it. At least, not all of it."

Huffing a breath out in frustration, Aiden shoved his fingers through his short brown hair. "Look, I'm doing the best I can. I've been waitlisted for this therapist for months and I finally got in to see her. She's apparently *the best* for

PTSD and anger. So that's gotta count for something, right?"

"It definitely does. But you need to actually go to your appointments with her for the healing to begin. And you need to actively participate in anger management as well." Greg pulled out his phone from his pocket. "Let me call around and see if I can pull some strings to get you into a class elsewhere, where you're less likely to run into people you know. People you've encountered while on the job."

Aiden grunted. He appreciated Greg's effort and understanding, but the whole situation just pissed him off. Yes, he'd over-reacted when he punched that drunk driver he pulled over. But the guy had his fucking nine-year-old daughter in the car with him. They'd been at a friend's barbecue and the dad tied on one too many, thought he was fine to drive home and was swerving all over the fucking road.

Aiden pulled him over and was furious enough to see the man had been drinking and was driving, but when he noticed the kid in the back, Aiden lost it. He lost his temper. He lost his cool. He lost all sense of composure, reached into the car, hauled the man out and decked him hard across the jaw.

That's when he saw the camera-phone vigilante who'd pulled over behind them and was filming the entire thing.

It went viral and Aiden was cast and the villain in the story.

Not the negligent father who could have killed his daughter.

Aiden was suspended from work and forced to attend mandatory therapy and anger management classes.

But everything was full and waitlisted because the world was an angry fucking place.

He'd been out of work for four and a half months and was going stir-fucking crazy doing nothing every day as we waited for the call that he was next on the list to see the therapist.

He was even willing to see other therapists. And travel to do so. He didn't *have* to see this Dr. Young. But apparently, she was the best and who was recommended for him. So he had to at least try to see her first. And besides, all other therapists were booked, too.

"If you want to come by and just chat one-on-one, I'm happy to listen," Greg said. "I understand what you're going through."

"Do you?" Aiden bit back, his voice loud enough that it echoed around the room. All other conversations halted like cars screeching to a stop so a mother duck and her ducklings could cross the road, and every set of eyes in the room pivoted to him.

Greg swallowed and his eyes darted sideways.

With his face on fire, Aiden squeezed his fists even tighter, shifted his eyes around the room for a hot minute, then spun on his heels and stalked out of the rec center basement into the frigid early December evening in Montreal, Quebec.

He hit the fob for his truck and the auto-start button so the engine roared to life before he was even at the door.

Normally, an event like this would make a person turn to booze. Hit up a bar and grab a drink—or several—to numb their feelings. But Aiden didn't drink.

He didn't do any kind of substance, illegal or legal.

His only *vice* was coffee. He liked his coffee and he drank at least four cups a day. But he was also strict about that consumption and never took a drop after three o'clock since it would just keep him up. And as a cop who worked two day shifts, then two night shifts, his sleep cycle was already fucked up enough.

He climbed into his truck which was already getting toasty warm, since he made sure to leave the heaters on full-blast before he got out earlier, and the seat-warmers were at max, too.

He might not drink alcohol, but that didn't mean he couldn't just go sit at a bar, watch the hockey game on the screen, indulge in some nachos and just exist among the carefree.

Besides, it never hurt to have a cop in the bar in case things got rowdy. More than once, he'd had to jump in and help a bartender throw out some degenerates who were getting obnoxious after one-too-many beers and their team lost the game.

He did a quick Google search for a nearby bar with televisions and nachos and low and behold, there was a hotel only two and a half kilometers away with just what he was looking for.

With his face still full of flames from that outburst in the rec center, he put the truck into gear and pulled out of the parking lot, careful to keep his eyes peeled for black ice. They hadn't had a big dump of snow yet, but it was coming and soon. He could smell snow in the air and the clouds above were a dense, dark and gray blanket. The thermostat on his dash said it was minus eleven.

Fuck, he hated the cold.

He drove to the hotel, parked his truck further away than right in front of the front door, so that hopefully nobody would park right beside him and scrape his shiny black Dodge Ram, then he hoofed it across the slick parking lot to the front door.

The hotel wasn't huge, but the parking lot was absolutely packed.

As he opened the front door to the lobby, a roar of a crowd, followed by applause made him pause.

The bar was to the left, but the cheering was coming from the right.

"What's going on in there?" he asked the red-vested hotel staff behind the front desk.

"Monthly pole and burlesque show," the front desk guy with the nametag Rakesh, replied with a big smile. "Always pulls in a huge crowd."

"A what?"

"Pole and burlesque. You know, pole dancers."

"Like strippers?"

"Well ... it's more than that. In fact, I don't think they take their clothes off at all." He scrunched his nose. "I mean, they're not wearing a lot to begin with, but it's not a strip show. We're not licensed for that." He tipped his chin toward the door to the show just as another cheer made the pictures on the walls tremble. "You should go check it out. These woman are crazy-strong and fit. It's an artform. I couldn't do it."

Aiden grunted and was about to scoff at the idea when he was interrupted by a loud announcement from inside. "And please welcome the beautiful, the talented, the brilliant ... *Luna Love*."

The crowd went bananas.

"How much?" Aiden asked.

"Fifteen, or twenty and that gets you two drink tickets. Otherwise, drinks are five bucks each."

"Don't drink," he said, reaching into his wallet and pulling out a ten and a five. He took a step toward the room filled with music and more cheering, but then paused. "Can I order food from the bar and have it sent in there?"

"Afraid not, sir, but the show in there will be over in an hour, then you can move to the bar."

Aiden grunted again, nodded, said a quick *thanks*, then headed toward the music and cheers.

The place was dark and filled with round tables that sat four people. All the tables were full and people stood around the edges, drinks in their hands, eyes glued to the stage as a caramel-haired beauty with a super-sexy silver bathing suit thing that was up her ass crack like floss and with giant cut outs on her abdomen, hung from a metal pole by nothing more than one bent leg.

Her body was at a ninety-degree bend outward and she was spinning around the pole—or the pole was spinning her around—backward, her arms out.

"Fucking hell," he murmured under his breath.

"Drink, sir?" a chipper-voiced male server asked.

He glanced down at the kid who was probably no more than twenty and weighed less than a Great Dane. "Club soda with lime," he said.

The kid nodded. "Be right back."

Aiden meandered through the crowd, his eyes glued to the woman on stage. This, Luna as the announcer called her. She was in ridiculously high clear, plastic, chunky heels and had just hoisted herself into the air by holding onto the pole with her arms, she spun around a few times, continuing to stay off the ground, then while still in the air, she flipped herself upside down, hooked one leg around the pole, maneuvered her body around so her head was hanging below her legs and bent the other leg so that she could grab the heel of it with both hands. All while still spinning. All while holding onto the pole with just that one leg at the knee. Squeezing it with her calf and hamstring.

Then, still just using her arms, she lifted her bent leg back up and held herself on her back in the air in the splits with the pole between her legs, before finally dropping to the ground to her knees in a sexy way, then standing up by pushing her ass up first and flipping her high ponytail.

The crowd went apeshit.

Aiden hadn't fucking blinked and when he finally did, his eyes stung and he realized he had dry mouth from standing there with his mouth open.

"Club soda, sir," the server said, approaching him with his drink on a tray.

Aiden grunted. "Thanks." He handed the kid a five, knowing that the drink was probably no more than three bucks since there was no booze in it and leaving a generous tip.

"Thank you very much," the server said, his grin getting bigger before he disappeared into the masses.

Luna continued to do tricks and spins on the pole, defying gravity and all other laws of physics, while simultaneously blowing Aiden's mind.

He'd been looking for nachos and a hockey game to ease his temper, but this was somehow doing the trick, too.

Eventually, Luna's time on stage was over, but as she bowed and left, the crowd stood up from their seats and gave her a standing ovation.

She bowed deeper, then hopped back up onto the pole for an encore. This time, the move she did certainly had to have wires or something because nobody had that kind of upper body strength. Especially someone who didn't have enormous biceps. She went upside down, parallel to the pole, hooked on foot around it just at the ankle, then held on with one hand and spun around, giving him a clear view of the tattoo she had on her left shoulder blade, as well as her right tricep. Her other hand and leg just hung out away from her body.

How?

Just. Fucking. How?

Then she did a move where she held onto the pole with one hand, made her body go parallel with the floor, split her legs like chopsticks and grabbed one foot. Only to then slide to the floor, almost lick the ground with her body, stick her ass in the air again, and finish in the fucking splits.

The crowd continued to go insane and the applause followed Luna off the stage and for another thirty seconds after she was gone and her pumping music had changed to something else.

The performers that followed Luna were good, but they were no Luna.

The woman had a presence about her. An almost aloofness that Aiden felt in his very marrow.

She made eye contact with the crowd, but in a way that he was sure every person in there thought she was looking at them. That she was performing only for them. Like Mona Lisa's eyes, they followed you no matter where you were in the room. And even though he was sure she was doing it all for show, that it was just part of the performance, the way she looked at him, the way her light brown eyes bore into him had him believing that this was all for him. That he was the only person in the crowd and this was a private show.

He stuck around, hoping that the lovely Luna Love would return to the stage. He'd paid his ticket and the front desk guy said there was only an hour to go, so he may as well see the hour through.

After his second club soda with lime and the third performer after Luna, there was a ten-minute intermission where the lights came on, and people quickly grabbed more drinks or used the washroom.

Aiden took this as an opportunity to find a better vantage point.

He didn't want to steal a seat from anyone, but he made his way closer to the front along the side wall, picking a spot that would give him a clear view of the stage.

A man wearing all black wandered onto the stage and removed the pole, then other props were dragged onto the sage. All gold, black and red, as well as five black folding chairs.

Everyone returned to their seats and the lights dimmed. The stage went completely dark and the crowd went silent. Five dark shadowy figures stepped across the stage and took their places in the chairs.

Then there was a thump from the speakers, followed by another and the lights on stage came on, revealing five beauties—with Luna in the center—all decked out in lingerie and feathers.

This was the burlesque part of the show.

Aiden's heartbeat mimicked the thumping of the bass.

The music picked up tempo and the women started to move, giving the chair a lap dance.

Four of the five removed a few articles of clothing as the song and dance progressed, until all that covered their chests were black flower pasties, but Luna remained dressed. She kept all her clothes on. But the clothes she kept on were sexy as fuck. Black fishnets, mile-high black heels, a black and red corset with lace and bows, and a black thong that went up her ass crack to show off her taut, round cheeks. Her hair was pinned up in a glam kind of way with red and black feathers in it. She was stunning.

Her makeup was dramatic and the jewelry on her neck and ears was sparkly as hell and probably added a couple of pounds to her fit frame, but she was breathtaking and for the second time that night, Aiden's mouth was dry and his eyes burned from not blinking.

The way she moved on the chair, doing a handstand then the upside-down splits, sticking her ass in the air, caressing her body in a seductive way. He was mesmerized, transfixed.

Before he knew it the show was over. The five women on stage held hands and bowed while the entire crowd stood up and rattled the rafters with their applause and cheers.

"Give it up for Margo, Juanita, Cherise, Daphne and *Luna!*" The way the announcer said Luna made it clear that she was the center of this show. The star performer and the reason everyone came to watch. Even if he hadn't emphasized her name that way, Aiden wasn't an idiot and could easily tell that Luna carried that group. But maybe she was the leader and their teacher? Everyone had to start somewhere.

He set his empty drink down on a ledge and clapped, then put two fingers in his mouth and whistled. His whistle was loud enough to pull Luna's attention and her heated gaze pivoted toward him.

She batted long, fake lashes at him and smiled demurely. Almost shyly.

The women bowed once more, then stood up, waved and filed off stage.

Aiden elbowed his way through the crowd to the door, then booked it across the lobby to the bar. He needed to grab a seat before all those people at the show followed their rumbling bellies next door and he was once again without a place to put his ass.

He grabbed a stool at the bar which gave him a perfect view of the television overhead. The Maple Leafs were playing the Rangers and it was the second period. Maple Leafs were up by two.

"What can I get you?" the bartender asked.

"Nachos. Loaded with extra guac and a club soda with lime," Aiden said, settling in for a bit.

"You got it."

He tried to focus on the hockey game overhead, and his nachos when they came, but his mind kept drifting back to Luna.

The way she moved, the way her eyes filled with fire. But he already knew there was an incomparable intelligence behind those eyes. He was exceptional at reading people, and he could see that there was a hell of a lot more to the lovely Luna Love than just plastic high heels and a lot of makeup.

With a chip hanging mid air loaded with far too much guacamole for any sane person to put on one chip, he was lost in thoughts of Luna and staring blankly ahead when the bartender's voice broke through his fog.

"Usual?" he asked.

"Please, Pedro," said a soft female voice.

Aiden's chip broke and the guacamole plopped back onto his plate. He turned his head to find Luna Love of all people beside him at the bar. There was one empty stool between them. She had removed her makeup, put her hair caramel-colored up in ponytail midway down the back of her head, and was dressed down in dark jeans, a gray sweater that fell off one shoulder revealing the strap of a red bra, and black ballet flats.

She was beautiful on stage all dressed up, but holy fucking shit. Now, she was ... he was speechless.

Swallowing, he cleared his throat. "Saw the show."

She glanced at him and her dark brows lifted. "Yeah?"

"Impressive. Not sure I have the upper body strength to do that and I work out every damn day."

Her smile was small, but also tired, like she'd heard that line more than once and wasn't exactly impressed with it.

The bartender placed a drink in front of her and Aiden knew immediately that it was a Shirley Temple. Non-alcoholic and fruity.

"Not drinking?" he asked.

"I don't drink very often. And not when I'm out. Only home or with friends and maybe one or two glasses of wine. Besides, the adrenaline is more than enough for me."

He could believe that.

"You ordering food tonight?" Pedro the bartender asked Luna.

She nodded. "Yam fries, gluten-free chicken strips and chili prawns, please."

Pedro cracked a smile then tossed her a wink. "Luna Love appie platter, coming right up."

"You're welcome to share my nachos," Aiden said, sliding the platter normally meant for four people, closer to her. "I *could* finish it myself, but I probably shouldn't."

She eyed him suspiciously for a moment, then her gaze fell to his drink. "What's in the glass?"

"Club soda and lime. I don't drink—ever."

Her brown eyes flecked with different shades of gold, flared and she held his gaze for a moment, then reached forward, grabbed a chip and dipped the corner of it into the sour cream. "Thanks ..."

"Caden," he said. He liked this woman, but he already knew there was no future for them. He was a broken human being and she deserved so much better than him. No sense getting attached with real names and torrid pasts. He stuck out his hand.

She took it. "Luna."

ACKNOWLEDGMENTS

There are so many people to thank who help along the way. Publishing a book is definitely not a solo mission, that's for sure.

To Nicola Jackson whose firsthand knowledge and experience dancing on the cruiseships was vital to the realism and accurate depiction of a dancer that I wished to portray. Thank you so much, Nicola for answering all of my questions, sharing your experiences and tales of your adventures with me. It really helped bring vitality and truth to Mieka's story.

To my editor, Proofreading by the Page, thank you so much for the beta and editing on this once, I really appreciate it.

To Postive Proof Author Services, thank you for your beta-read, your questions and incites were so important and appreciated.

Megan J. Parker-Squiers from EmCat Designs, your covers are awesome. This cover is beautiful.

Author Ember Leigh, my author bestie, I love our bitch fests—they keep me sane.

My fabulous assistant, Megan MacPhail of Kiss My Smut, what would I do without you? You are amazing and I SO appreciate all your hard work, beautiful graphics and organization. Thank you!!!

My parents, in-laws and brother, thank you for your unwavering support. The Small Human and the Tiny Human, you are the beats and beasts of my heart, the reason I breathe and the reason I drink. I love you both to infinity and beyond. And lastly, of course, the husband. You are my forever, my other half, the one who keeps me grounded and the only person I have honestly never grown sick of even when we did that six-month backpacking trip and spent every single day together. I never tired of you. Never needed a break. You are my person. I love you.

FIND WHITLEY HERE

Website: WhitleyCox.com
Email: readers4wcox@gmail.com
Twitter: @WhitleyCoxBooks
Instagram: @CoxWhitley
TikTok: @AuthorWhitleyCox
Facebook : https://www.facebook.com/CoxWhitley/
Blog: https://whitleycox.com/fabulously-filthy-blog-page/

Exclusive Facebook Reader Group:
https://www.facebook.com/groups/234716323653592/
Booksprout: https://booksprout.co/author/994/whitley-cox
Bookbub: https://www.bookbub.com/authors/whitley-cox
Goodreads:
https://www.goodreads.com/author/show/16344419.Whitley_Cox
Subscribe to my newsletter here:
http://eepurl.com/ckh5yT

ABOUT THE AUTHOR

ABOUT THE AUTHOR

A Canadian West Coast baby born and raised, Whitley is married to her high school sweetheart, and together they have two beautiful daughters and a fluffy dog. She spends her days making food that gets thrown on the floor, vacuuming Cheerios out from under the couch and making sure that the dog food doesn't end up in the air conditioner. But when nap time comes, and it's not quite wine o'clock, Whitley sits down, avoids the pile of laundry on the couch, and writes. A lover of all things decadent; wine, cheese, chocolate and spicy erotic romance, Whitley brings the humorous side of sex, the ridiculous side of relationships and the suspense of everyday life into her stories. With single dads, firefighters, Navy SEALs, mommy wars, body issues, threesomes, bondage and role-playing, Whitley's books have all the funny and fabulously filthy words you could hope for.

OTHER BOOKS BY WHITLEY COX

SECOND CHANCE WITH THE RANCHER

·

Hard, Fast and Madly: Part 1
The Dark and Damaged Hearts Series Book 7
https://books2read.com/HFM1-DDH
Freya and Jacob

·

Hard, Fast and Madly: Part 2
The Dark and Damaged Hearts Series Book 8
https://books2read.com/HFM1-DDH
Freya and Jacob

·

Quick & Dirty
Book 1, A Quick Billionaires Novel
https://books2read.com/QDirty-QBS
Parker and Tate

·

Quick & Easy
Book 2, A Quick Billionaires Novella
https://books2read.com/QEasy-QBS
Heather and Gavin

·

Quick & Reckless
Book 3, A Quick Billionaires Novel
https://books2read.com/QReckless-QBS
Silver and Warren

·

Quick & Dangerous
Book 4, A Quick Billionaires Novel
https://books2read.com/QDangerous-QBS
Skyler and Roberto

·

Quick & Snowy
The Quick Billionaires, Book 5
https://books2read.com/QSnowy-QBS
Brier and Barnes

·

Doctor Smug
https://books2read.com/DoctorSmug
Daisy and Riley

·

Hot Dad
https://books2read.com/Hot-Dad
Harper and Sam

•

Snowed In & Set Up
https://books2read.com/SISU
Amber, Will, Juniper, Hunter, Rowen, Austin

•

Love to Hate You
https://books2read.com/Love2HateYou
Alex and Eli

•

Lust Abroad
https://books2read.com/Lust-Abroad
Piper and Derrick

•

Hired by the Single Dad
https://books2read.com/HBTSD-SDS
The Single Dads of Seattle, Book 1
Tori and Mark

•

Dancing with the Single Dad
https://books2read.com/DWTSD-SDS
The Single Dads of Seattle, Book 2
Violet and Adam

•

Saved by the Single Dad
https://books2read.com/SBTSD-SDS
The Single Dads of Seattle, Book 3
Paige and Mitch

•

Living with the Single Dad
https://books2read.com/LWTSD-SDS
The Single Dads of Seattle, Book 4
Isobel and Aaron

•

Christmas with the Single Dad
https://books2read.com/CWTSD-SDS
The Single Dads of Seattle, Book 5
Aurora and Zak

SECOND CHANCE WITH THE RANCHER

WHITLEY COX

SECOND CHANCE WITH THE RANCHER

Snowed in with the Rancher
A Young Sisters Novel
https://books2read.com/snowed-in-rancher
Triss and Asher
March 4, 2023

•

Second Chance with the Rancher
A Young Sisters Novel
https://books2read.com/second-chance-rancher
Mieka and Nate
May 13, 2023

•

Done with You
A Young Sisters Novel
https://books2read.com/done-with-you
Oona and Aiden
October 13, 2023

•

Rock the Shores
A Cinnamon Bay Romance
https://books2read.com/Rocktheshores
Juliet and Evan

•

The Bastard Heir
Winter Harbor Heroes, Book 1
Co-written with Ember Leigh
https://books2read.com/the-bastard-heir
Harlow and Callum

•

The Asshole Heir
Winter Harbor Heroes, Book 2
Co-written with Ember Leigh
https://books2read.com/the-asshole-heir
Amaya and Carson